Still Life

By

Isobel Hart

Chapter 1

A pedestrian stepped out of the fog and onto the crossing, forcing me to brake hard. The seatbelt bit into my shoulder as it locked. Edward drew a quick breath, but didn't say anything. Just as well.

The man passed in front of the car, his skin and clothes shimmering with a pink film of whatever shit was inside the mist. The stuff was everywhere. Head down, he walked briskly and didn't look up – in too much of a hurry to get under cover, I presumed. I watched him, my hands still trembling, until he vanished back into the fog. Then, I inched the car forwards again, peering through the opaque darkness. The thick, swirling gloom made it difficult to see any other traffic on the Brighton streets.

I accelerated, my foot slipping off the clutch too soon, sending us lurching forwards. This time Edward's hands shot out, one grabbing the door handle, the other gripping the side of his seat. My next gear change wasn't much smoother. I sensed him looking at me, wanting to talk.

"Samantha–"

I jabbed at the radio button, to shut him up and avoid having to listen to any more of his bullshit. He was damn lucky I'd let him share the car home. The cool tones of the BBC news reporter soothed me, the day's events a welcome distraction:

"An unusually heavy fog has led to transport delays and disruption worldwide today.

Despite reports of an apparent 'luminosity', the Department of Health has issued a statement advising that the phenomenon is not believed to be a cause for concern – however they've recommended children and the elderly stay indoors as a precaution.

Continued travel disruption is expected while the fog persists–"

Edward flicked the off-switch.

I took my eyes from the road to glare at him. "I was listening to that."

"Sam, we need to talk–"

"Why? I was there, remember?" I slowed as we hit a mini-roundabout, the fog hiding it until the last moment.

"It was nothing. She meant nothing."

"You're still talking about it? Really?" I closed my eyes for a second, but found a perfect portrait of Edward fucking Serena over the table seared onto the backs of my eyelids. "She meant nothing? Doesn't that make it worse?"

He looked away. "Maybe if you weren't always being such a bitch to me, I wouldn't feel tempted to look elsewhere."

Typical Edward, trying to shirk responsibility even when he'd been caught with his pants down. I swallowed, blinking furiously to prevent my tears. "I'm done talking. I'm done . . . I'm just done." I fixed my eyes back on the road, accelerating onto the dual-carriageway. "We're done."

"You're overreacting."

I looked across at him. "You fuck someone else and I'm overreacting?" I gripped the wheel tighter. "We both know this has been a long time coming. I don't believe for a minute she was your first."

"Sam, don't do this. Don't throw everything away over a meaningless fuck . . . she meant nothing to me."

"So you keep saying. She meant something to me though. I'll move out when we get home. Heidi said I could stay at her place."

"Fucking hell! Fucking Heidi . . ." He hammered his fist against the passenger window, throwing himself against the headrest.

I pulled my attention back to the road, drawing a deep, calming breath to quell the rage he'd provoked, to be met with a wall of haloed lights looming red in the pink fog ahead.

I was going way too fast to stop. I turned the wheel hard and stamped my foot on the brake, praying I'd reacted in time to avoid ploughing into the back of anyone. Edward screamed – or was it me? – as we clipped the back of a stationary vehicle. Airbags exploded towards us as the car lurched. We lifted and the world tilted. For a moment we were flying, then we hit the ground, hard. The impact sent a jarring pain through my leg and neck. Glass imploded as the windscreen shattered and metal shrieked as it twisted beyond endurance. My head rolled first one way, then the other, as we turned over until, at last, it all stopped.

Silence. Then slowly, I became aware of a dripping sound. "Edward!" I turned to look at him. Like me, he hung upside down by his seat belt, his full weight supported by the thin strap. He didn't respond. "Edward!" I reached over to shake him. Blood covered his face, a small pool already forming below him.

"Help!" I screamed, when he still didn't move. I couldn't catch my breath, managing only short, ragged gasps. *Am I going to die here?* Not if I could help it.

I pulled at my seat belt, trembling hands fumbling with the buckle, lightheaded and disorientated as the blood rushed to my head. It didn't move. I tried again; nothing happened. My leg throbbed as I twisted, looking for another way to free myself, a wave of pain forcing me to stop until the nausea passed. My skin slickened with sweat. Then I smelt fuel. I pushed away thoughts of fire.

"Hey!" a voice called from outside the car. "You okay in there?" Someone was out there – a man. His feet outside my window.

Relieved, I started to cry. "Here," I sobbed. "Down here. My boyfriend's hurt. Please, call an ambulance."

"Already done. Let's see if we can get you out of there." He bent down and peered into my broken window, reaching inside to take the key out of the ignition. "That was a hell of a crash. I couldn't believe it when you shot past us into the barrier–" He talked on, but I heard little else until, "I think I can release you." The seat belt moved a fraction. "Before I do, tell me where you're hurting?"

"My leg. I think it might be broken."

"Maybe we should wait for proper help. I don't want to damage you more. You might've hurt your neck. I can hear the ambulance." Sirens drifted towards us on the still, night air.

"Leave me, I'm okay," I said. "Check Edward. He's bleeding."

"I can't get to him. We need to move you first."

"Well, fucking move me then." I pushed relentlessly on the release button until it gave way, the strap recoiling in a rush, dropping me in a heap onto the debris from the windscreen. My leg protested agonisingly at the sudden movement, and I moaned as darkness swallowed me.

***

I blinked my eyes open. "His pulse is thready," a voice said from somewhere nearby. "We need to get him in fast or he's not going to make it."

"Miss? Miss? Can you hear me?" A man leant over me and shone a bright light into my eyes. I flinched and tried to move away, my movement restricted by straps and a neck brace. Paramedic, I realised. I twisted my head as far as the brace would allow. Edward lay near me, motionless, visible through a crowd of medics surrounding him, lit by the flashing blue lights turned purple in the mist.

Snatches of conversation drifted past: "His blood pressure's through his boots . . ."

". . . internal bleed . . ."

"Air ambulance can't land in this fog. He'll have to go in by road."

"Let's go," the voice closest to me said. My stretcher lifted. Pain shot through my leg, and my vision faded again.

***

"At least let someone wheel you up there," the nurse said, as I grabbed my new crutches and tried to insert my arms into the cuffs. Pain shot down my neck, the throbbing in my head making me want to vomit. "I'll call a porter."

"They'll take forever to come. I've been down here for hours. Anything could have happened to him."

"I told you, he's still in surgery."

I ignored her and took an unsteady hop forward.

"Oh, for God's sake, woman, let me take you." She huffed and grabbed hold of the wheelchair. "You have concussion, whiplash and a broken fibula. You should be resting, not running about the hospital on crutches."

I tuned her grumbling out, the hospital corridors passing in a blur, focused instead on what I knew: He'd been in surgery since arriving at the hospital, but was, according to the last report at least, still alive. They'd told me this like it was good news. I guessed it was, in the context of the alternative.

"Here you go." The nurse pushed me into a room filled with moulded orange plastic chairs. A small television fixed to one wall flickered with silent images of the worldwide chaos caused by the fog.

Edward's parents rose in weary symmetry. "Samantha, my God! Thank goodness – I'm so glad you're okay. It's all so awful." His mother wiped at red, blotchy eyes with a tissue disintegrating from overuse. "He's in surgery," she said, telling me again what I already knew. "Your poor leg." She looked down at my cast and then back up at the neck brace. "The pair of you are lucky to be alive. The policeman said the car was ruined. It's just awful. Awful. Poor Edward." She sniffed, her voice wobbling as more tears slid down her papery cheeks.

"Can you tell us what happened?" Edward's father stepped towards me. "I believe you were driving?"

I swallowed, guilt paralysing my vocal cords. My inattention to the road had, if not caused the accident, at least worsened the outcome. Plus, I may have wished him dead, right about the time I caught him fucking Serena. If it happened . . . I wasn't sure I would be able to live with myself, regardless of what he'd done to me.

"You were at a wedding?" his father prompted. I nodded as much as the brace allowed. "Were you drinking?"

"No. I was driving, so I didn't drink." I didn't feel the need to add I wasn't looking at the road because we were in the middle of a row about their son's infidelity. "You can check my blood results." He nodded, and seemed somewhat reassured. "It was the fog. The cars had stopped, but I didn't see them until it was too late. I swerved . . . I tried to miss them, but then we rolled. The car turned over–" I sobbed as I relived the terrifying memory.

Edward's mum rushed over to hug me. "Oh, this awful fog! They still don't know what caused it. It's havoc out there." She turned on her husband. "Leave her alone, Patrick. Hasn't she been through enough today without you giving her an inquisition?"

"I just want to know what happened. I want to understand how our son–"

The door opened, and a doctor entered. He looked tired, his green scrubs creased from long hours in the operating theatre, mask pulled down so it hung loose around his neck. Young, probably in his early thirties like me, he also looked familiar. Very familiar. I'd met him through work. I remembered him attending a couple of my lunchtime presentation meetings. He had the kind of looks that made him hard to forget.

He nodded at me before shifting his attention back to Edward's parents. "Mr and Mrs Patterson . . ." He sounded serious. Ominous. It didn't bode well. ". . . I'm Dr Harvey. I've been looking after your son. I wanted to update you on his progress." He paused, and I feared the worst. "Your son is critical but stable. We've done what we can for now. He has several injuries; a head injury, as well as a severely lacerated liver – from the abdominal trauma he received during the accident. We've patched him up as best we can, but the next couple of hours will be critical." He took a deep breath, releasing it slowly, running a hand through his hair. "If we're lucky the patches will hold. The liver is a remarkable organ, but I need to prepare you . . . they may not. He may start to bleed again internally. If he does, then our chances of being able to patch him up a second time would be slim."

The blood drained from Edward's parent's faces.

"Can we see him?" his mum asked.

"He's in ITU, heavily sedated, but you're welcome to sit with him. No more than two visitors at a time." Doctor Harvey glanced at me in my wheelchair.

I swallowed. "You two go first, Brenda, I'll see him after."

They nodded. Brenda squeezed my shoulder, then followed her husband and the doctor out of the room, leaving me alone with my thoughts.

If only Edward hadn't drunk a whole bottle of merlot at the wedding breakfast.

If only I hadn't imagined him choking on his own vomit in a corner when I couldn't find him, and gone looking. Or, hadn't heard a noise from inside the hotel conference room as I walked past.

I should've listened to my instincts the first time I suspected he might be fucking around on me. But the thought of starting all over again, with someone new, when I was already over thirty . . . I shouldn't have settled for the Devil I knew.

I glanced up at the rolling images on the television. If only there'd been no fog.

***

Patrick walked back in ten minutes later, he'd aged. "You can go and see him now." His glassy eyes shone with unshed tears. "Follow the corridor to your right–" He looked down, as if seeing my wheelchair for the first time. "I'll take you." He grabbed hold of the handles.

He left as soon as we reached his son's room. It took a couple of moments for my eyes to adjust to the lighting. Edward lay motionless amidst a mass of wires and monitors, that bleeped and flashed around him. The background rasp of a ventilator punctuated the passing seconds.

Brenda sat beside him, clutching his hand, her desperate eyes fixed upon her son. "I'm here, darling," she whispered, reaching out to brush her fingers through his fringe. A mother's comforting touch.

Alarms sounded from every monitor simultaneously.

Brenda dropped Edward's hand as if she'd been scalded, and staggered backwards, horrified. "I'm so sorry . . . Did I do something? I didn't mean to."

The nurse pushed her aside and slammed her palm against a panic button behind the bed on the wall, calling for help in an urgent voice. People came running; the doctor we'd met earlier – Dr Harvey – barked instructions as they bent over the bed, preparing him to go back into surgery.

"Get them out of here!" someone shouted. A nurse grabbed my wheelchair, and Brenda and I were pushed out the room and deposited in the hallway. The sounds of frantic activity echoed out to where we'd been left. A monitor's single tone, the soundtrack to death, announced the moment Edward's heart gave up and stopped beating.

For twenty minutes, Brenda and I could do nothing but stare at one another in horror. Then the commotion stopped, its absence even more terrifying: "Time of death, two twenty-seven."

Brenda clasped a hand to her mouth and moaned.

I couldn't speak, couldn't think. Instead, I pushed myself into the doorway in time to see a nurse reach towards the heart monitor. Renewed sounds of bleeps halted her hand in mid-air.

Heads swivelled round. No one moved, as if waiting for the monitor to stop a second time. When it didn't, pandemonium broke out again.

Twenty minutes later, Dr Harvey stumbled into the hallway, his ashen face covered in a sheen of sweat. "He's stable again . . . for now."

Chapter 2

A week later, Edward continued to confound his doctors. Whilst not out of the woods, the signs were positive. His parents and I maintained a permanent vigil at his bedside. I couldn't speak for Brenda and Patrick, but I stayed because I believed no one should have to die alone. That, and the guilt that still choked me. After the first day, I had been convinced he would die. Now, I felt less sure. There had been no further heart-stopping moments, for him or for us. Today they intended to remove the ventilation to see if he would breathe independently.

I flexed my head from side to side, enjoying the sensation of mobility after the removal of my neck brace, despite muscles still tight with tension. Dr Harvey looked up from reviewing Edward's notes with the anaesthetist, and we shared a small smile. I glanced over at Brenda and Patrick who were already positioned beside the bed, eyes fixed upon their only son. Both appeared a little more stooped, and greyer.

"Okay," Dr Harvey began, "It's a simple enough procedure. We're happy to give this a try based on the improvement we've seen in Edward. You have a remarkable son, Mrs Patterson."

She gave a thin smile. "If it doesn't work? What will you do?" She clasped her hands, pulling at the rings on her fingers. Twisting them off, then pushing them back on. I understood her anxiety: she'd already seen her son's heart stop beating. No one should have to watch their child die, and certainly not more than once.

"Then we ventilate again. We have everything here we need to re-intubate." He pointed towards a prepared tray. "His body will tell us when it's ready." He smiled with more confidence than I imagined he had to be feeling. "Okay," he said, "if you wouldn't mind standing to the side?"

"Do we have suction?" the anaesthetist asked. A nurse confirmed they did. "Levels?" When they were both fully satisfied, Dr Harvey gave the instruction to proceed.

As the tube slipped from his throat I held my breath, watching as Edward stilled without the artificial action of the ventilation machine. Then, a faint breath reinforced by the rise of his chest as his lungs inflated. His heartbeat elevated briefly, and then just as quickly returned to normal.

"Remarkable," the doctor said, the steady beat of the heart monitor reassuring all was well. "He's doing brilliantly, all things considered. Extraordinarily well. We'll keep a close eye on him for the next few days, but I'm delighted with his progress." Dr Harvey gave them a broad smile, it faltered when he looked at me.

Brenda and Patrick turned, taking their eyes away from their son for the first time in what had been an excruciatingly long week. "You look exhausted, Sam," Brenda said. "You should rest too–" I started to protest, but she stopped me with a raised hand. "Edward will need you when he comes home. He's got a long recovery road ahead. While we're here take a little time and get some rest. You're nearly dead on your feet."

"I just need a bit of air. I'll be alright. Is it okay if I step outside for a few minutes?"

They nodded. "Of course dear, whatever you need."

With some relief, I let myself out the hospital room and limped my way down to the ground floor. I exited through the hospital's reception doors, and I pulled myself up onto a low wall.

My phone beeped with an incoming text. *Where are you?*

It was Heidi. *Sitting on the wall outside reception*, I texted back.

"Hey stranger," she said, when she walked up five minutes later.

I leant over and hugged her. She was a good friend. My best friend. She was also the only other person who knew the full details about the events preceding the accident.

"Sorry I'm a bit later today. Good to see you outside. You okay?" She pulled herself up onto the wall beside me. She'd visited the hospital daily since the accident – to see me, not Edward.

"No," I admitted.

"Want to talk about it?"

"Not really. Not yet. Just give me some time."

"As much as you need." She gave me a reassuring squeeze on my good knee. "Just breathe, honey."

Like Edward, it felt as if I was taking my first real breath since the accident. I closed my eyes and turned my face to the sun, feeling some of the tension ease a little.

"How's the shit-bag doing?"

Keeping my eyes closed, I said, "He wasn't always a shit-bag, but . . . good. They removed his ventilation. He's breathing on his own."

"That's great. I'm glad. I need him to hurry up and get better so I can kick his arse for hurting my best friend."

I opened my eyes and smiled at her, watching as she trailed her finger through the pink coating on the wall. It was everywhere. The strange fog had cleared after that first awful day, leaving behind its residue. The clean-up would take weeks.

She looked at her finger. "Hey, did you hear they said the pink stuff in the fog was some sort of airborne protein?"

"What?"

"The pink fog."

"Yeah?"

"It was an airborne protein. You're the medical rep, you know about medical stuff. I thought you'd know what that meant."

"Like an agar? An airborne agar?"

"I guess. If you say so."

"What caused it?" I felt woefully out of touch with the rest of the world.

"They still have no idea. Not Isis though, despite their claims." She snorted. The news had been rife with fears of biological attack on the morning of the fog. Scientists had been quick to reassure the public there were no known harmful elements contained within it, despite its strange luminosity. It had helped stop the finger-pointing when the fog enveloped the globe. Our accident had been one of hundreds caused by the poor visibility. My inattention hadn't helped though.

"It wasn't your fault," Heidi said.

"Are you a mind reader now?"

"No. I know the look. It wasn't your fault," she insisted. She had that stubborn set to her jaw I knew meant she wouldn't be budged on the subject.

"I crashed the car."

"The visibility was crap, and you were . . . distracted."

I snorted this time.

"He fucked another woman. You were entitled to be pissed off with him."

"I was certainly that." And hurt. All those weeks of believing his lies about where he'd been. The late-night texts I'd ignored. The perfume that wasn't mine. I'd been such a fool. "I wished him dead," I admitted.

"Hmm, I can't say I blame you. He treated you like shit the last few weeks. Maybe it's karma." She looked at me. "You need to eat something, Sam. You're getting too skinny. You're going to need your strength for what's to come."

The knot in my stomach tightened another notch.

***

"No, the liver seems fine. They're worried about his brain now." I pressed the phone to my other ear, as I sat on the bed beside Edward, looking down at his too-still form. He was so handsome. Perfect really. I traced my fingers along his stubble line until I reached the little cleft in his chin. He'd loved it when I did that. He'd loved a lot of the things I did. I'd loved a lot of the things he did for me too. In the beginning, we couldn't do enough for each other. I hadn't been able to believe my luck when he liked me too. I should have known it was too good to be true. I dropped my hand back into my lap.

"What's wrong with his liver?" Heidi sounded breathless, noisy traffic audible in the background.

"They don't know yet. They won't know until he wakes up, if he wakes up." There was no evidence of any swelling in the most recent scans, which they deemed to be very good news. Good enough to have made them suggest removing all anaesthetic in the hope he'd wake up and enable them to assess his cognitive function. So far, after a massive build-up of expectations, we'd waited a day but nothing had happened.

Edward had been moved to a different room now that he needed less one-on-one nursing. A private room, thanks to the bank's health insurance. Just as well, he didn't cope well with 'the masses'. He'd hate to wake up on a public ward. My eyes ran over the unrelenting white walls, broken only by the blue curtains, gaping in places where the hooks were missing. The NHS version of private healthcare. "I'm meant to talk to him."

"Isn't he in a coma?"

"Yes, but the nurse said he may still be able to hear us." His parents had certainly taken them at their word. I'd had to listen to a continuous stream of all the things they wished they'd thought to say to him. I felt like such a fraud. They'd chattered away to the both of us, as if they'd popped round for afternoon tea, seeming to have forgotten he was a thoughtless bastard who only bothered to see them twice a year – to collect his birthday and Christmas presents. I explained as much to Heidi.

"I don't know how you keep a straight face."

"Tell me about it. The thought of listening to it all day again today is almost enough to make me want to go back to work."

"Steady on."

I laughed. "I said *almost.*"

The door opened and Brenda breezed into the room, a wake of Estee Lauder fragrance washing in behind her. With the quantity she used, it was cloying in the small, unventilated space.

"I'll speak to you later, Heidi, Brenda's here," I said, not waiting for a reply as I disconnected. "Hi." I smiled up at his mum.

"Samantha, how are you doing, darling? How's our boy today? He's so lucky to have you." She patted my shoulder as she gazed down lovingly at her son. Guilt stabbed at me. The crash aside, I hated him for what he'd done to me – to us. I loathed all the pretence.

"I'm fine. He's fine. No change." I reeled off the required status update. "I'll go and get a coffee if you're happy here alone for a minute? I'm gasping." I couldn't wait to get away.

"Of course, darling. I won't be alone. I'll be with Edward. We'll be just fine together, won't we, my love?" She chattered away to him as she unpacked her bag. "I'm here for the day," she assured me, as I dithered beside her. "Patrick will be in to visit this evening too. You go and get your coffee, and rest that leg. Make sure someone carries it to the table for you."

I smiled gratefully. She'd been very kind to me. "Do you want anything?" She shook her head, already focused on Edward.

I dragged my coffee out for nearly forty-five minutes before limping slowly back to Edward's room, a room that became more and more like a cell. As I shuffled inside, Brenda spun towards me, her eyes bright. "Sam, thank goodness you're back! He's awake!"

My gaze darted towards the bed. Edward's eyes were open and staring straight at me. I saw no flicker of recognition. His dead-eyed stare sent bone-numbing fear running through my veins.

Chapter 3

For a second, the fear paralysed me, then sense kicked in. "Edward, how are you? How are you feeling?"

He said nothing.

I looked at Brenda. "Has he spoken yet?" I turned back to the bed, scanning his eyes and face for any signs of cognitive deficiency.

"Not yet, but he will," she said with confidence as she beamed down at her son.

"Samantha?" Edward's voice sounded husky from the intubation and lack of use.

"Oh my God!" I clasped a hand to my mouth. "Nurse!" I bellowed towards the closed door. "Nurse!" I shifted closer to the bed. "Edward, thank God you're okay."

The door burst open as medical staff poured in. Pushing me aside, they began to take his observations. "How do you feel, Edward?" a small man with bright red hair asked, as he shone a light into Edward's eyes. He wore a stethoscope around the neck of his white doctors' coat.

"Tired. Sore. Samantha?" Edward sounded anxious.

"Still here," I said from my position beside the wall. The crowd moved, making a space for me next to him. I struggled to meet his eyes, guilt and anger warring with my relief he'd woken.

"What do you remember about the accident?" the doctor asked, setting off more bursts of adrenaline, like fireworks, inside me. Did he remember asking me to slow down? Did he remember our fight? Did he remember fucking that girl . . . Serena?

Edward stared up at the doctor, returning his gaze to mine a second before answering. "Nothing. I don't remember anything."

The doctors exchanged a look. It was the neurologist who answered. "You've had a severe trauma to your head. It's to be expected you might have some temporary memory loss. I don't think it's anything much to worry about, all things considered, but we'll run some tests. I expect, over the next few weeks and months, things will improve naturally."

Edward nodded, appearing unconcerned.

Someone found him a cup of water and a straw. I watched as his mother helped raise his head to take a sip. His eyes drifted closed as soon as he rested back against the pillow, his breathing slow and measured. I sagged with relief.

"Oh, my darling, I'm so happy for you." Brenda pulled me into a tight hug. I pressed my face into her shoulder, glad it gave me the moment I needed to get a handle on myself. I wished desperately I could feel happy too. It was certainly good news that he'd woken up, but it forced me to face the terminal state of our relationship. I wondered if he even remembered hammering the final coffin-nail in with his wayward dick? Worse, what might happen if he didn't remember? I fixed a smile on my face as his mum gushed about how wonderful it all was.

"Maybe you should tell Patrick?" I suggested.

She gasped. "Patrick! My God, yes." She rushed out of the room.

As soon as the door closed, I collapsed onto a chair, my head clasped in my hands.

"Are you okay, Sam?" Edward's question startled me. I swung to look at him. His eyes were open again, and staring straight at me. "Are you okay?" he asked again.

"Fine," I replied automatically. I couldn't face the truth yet. "I'm sorry . . . I really have to go." I stood, my legs swaying as I tried to find my balance, before limping my way out of the room, hoping like hell he wouldn't ask me to stay. I didn't have the strength for more; my head spun. Outside the room, I leant heavily against the wall and closed my eyes, praying I'd find some strength from somewhere to get me through the next few weeks.

"Are you okay?" a voice asked.

What is it with people asking me that? I opened my eyes resentfully, to find Dr Harvey looking down at me.

"Do you need to sit down?" He sounded concerned.

"What I need is a stiff drink."

He smiled. "I know that feeling. I can't offer you alcohol, but I'm due a break if you fancy a coffee?"

***

"Triple shot. I probably shouldn't condone the abuse of your body with so much caffeine, but what the hell. I think you've probably earned it." He placed a cup down in front of me, followed by a scone and a small pot of strawberry jam. "You look like you're not eating enough." I protested, but he held up his hand. "Humour me, I'm the doctor."

My stomach rumbled and decided the matter.

"So," he began, after we'd both taken a sip of our respective coffees and I started smearing an excessive amount of jam over my fruit scone. "Edward's woken up and spoken. That's good news. He was lucky." He paused, tapping his index fingers together as he looked at me intently. "You must be delighted."

The tension returned, my shoulders stiffening at his words. "Yes. I am. Of course." The words tripped out of me. Each pause betraying my true feelings.

He frowned. "Look, forgive me if I'm overstepping the mark here. Please don't think you need to talk to me at all. Hell, you don't even need to sit at the same table as me to drink that." He nodded towards my coffee. "You just look so unhappy. In fact, you look ill. Chewed nails, rigid posture and clenched jaw; you look stressed beyond belief. Believe me, I didn't need seven years training to diagnose that. Is everything okay?" I opened my mouth to deny his observations, but he cut me off. "It can help to talk . . . especially to someone you don't know well, someone who isn't emotionally attached to the situation. I'm volunteering." He sat back in his seat, as far as the moulded orange plastic would allow, and stared at me, arms folded across his chest.

I stared down at the stubs that existed where I used to have fingernails, before looking up into his beautiful sky-blue eyes – my favourite colour blue. Beautiful blue eyes that appeared clouded with concern. There was no doubt he was a handsome guy. Not much older than me, I guessed, with unusually shaggy blonde hair. Unusual for a doctor. He looked the way I imagined a doctor in one of the Australian soaps might look, rather than the sun-starved, sleep-deprived NHS doctors I normally encountered through work. He was also right about my stress levels, and my need to talk to someone other than Heidi. Something about him made me want to trust him. "If you really don't mind?"

"I really don't," he assured me, his gaze steady on mine.

"Well, okay then." I took a bite of my scone.

"Okay then," he said. He tilted his head to one side as he looked at me. "So . . . if we start with the premise that it's a good thing Edward has woken up?" He paused, waiting as I chewed.

I nodded.

"Then explain to me why you don't look happy about it."

Guilt flooded my cheeks with heat. "Of course I'm pleased he's getting better. I'm not a monster!" I stopped, aware people were looking at us, and took a deep breath. "I can assure you, Dr Harvey–"

"Elliott, please."

"Okay, well I can assure you – Elliott – I would have been eaten alive by the guilt if he hadn't survived . . ." I paused, looking up from my coffee, ". . . I was driving when the accident happened. The thing is, Edward and I had just broken up."

"Why?"

"Simple, really. I caught him shagging another woman. You'll forgive me if, as a result, I'm not quite the gushing girlfriend everyone expects me to be." I had no idea what possessed me to be quite so brutally honest with him.

Elliott's eyebrows rose a little, then his expression softened. "Well, I guess that explains why you've appeared a little strained at times."

"Probably it," I agreed.

"More fool him, by the way."

"Sorry?"

He shook his head, unwilling to repeat himself. It didn't matter; I'd heard him. My cheeks bloomed for a second time. "Do his parents know you'd broken up?"

"No. It all happened on the day of the accident. We went to a wedding, he got pissed and then shagged someone else. I finished it, then we crashed on our way home. That was my day in a nutshell. Oh, and there was that fog."

"How long had you two been together?"

"Two years."

He whistled. "Two years – that's a fair while."

"Yeah, long enough to learn every little thing that pissed me off about him. The fact he fucked at least one other woman was a biggie, but it was just top of a long list."

"Sounds like you're glad you finished it."

"I was at the time. I am . . . I am." I said again, with more certainty. "The problem is, he doesn't remember the accident, so I don't know if he remembers we broke up. Then there are his parents to manage. Someone will have to look after him when he gets discharged. I'm guessing everyone assumes that will be me as we still live together."

"You don't have to do any of that if you don't want to. You can remind him you broke up. You can explain why to his parents, and then you can move out and start again with . . . someone who'd appreciate you a bit more." He looked at me intently.

Was he flirting with me? It had been so long since I'd paid any attention to the opposite sex, I didn't know for sure. "You make it sound so easy." I sighed.

"It is. Life's short. Don't waste it with someone who doesn't value you."

I swallowed down the last of my coffee and smiled. "You know what, maybe you're right. I just need to grasp the nettle, so to speak."

"It'll be easier to do it sooner rather than later," he assured me. "I've found it's better to call it a day early, rather than allow a failed relationship to limp on."

"I'm afraid I'm a bit of a limper." I popped the last piece of the scone in my mouth.

"Well, don't be this time. You were brave enough to finish it before the accident." We both stood. He picked up our tray and returned it to the carousel. "Just tell him what happened," he said, as he held the canteen door open and then followed me out to the lifts.

"*Just* tell him."

"It can be easy if you let it be. He's a big boy." He reached to hold the lift door open while I stepped in.

"Shouldn't you be telling me to avoid breaking his heart, given how much of the rest of him has been damaged recently? Not that I think he'd even care. He'd have a replacement installed before the lift doors closed. Girlfriend, I mean, not heart." I laughed, but the sound oozed with my bitterness.

We rode the lift in silence, stepping out into the corridor together. "I'm just trying to think about your long-term well-being, as well as his. You seem so stressed. It can't be good for you. Give yourself a break from all the responsibility."

I looked at him. "But that's the problem. I am responsible – at least for him being in that bed," I nodded my head towards the door to Edward's room as we paused outside. "I was driving. I'll always feel guilty he was hurt like that. At the end of the day, I crashed the car."

Elliott sighed. "I guess I'll see you around." He seemed reluctant to leave.

"Yeah, I imagine I'll be here a lot until he gets let out." I leant my shoulder against the door to Edward's room and pushed it open. "Oh, sorry," I said quickly, as a man jumped up from the chair beside Edward's bed. "I didn't mean to disturb you. I can come back later."

Edward glanced at the man, then me.

"I'm sorry," I said again, awkward tension filling the room.

"It's fine. I was just leaving." The stranger tightened the cord of his blue *Star Wars* dressing gown.

"Oh, you're a patient too?" The man nodded, then rushed past me with his head down. I turned to watch him leave, finding Elliott still framed in the doorway, a frown carving deep lines into his forehead, before the door closed on him. I turned back to Edward. "Who was that man?"

Edward ignored my question. "Should I be jealous you were hanging out with one of my doctors?" he said, his mouth set into a thin line.

The door opened again and prevented me from having to answer. I spun around, in case it was Elliott. It wasn't. "Darling, you're awake!" Brenda cried as she rushed to Edward's bedside. Patrick followed on her heels.

Relieved, I inched back towards the wall and spent the rest of the afternoon trying to ignore Edward's looks in my direction.

Chapter 4

A week later I arrived at the hospital and the place was heaving. People spilled out into the car park, as medical staff tried to direct them into some sort of order. The first person I recognised was Elliott. "Still limping along?" he said. I knew it wasn't a reference to my crutches and broken leg.

"What's going on?" I nodded towards the overflowing Reception.

"Mass panic."

"Why? What have I missed?"

"Don't you listen to the news? They found a virus in the fog. A retrovirus. It's integrated itself into our DNA . . . well, *male* DNA."

"God, really?" I looked around again. The place was full of men. "Is it harmful? Contagious?"

"They don't think so. It appears to be inactive, for now. Dormant in the cells of anyone who was exposed to the fog. I'm not sure everyone's convinced though. A&E are full to bursting. I haven't been home in thirty-six hours."

"Has anyone become ill?"

"Not yet, not as far as I've heard. The great and the good say there's nothing to worry about. I'm too busy to worry anyway." He looked at me. "So, it's been a while. What's your news?"

An awkward silence settled as I shuffled my feet, feeling my cheeks redden with what I could only imagine was shame at not having addressed my issues. "Nothing new." I didn't want to look up and face his disappointment, so I stared at my shoes whilst we waited for the lift to arrive. "Look, I know what you must think of me," I said finally, as we stepped in together.

"No, you don't, Samantha. You don't know what I think of you at all."

The doors opened on my floor, and I walked out into the long hallway, thinking to halt the conversation; Elliott followed, matching my pace. I thought he might say something more, but he hesitated as soon as we saw Edward in what looked like an intense discussion with the same man we'd seen in his room. The man with the *Star Wars* dressing gown. This time the man was fully dressed. Their heads were bent close together, their words spoken with some urgency from the sounds that drifted down the hallway towards us.

"He's out of bed already?" Elliott looked at me.

"Yes, the last day or so."

We walked slowly towards them. The two men were so intent on their conversation they didn't even look up. "That's amazing. By the way, how does Edward know Mr Rawlings?"

I glanced at Elliott, surprised by his question. He frowned, his attention fixed on them. He slowed his pace a little more and I matched him. I had no desire to reach Edward.

Elliott looked at me, waiting for my answer.

"That man? I have no idea." I shrugged, looking at the two men. "I'd never seen him before the other day; the day we saw him in Edward's room." Elliott's frown deepened.

When we got to within twenty paces, Edward heard us and looked up. He glared when he saw who walked beside me. "Samantha," he said, pulling me into his arms as soon as I moved within reach. "I missed you." He pressed a kiss onto my lips, cupping my face with his hand. He'd never liked public displays of affection; his greeting was so uncharacteristic it caught me by surprise. Shocked, I did nothing to resist.

Elliott had walked on by the time I managed to pull away. "You're feeling better," I said, flustered. I took a step back to put some much-needed distance between us. Edward grinned and exchanged a look with his friend. "We haven't properly met." I put out my hand.

"Richard," the man replied, smiling as he took it.

"How do you guys know each other?"

"We met in here," Edward said.

"Really? But I thought—"

"Well, I need to be off." Richard shook Edward's hand before smiling at me. "It's lovely to have met you. I'll see you soon," he said to Edward, who nodded.

Edward prevented any more questions by pulling me back into his arms and kissing me again. "God, I missed you."

"Stop." I tried to push him away, but he walked me backwards, my crutches dragging on the floor as they hung off my forearms, stopping when my back hit the wall. "Edward!"

"I can't wait to get home." His breath warmed my cheek as he pressed himself against me, making sure I knew for certain what he was looking forward to.

"I don't think you'll be well enough for any of that for a little while longer." I laughed, to cover my discomfort, as I attempted to move away from him again. He grabbed hold of my hand, and led me back into his room.

"I can't keep my hands off you. You're so beautiful." He pulled me towards him and tried to kiss me a third time, hands running over me. One of my crutches fell off my forearm and clattered onto the ground.

"Oh gosh, I'm sorry to interrupt," Brenda said with a laugh from the doorway.

I bent down and picked up my crutch, hobbling away from Edward, trying to catch my breath and hopefully my wits. He followed, folding his arms around my waist, pinning me against his chest as his chin rested on my shoulder.

"It's good to see you feeling so much better, Edward." Brenda laughed again, looking delighted.

I squirmed, but Edward held on tight. "I can't wait to get out of here. The doctor said maybe today if I promised to be good." He pressed against me again.

"That's wonderful, darling. And are you sure you and Samantha will be able to manage while she's still on crutches? Do you need me to come and stay for a bit?" I shuddered at the prospect.

"No. Thanks, Mum, really. Sam's getting around okay. She barely even uses the crutches – except as support – and I'm more mobile than anyone expected me to be. I think we'll be fine."

"Darling, please make sure you don't overdo it." She took a breath, but it turned into a sob. "To think I could have lost you," she said, voice trembling. She rummaged inside her handbag to find a tissue and then dabbed at the corners of her eyes.

"I'll take good care of him," I promised Brenda, "I'm happy to do it." I hated the lying words as they poured out of me like sewage from an overflowing toilet. I knew in my heart, no matter how lovely he was being to me now, or whatever he did, I couldn't forget what he'd already done to me . . . to us. So, as I listened to them plan the weeks ahead, I resolved to get him better, then get myself the hell out.

***

Forced to wait for hours until they completed the discharge paperwork, it took even longer for his medication to be brought up from pharmacy, so by the time the nurse announced his antibiotics were missing I wanted to scream with frustration.

"Do we really need them?" Edward groaned, as bored with waiting as me.

"You're at risk of infection until that wound is healed. I can't allow you to leave the hospital unless you have them."

"Really, I think this is quite unnecessary–"

"I'll get them," I said, keen to volunteer because it would allow me some much-needed space from Edward. His constant touching and stroking had left me on edge.

Elliott materialised as the lift doors were about to close. "We've got to stop meeting like this." He grinned, flashing me a dimple. "Are you going down?"

"To the pharmacy, yes," I said, unaccountably happy to see him. "Were you?" But he'd already stepped into the lift, moving far closer to me than social norms permitted. The hairs on my arms lifted in response. "Edward's allowed home today."

"So soon? That's amazing."

"I know. Everyone says that." The lift doors slid open.

He stepped out beside me, but grabbed my arm, halting me before I could move away. "Samantha." His expression looked intense. "I know you barely know me–" I opened my mouth, but he cut me off. "–Just because he nearly died, it doesn't excuse what he did. To you. You deserve better."

"I know. I haven't forgotten. I just need to see him well again, it's the guilt."

He nodded in understanding. "I get it. I do . . . But after?" His words hung between us. I shifted. "It's fine," he said, holding up a hand before I could speak. "Don't say anything. You know where to find me." He backed away, giving me another grin – one that showed off more dimple. Then he hesitated. "Just . . ." He looked uncertain. ". . . One more thing. If you notice anything . . . unusual . . . with Edward, I mean. Will you let me know?"

I frowned, thinking everything about Edward seemed fairly unusual at the moment, wondering how I might pick out a single unusual event when there were so many to choose from. Instead of voicing my thoughts, I found myself nodding.

He smiled a final time, and I noticed again how handsome he was. How tempting.

But Edward still needed me after everything he'd been through. The accident I'd caused. The least I could do was see him back to full strength. Maybe then I'd think about what I really wanted.

And what else might be possible, I thought, with a last look towards the retreating form of Dr Elliott Harvey.

Chapter 5

"I've been thinking," Edward announced. I turned my unseeing gaze from the blur of the passing high street and focused on the man beside me. The bus was full, crowded. Heads tilted our way, listening.

I flexed my newly liberated calf. It felt good, despite the forest of hair that adorned my lower limb and the obvious shrinkage of the muscle from lack of use. In another week or so I'd be able to drive again, and get back to my beloved kickboxing classes. Ironically, Edward, who had died – albeit briefly – had recovered even more quickly than me. Back to full strength, he'd bounded around the hospital earlier, greeting staff like old friends.

"Hmm?" I replied, my gaze swinging back to watch the people on the pavements. Edward's presence distracted me. He hadn't needed to come with me today, but it was yet another example of how much more thoughtful he'd become since the accident.

"Maybe you shouldn't go back to work."

I swivelled my head around to stare at him. "Sorry?" I managed. "Where did that come from?" I ignored the interested looks from nearby passengers.

"Well, it's not like we need the money. We can easily get by on what I earn, and I know you hate your job. Why don't you give the photography a proper go? What have you got to lose?"

I stared at him in shock. "But you always insisted we needed to maintain our income level . . . that you didn't want to support me." Who was this considerate, caring man? Only a few weeks ago he'd argued against me dropping down to four days a week to spend a day attending a photography course.

I pressed the button for our stop and stood as the bus slowed. "Samantha," he called as I moved out as quickly as my stiff leg would allow, needing to get off, avoiding the stares of the other passengers as I used my crutches to clear a path. I ignored him, forging through the crowd, until I reached the front and hopped down onto the pavement. "Samantha," Edward called again, a moment or two behind me. I ignored him again, setting off towards the apartment.

He caught me easily, pulling my arm until I stopped and turned towards him. Behind us, the passengers watched, enjoying our display, making me grateful when the bus moved off and gave us some privacy.

"What?"

"What was that? Why are you not talking to me?" He sounded confused.

"I am talking to you. Just not about this. Not right now."

"Why not? It's a good idea. When we're married–"

"Stop! Who said anything about marriage?"

"Samantha . . ." His use of my full name in that long-suffering tone, the one that always implied he thought I was being stupid, irritated me. What right did he have to sound exasperated when it was him who kept saying and doing things entirely out of character? "You know it's inevitable." He tried to pull me into a kiss, but I held myself away, tense and unyielding.

"Stop it." I pushed against his chest. "Stop trying to distract me. You keep doing this."

"I want to be close to you. I like being close to you."

"You just want to get your end away, and I'm the closest thing on hand."

"I can't help it if you turn me on." He grinned, his expression boyish.

Handsome, I found myself thinking. I caught my breath as the pain of his betrayal hit me again. "Everything turns you on at the moment. You're horny. I could be a blow-up doll for all you care."

"Not true. I want to be close to you. I miss being intimate with you. It's been too long."

"Because you nearly died. You had major abdominal surgery."

"I'm better now."

"So you say. Excuse me if I listen to the doctors' opinion, rather than yours."

"Well, he said it's all systems go, and now you've had your cast off. So . . ."

His willingness to wait until my cast had been removed, to put my needs before his own, had been yet another unexpected and oddly touching gesture. It meant today signalled the end of my last good excuse. I still didn't feel ready for anything like that. I didn't think I ever would again. I found it hard to imagine a time I wouldn't have the mental image of Edward and Serena together whenever I thought about having sex with him.

"When we're married—"

"Stop saying that!" Despite some better moments between us over the last few weeks, I had no idea where the sudden talk of marriage had come from. The prospect washed over me like a cold shower. I would not let myself fall for his sweet lies again. "Believe me, there is no chance of us getting married." I pushed past him, running up the steps and into the apartment block as fast as my stiff leg would allow.

"Why would you say that?" He sounded bewildered as he followed me into the building. "We're perfect together. You're beautiful, sexy, intelligent, kind, caring. What more could I want in a wife and the future mother of my children?"

"I'm not having this conversation!" I rummaged inside my bag to find my keys, propping it up on my knee to get better access. It was too big and too full for me to locate them. Edward moved me gently aside and unlocked the door with his own set.

"I'm able to provide for you, I'm fit and healthy – well, almost – and handsome, so I'm told." He smiled.

I snorted at that.

"What?" He seemed surprised by my response.

"Do you really want to have this conversation now?" I slammed my bag down on the sideboard just inside the front door, knocking over the carved wooden elephant, a gift from my mother after her safari trip.

I'd avoided going near this whole subject for weeks, much to Heidi's open disapproval. She'd told me, in no uncertain terms, that I needed to remove my ostrich-like head from the sand in which it was currently placed and face up to the elephant in the room. When I'd pointed out her overuse of animal metaphors, she'd raised a well-plucked eyebrow at me – as much as her recent Botox session would allow – and told me not to try and change the subject. That I was deluding myself if I thought Edward had really changed at all, telling me a leopard didn't change its spots.

I didn't know if I wanted to have this conversation. It had been civilised between us since we'd been home, like the early days of our relationship. He'd been kind, attentive. Loving. I'd liked it. It seemed a shame to bring it all to a crashing end.

"So, why don't you think you can see yourself marrying me?" Edward persisted, as he switched on the kettle to make me a cup of tea. Another thing he did for me all the time now. All this thoughtful behaviour was freaking me the fuck out.

"I'm not ready to talk about this." I stalked out the kitchen and into the bathroom, turning on the taps to run a much-anticipated bath, the desire to shave my leg overriding everything else. I rolled my shoulders back to ease a little of the tension, ignoring the anxiety twisting in my stomach. An all too familiar state since the accident.

Once the bath and bubbles had reached a sufficient volume, I stripped and stepped into the warm water, immersing my leg for the first time in weeks. I groaned as I fully submerged my body, ducking my head below the waterline, cutting myself off from everything but the muffled sounds within my watery sanctuary.

Eyes closed to protect them from the bubbles, ears blocked by the soapy water, a change in the quantity of light filtering through the backs of my eyelids alerted me to another presence in the room. I opened my eyes to find Edward hovering over me, inches from my face. "Jesus, fuck!" I gasped, spluttering, slipping as I scooted away from him within the confined space of the bath. My arms rose to cover my chest. "What the fuck are you doing in here?" I demanded, anger replacing the initial shock and fear.

"I wanted to check you were okay. I called, but you didn't answer. I was worried."

I frowned. "Well, as you can see I'm perfectly fine." I crossed my arms tighter over my chest to hide my breasts when his gaze dropped towards them. We'd slept in the same bed for the last few weeks, but I'd made a point of never changing in front of him. Thank God for the bubbles that obscured me.

"You look fine," he said, his voice low and heavy with meaning. Desire flared in his eyes as he stared at me.

"I want to shave my leg," I blurted. "Then we'll talk . . . I promise," I added, when disbelief replaced lust.

"Okay." He exhaled heavily. "We'll talk. Then later . . ." He let the words hang before he walked out.

***

I was so pruned by the time I got out the bath, my skin looked crenelated. I spent another thirty minutes drying my hair. With all my delaying tactics deployed, I emerged from the bedroom wearing clean underwear and my bathrobe, to find Edward in the lounge reading one of my books. I knew it was one of mine because the most he normally read was the walkthrough guide of one of his Xbox games when he was stuck on a level.

"What are you reading?" I asked when he looked up.

"*The Road.*" He held it up for me to see the cover.

"Depressing."

"But good. Father and son, trying to survive against the odds. It's really good. Moving."

I waited for him to add a stupid one-liner. It didn't come. "Yeah." I sat in the chair beside him, and took a deep breath. "I'm sorry I shouted at you. You made me jump."

"I understand. I frightened you. I don't want to frighten you." He reached out and took hold of my hand, squeezing it. "Are you ready to talk?"

I nodded.

"So?"

I took a deep breath, wondering where the hell to start. "What do you remember about us? Before the accident, I mean."

"What do you mean?"

"Do you remember being happy?"

"Yes."

"Well, I wasn't."

He frowned.

"We weren't."

"We weren't?" He sounded genuinely surprised. "I was. From what I remember."

I stared at him. His eyes met mine. There was no sign of the shiftiness I'd come to know so well. "You're different."

His eyebrows shot up this time.

"Since the accident."

He swallowed, his Adam's apple bobbing with the motion. "I am?"

I considered a moment or two longer. "Yes. Nicer. More thoughtful. It's . . . odd."

"Good odd or bad odd?"

I thought about it for a moment. "Good odd, I think."

"Is that why you don't want to marry me? Because I've changed?"

"No," I said quickly. "In fact, if anything, I'd be more likely to marry the man you seem to be now, than the man you were." I let that hang for a moment. He looked relieved. "Do you remember anything about our argument at the wedding?"

"We argued? At the wedding?"

"Yes. We broke up at the wedding."

He stared at me, eyes wide. "We broke up?" he said, as if hearing it for the first time. "Why? What happened?"

"I caught you fucking another woman."

His mouth opened, then closed again.

"Edward, I don't think it was the first time you'd been with someone else. You admitted as much to me just before the crash. Only it was the last time, as far as I was concerned." I paused, letting him take a second.

He nodded for me to go on.

"That's it really. I caught you with her and we left. I told you I'd had enough, and that we were over. Then we crashed in the fog on our way home. You didn't remember any of it, and I didn't know how to tell you."

"Jesus." He exhaled, running his hands through his hair. "Jesus." He looked at me. "Samantha, I'm so incredibly sorry."

Out of everything I'd expected him to say, all the defensiveness, denial and lies I'd anticipated, like the ones I'd already heard on the day of the wedding, I'd never once imagined he might apologise. "You really don't remember any of it?" I said again, less certain now.

"Not the wedding. I remember ... before that," he admitted. "I didn't know you knew. I didn't want to say anything because I didn't want to lose you. I can't believe I was so stupid. Not one of them held a candle to you. I've been such a fool." He grimaced. "I didn't remember the wedding ... Jesus, no wonder you don't want to marry me. I don't blame you."

I nodded, unsettled by his remorse.

"You actually caught me? With the girl?"

"Yes."

"Jesus." He ran his hands through his hair again, looking anguished. "So, we argued? In the car?"

I gave a short nod.

"And then we crashed?"

Again, I could only nod.

"I caused the accident? I distracted you?"

I took a deep breath. "We were arguing. The fog was bad. I was distracted. It was no one's fault, really, just a bad combination of factors, which made for a crappy ending to an even crappier day."

"God, Sam. Can you ever forgive me?"

That was the question, really. I'd never imagined he'd even ask. He'd been so adamant, the last time we'd discussed the subject, I'd been as much to blame as him. He'd almost convinced me it had been my own fault he'd needed to look at other women in the first place. I'd never considered any other option than splitting up. His remorse was totally unexpected.

"I don't know." I pushed a tear away from my cheek with the back of my hand, irritated to find it there in the first place.

"Babe." He slid next to me and pulled me into his arms. "God, I am so, *so* sorry. I know I don't deserve your forgiveness, but I want to try to earn it. I want to be with you. Nearly dying like that has made me appreciate what we've got together. I want to hold on to it . . . hold on to you." He stroked my hair, soothing me. For the first time in weeks, the tension I'd held curled inside – my guilt over the accident, my feelings about his infidelity – uncurled and released. Unbidden, a sob choked out of me, and then another. All the pent-up anger and guilt about the accident spilled out in a flood of tears I seemed unable to stem now the wall had finally been breached. Throughout, he held me and whispered words of apology and comfort.

Sometime later, I stopped crying, his chest damp beneath my cheek, and turned to look at him.

"Please give me a second chance, Sam. I've been given a second chance at life. I love you. I've always loved you. I was a stupid, immature fool. I didn't appreciate what we had. I need you – only you – and I won't make the same mistake again." He held my gaze, his expression clear, the words acting like a balm, soothing away some of the pain and hurt of his betrayal and rejection. I wanted to be wanted again, needed it, despite everything.

Desire coiled within me, and he saw it. He lowered his head and kissed me. The salty taste of my tears softened our lips as the growing urgency took away thoughts of anything but what I needed from him right then.

Chapter 6

My senses returned one-by-one after what felt like minutes, but may have been hours. Edward's body lay across mine, inside mine.

The sensation of warm trickling fluid as he withdrew from me broke through my blissed-out state. I sat up quickly and stared at him in horror. "You didn't use a condom?" I gasped at the tell-tale evidence now coating the insides of my thighs.

"Fuck, you're beautiful." He reached for my breast, his finger teasing my nipple.

My eyes closed for a second as the sensations took hold. Then I remembered. "Edward, stop. You didn't use a condom. You know I don't use anything else. We could get pregnant."

He moved towards me again and pushed me back down on the bed. "I don't care," he said. "I want to feel you like this." He moved slowly. "I need to be close to you."

"Edward–" I protested, but it sounded feeble. Instead, my body responded, pulling him closer as I pushed away common sense, and gave myself over to base instinct.

***

When I woke, my body ached deliciously. I reached across, but Edward's side of the bed was empty, the sheets cold to my touch. Flopping back against the pillows, I allowed myself to wallow for a moment in the memories of the night before. For a man only recently recovered from a major abdominal operation, his sexual endurance had been phenomenal. It bore no relation to other recent times we'd had sex – as exciting as our relationship in its earliest days, when we couldn't leave each other alone. Although the sex had never been bad. I shivered, feeling aroused all over again. His apparent unconcern at the prospect of getting me pregnant had lit the blue touch paper of my libido. I couldn't get enough of him. Perhaps my thirty-something ovaries were more aware of the need to procreate than I was willing to admit.

But, in the cold light of day, the prospect of having a child with Edward felt slightly less appealing. Even worse, the more I thought about it, were the potential consequences of having unprotected sex with a man who may have stuck his dick in a virtual whorehouse of other women. I had no idea if he'd always covered himself up.

Mood somewhat dampened, I slid out of bed, grabbing my bathrobe, and headed for the shower. The evidence of my irresponsible behaviour coated my thighs, making me feel sticky and uncomfortable. With relief, I washed it away, removing all externally visible traces, as I promised myself I wouldn't let it happen again.

Determined to sort it out, I applied a quick layer of foundation and some mascara, dressed in my comfiest jeans and an old shirt, and quickly plaited my still-damp hair.

Edward still hadn't come home by the time I was ready to leave, so I scribbled him a quick note, then pulled on my jacket and hurried out the door.

***

Leaving the pharmacy, I looked down at the packet of small white pills clasped in my hand and experienced a moment of doubt, wondering whether I wouldn't quite like to have a baby. The thought lasted no more than five seconds. Then I remembered just how bad our relationship had been before the accident, and how hard it would be to raise a child alone. I unscrewed the top of my bottle of water, popped the first of the pills from the packet onto my tongue and swallowed it down, telling myself Edward was far too selfish to be a good dad, no matter how well-intentioned he might be right now.

The warm, spring-like weather made it an easy decision to walk back to the apartment rather than catch the bus, the gentle exercise feeling good on my underused leg muscles. Unfortunately, the removal of my cast also meant I needed to start thinking about returning to work again. My sick note only covered another week, leaving little time to decide about Edward's offer. I hated being a wage slave, but, without the support of someone like Edward, I couldn't afford to follow my love of photography and still eat. Even blissed out from great sex, relying on Edward – a man with whom I'd been on the verge of splitting up – seemed like a bad idea.

In a Voldemort-esque coincidence, as if by thinking of him I'd wished him there, Edward materialised in the window of the Costa in front of me. The closest coffee shop to our apartment, he was sprawled across one of the large brown leather armchairs beside the window.

I stared at him from across the street while I waited for the crossing to flash green, wondering who he was drinking coffee with. He threw his head back and laughed, sending a dread through me that embedded itself in the pit of my stomach. Kicking myself for falling for his charms again, I tried to remember the last time I'd seen him laugh like that at anything I'd said – so long ago I couldn't recall it – until the light changed and I crossed the road towards him.

He looked up as I stepped onto the pavement. I raised my hand in a half wave, feeling awkward and embarrassed. His gaze flickered towards whoever he was with. Then he looked back at me and smiled. Despite the warmth of his smile, the momentary delay was enough to sew doubt. Determined, I walked towards the door of the cafe and pushed inside.

The place was busy, the tables filled with women and their noisy preschool children. "Babe," Edward stood and moved to intercept me, bending to press a kiss onto my lips.

Surprised, I became aware of the people around watching us and pulled away, cringing.

"What can I get you? Come and meet the guys," he said, as if nothing unusual had occurred.

I looked over his shoulder, towards the window, relieved to find a group of six men seated in a circle of the chocolate-brown armchairs. They stared back with equal interest. The only face I recognised was Richard's.

"Hi," I said with a small wave, feeling shy, as Edward took hold of my hand and led me over to make the introductions.

He fussed around me, waiting until I was seated before running off to fetch me my favourite coffee – a vanilla spice latte, my ultimate coffee indulgence – while I sat in the chair he'd vacated.

"Nice to see you again. How are you doing? Are you fully recovered?" I peppered Richard with questions to cover my awkwardness, as the group continued to stare at me in silence.

"Oh yes, thank you, yes. Yes, I'm perfectly fine. How kind of you to remember."

"What was the matter?" I asked, struggling to think of another topic for conversation.

"I had a heart attack."

"Goodness! But you're okay now?" It amazed me he'd been discharged so soon after something so serious. He was young to have had a heart attack; it suggested some sort of heart disease, possibly heart failure – not the kind of thing you just "got over" easily.

"Yes, thank you for asking, much better. Fine really, not that my parents are convinced, they fuss dreadfully." He looked old to still be living at home with his parents. Given he was dressed like a bit of a geek, and seemed somewhat socially awkward, I imagined his heart problem meant he'd relied on them a fair bit.

"Edward's lucky to have you to take such good care of him," Richard said, adding an unexpected wink. From the shared smirks round the table, the reference had little to do with my nursing skills. Edward had clearly been telling tales.

The exchange left me feeling uncomfortable, cheeks heated with embarrassment. The whole group made me uneasy with their silent staring. Their oddly matched clothes in outdated fabrics gave the impression of a meeting of the math club, at odds with the sort of people with whom my appearance-conscious partner usually associated. "So, how did you all meet?"

Richard's eyes darted towards one of the other men as his hands shredded the paper napkin on his lap. He hesitated a moment longer than felt comfortable. "We're part of a patient support group. For people who've survived a medical trauma. It helps to talk to others who've been through the same thing."

"Oh, of course."

Edward placed my latte down on the table in front of me, complete with a spontaneous caramel slice, making me scowl despite it being my favourite. "I can't start kickboxing or running for another few weeks," I complained. "You'll make me fat."

"Baby, you're gorgeous, whatever weight you are." He pulled up a chair beside mine, his hand caressing my thigh through my jeans.

I stared at him in shock, then snorted. "Is this the same guy who can't even watch fat people on T.V?"

"Don't be so dramatic."

"When I sold that weight loss product, we had a row about whether it should be funded by the NHS. As I recall, you insisted people should just 'stick less in their gobs'."

"I'm not that bad—"

"What about that crack you made about the bridesmaid at Victoria's wedding."

"I don't remember the wedding."

I let the subject drop, feeling guilty, as he launched into a discussion with one of the other guys about the new car he planned to buy.

"Jamie, watch out!" a woman called from behind us. Her frantic tone making me turn just as a small boy, holding a tray that contained a single cup of hot chocolate, failed to notice the acute tilt that had developed. In slow-motion, the cup slid towards the edge, hit the lip of the tray and then tipped forward, depositing its scalding contents down Edward's back. He launched to his feet with a bellow of rage.

"What the fuck!" The boy stood there, frozen in shock, as Edward towered above him. His lower lip trembled as his mother rushed to his side.

"God, I'm so sorry." She dabbed at Edward's sodden back with napkins.

He flinched as she touched his scalded skin. "Don't fucking touch me."

"It was an accident," she tried again. "He didn't mean to do it."

"What the fuck were you thinking, getting a child to carry a tray containing a cup of boiling hot liquid?"

"He wanted to be a big boy. I thought he'd be okay with the tray."

The coffee shop staff rushed over at the commotion, in time to witness Edward pulling the soaking shirt away from his scalded skin and slipping it off over his head. A couple of them started to dab at him again with paper napkins.

"Well, clearly he *wasn't* fucking capable," Edward seethed, as the kid sobbed, devastated, the coffee shop staff still dabbing.

The skin on his back looked red, from where the hot liquid had scalded him, but there were no blisters. I reached out and placed my hand on his arm, hoping to take his anger down a notch. "Edward, calm down a bit."

"Calm down?" He turned towards me, outraged. I cringed, feeling the full force of his ire.

"Edward!" Richard said. His tone of voice unexpectedly assertive for someone wearing corduroy.

Edward flinched and appeared to shake himself. He took a step back, apologising for being so angry, as the woman gratefully led the still-weeping child from the shop and ushered him into a car outside.

Whilst I reeled with emotional whiplash, Edward pulled on a spare t-shirt one of the staff had found to replace his own sodden one which lay forgotten over the back of a chair, then sat down and continued to drink his coffee as if nothing had happened. He thanked the staff effusively when they brought over a complimentary round of drinks. Within minutes, it was as if nothing had happened. It took me a while longer to settle.

"You look tired," Edward leaned over to whisper. We'd been there for more than an hour. I rubbed my leg, the recently mended bone protesting at my earlier activity. "Shall we go?"

I nodded, more than ready.

"I'll call you," Edward promised Richard as he helped me into my jacket, reaching down to take a hold of my hand, the pad of his thumb brushing gently over the top of my knuckles. I looked down at it, and then up at him. He smiled. "Ready?"

I nodded, unable to speak, berating myself as I fell a little more for his charms. *You can't trust him*, my subconscious admonished me, even as I let him lead me out the café and back towards the apartment.

I needed distance. I needed time to get my head together, to remind myself why we'd broken up all those weeks ago. "I'll pop in here and get something for dinner," I told him, pulling my hand away from his as I stopped outside the entrance to the local supermarket. "You go on back. I'll be right behind you." He'd always contended that I was 'cooking and cleaning', whilst he looked after 'gardening and maintenance'. The fact we didn't have a garden and he didn't own a toolbox, just knew the number of a man who would happily do all his odd jobs for a fee, never struck him as a problem.

"Sam, you're tired. You need to put that foot up or it'll swell. You heard what the doctor said. Come home with me. We can do an online order later, I'll get us a takeaway if we're hungry. You've done enough for one day. Come on, let's watch a film and just chill." Astonished, and feeling oddly emotional, I let him wrap an arm around my shoulders and pull me against him.

Inside, he settled me on the sofa with my leg up, before retreating to the kitchen to make us both a cup of tea. "What do you want to watch?" he asked.

I shrugged.

"I know." He grinned, disappearing for a few minutes and returning with my copy of *Gladiator*. It was one of my all-time favourites. He settled in beside me on the sofa, turning my body so that I leant against him, my head on his chest, his arm draped easily across me.

We'd only reached a quarter of the way through the film when his fingers brushed my thigh, light at first, the whisper of a touch that made me wonder if I'd imagined it, until I felt it a second time. Then a third, as he started to stroke me, his hand drifting higher. As the pressure increased I turned to look at him. He met my gaze, eyes dropping to my lips a second before he kissed me. The kiss escalated quickly, until we were pulling at one another's clothes. I didn't know who had started it, only that I needed access to skin. Within minutes, we were naked. "Condom," I gasped.

"Next time," he promised.

"No," I groaned, even as my body opened for him. "I don't want to have a baby. Not yet, anyway. Get a condom."

"Sssh, baby, it feels so much better like this."

My body moved in response, betraying my brain again. "Pull out before you come," I gasped. It felt so good. It was hard to remember to be angry with him. The element of risk made it sexier somehow.

As my body contracted around him, his own groan penetrated my bliss. He shuddered and released, making no effort whatsoever to pull out.

"Fuck! You didn't pull out."

"God, nothing has ever felt this good." He sounded happy.

"I asked you not to. I don't want a baby right now." I pulled away, annoyed with myself as much as him. I prayed the pills I'd taken would work against this episode too.

"Well, I do," he said, matter-of-factly.

"You hate children! Why on earth would you want one now?" I said, confused by his turnaround on the subject.

"A man can change his mind. Nearly dying will do that to you."

"We have plenty of time – there's no rush."

"Life's short. We need to make the most of it, so why wait?"

"Because I'm not ready."

"You'll love it when it arrives. You'll be a great mother."

"I'm not ready for that yet. I'm not even ready to commit to you long term, let alone have a child. You might have done a life one eighty, but that doesn't mean I have. I don't know for sure that we even have a future together. Only a few weeks ago I was certain that we didn't. Anyway," I continued, getting into my groove now, "that wasn't exactly an audition for Father of the Year back at the coffee shop earlier. That kid nearly wet himself, he was so terrified of you. Don't push me on this. I want you to use a condom from now on."

"No," he said, his face set with a stubborn expression I knew only too well meant he wouldn't be moved on the subject.

"Then no more sex," I countered, being equally stubborn.

He grinned at that. "We'll see." He looked smug.

That pissed me off. By the expression on his face, he assumed I'd be gagging for it soon enough. I determined to get straight back down to the doctor's and onto a longer-term contraceptive solution, now it seemed I could no longer trust him to wear a condom. That would put a stop to the silliness.

Chapter 7

Edward veered from cajoling one minute to angry the next, and back again, several times. Relentless, he tried everything to woo me back into the sack; flattering my appearance, touching me at any opportunity – sometimes highly inappropriately. He didn't want to take no for an answer. I stood my ground.

When he was being nice I almost felt tempted. The sex had been good – I missed it. But, more often than not, my refusal made him angry with me. Then, I found myself a little afraid of him. Edward had always been moody, but I'd never known him to be quite so emotionally volatile.

A week later, I was on the pill. I had woken to light bleeding, which meant I could start using them immediately. I stashed the packet I was taking deep in my handbag and was in the process of secreting the other two packets in the back of the bathroom cabinet, inside an old wash bag we never used, when Edward walked in. "What are you doing?"

Flustered, I knocked over a can of shaving foam. "Looking for these," I said, pulling out a packet of tampons.

"You got your period? Are you sure?"

I laughed, unable to meet his eyes. "I think I know when I get my period." My flippant remark didn't help matters.

"You're so fucking selfish. It's always about you, and what you want. What about me? How about giving a shit about my feelings for once?" He towered over me, jabbing his finger into my chest, making me cringe away from him. "Fuck this!" He stormed out the bathroom. I heard him pick up his keys from the bowl in the hall, before the apartment door slammed closed, sending a tremor through the building that rattled the windows.

"I'm sorry baby," he said, breezing in through the door later as if nothing had happened. "We'll be luckier next time."

I nodded, a pleasant smile fixed on my face, relieved he seemed calmer. His earlier rage had frightened me.

He bent and kissed me gently.

I didn't miss the waft of a floral fragrance I didn't recognise, wondering where he'd been for the last four hours – or who he'd been with.

"Do you need a hot water bottle for the cramps?"

I forced a smile, and nodded again, my mind whirling when he left me to fill the kettle. One thing had become clear; there was no way I wanted a baby with him right now. Great sex did not provide reason enough, despite the generally positive change overall in our relationship. I still didn't trust him.

***

I stared down at Edward's unmoving form, burrowed beneath the duvet. He looked out for the count. Rather than disturb him, I scribbled a quick note, letting him know I'd gone out for a coffee, and propped it on the table so he'd see it when he woke. On a whim, enjoying the warmer weather, I walked a little further instead of going to the Costa, snapping photos on my Nikon D850 as I went.

I ordered a skinny latte then flopped into an armchair to read the paper someone had left behind on the chair. As expected, the news continued to be full of reports about the unknown retrovirus particles they'd found within the fog's residue:

Scientists have confirmed the new virus is a viral vector; a carrying mechanism that can deliver viral genetic material straight into human cells. To date, infection rates suggest any men exposed to the fog have tested positive for traces of the virus.

Despite high levels of public alarm, The World Health Organisation have reiterated there has been no evidence to date of any immune response to the virus. Tests have shown the material as dormant within their human host cells. Officials have dismissed claims the virus is cytocidal or infectious as 'scaremongering'.

Several pharmaceutical companies have filed patents for the viral material, which it is hoped may offer new options for treatments against cancer—

I put the paper down, depressed. I was due back at work soon. The article provided a timely reminder of why I hated my job – making profit out of ill health had always made me uncomfortable, however laudable the treatment being sold. Unfortunately, I needed to work, because having no income made me even more uncomfortable. I'd allowed money to trump my morals.

I sighed and pulled out my phone, texting Heidi my location in the vague hope she might be free to come and join me. We'd failed to meet up since Edward had come out of hospital. He'd demanded all my time and attention, his needy behaviour leaving little of anything for anyone else. Twenty minutes later, she walked through the door of the café with a big grin on her face, wearing stylishly old jeans and a jumper with designer holes in it. "Look at you," she said as she sat down. "Beautiful as ever. Have you left fuckwit yet?"

"No, but I'm getting close."

"What's stopping you? I thought he'd fucked one too many other women, even for you."

"Yeah, well, he's changed."

She raised a single eyebrow.

"Really, he has. Since the accident. He's like a different bloke. Edward Mark II – the new, improved version."

"Whatever. I've heard it all before – the last few times you suspected he'd slept with other women. He's just turning on the charm again, trying to hold on to you, using whatever manipulative means he can. Who can blame him? You're gorgeous."

"This time he really seems different. He wants to have a baby." This was a sore subject for Heidi, who'd been trying to get pregnant since she and Paul had married eighteen months ago, with no success.

"Fucking hell. He's barely able to wipe his own arse, and now he wants to inflict himself on another human being." She snorted, then rocked backwards in her chair when she saw my face. "Don't tell me you're actually considering it?"

"No," I said quickly. "I thought about it for maybe a nanosecond." She started to react, so I continued: "No, honestly, he really has been at his most charming recently – most of the time – and the sex has been amazing. But then I remembered how bad it was before." I paused. "Seriously, though, you'd hardly recognise the guy. He's different. I can't tell if it was the blow to his head in the accident or just knowing that he nearly died, but he's like a completely different guy. Sadly, I fear he's just replaced a load of fucking annoying habits with a whole new set of different but equally annoying ones."

"I need to see this 'new Edward'. When are you free?" Heidi grinned. I laughed, but the idea of getting some of the old gang together appealed. Friday nights in the pub, with whoever could make it, drowning work woes in excessive amounts of alcohol had been our thing. It would be nice to do something normal again.

An hour later, having made plans to meet, I was happy and relaxed, feeling far more myself. "Text me and let me know how work goes," she said, hugging me tight.

Stepping out of the coffee shop, I felt lighter than I had in weeks. It was warm enough to take my coat off for the walk home. The sun heated my skin, signposting summer just around the corner. I'd always been a sunshine girl; it worked wonders on my mood.

Happy, I pulled out my camera and snapped some more pictures in the park – people were out in force, making the most of a rare sunny weekend – and then, content I'd got some good shots, I meandered my way back to the apartment, in no hurry to get home.

I'd barely put my key in the lock when the door swung open. "Where the fuck have you been?" Edward growled as he pushed me against the wall and pinned me there with his body.

"What the hell?" I laughed, assuming he was joking, confused by his aggressive greeting.

"I asked where the fuck have you been? You've been gone all morning, and you weren't in the Costa like you said. So, where the hell were you?"

"I never said I was going to the Costa. I said I was going for a coffee. I went to the French café. I met Heidi there. Then I walked home and stopped to take some photos in the park. Not that it has anything to do with you." I tried, unsuccessfully, to push him away from me.

"Wrong. It has everything to do with me. We're a couple. I look after what's mine."

"No, you're wrong. What's with the caveman impression? We might be a couple, but that doesn't make you my keeper. Last time I checked, I was a free woman, allowed to go where I want, when I want. So back the fuck up, or we won't even be a couple."

He ignored me; "Are you still bleeding?"

"No," I said, bemused by the sudden change in conversational direction. The bleeding had stopped this morning, having been briefer than normal because of the pill. Without a word, he swept me into his arms and carried me into the bedroom. "Put me down," I protested as soon as I realised what his intentions were. "I'm not in the mood."

"I'll get you in the mood," he promised, as he placed me on the bed and started to undress me, ignoring my protestations. When the buttons on my shirt didn't release quickly enough, he pulled it apart, sending them flying towards the corners of the room.

"Fucking hell, Edward!" I yelled, irritated by his destruction of a favourite item. He silenced me with a kiss as he pushed my skirt up and fumbled with his jeans, trying to release himself.

I pulled away. "No! Stop!"

He froze, my words at last penetrating his lust.

I pushed him off me and slid from the bed, pulling down my skirt as I grabbed a clean t-shirt, and headed into the bathroom, slamming the door closed behind me.

"Sam," Edward called from the other side of the door. "Are you okay?"

"What do you think?"

"I'm sorry, I was mad. I didn't think."

I opened the bathroom door, wrapped in a towel, the shower steaming behind me. "That was not okay. Being mad does not excuse you. I hadn't done anything wrong."

"I know, I know. I just see red where you're concerned. You're so fucking beautiful, whenever you're not with me I imagine other guys wanting to take you from me. I mean, why wouldn't they, given half a chance?"

"Well, I guess it's true 'cheaters think everyone cheats'. You shouldn't judge me by your own low standards." My shallowest-self took some pleasure in seeing him struggle with his insecurities. It made a change for the shoe being to be on the other foot for once.

He stepped towards me, eyes darkening as they ran over me, his body stiffening in response. He walked me backwards towards the shower. "Don't ever try and force yourself on me again. No means no. If you do, I'll leave."

"I won't. I promise. I just . . . want you so much." He looked at me as if I were the most beautiful woman on earth.

Hell, I could enjoy the sex, couldn't I? It didn't need to be more than that. As for the condom issue, the pills would cover me there. I could let him believe he was getting his way, that we were trying for a baby. He dropped to his knees in front of me, and my resolve wavered. He kissed me, and I melted. *Fuck it*, I decided, resistance was futile.

Chapter 8

Work was as shit as I remembered it to be. In fact, it was worse. I spent long days trying to see clinicians, who frankly couldn't care less about what I had to say, even when they did give me some time to talk to them about our products. Given what I knew from firsthand experience they did for patients, I felt bad about taking up their time. When I wasn't stalking doctors in hospital corridors, I sat in interminable internal meetings discussing strategies to see the same doctors who still wouldn't want to see me.

Then there was my manager. The man was an arse.

"So, tell me about the crash," he said at our first meeting, head tilted to one side.

I had. I'd told him how close Edward had come to dying. I'd explained how his heart stopped beating for a time, my eyes brimming with tears as I recalled the horror. When I'd finished, wiping my tears away with a tissue and then blowing my nose noisily, he'd shifted in his seat, eyes scanning the room as if looking for an escape. "Yes, well, I think we should park that now," he managed. "What anaesthetic products were they using? Did you notice? Sales are down in that part of your territory."

I somehow stifled the urge to scream into his corporately composed exterior. Instead, I nodded, and we acted as if nothing had happened.

Back in the same hospital coffee shop that had been my respite for so many weeks, while Edward had been an in-patient here, I watched the flow of people as they arrived. They sought solace in the caffeine and sugar, just as I had, before stoically returning to whomever they were here to see, their faces a palette of despair through to boredom. Patients in dressing gowns and doctors in white coats peppered the tables. I knew only too well the need to escape the monotony of the sickbed.

"Samantha?"

I jumped, and looked up. "Oh, thank God, it's you," I laughed with relief at the sight of Doctor Elliott Harvey standing beside my table.

"How are you? How are things?" He smiled, flashing his dimples as he looked down at my leg. He looked as good as I remembered. Handsome, I found myself thinking, his perfectly straight white teeth co-ordinating with his coat.

"Okay. . . Better . . . Good." Elliott seemed unconcerned by my inability to speak sentences, looking longingly at the chair opposite me. "Do you want to sit down?" I offered.

"Great, yes," he said with another blinding grin.

I kicked myself, as he slid into the seat, placing his herbal tea on the table in front of him. "Nice." I nodded at the tea.

"It is. Triple shot?" he said, looking into my empty cup.

"Mocha." It touched me he'd remembered.

"Coffee *and* chocolate?" He raised an eyebrow. "Do you need to talk about it?"

"Jesus, don't start me off." There was more wobble in my voice than I'd intended.

"Work?" He looked at my briefcase. "Home?" Maybe I imagined it, but he sounded hopeful.

"A bit of both," I said, wondering why I was always so honest with this guy.

He placed his elbows on the table and steepled his fingers together, resting his chin on the top as he looked at me. "Would it help to tell me about it?" I found myself wanting to.

"It's very dull and self-obsessed. Don't say I didn't warn you."

"I'd like to think we're friends now." He was ignoring the fact we'd spent less than a couple of hours together in total, and most of that had been whilst he cared for Edward. "Friends listen to what's going on in each other's lives. I'll tell you about my car problems if you tell me about whatever has you skulking down in this godforsaken coffee hole."

"Car problems?" I looked up at him. "I had you down as more of a skateboard kind of guy."

He smiled more broadly. "It's been known," he confirmed, "but they cause too many accidents. These hands are precious." He waggled his fingers at me. "Anyway, enough of me. What's going on?"

"I hate my job. Always have, always will. Oh, and Edward's had a complete personality transplant."

"Okay . . . Work first. Why do you do it if you hate it? You don't seem the kind of person to waste your life doing something you hate."

"I am if it means I can afford to eat. If money were no object I'd do photography, but it doesn't pay enough. Not straight away, anyway. If everything were great with Edward, then maybe . . ."

"But it's not?"

"It's better-ish. I don't know. He's different since the accident."

"Different how?" He sounded like a doctor again now.

"Umm, I don't know." This stuff was personal. I fidgeted on my seat. "He just doesn't do the same things he used to. He's more . . . thoughtful."

Elliott frowned. "That doesn't seem so bad." He sounded sorry as he said it.

"You'd think. I don't know, I can't really explain it. He just doesn't seem like the same guy. Things are different . . . between us . . ." I hesitated to tell him, but in the end decided to anyway, "intimately."

"What do you mean?"

"It's like being in bed with someone completely different."

His eyebrows nearly vanished through his hairline. "Good different or bad different? I'm impressed he's even rediscovered his libido after what he went through. That was some major surgery."

"Oh, he's discovered it alright. In fact, he wants to have a baby now. He hated anything to do with kids before."

For a moment, Elliott couldn't hide his horrified response. It took him a full five seconds before he masked his expression. "Well, it sounds like you two are making a go of things. If you're worried, you should mention it to the neurologist at your next outpatient appointment. I'm sure it's nothing to worry about – just the after-effects of a near-death experience, I would imagine." He sounded professional; a doctor's voice, cold and impersonal. "It tends to make people appreciate what they have a little more," he added, looking at me for a second before staring back down at his tea.

An awkward silence settled between us before I finally broke it. "Well, I'd better–"

"Yeah," he agreed, before knowing for sure what I was going to say.

We both stood, chairs scraping as they slid in unison across the linoleum floor. We hesitated, uncertain who would move first, resulting in yet another awkward standoff. "After you," he offered finally. Ever the gentleman.

We walked in silence along the sterile corridors. Side-by-side, as Elliott stared at his feet and I scanned the faces of the people around us. It was a rep habit, just in case any of the doctors I needed to talk to unfortunately – for them – happened to be walking along the corridor. "Richard?" I said, surprised to see his familiar face exiting a ward as we walked past.

He jumped, turning towards us, face flushed. "Oh . . . Hi . . . Sam."

He scanned the corridor, seeming unable to look me in the eyes. "What are you doing here?"

He squirmed. Elliott looked on with interest beside me.

"A check-up," he managed after a long pause.

"Here?" Elliott sounded surprised. "This is a general medicine ward. I think you'll find your check-up is in Outpatients."

"Oh, yes." Richard looked relieved. "That's what I was looking for. Do you know where I'm meant to go?"

Elliott frowned, but gave directions, then we both watched as Richard walked off in the direction Elliott had pointed. "That was odd," I said, once he'd turned the corner.

Elliott nodded thoughtfully. "Did you ever find out any more about how Edward got to know him?" he asked as we carried on walking.

"He met him in here. The hospital put them in touch . . . a patient group for people who'd survived medical trauma, or something."

Elliott made a surprised noise.

"Why?"

"I've never heard of a group like that. It's true though . . . that guy, Richard, he had a really similar outcome to Edward."

I stopped walking and turned to look at Elliott. "What do you mean?"

"On the night Edward came in – the night his heart stopped and then started again?"

I nodded.

"Richard came in having suffered a massive heart attack. He was in acute heart failure, his second heart attack in a month. The prognosis was poor, really poor. I didn't think he'd make it – no one did – because his heart was so damaged. He was on the transplant list, but none of us thought he'd be alive long enough to get one. But then, like Edward, his heart stopped and then started again. He's made a complete recovery. His cardiologist told me his heart has never been so healthy."

I stared at Elliott, trying to make sense of what he'd just said. "His heart stopped and then started again?"

"Look, I probably shouldn't have told you that. His medical history is confidential.

"I won't tell anyone."

"It just seemed so odd."

It was odd. "Maybe, like they said, they made friends because they both had that experience? Maybe the hospital told Richard about Edward, and he made a point of introducing himself."

"Maybe," he agreed, but he didn't sound convinced.

A thought struck me. "Wouldn't a guy who'd had heart failure most of his life, and needed regular hospital check-ups, know where the outpatient's department was located?"

"You'd think so." Elliott looked at me for a moment as we both tried to wrap our brains around what had just happened.

"Is it me, or was all that a bit weird?"

"Definitely weird." We'd reached the hospital reception area. "Well." He turned to face me, "look after yourself. Don't forget to come and see me if you're in again."

"You might regret saying that if I'm down on my numbers. I'll be in every day."

"I wouldn't mind. A small smile twitched at the corners of his mouth.

Another of those awkward moments arrived, where what we both wanted to say seemed somehow inappropriate, and we couldn't hug, but shaking hands seemed too formal for the friendship we'd already formed. In the end, we said and did nothing, just looked at each other for a long moment. I had enough complications in my life right now without adding to them.

"Hey, at least take my number so you can let me know if you're going to be coming to the hospital," Elliott said, trying to lighten the moment.

I delved into my oversized handbag and found my phone. Pressing my thumb to the pad I unlocked it, then handed it to him, watching as he entered his number and then called his own phone.

"Well . . ." I wanted some distance now, needing to think. I walked backwards, away from him, while he watched me. "I'll see you soon," I promised.

"I hope so."

I turned and stepped quickly out into the car park. It was warm again, making me regret the black trouser suit I'd chosen this morning, as I made my way over to the row where I'd parked my car. I slung my briefcase onto the back seat, before sliding in behind the steering wheel. Inserting the key in the ignition to start the engine, my radio blaring to life. A familiar figure walked with undue haste in front of my car, towards a silver Ford parked a couple of rows over – Richard.

He would have barely had time to reach the reception of the outpatients' department, located on the other side of the hospital, in the time since he'd left us in the corridor. He would definitely not have had time to wait to be seen by anyone. His presence in the car park made me wonder what he'd actually been doing in the hospital, because it sure as hell hadn't been to attend an outpatient appointment. And, more importantly, why he'd felt the need to lie to us.

Chapter 9

"I don't know what you were thinking, setting this up." Edward dragged his feet, forcing me to slow down. He'd been moaning since we'd left the flat. I was already in a bad mood because my jeans were tighter than usual – a symptom of my inability to exercise for weeks. I felt fat and ugly, despite having made the effort to dress up and make myself look good.

Our first excursion out as a couple since the accident, it had taken longer than I'd planned to get everyone together thanks to Heidi's husband Paul's work commitments. More than three weeks had passed since I'd last seen Heidi, and in that time Edward had shown no interest in going out – with or without me. He'd seemed perfectly content to stay in with me every Friday night. And every other night of the week. I'd found his company surprisingly pleasant.

"Heidi and Paul will be there, and I invited Julian and Victoria too." Julian and Victoria were the couple whose wedding we'd attended. His friends, not mine, I'd invited them to please him. "I've got the photos I took at the wedding. They felt terrible when they heard about the accident. They've been trying to get over to see us since they got back off honeymoon."

"I would imagine Victoria just wants to get her hands on your pictures, in case they're better than their professional shots."

"Well . . . anyway, they were worried about you." I tugged at the bustier top I'd chosen to wear. In the light of my too-tight jeans, it now seemed a bad choice.

Edward grabbed hold of my hand, forcing me to halt, then turned me to face him. "Have I told you how fucking amazing you look tonight?" He pulled me against his chest. I giggled as he spun and walked me backwards until my back hit the rough brick wall. Then he reached for my knee, lifting my thigh, fitting himself against me, only our clothes separating us. "I'd rather get to appreciate you alone than have to sit in a crowd." He kissed me. "I'm not going to be able to think about, let alone look at, anything but you in that top tonight." He pressed more gentle kisses against my neck, his breath hot on my skin. "All I can think about is what it'll be like to unwrap you."

Tempted for a second to turn around and go straight home, I remembered Heidi's text, telling me know she couldn't wait to see us, and guilt dampened my ardour. "We can't. They're waiting, come on." I twisted out of his grip and pushed away from the wall, grabbing his hand and tugging him across the road behind me, towards the bar.

It was just as well we hadn't ditched them, because the group had secured a window table, watching our little street display from their front row seats. We walked in to a round of applause. "Jesus, Sam," Heidi said, as I took the chair she'd saved for me beside her own, "I thought he was going to fuck you

against the wall. I was actually a little turned on watching you."
She laughed.

She laughed even harder when, in my mortification, my face heated, presumably turning me the colour of a raspberry.

"Can you blame me?" Edward pulled up a stool from another table, slipping it in beside my own. He leant across and kissed me. Heidi's eyes bugged out, while I squirmed with yet more embarrassment.

"Come and help me get the drinks in," she said, as soon as he released me, yanking me up by the arm and pulling me along behind her.

"Can I help?" Edward called after us, standing in readiness.

"No," Heidi squeaked. "We've got this." She towed me towards the bar. "What the fuck was that?" she said, when we had enough distance that we weren't within earshot.

"I told you, he's different since the accident."

"Different is one thing, but that's a complete personality transplant. What's with all the PDA? Edward hates PDA. He used to give Paul and me a hard time just for holding hands, and now he's practically humping you in the street. What the fuck?"

"I know. It's hard to get your head around, but he's all about displays of affection now, public or otherwise. It's all a bit overwhelming," I admitted, as we ordered drinks.

"And sitting next to you like that!"

"I know," I said with a groan.

"Can I offer to buy you lovely ladies a drink?" a guy beside us offered, his eyes glued to my bosoms. They were busy trying to push their way out the top of my corset again.

"Thanks, but—"

"Back off," Edward said, materialising beside me, shouldering between us and the now slightly bewildered guy. "Look elsewhere." He fixed the poor man with a stare, his fists clenched at his sides.

"Edward," I scolded, embarrassed by his unnecessary level of aggression.

He ignored me and continued to face the other guy down.

The man looked like he might make a stand, but then must have seen something in Edward's expression that made him step away. "Sorry, love," he threw over his shoulder as soon as he'd been served. "Maybe next time, when you've got rid of The Hulk here." He nodded towards Edward, who tensed as if he planned to follow him.

"Edward, please." I placed a hand on his arm. "Stop, I'm begging you."

He turned to look at me, his face still tight with anger. "Just so long as they know who you're with." He pulled me against him, pressing his forehead against mine, closing his eyes and breathing deeply. His tension eased, as if my presence calmed him somehow.

I swallowed and nodded, stepping away to collect our drinks from the bar. I handed a couple to him. He took them then walked back to join the others.

Heidi stared at me open-mouthed. "What the fucking fuck!"

"I did tell you," I said, exasperated. I'd gotten used to the new Edward; it was kind of weird being reminded just how different he seemed now.

"That was the hottest freaking thing ever," she said. "He was like all grrr, and the other guy was like all grrr, and you were all swoony, and they nearly fought over you. Fucking hell." She laughed, fanning herself.

"It's not funny. Don't encourage him. He's still a philandering bastard, remember?"

"I'm trying hard to but I have to say the 'new' Edward is making my girly bits gush."

"Oh, please Heidi! Too much information."

"Do you think if I drive the car into a wall and Paul bangs his head he might come back all growly alpha male like that too?" she mused.

"Maybe, or all dead, like Edward nearly was."

"Good point." She sighed.

Edward hadn't taken his eyes off me. As soon as I reached my seat, he placed a hand upon my thigh, leaned over and kissed my cheek. Victoria huffed a little breath of annoyance. Heidi grinned, making gushing gestures with her hands under the table.

***

"They're so much better than the professional ones," Victoria raved about the photos for the tenth time. I fidgeted, unused to her praise. "With that fog shit all over us we looked like we were made of Play-Doh in the ones taken out front. Thank God for yours, at least we still look like human beings. Oh, thank you so much."

The boys had moved out into the beer garden, to allow Julian to have a cigarette. At least that was their excuse. I suspected Julian was also sick to death of talking about the wedding, a subject of which Victoria never seemed to tire. Edward appeared reluctant to leave my side, but eventually the other men had ribbed him so much he'd been forced to go.

"Julian will have to stop smoking soon," Victoria said. "We're trying for a baby." She smiled, looking like the proverbial cat. Heidi and I smiled back at her, making appropriate sounds of approval, but Heidi's was forced, her eyes tight. I knew their difficulty getting pregnant was starting to seriously worry her, to the extent she'd texted me to say they were planning to start investigations. I wondered if her reaction to Victoria meant the news was bad.

"I bet she falls straight away," Heidi groaned when Victoria excused herself to go to the bathroom. "She'll probably have fucking triplets naturally or something, the cow."

"Yes, but they'll have her for a mother, and you know Julian's family have a tradition of calling all the boys Roman names, so she'll call them Brutus or Maximus, and they'll be tormented at school and be terribly miserable. Did I mention they'd have her for a mum?" Heidi smiled at me gratefully, as I reached over and squeezed her hand.

"Paul's in the clear," she admitted. "He got checked first. If there's a problem, then it has to be with me." Her shoulders slumped.

I hugged her. "Don't assume anything. You don't even know for sure there's a problem yet."

"If it isn't the very lovely Samantha! Good to see you're still alive." The voice boomed across the crowded bar, halting our conversation and making everyone in the vicinity turn and stare.

I groaned. Harry, one of Edward's most obnoxious friends.

"What are you doing here? I heard you were both at death's door, but you're looking as alive and delectable as ever." Harry's voice demanded attention. He moved purposefully through the crush, which parted in anticipation of the second part of his act, pulling himself out a seat as soon as he reached the table.

"Sit down, why don't you, Harry," I said.

He looked over at Heidi and raised a querying eyebrow.

"This is Heidi." I nodded towards her. "Heidi, this is one of Edward and Julian's friends from the bank."

"Pleasure to meet you," Harry said, with practised charm.

"Harry," Victoria cooed as she made her way back to our table. She fluttered her eyelashes. "How are you?"

"Victoria, you look lovelier than ever. I hope Julian appreciates just what a gem you are." He added a leer. "If not, then let me know. I'll be happy to step in and pick up any slack."

"Oh, Harry, you are naughty." She tittered, clearly loving every minute of the attention. Heidi looked across at me and rolled her eyes.

"Where are the boys?" Harry asked, looking around. "Sharking in another part of the bar?" He grinned. In the past, Harry had always been one of Edward's wingmen. Given what had happened at the wedding, Edward could have been doing exactly that. But his more recent behaviour – the thoughtfulness and general attentiveness – made me less sure now. "He's a fool, Samantha." He sidled closer to me, leaning in so he could whisper in my ear, "I've always told him he was mad to be sipping cava when he had Champagne at home."

"Harry," Edward said, his voice cold, his timing impeccable.

Harry jumped away from me.

"Good to see you." I'd never heard Edward sound less sincere.

"Edward." Harry stood, and shook his hand, before turning to greet Julian and Paul.

Edward moved his stool back in beside my own, pulling me towards him for another kiss. This possessive behaviour was getting old fast – no matter how annoying Harry was.

Curious eyes watched us whilst we chatted, especially every time Edward reached out to touch me – which was often. Harry sat back and made himself comfortable, seemingly disinclined to move on, despite the hard looks Edward kept throwing his way. He had the hide of a rhinoceros, his choice to squeeze in next to me a deliberate "fuck you" to Edward. In the meantime, Heidi had a huge grin on her face and looked like someone who'd settled in to watch a good show.

Edward placed his hand on my thigh, fingers caressing me gently, as the conversation wove a familiar path through news about mutual friends and acquaintances; who was seeing whom, who was engaged or expecting. There was even our first divorce.

"Hopefully we'll be next," Edward piped up, squeezing my hand.

A silence settled around the table, then everyone spoke at once: "What, marriage or a baby?" Heidi said.

"You have to be kidding me! You've certainly changed your tune," Victoria spluttered.

My mouth, which must have been hanging open at his words, snapped closed as I turned toward Victoria. I'd had a suspicion she and Edward had had a thing together a year or so before. About the time every other comment Edward made had been to tell me how wonderful Victoria was compared to me. I guessed, from her reaction to Edward's remark, I'd just gotten my answer. She blushed under my scrutiny and Edward's scowl. Julian smiled on, oblivious.

"Both," Edward replied to Heidi, choosing to ignore Victoria's outburst. "As soon as possible." He rubbed my tummy as if we were already incubating something in there. For all he knew we were, I supposed, considering all talk of condoms had long been forgotten and I'd yet to confess my use of the pill. Heidi's horrified expression mirrored exactly how I felt.

"Who the fuck are you? And what have you done with Edward?" Harry said. "Seriously, man, what's the matter with you?" It was funny to hear someone say exactly what I'd been thinking, along with everyone else around the table. The rest of us were just too polite to say anything out loud.

"You're not funny, Harry," Edward said, an edge to his voice.

"Neither are you, man. I mean, I know you nearly died, but shit . . . really? Oh, Serena asked after you the other day. I passed on your number." He necked what was left of his pint and stood to leave.

My cheeks heated with embarrassment as all eyes swivelled away from Harry towards me, a uniform look of horror on their faces. Only Edward appeared confused. "She's the girl you shagged at Julian and Victoria's wedding," I supplied, before finishing my own drink, then standing and pulling on my jacket. I nodded to Heidi, who smiled in understanding, then pushed my way out through the crowd, pausing to catch my breath once I'd broken through the fog of smokers huddling in the doorway.

"Look, I'm sorry for hurting you, Sam," Harry said, sidling up beside me. I hadn't noticed him standing there, imagining he'd made a hasty getaway. "I mean, I couldn't take all his hypocritical lovey-dovey shit when he was shagging that other girl only a few weeks ago."

"Pot, meet kettle. Nice of you to bring it up in front of everyone."

"Yeah, well, at least I'm single. I've never lied to the women I've slept with. I've never told any of them that it was anything more than a mutually satisfying shag. Not like him. You're better than that schmuck. He doesn't deserve you. Certainly not as a wife, for fuck's sake."

"Oh, and you do?" I laughed at the absurdity of the conversation.

"Probably not," he admitted. "But if I had you waiting at home for me, I'd treat you a damn sight better than he ever has."

The punch came out of nowhere. Next thing I knew, Harry lay flat out on the ground as Edward pummelled him. "Edward, stop," I screamed, pulling futilely at his shirt while he continued to rain punches and kicks down on Harry's foetal form. Harry remained still, his arms wrapped protectively over his head.

People shuffled closer to watch, but no one stepped in to help, as I screamed for Edward to stop, still tugging on the back of his shirt to little effect.

"Alright boys, pack it in." Two bouncers arrived and pulled Edward off. Harry's face looked bloody, one eye already swelling.

"Stay out of my fucking life!" Edward shouted, his face reddened, spittle flying, eyes bulbous with rage, as he pulled against the bouncer's grip to free himself.

"You're a fucking madman," Harry shot back. "She'll see through your act. She doesn't know about half the women you've fuc–"

Edward lunged again. My heart plummeted. The confirmation that there were more than I knew about made me feel sick again. I turned and left, knowing Edward would be forced to wait while the police were called.

As I walked home, I tried to work out why it still hurt so much. I'd known Edward was an arse. I'd known he was shagging around. Hell, I'd broken up with the guy because of it. Somehow, since the accident, I'd allowed him to flatter and charm me into loving him yet again. *Stupid,* I scolded myself. *Stupid, stupid, stupid.*

Once home, I showered and washed the makeup off my face, slipping into my pyjamas, hugely relieved to take off my jeans before climbing into bed and curling up into a foetal position of my own. Maybe it would protect me from the hurt Edward continued to inflict on me. I ignored the relentless texts and calls from Edward, Heidi and even Victoria that had been blowing up my phone since I'd left the pub. Instead, I switched the phone to silent. They could all wait until tomorrow, when I'd decide what the hell to do.

A couple of hours later Edward arrived home. I kept still and pretended to be asleep. He undressed and showered, before climbing into the bed beside me, his smell familiar and comforting. His arms enfolded me, his lips pressing against the back of my neck.

Silent tears slipped down my cheeks and onto my pillow as he held me, until the emotion became too much. I took a sobbing breath.

He turned me slowly, forcing himself into my line of vision. One of his eyes looked blackened, and his nose showed evidence of swelling. I tried to turn my head away. "Look at me, Sam. Please. I'm sorry. I don't want anything between us anymore. Nothing." He drew a deep breath. "Before the accident, I didn't appreciate you like I should have. I know that. I was a fool. But it's different now. I'm different. You've seen that, haven't you?"

I nodded slowly.

"I don't want anyone else. I'll prove it to you, again and again, until you believe me. It's different now . . . I'm different now."

"Why? Why are you different?"

Chapter 10

Edward never answered my question. Instead, he'd kissed me, then made love to me, until my concerns became whispers in the back of my mind. Just under a week later, I was beginning to believe him when he said he only wanted me. He'd continued to be attentive, almost overly attentive. This evening I'd escaped with Heidi for drinks, but it had taken a lot of persuading. He'd wanted me to stay home with him for fear I'd meet someone else. In the end, I'd lost it with him and told him he'd have to trust me, the same as I was trying to learn to trust him, which had shut him up.

Heidi was full of beans, excited to share her ovulation status and the copious amounts of sex she'd been having with Paul as a result. "It was only the number of kids who get knocked up after a drinking a couple of WKDs that dragged me away tonight," she said. The result of her graphic oversharing was I'd drunk a lot more than I'd intended, especially given I had to work the next day.

We were on our second bottle of wine in an obscure little bar in the middle of Camden when Harry walked through the door. *What were the chances?* I grimaced, shrinking down in my seat in the hope he wouldn't notice us. He stopped in the doorway, his gaze sweeping the bar until his eyes landed on mine. Then he cut an immediate path through the post-work city crowd, straight toward our table.

Heidi caught sight of my horrified expression and turned. "Is that the same guy from the pub?" I'd filled her in on the whole Harry versus Edward streetfighter episode.

"Sorry to bother you ladies," Harry said, sliding into one of the free seats at our table without asking permission. "Can I get either of you a drink?"

"No, I think we're good, thanks." I nodded towards the new bottle of red wine in front of us. "Are you okay?" I stared at the already yellowing bruises on his face. The ones around his neck seemed worse, a vivid red band circling his throat. I shuddered, imagining how angry Edward must have been to have throttled him that hard.

"Yeah, I'm fine, thanks." He certainly looked fine – well, apart from the fading bruises – far better than I'd imagined he would, given the beating I'd seen him take. "Actually," he said, sounding embarrassed, "I'm glad I bumped into you. I wanted to apologise for what I said the other night."

Astonished, I waited for the punchline. It didn't come.

"I shouldn't have butted in where I wasn't wanted. You and Edward seem to be making a go of things. He's a good guy, and he cares a lot about you. I deserved a beating for sticking my nose in. I should've known better."

I stared at Harry, wondering if my mouth was hanging open like Heidi's.

"Well, anyway, that's it, really. I was jealous . . . I envy what you've got together . . . I hope I'm half as lucky one day. Have a good night, ladies." He nodded at us in turn before standing up and walking off.

"What the fuck was that?" Heidi said.

"Who the fuck was that, rather?" I murmured. "I mean, Harry's always been a manwhore and proud of it. 'I hope I'm half as lucky', my arse. He'd run away screaming if a woman suggested a second date, let alone marriage."

"Did Edward set that up? Even if he did, why on earth would Harry go along with it?"

"Maybe. I don't know. I was waiting for him to press GBH charges. Edward kicked the shit out of him the other day – in front of a pub full of witnesses. Instead, Harry's here talking about how the beating was understandable, and how Edward was within his rights. Bullshit. It's a complete and utter mind fuck. There's a lot of it about."

"Tell me about it," she agreed, pouring us both another large glass of wine. "I suggest we block all the stress out with copious amounts of alcohol." She raised her glass. I clinked my own against it before taking a hearty gulp.

By the end of the second bottle, my head was reeling. I giggled, sitting on the toilet, the cubicle walls spinning around me. The night had been the most fun I'd enjoyed in ages, but for the nagging voice reminding me I needed to go home soon if I wanted any chance of making my customer appointment. Thankfully the meeting was a local one.

"Spoilsport." Heidi pouted when I explained as much to her.

"What about Paul? He's waiting at home to make beautiful babies with you." That was all it took.

My head was doing a good impression of a Waltzer ride as I hunted for keys in my oversized bag. I wished I'd thought to take a smaller one out with me, instead of the monster I used for work. I leant against the door, propping the bag on my knee as I rummaged, knowing they were hidden somewhere within its depths. When the door opened suddenly, I fell forward, straight into Edward, the bag and all its contents scattering inside the hallway.

"Hey, baby, have a good night?" He grinned at me as I staggered against his chest.

"Hi." I grinned back, peering up at him, registering again just how handsome he was. "Did you miss me?"

He swept me into his arms in response, kicked the front door closed with one foot, and carried me into the bedroom.

"Like Richard Gere." I giggled.

"Is that good?" He laid me carefully down.

"Very," I purred. Any inhibitions had long since been dissolved in red wine. "I want you."

He grinned. "You've got me." He unbuttoned my blouse slowly, worshiping each part of my body as he revealed it.

Afterwards, he pulled me into his arms, my body sated, holding me until I fell asleep. In the last moments between sleep and wakefulness, I felt as near to happy with Edward as I ever remembered being.

***

The light seemed brighter than it should have been when I opened my eyes. My head throbbed, my mouth feeling parched, almost as though I had been desiccated during the night. I rolled over and found nothing, the bed beside me empty and cold. My eyes flickered towards the digital display on the clock radio Edward kept on his bedside table. It was twenty-five to ten.

"Fuck!" I flung back the covers and stood quickly. My head protested the movement a beat after I hit upright, a wave of nausea rolling over me. I had a midday appointment with a consultant anaesthetist I couldn't afford to miss. I'd been trying to see him for ages, but this was the first time he'd granted me an actual appointment. I squinted at my watch, confirming the time, and then ran to the shower, trying to ignore the pounding in my brain. Edward must have switched off my alarm, or I'd forgotten to set it in my drunken stupor.

I rinsed myself, stepped out and then dried off quickly, noting that even the towel hurt today. I was grateful to have not needed to wash my hair as I pinned it up into a messy bun. I tried to hide the skin-ravaging after-effects of too much alcohol, but it was very much a patch job. My eyes looked bloodshot, and my skin parched.

I dug inside the bathroom cabinet for paracetamol, relieved when I found a packet with a couple left in it. I necked them quickly, washing them down with water straight from the bathroom tap, my head tilted to one side as I tried not to remove my recently applied foundation. Then I ran back into the bedroom and found a clean white blouse that I paired with a favourite black shift dress which forgave everything. I dressed, promising myself I'd sort my shit out at the weekend. Thank God it was Friday.

Another glance at my watch told me I had twenty minutes before I needed to be out the door, if I wanted to make the twenty-minute drive to the hospital and arrive at my appointment in good time.

I hurried into the lounge but stopped short when I found Edward sitting silently on one of the chairs, his body hunched forward, hand clutching something, his head bowed. "Oh, you're here. I assumed you were at work you were so quiet," I said as I wandered into the kitchen and flicked on the kettle. "I overslept," I called through to him. He didn't reply. I walked back into the lounge while the kettle boiled. Edward sat motionless and stared down at his hands. "Why aren't you at work? Do you want tea? Hey, are you okay?" I added, concerned when I got no response. "Are you feeling okay?"

He looked up at that. His eyes were cold and angry. I took a step back instinctively.

"No, Samantha, I'm not okay." His voice sounded clipped. Okay, he was really angry; really, really angry – thermonuclear angry, I suspected. I cast my mind back, trying to figure out what I might have done, but came up with nothing.

"What's the matter?" My voice sounded small. The kettle reached maximum boil and then clicked noisily from inside the kitchen, the still-moving water the only sound in the room as he stared at me. Then he stood and stalked towards me, and for the first time I saw what he held in his hand. My contraceptive pills.

"You dropped your bag," he said in a menacing tone, "and there was shit all over the floor. Imagine my surprise when I picked all your crap up to find these." His voice sounded strange, hard, as he loomed above me. I shrank away from him, walking backwards until my back hit the sideboard.

"I can explain–" I started, but he grabbed me by my neck and cut my words off.

"I don't want to hear any more shit from you, Samantha. You've been lying to me all this time. All you needed to do was let me fuck you. It was good. We were good together. You just needed to let me fuck you." His voice sounded unrecognisable, like a stranger. "But you couldn't do that. You had to take these." He waved the packet at me with his other hand. "So now you're forcing me to do this."

He squeezed my throat, cutting off my air supply. I clawed at his hand with both of my own, fear making me forget everything else but the desire to survive. *He's going to kill me*, I thought, as black spots started to cloud my vision. If I passed out, I knew I was done for. Unable to prise his hands from my neck, my own hands flailed blindly out sideways, trying to find something, anything, to hit him with. My fingers brushed the sideboard, solid and smooth behind me, and on it the carved wooden elephant. Without thought, I grabbed it and swung it hard against his head. It hit his skull with a sickening crack, then with a duller thud when I hit him in the same place a second time. The pressure on my throat eased, and he slid to the ground. I gasped for breath, bent over as I forced oxygen back into my lungs, until gradually the black dots cleared and I could see again.

Edward lay very still on the floor in a pool of his blood. I bent down and touched my fingers to his neck gingerly, feeling for a pulse. Faint, but there was one. I debated what to do next, my mind still foggy. *Call the police*, I thought immediately, but would they arrest me for hitting him, or was it self-defence? *Run away* . . . but where to? If he died, I'd be a murderer. *Call an ambulance?* Then the police would look for me anyway, but they might not know I had hit him. Would he remember? Nausea rose, the cloying, metallic scent of his blood turning my stomach. I leant back against the sideboard and took some deep breaths. Edward groaned, and reminded me he had just tried to kill me. I needed to get away from him.

I grabbed my handbag off the side where he'd placed it and ran out the door, not even picking up my coat as I went. My keys were in my bag where I kept them, where Edward must have replaced them, so I jumped into my car and drove, uncertain where I was going, until I reached the hospital. All the time my mind flickered over who I could call, who could help me. Who would even believe that Edward had tried to kill me? I didn't believe it myself.

Once I'd parked, I sat there, behind the wheel, shaking. My head throbbed as the immediate hit of adrenaline left my body. The memory of Edward lying in a pool of his blood sent nausea roiling through me again, and I opened the door and vomited onto the ground beside the car.

"Are you okay, love?" a concerned voice called over. I looked up; an elderly man and his wife had stopped and were both staring at me. I must have looked a mess. I wiped the vomit from around my mouth with my sleeve, but could still taste it. I needed to think clearly, and I needed a drink of water.

I got out the car and locked it, nodding at the couple with what I hoped looked like a smile, before making my way inside the hospital, my appointment with the anaesthetic consultant no longer important. I clutched my handbag to my chest and strode, head down, towards the cafeteria, where I bought myself a coffee and a bottle of mineral water. I drank a sip of the mineral water first to remove the taste of vomit, wincing as I tried to swallow and my throat protested painfully. Then I sat and stared at my coffee.

People drifted in and out as I sat there, watching my coffee growing cold in front of me. Then finally, I picked up my phone and texted Elliott. *I need help.*

Chapter 11

He'd texted me back almost immediately. I hadn't said who I was in the message, so he must have entered my name in his phone when we'd exchanged numbers.

Where are you?

Canteen, I replied. Five minutes later, he stood at the table in front of me.

"Wow, things must be serious – you let your coffee go cold," he joked, until I looked up at him. "Jesus, Sam, what happened to you?" He slid in beside me and took hold of my jaw gently. "The blood vessels in your eyes are blown . . . and your throat." He lifted my chin. I winced, and he let go quickly.

"Did he do this to you? What the fuck happened?"

Tears welled up in my eyes, and I nodded before trying to speak. "He tried to . . ." My voice sounded hoarse and breathy. It hurt.

"Don't speak, and don't drink anything else," he said as I reached for my water. "Come with me." He took my hand and led me to A&E.

"I don't want to . . ." I croaked at him.

"Sam, you need to get checked out. You have a serious throat trauma. He could have damaged your airway. That's not something you mess about with." He sounded very authoritative, but frankly I felt relieved to let someone else make the decisions.

We walked in through the back door, and within minutes I lay on a trolley being examined. The benefits of knowing one of the doctors.

I caught the staff looking each other, and Elliott, when they examined my injuries. Eventually a female doctor asked what they all wanted to. "Try not to speak. I'm going to ask you some questions about what happened. I just want you to gently nod or shake your head to reply, okay?" I nodded, the movement sending pain through my neck. "Were you attacked?" I nodded again. "Elliott said you told him it was your boyfriend. Is that true? Was it your boyfriend?"

"Edward Patterson," Elliott supplied, and I bobbed my head again, wincing.

"Can you show us what he did?"

I mimicked the way he'd held my throat using Elliott's hand around my neck.

"We'll need to get some photos of the bruising," the doctor said to one of the nurses. Then to me, "Samantha, we'll need to let the police know about this." My eyes filled again. "He can't be allowed to do this to another woman," she said.

A tear rolled down my cheek. I gave her a small nod, terrified at the thought of seeing him again. Worse, I had no idea what would happen when the police found out I'd hit him. I knew I needed to tell them – it was now or never. "I hit him," I whispered, and they all turned back to look at me. "To get away.

I couldn't breathe. I reached out and found something, a wooden elephant, and hit him with it."

They were all wide-eyed now, including Elliott.

"Did he collapse?" the doctor asked.

I nodded.

"Was he moving when you left? Did you call an ambulance?"

"I heard him groan. I couldn't stay to help him. I just had to get away. I was scared," My voice croaked, the tears coming in earnest now, dripping off my chin onto my dress.

"It's okay, Samantha, don't strain your voice any more. We'll let people know, and they'll go round there and see that he's okay. I'm sure the police will want to speak to him anyway." The doctor's tone of voice sounded professionally comforting.

They applied ice and then X-rayed me to make sure the damage wasn't worse than it seemed to be. I'd damaged my vocal cords, but seemed to have escaped more serious harm. Elliott stayed by my side the entire time, like my own personal guard dog. Then the police arrived.

In short, breathless whispers, I described what had happened. When they asked why he'd been so angry, I told them about him finding the contraceptives. They'd nodded as if it were entirely normal for a guy to try and kill his girlfriend because she didn't want to have a baby with him.

Officer Frank Murray – a taciturn mountain of a man, who said little but whose eyes never seemed to leave me – stepped out to make a call. When he came back inside, he told us, in a matter-of-fact way, that Edward had not been found.

Stunned, I could only think about the viscous texture of the pool of blood I had left him in. "Are you sure?"

Officer Murray nodded. "We found no evidence of any struggle in the apartment. There was no sign of a body, or any blood. In fact, we found nothing to indicate anything untoward happened at all."

Relieved I wasn't a murderer, I couldn't hide my surprise. "How can he be well enough to be walking around?" I looked at Elliott, confused. Then the fear hit; he was out there, pissed off with me enough that he'd tried to strangle me.

"Do you have somewhere to stay?" Elliott said, when the staff announced they were happy to let me go home. "You can't go back to the apartment, not while he's still out and about. You need to wait until the police pick him up." I couldn't have agreed more; there was no way I wanted to be anywhere near him. Flashbacks sent tremors of fear through me every time I thought about him. My choices consisted of a safe house for battered women, a friend or a local hotel.

"I'll call Heidi," I decided. I'd texted her earlier but hadn't got any sort of response yet. I dug my phone out of my bag, aware of Elliott watching me as I waited for the phone to connect. It rang with the single tone of an international call.

"Paul's taken me on a surprise trip to Italy for the week," Heidi squealed as soon as she picked up. "We're hoping we'll get pregnant."

I didn't have the heart to tell her what had happened to me. I knew she'd feel obliged to pack up and come home, and I didn't want her to do that. "Have a lovely time," I said instead.

"What happened to your voice? You sound like Bonnie Tyler."

"Hangover," I improvised. "Have fun." Tears threatened again. "I've got to go," I said quickly, and disconnected the call. I looked at Elliott. "I'll stay at the Travelodge."

"You won't be safe there. Most of them don't even have receptionists anymore. He could walk into the place."

"Why? Well anyway, I don't have much of a choice." Weary, feeling overwhelmed by everything that had happened I was at a loss. "Most of our friends are exactly that – *our* friends. I don't want to put them in the middle of this."

"Come home with me."

"What?"

"Come back to mine. I have a spare room, and you'll be safe because he won't know where to find you. I can make sure you're okay. I have a coffee machine," he added when I hesitated. "Come home with me." Insistent, he almost seemed excited by the prospect. I didn't have the strength to fight him. It wasn't as if I had many other choices.

The policeman barely lifted an eyebrow when we gave him the details of where I'd be staying, jotting the address down in his pad. The medical staff were another matter. I ignored the curious glances and excited whispers that followed us when Elliott helped me out to the car.

We'd agreed he'd drive my car back to his place and leave his own in the staff car park. His place turned out to be a small maisonette, occupying the upper two levels of a three-storey house. It was a good area. I had nothing with me, but he found an unused toothbrush, and then showed me where to find the bathroom, while he made up the bed in the spare room.

It was late afternoon by the time I fell gratefully into the cool cotton sheets, wearing a borrowed t-shirt that reached nearly to my knees. The throb of my throat acted as a constant reminder of events, but, despite all the trauma of the day, I fell asleep in minutes. My last thoughts were of the look in Edward's eyes as he'd gripped my throat.

***

I woke late the next morning, surprised I'd slept straight through dinner. I must have been asleep for fifteen hours or more, and yet my body still felt the pull of fatigue. Initially confused, it took several minutes to remember where I was, and then why. Memories of the attack flooded back. I stood quickly, determined not to allow myself to become a victim, stumbling a little as dizziness made my head swim. I knocked into the bedside table, sending the lamp toppling over.

"You okay?" Elliott asked from the doorway, as I sat back down heavily on the end of the bed, one hand on the bedframe to steady myself.

"Been better," I admitted. My voice sounded a little stronger, though still hoarse. I gathered my legs beneath me and tried to stand a second time, noting my bloodshot eyes as I caught my reflection in the dressing table mirror. "Don't you have work today?"

"No, I took a day off."

"God, not on my behalf, I hope?" I picked up the lamp and set it back down on the bedside table. "It's bad enough I've already involved you in all this shit. You must regret the day you ever spoke to me."

"On the contrary," he said, with a slight smile. "Anyway, I'd already planned to take some time off today. I've been doing some research – I thought, as you were here, I could run it past you, and maybe introduce you to a friend of mine."

"I only work as a rep. I don't have anything to do with allocating grants for research." This was not the first time I'd been approached by someone who wanted pharmaceutical company sponsorship cash for their work.

"No, no, it's nothing like that. Look, before we get into it, let's get some food inside you. You didn't eat last night. You must be starving."

I thought about it, feeling the familiar ache of hunger from my hollow stomach, and nodded. "Scrambled eggs?"

He smiled. "I think we can rustle something like that up. It needs to be soft. Tomatoes too?"

I nodded again.

He moved around the kitchen with ease, serving the eggs in minutes, then pulling out the chair opposite to share the small meal. They tasted good, good enough to ignore the ache in my throat on every swallow. I finished quickly, placing my knife and fork together with some regret.

"Someone was hungry," Elliott observed with a grin, pushing what remained on his own plate towards me.

"No, really," I protested.

"Go on, have it. You need it more than I do." He slid the plate in front of me again, watching while I wolfed down the contents.

I leant back on the chair with a contented sigh. "Thank you."

"You're welcome. How's your throat?"

"Not too bad," Thinking about it brought flashbacks of Edward's face. I couldn't rid myself of the memory of his crazed expression; his anger, directed at me.

"Hey, stop," Elliott placed his hand over mine. "Don't go there, not now. It won't help anything. Don't think about him."

I nodded and stood, intending to scrape off the plates. The muffled beep of a text arriving on my phone, from within the depths of my handbag, diverted me. With a quick look at Elliott I placed the plates back on the table, retrieving my bag from the side in the hallway and rummaging inside until I located the phone. Edward's name sat beside the new message icon. My hand shook as I unlocked it and read the message:

I hope someone is looking after you. You need help, Samantha

"What the fuck! He's a bloody lunatic. What does he mean *I* need help? He's the one who tried to fucking strangle me!"

Elliott reached for the phone, his eyes dropping to read the message. "He's playing mind games with you. We just need to work out why. You have to show this to the police. Maybe they can use this text to track down his cell phone or something. The sooner they have him in custody, the sooner you can stop worrying. What you can't afford to do is lose it right now."

My heart raced. "You're right." I took some deep breaths, trying to slow my breathing as I rummaged for the card the police officer had given me, the one with contact numbers on it. My hands were trembling badly now. "Here." I held it up. The small card shook in my hand.

"You're doing the right thing, Sam." Elliott placed a hand on my shoulder. "Call them."

I took another deep breath, then punched in the numbers.

The phone answered on the second ring. "Officer Murray." I briefed him quickly on the text I'd received. "Do you know what he means by that?" he asked when I'd finished.

"No. No idea."

"Are you still staying with Dr Harvey?"

"Yes, for now," I confirmed.

"We have a car in the area," he informed me. "If you see any sign of Mr Patterson, or if you receive any more texts or phone calls, I want you to contact me immediately – or tell my officer."

"I will," I promised. Feeling safer knowing there were other people looking out for me.

"I'll get someone to make enquiries into the mobile phone information. We'll be in touch when we know more."

"Better?" Elliott asked, when I ended the call.

"Much. They seemed confident they can trace him through his phone. Did you know they've got a car in the area?"

"They mentioned they would. Only until they pick him up – it shouldn't take them much longer." He paused, shifting a little. "Um, my friend will be here in about twenty minutes."

I looked down at the borrowed t-shirt and the knickers from yesterday I still wore, and my cheeks heated. I'd been so at ease in his company, it had never crossed my mind to cover up. "I'm sorry," I said, backing towards the hall. "I'll go and get dressed." A thought struck me – maybe he had a woman coming around. "I can get out of your hair completely if you'd like? Give you time to talk to your friend . . . without me?" I kept my eyes fixed on the ground, reluctant to reveal how oddly unsettled the thought made me.

"I don't want you to go anywhere," he said. "*He's* a microbiologist. A friend from work. He's great, just not really used to being around half-naked beautiful women. I'll dig out some clothes for you. An ex of mine left some stuff here in a box she never collected, so hopefully something in there will fit you. Why don't you grab a shower and I'll leave the box in your room?"

I scurried into the bathroom, peeling off my shirt and knickers before stepping into the shower. I lifted my face to meet the warmth of the powerful spray, enjoying the cleansing feeling. When I stepped out again, reluctantly, I felt better than I had done in the previous twenty-four hours. I avoided my reflection, unwilling to witness the bruises circling my neck, the thought alone sending my heart racing.

With my back to the mirror, I found a comb and untangled my hair, before brushing my teeth. Wrapped in a large bath towel, I padded across the hallway, back to my room. Voices drifted towards me from the lounge; Elliott laughed at something the other person said.

Back in my room, I fished out a t-shirt and some jogging bottoms from the box of clothes Elliott had left on the bed for me. I looked down at myself; clearly the previous owner of the clothes possessed a smaller bust size than I did. The t-shirt hugged my chest in a most distracting way, stopping well short of the waistline of the jogging bottoms, somewhere near my belly button. I rummaged through the rest of the box for an alternative, but found nothing any larger. The jogging bottoms were fine, but together I feared the whole ensemble made me look like I planned to parade a number around a boxing ring. I contemplated putting the t-shirt I'd worn to bed back on, but, since that came nearly to my knees and carried a faint whiff of sweat, decided to make do until I could get back to the apartment to collect some of my own stuff.

Taking a deep breath, I walked out into the lounge to meet Elliott's friend.

Chapter 12

He turned out to be everything I imagined a microbiologist should be. Small and thin, with premature baldness, leaving only curly wisps that stuck out over his ears. I grinned as soon as I saw him.

In return he gawped at me, in a decidedly un-paternalistic way, his eyes sweeping over my inadequately clad form and coming to rest somewhere between my exposed midriff and my chest. Elliott didn't perform much better but recovered more quickly, especially when I crossed my arms to cover myself.

"Malcolm, roll your tongue in," Elliott grumbled at his friend, who blushed. "Malcolm, meet Samantha. Sam, this is Malcolm."

Reluctantly, I unwrapped an arm from around my middle to shake the offered hand.

"Sam, can I get you a coffee?"

"Umm . . ." I didn't fancy a coffee for once. "Maybe water? Or orange juice if you have any?"

"No coffee! Are you sure you feel okay?" Elliott laughed as he reached for a carton from the fridge and poured me a large glass of fresh orange juice.

"I feel much better." I took the glass he handed me. "Thank you," I said, giving him a smile as I took a sip.

"Your voice sounds a lot better today," he noted. "And it's my pleasure."

I put my glass down after taking another sip and wrapped my arms back around my chest.

"Right, now we're all here, and focused," Elliott gave Malcolm a meaningful look, "how about we talk about the samples?"

"Samples?"

"Ah yes, the samples," Malcolm said.

"Malcolm and I were interested in the news about the retrovirus they found in the fog. We've been looking at patient samples to see what more we could discover about it." I nodded to show I understood so far, as he continued; "From what Malcolm can tell, the virus is present only in men, exactly as the initial reports suggested, seeming to lie dormant within the cell. I had a hunch, so I asked Malcolm to look at samples from a varied population of patients within the hospital to see if he could find any differences in the virus activity among them."

"And did you?" I looked at Malcolm.

"I did." Malcolm grinned. If he'd been a dog, his tail would have been wagging. "Two of the samples you gave me were very different. In those the virus was active. It had integrated itself into the cell DNA entirely. In fact, I'd say the new DNA had become dominant."

"What does that even mean?" I asked.

"I don't know," Malcolm admitted. "We don't know what impact it had on the patients, if any. All we know for sure is that under certain circumstances the virus becomes active, despite what the media is saying, and the DNA in those patients is genetically different as a result."

"Okay, well then, I need to look at the records to see more about what happened to the patients . . . to understand if there was a trigger for activation." Elliott sounded thoughtful.

"I have a theory," Elliott continued. "I'll tell you about it if it appears to be right, but for now, if it's okay with you, I want to keep it to myself." He glanced quickly over towards Malcolm, as if to warn him to keep his mouth shut. "We could go today?" Elliott suggested, looking at me. "If you don't mind – and if you feel up to it? I mean, you don't have to come at all. You could stay here if you prefer?"

"I want to come with you," I said. The prospect of being on my own today was more terrifying than the thought of being outside the safety of the house. "It's not like I've got anything else to do, although I wouldn't mind stopping by my apartment first to get some of my own clothes." I looked down at my outfit. "Before we go anywhere public I mean." I laughed. The sensation hurt my throat, bringing with it the realisation it must have been the first time since my attack that I'd managed to laugh. I supposed that had to be some sort of progress.

***

Less than an hour later, we were all sitting in my car outside my apartment block. Elliott insisted we let the police know our intentions, and they had in turn warned the officer stationed outside – I presumed he was there to wait for Edward's return. I still struggled to believe Edward could be up and walking around after the way I'd hit him with the wooden elephant. But the fact remained that, as yet, no body had been found, and there hadn't been sight nor sound of him apart from the text I'd received.

Leaving Malcolm in the car on lookout, we walked up the stairs to the apartment, Elliott in the lead, muscles tense, half expecting Edward to jump out on us at any moment. The neon bulb in the hallway flickered. Every instinct inside me screamed *run*. Instead, I followed like the proverbial lamb.

Elliott banged on the door, the sound echoing along the hallway. I froze. My heartbeat sounded nearly as loud as it pounded in my ears, adrenaline making my pulse race as I fought the urge to flee. I rubbed my neck, as we waited for any sort of response from within.

Elliott placed a hand on my arm. "He's not here, that officer said so. And even if he was, I won't let any harm come to you."

I nodded, unable to speak, my breaths coming short and fast as anxiety threatened to overwhelm me.

He waited another minute without response, then used the key I'd given him earlier – the one the police had given back to me – and unlocked the door. We stepped inside, stopping close to where it had happened. My eyes found the spot where I'd last seen Edward. As expected, exactly as the police had reported, there was nothing there. No blood. "He was there." I pointed to the spot where I'd left him. I swivelled towards Elliott, my fear palpable. "He was just there. I left him lying there . . . he was in a pool of his blood."

"I believe you," Elliott reassured me, taking hold of my hand. "Hey," he said, feeling my racing pulse, "He's not here, he can't hurt you. You're safe." But I didn't feel safe. Memories of the smell and appearance of the blood drowned my senses, making me gag, the nausea threatening to overwhelm me. I pushed away from Elliott and sprinted into the toilet, reaching the bowl as I gagged again. I broke out in a sweat, clutching the sides of the pan for dear life, taking deep breaths until the feeling passed.

Elliott walked into the bathroom and bent to rub my back. "You're safe," he soothed. "It's just the adrenaline making you feel like that. It's shock. Take some more deep breaths. As soon as you feel better, we'll grab your stuff and get out of here, okay?"

I sat back on my knees, wiping the beads of sweat from my forehead with a piece of toilet roll before throwing it into the bowl and flushing. My legs wobbled, as I stood and the world spun around me, threatening to collapse. Elliott reached a hand under my arm and steadied me. "Stay there," he said, when he was satisfied I wasn't going to crumple again, disappearing from the bathroom for a minute, reappearing with a glass of water. "Drink this."

I took a long drink of the cool water.

"Better?"

I nodded.

When the world stopped spinning I grabbed my wash bag and started filling it with toiletries, before moving to the bedroom, grabbing one of our big holiday cases, and throwing everything of mine I could find into it. I did not intend to come back.

Slipping off the borrowed t-shirt I replaced it with a better fitting version and V-neck sweater, pulling on the trainers I usually wore to run in. As the minutes ticked past without any sign of Edward, anger replaced my fear; anger that he'd hurt me, anger that I'd let myself become a victim, anger I'd stayed with him when all my instincts had told me to get the hell out of the relationship months ago. I almost felt sorry he wasn't there for me to give him a piece of my mind – almost.

I moved out of the bedroom, back into the lounge, and collected the only other important items to me; my camera and a couple of photos in frames that I'd taken and deemed good enough to hang on the wall.

"That's everything," I said, zipping up the bag. Elliott had followed me into every room, guarding me. He nodded, lifting the suitcase as I shouldered the smaller bag.

I paused in the doorway to take a last look around at the place I'd called home for nearly two years of my life. My eyes touched upon the elephant, still on the sideboard. Its position was slightly off, evidenced by the darker ring of wood where the dust had settled less heavily. I moved towards it and picked it up, inclined to take it with me – after all it had saved my life. A smear of dark fluid on the corner of its rump caught my eye, and my breath hitched. "There," I breathed to Elliott, pointing. "That's what I hit him with . . . there's blood on it, and some hair, I think."

Elliott stared where I pointed and nodded. "Have you got a food bag or something? Something that will seal up? He's gone to great efforts to hide the attack; I think you should keep this."

I nodded and ran into the kitchen to find one of the large sealable Ziploc food bags we kept in the drawer. Elliott picked up the elephant and dropped it into the bag, being careful not to dislodge the hairs, before handing it to me.

I slipped the bagged elephant into my smaller bag, then shouldered it again. Elliott picked up the suitcase, and we both walked out of the flat. This time I didn't hesitate. As I pulled the door closed behind us, locking it, I released a thread of the tension I'd held since we'd walked in there. I didn't relax completely until we were back in the car and pulling away.

Chapter 13

Elliott led the way through the hospital hallways, having let the three of us in through one of the rear entrances using his staff pass, up the two flights of stairs to his departmental offices. They were situated close to the surgical theatres.

At the door to his office, he entered a code into an electronic keypad. I couldn't help noticing as he punched in one through to six in numerical order. "Not worried about security?"

"I already have too much to remember without adding entry codes to the list," he muttered, pushing open the door.

The small office appeared sparsely decorated: bare magnolia walls competed with a shade-less lightbulb to see which could be less visually stimulating. Two desks occupied the small space, both covered in large piles of poorly stacked files that I recognised as patient notes. It appeared he shared the office with another consultant – someone equally unkempt, if appearances were anything to go by. It looked chaotic and disorganised – and exactly like every other consultant's desk I'd ever seen in the NHS. And, with my job, I'd seen a few.

Elliott mumbled apologies as he pulled the chair over from the second desk to a position beside his own, indicating I should sit in it, before unearthing a third chair that had been hidden at the side of the room under a further pile of patient files. When we were all seated, he turned on the antiquated monitor that occupied prime position on his desk, which proceeded to wheeze and click slowly into life.

"I think you should have a word with your secretary," I suggested, pointing at the piles of notes that needed filing.

"She quit," he said, tapping in a password. "Said I was too disorganised."

"Hmm, I wonder why." I grinned, scanning the room. "I'm amazed you can ever find your patients' notes when they come in to see you."

"Okay," he said, ignoring me, as the screen came to life slowly and a green cursor flashed, "give me the first patient's number and let's see what we've got."

Malcolm slowly read out the long numerical sequence from the sample he'd found with the active virus as Elliott typed it in. When he pressed "return", a patient's record appeared. "Hmm . . ." He scanned through the case notes. "Okay, he's an acute allergic asthma patient, brought in with chronic breathing problems . . ." He went silent as he read further. "I can't see anything that jumps out at me. Nothing that explains why he'd have a different response to the virus compared to the rest of the population." He talked to himself under his breath as he scrolled through the screens, his eyes tracing backwards and forwards across the lines as he looked for anything that could explain it. "Hold on . . . here! He went into respiratory arrest when he was down in A&E. They resuscitated him." Elliott looked at

Malcolm, his expression triumphant. I was missing something. "What's the next one?" Elliott asked.

Malcolm read out the second sequence of numbers, and again Elliott tapped them in. This time it was an acute heart failure patient, brought in with a suspected heart attack – a readmission following an attack only a month before. The case sounded familiar. "Who is the patient?" I asked. Both Malcolm and Elliott squirmed in their seats – it was a massive no-no to reveal any patient-identifiable details. I saved them from their professional dilemma and peered over Elliott's shoulder. As I expected, Richard Rawson's name sat at the top of the screen. "That's Richard," I said.

Elliott nodded.

"They brought him back too, you said."

He nodded again.

"So, hold on a minute, you're telling me you've found the virus has become active in a couple of the samples you've looked at, and now you're looking at what those patients have in common?"

They both nodded this time.

"And what they seem to have in common is the fact that they were both resuscitated after their hearts stopped."

Again, they nodded.

"So, what does that mean?"

"I'm not sure," Elliott said finally.

"Edward's heart stopped. Does that mean the virus is active in him?"

"Maybe. But we won't know until we check his sample."

"But what does it mean?"

"I don't know." Elliott couldn't look at me.

"You don't know, but what do you think?"

Malcolm and Elliott exchanged a look. In the end, Malcolm spoke. "The virus is nothing we've ever seen before." He hesitated. "When I found the active virus, it wasn't just occupying part of the cell. It's a retrovirus – it blends with the cell, or in this case actually takes the cell over. It seemed, from the samples I looked at, like the original DNA had been replaced by this new viral DNA – it's that different."

"But what does that even mean?" I couldn't get what they were saying straight in my head.

"They're different. *Genetically*." Malcolm emphasised the words as if I were being especially dense.

"They're different?" I echoed.

"It's changed them," Malcolm agreed.

"We just need to understand how ... and why," Elliott added.

"Let me get this straight. You think they're different, that the virus has become activated and changed them."

Elliott and Malcolm nodded.

"And what you think changed them into having activated virus in them was the fact they both needed resuscitation?"

"I'm not sure. We're looking at what they have in common . . . that seems to be a common factor, but we need to find more people who are the same, who also have activated virus. I'm not so sure it's the resuscitation per se . . ." Malcolm paused, seemingly reluctant to say what he really thought.

"Just fucking tell me!"

"I think it's that they died," Elliott admitted finally.

I stared at him, struggling to process what he'd just said. "They died, and that's what caused the virus to activate?"

"Yes, exactly. Like a backup generator, the virus kicked into life."

"And if that hadn't been there? What would have happened?"

"Honestly?"

"Of course fucking honestly," I said, aware my language capabilities had taken a nosedive but frustrated he'd think I'd want anything but honesty at this point.

"I think they'd all have died. I think they did die. I think the virus brought them back."

I stared at him, waiting for the punchline. When it didn't come, I started to laugh anyway. "Oh my God . . ." For a good minute those were the only words I could manage, laughter bubbling up each time I considered what they'd told me. I gasped in a breath after each episode, my neck throbbing from the movement. Elliott and Malcolm sat and watched me in silence. "You're telling me you think this is some sort of zombie shit? You have to be kidding me . . . Seriously? Where are the cameras?"

Elliott frowned. "Look, I don't know anything for a fact yet. That's what we're trying to find out. All I do know is that two of my patients came back from the dead that night and I've had one other since then. Patients that, honestly, I thought didn't stand a chance. It made me ask questions, especially when they found that there was a virus in the fog that had assimilated itself into these same patients. So, I asked Malcolm to do me a favour and look at some of the samples of the cases that seemed unusual, and now he's found active virus in two people who also had an atypical outcome. Is it statistically significant? Probably not, not yet – we need a bigger sample. But it is almost a trend."

"You think Edward should have died that night?"

He lowered his head, his shoulders slumped, and then lifted his eyes to look at me. "I'm sorry, Sam, I shouldn't have told you like that, but I won't lie to you. I do. I was amazed he even survived the surgery. His liver was shredded in the accident. He was barely alive when he got to me. Then, when his heart crashed, he was flatlining for more than ten minutes. We'd done everything to bring him back but there was no response. And then his heart just started again on its own? Seriously? Apart from on the occasional TV medical drama, that just doesn't happen."

"So the virus saved him?"

"I don't know. Maybe. We need to look at his sample, maybe use that blood from the elephant ornament you took from the flat, and of any others who seem to have survived against the odds. Then perhaps we'll understand a bit more about all this."

I nodded, unable to speak as I tried to process what he'd told me. It didn't seem quite so funny anymore.

"Hey, let's get out of here. I think we've done all we can for now. Malcolm, can you get on to the records department and pull any records that were coded for resus activity? Then can you look at death rates? The end-of-year datasets should be in any day, but we need to look at the statistics for incidence of death after the fog in the different populations, to see if there is any noticeable change. It would be worth looking at males and females for comparison." He printed off copies of the two records we'd looked at, using an old printer that groaned into action in the corner of the room, spitting out the paper straight onto the floor.

"Won't the Public Health people pick this sort of information up?" I said, as he scooped the papers up from the pile at the bottom of the machine. "Why do *you* have to do it? Can't we just tell someone?"

"We will tell people. I think we just need to know a bit more first before we do. Public Health won't have that sort of data yet, or be able to pick out the trends for another year at least – by that time we might already be too late."

"Too late for what? What are you worried about?"

"I don't know," Elliott said, running his hand through his hair. "I can't think that far ahead. I need to take this one step at a time right now. I just know we need to get answers to some questions first. And then, once we have them, we can decide what to do next."

I shuddered, feeling uneasy. Elliott powered down the PC, before we filed back towards the hospital entrance, the mood more sombre, each caught up in our own thoughts. From the reception area Malcolm headed off to the records department, while Elliott and I walked the short distance back to my car.

"Samantha?" a voice called to me from across the car park. I stopped, frozen in my tracks, Elliott tensed beside me. Without asking, I knew we were both thinking the same thing; Edward had found me.

Elliott glanced over his shoulder. "It's not him," he said under his breath.

The voice called a second time and I turned. A guy approached us from the other side of the car park. I recognised him, but for the life of me couldn't place him or recall his name.

We stayed rooted where we were, waiting for him to reach us. He walked quickly, with purposeful strides, a big smile directed at me.

"Oh, hi," I said when he was still more than ten paces away, embarrassed to be unable to introduce him to Elliott. "I can't remember his name," I whispered out the corner of my mouth.

"Hi," said Elliott, when the guy got close enough. "Elliott Harvey, nice to meet you."

"Hi," he replied, his eyes sliding from me towards Elliott. "Damian Fisher. I'm a friend of Edward's. We met at the coffee shop a couple of weeks or so ago," he reminded me, picking up on my lack of recall.

"Of course." I offered him a big smile, kicking in to professional mode. "It's great to see you again. Were you visiting someone?"

"Yeah, a couple of people I know in here. Where's Edward?" he looked around as if he expected him to appear at any moment.

I scanned the vicinity too in case he knew something I didn't. My hand moved towards my throat unconsciously, drawing Damian's attention to my neck. He couldn't fail to notice the bruises there. I didn't miss the faltering smile and the darkening of his expression. Neither did Elliott, who took hold of my arm.

Damian scowled at his touch.

"Well, it was nice to meet you, Damian. I hope to see you around sometime," Elliott started to pull me away. "We need to go, Sam," he said, almost dragging me along by the arm.

"That was rude!" I hissed when Elliott and I were back in the car and the doors were closed. He locked them. The man, Damian, hadn't moved, he was still standing on the kerb, watching us.

Elliott started the car and pulled away slowly, pretending indifference, but his hands shook as he held the wheel. "You met him – Damian – at a coffee shop with Edward?"

"Yeah, so?"

"Who else was there?"

"Umm . . . about six others and us. Richard was there too. Why?"

"Because Damian Fisher was the name on the acute asthma patient record I just pulled."

Chapter 14

"Can you remember the names of the other people who were at the coffee shop with you?"

"I don't know. I doubt it, since I didn't remember that guy's." I tried to think. "I could recognise faces, I reckon, but not names. I'm sorry." I felt like a failure. "They were all men, if that helps?"

"All of them?"

"Yes. Why? Do you think they had the active virus too?"

"I don't know. It could be. It possibly links them to the virus. If we knew their names, we could look at their medical records for any anomalies."

I nodded. It made sense.

"Hey, when we met up before, you told me Edward was different after the accident. Can you tell me a bit more about how he was different?"

I sighed. I didn't want to talk about Edward. "I told you we'd been going to split up?"

Elliott glanced over at me and nodded.

"The Edward I knew was an arse. Handsome, but lazy, selfish and unfaithful in a nutshell. Then, after the accident, it was like he couldn't do enough for me. It was weird. He was so thoughtful it was disconcerting. A complete one-eighty in personality."

"Did you like him?"

"Yes, sometimes ... more than sometimes. When he wasn't trying to strangle me," I added, unable to resist the sarcasm.

Elliott ignored my feeble attempt at humour. "We need to speak to someone else who knew a person affected by the virus before it activated. We need to know if any of the others have noticed a difference."

"Well, Richard lives at home with his parents. I remember him telling me that. If you can get his address off the records you printed, we could talk to them. I don't know anything about this Damian guy."

Elliott pulled over and retrieved the medical records from his inside pocket. He scanned through them until he found Richard's home postcode, which he quickly entered into Google Maps. It turned out Richard only lived a couple of miles away.

"We're going now?" My voice sounded an octave higher than normal, despite my still tender throat.

Elliott nodded, on a mission, making a quick U-turn across the traffic. As we drove the diminishing distance to our destination, I couldn't escape the feeling that this probably wasn't the greatest idea we'd ever had.

We pulled up, all too quickly, on a road outside a large detached house. It was a quiet, affluent area, each house set back from the road and ringed by a privet hedge. Private and secure. I figured Neighbourhood Watch were active in the area when more than one upstairs curtain twitched in the adjacent houses during the time we sat in the car and observed the house. Two cars were parked on the gravel driveway, which seemed to indicate that at least someone was home.

"Hey," I said, as Elliott reached to open his door, "should you really be doing this?" This constituted a massive breach of patient confidentiality. If Richard's parents complained about Elliott turning up on their doorstep, and they traced it back to him accessing and using the notes from the hospital, he could lose his job. It seemed too much of a risk for him to take.

"What do you mean?" After I explained my thinking, he frowned at me. "I don't care. This feels too important."

"Why, though? Important enough to risk your job?"

"I can't explain it. It feels like there's something hidden in all of this. Something we need to find out."

"Well, Sherlock, I'm all for a bit of digging, but not at the cost of your job. Let me go in there and talk to them."

"No!"

"Seriously, I can tell them I know Richard from the hospital, that he's a friend of Edward's and that I wanted to speak to him about the fight we had. It's a reasonable reason to be there, and it won't end up with you losing your job."

"What if they try to do something to you?"

"What do you think they're likely to do? Really? Beat me with a soft floral pillow? I mean, look at the area." Flowery curtains with matching pelmets adorned every window visible from where we were sitting.

"I don't know. I don't like it. What if he's in there?"

"Richard?"

"Yes, what will you say?"

"The same as I planned to say to his parents. Look, if it seems bad I'll get out fast, but you've got to admit that it makes more sense than you turning up with a load of questions."

He huffed, then nodded with apparent reluctance. "Text me, let me know you're okay. I'll be right here. If you need me, I'll be straight in there."

"You gonna knock the door down, Hulk?" I grinned at him.

"If I have to." He huffed again, but with a small smile this time. I smiled back. He was really quite adorable, but I pushed those thoughts to the back of my mind as I opened the door and slipped out before he could protest any further.

The gravel crunched under my feet as I threaded my way past the parked cars, heading towards an intimidatingly large red front door. I couldn't find a bell, so I grasped the black metal knocker and rapped hard before my courage fled. As I waited, I glanced back towards Elliott. He watched me from within the shadows of the car, his outline dark. I tried to smile, but the moment was cut short when the door swung open.

I turned to find myself face to face with a small woman who, judging from the steely tint in her hair and the lines on her face, looked to be in her sixties. Her hair was styled into a sharp bob, her slim frame dressed neatly in a skirt and blouse. She looked educated and affluent. "May I help you?" she asked, her eyes darting to the car in the road behind me, as if sensing another presence. I sensed her trying to remember details in case she needed them for a Crimewatch re-enactment.

"Hi," I said, employing my most professional and friendly smile. "My name's Samantha Davis. My boyfriend, Edward Patterson, is friends with your son. I wondered if Richard was home. I wanted to talk to him about something."

"Oh . . . oh," she stammered, clearly taken aback by my request. "Oh, I'm sorry, he's out right now. You'll have to come back later, but I'll tell him you called." She started to close the door. I knew I needed to act fast if I wanted to get in there.

"Oh," I said, wiping the corner of my eye. "I'd so hoped to catch him. Can I leave you my card for when he comes back?" I reached into my bag and pulled out one of my business cards from work. It had my mobile number on it. I handed it to her. "I just don't know what to do." I dabbed at the corner of my eye again with a tissue from my bag. "I'm at my wits' end."

"Are you okay, dear?" she said solicitously, taking and pocketing my card, her natural concern when faced with someone in distress making her pause, the door widening again. Her kindness and empathy for others had won out over her caution of strangers. I felt bad for fooling her.

"Not really." At least that was the truth. "Edward and I had a massive row. I moved out. I don't know what to do about it. I thought Richard might be able to advise me since they seem to be such good friends these days . . ." I let my voice trail off. The pause lengthened between us.

"You can wait if you want," she offered finally. "Would you like a cup of tea?" She looked over my shoulder at Elliott waiting in the car. "Does your friend want to come in too?" She sounded more uncertain again given the prospect of a second stranger coming into her home.

"No, he's fine. He's a work colleague. He just offered to drive me over here because I was upset. He's doing some work in the car while he waits for me; he'll be fine where he is. Thank you so much, Mrs Rawson." I smiled as I stepped quickly through the doorway. She closed the door behind me.

I followed her inside into a wide Victorian hallway. Immediately in front of us, stairs ascended to the first floor. Everywhere I looked there were shelves and sideboards filled with porcelain figurines. I clutched my handbag closer to my chest, for fear of knocking something off, and followed her as she led the way into the kitchen directly ahead.

A country kitchen theme prevailed. Wood everywhere, only broken up by the hulking presence of a large Aga, completely at odds with its suburban setting, which warmed the kitchen to beyond comfortable. I sat where she indicated I should, at the large pine table that filled one end of the room, on a pine chair, gazing up at the pine cupboards while she filled the kettle and then set it upon the ever-ready Aga to boil. The silence became uncomfortable as the minutes ticked past, made more so by the heat. I unpeeled my coat and pushed my hair off the back of my neck to cool myself a little, watching her as she first warmed a teapot with the freshly boiled water, tipping it away before adding real leaf tea and then finally more of the water. She placed the teapot in the middle of the table on a cast-iron stand, and then covered it in a cosy.

I felt sorry for the pot, which must have been sweltering under there in this heat. God knew it didn't need the hand-knitted cover to keep it warm.

She decanted some milk from the carton in the fridge into a small jug and placed it onto the table along with two decorated bone china mugs. "Biscuit?" she offered, reaching for a packet of chocolate digestives in the cupboard. I nodded, and she emptied some from the packet onto a similarly decorated plate before offering them to me.

Finally, all required hostess courtesies met, she sat down beside me while we waited for the tea to steep. "How long have you been with Edward?"

"A couple of years."

"That's a long time." She straightened the teapot, fiddling with it until she had it perfectly centred on the stand. She appeared to be struggling to make small talk, seemingly unused to it.

I took a deep breath. It was now or never. "It is, but I think it might be over now. He's changed so much recently." She watched me as I stared down at my half-eaten biscuit. "That's why I'm here, really. Edward seems to see more of Richard than any of his other friends. His old friends, I mean. Since the accident, he seems to want to see different people. I thought if anyone knew what he was thinking . . ."

"I met Edward the other day," she said. "He came to the house. He's very handsome."

"Yes, he is," I agreed, wondering when he had come here. He'd never mentioned it. As far as I knew, when he left the house he went to work. It seemed there was a lot about Edward I didn't know.

Mrs Rawson stood, and collected a strainer that she placed over the top of one of the bone china mugs. Then she poured the tea, before repeating the process with the second cup. "Milk?"

"Please," I replied, wondering how to get the conversation onto Richard. I needn't have worried.

She held up a sugar cube with a small pair of tongs, and looked at me expectantly.

I shook my head.

"Richard has changed recently too." She fixed her eyes on a spot on the table, as if she were uncomfortable talking about it with me.

"In what way?"

"Oh, I don't know." She paused and looked over her shoulder as if she half expected him to creep up on her at any moment. "Since he came home from hospital the last time, he seems quite different." My heart thumped at her words. "He's always been such a quiet boy. He's been ill from a young age so . . . it's limited him a bit, I suppose . . . made him need us more than most boys his age would still need their parents. But we've always been happy, the three of us. He's always been very kind . . . thoughtful. But since he came back the last time . . ."

"He's different?"

"Yes," she admitted, sounding relieved to say it out loud. "He's always out now, and then when he isn't . . ." She hesitated, clearly uncomfortable with the topic.

"Edward suddenly wanted lots of things he'd never wanted before, like a baby. He'd always hated kids. It seemed like

I'd brought a stranger home from the hospital." I hoped she'd continue talking if she thought our experiences were similar.

She paused to top up our cups, and then spoke again, this time in a whisper. "Richard's always been very respectful of us, but then the other day he came home with a woman. A stranger . . . not really our sort of girl, if you know what I mean?"

I nodded, imagining the worst.

"They were upstairs together. It was just so unlike him – he's never even had a girlfriend before." She flushed with embarrassment, and I knew exactly what Richard had been doing with the woman upstairs.

"Edward nearly died. I keep wondering whether that made him think differently about life."

"Richard too. His father and I said the exact same thing."

"Do you know how they met?"

"No. I assumed they knew one another through the university. Richard is a researcher."

"No, Edward's a banker. I was told they met in the hospital–"

The front door opened then slammed closed, with enough force it made the windows rattle. Mrs Rawson jumped to her feet as my shoulders tensed, heart hammering in my chest.

"Richard," she said in a tremulous voice. "You've got a visitor, dear. We're in the kitchen." Footsteps approached before he appeared in the doorway.

He looked markedly different than the last time I'd seen him, wearing more fashionable clothes. He'd also restyled his hair into a modern cut. He'd even stopped wearing the glasses I'd seen him in before – I could only assume he'd replaced them with contacts. He stared at me, his eyes cold, and unconsciously I reached for my throat. "I . . ." My voice croaked as I struggled to get any words out. "I . . . I was hoping you could advise me. I thought you might be able to help Edward and me," I managed.

He raised an eyebrow; "You called the police on him, I'm not sure what help you were after. As I understand it, you're the one who needs help. You need to move on and recognise the relationship is over."

"Why is he being like this? He's changed . . ." I tried again.

Richard scowled at me, glancing quickly at his mother, then turning back to me. "I'd like you to leave," he said, with no trace of the friendliness he'd displayed during our previous encounters. "You need to leave Edward alone and stop making false accusations before you get into trouble yourself." His mother shrank in on herself a little more.

I gathered my coat and bag and stood. "Thank you for your hospitality, Mrs Rawson," I said, focusing on the small nervous woman in front of me while deliberately avoiding looking at Richard. "I'm sorry to have caused you any bother." It was a ridiculous understatement given the train wreck this visit had become.

"No bother," she said, as eager as I was to have this over and done with. "I'm sorry we couldn't offer more help. I do hope you sort things out with Edward, dear."

I nodded. I wanted to tell her to call me if she needed to, I knew she still had my card in her pocket, but I didn't dare. Richard stood and glared at me, remaining behind her like an ominous shadow all the while his mother showed me out. When we reached the doorstep, she turned to face me, and we shared one final look. I stood directly in front of her while she kept her back to him. She looked so afraid, I wanted to cry, or grab her hand and tell her to leave now and come with me; a small shake of her head told me she knew what I was thinking. Neither of us spoke a word. I squeezed her hands quickly, one last symbol of solidarity, before I turned, crunching my way back up the gravel path to where Elliott waited. Richard's eyes felt like lasers on my back as I moved away. Somehow, I resisted the urge to run.

Only when I had opened the car door did I allow myself one last look back. They were standing side by side, her posture rigid. Richard's expression chilled me, the arm he had slung around his mother's shoulder somehow menacing as they stood together on the doorstep. I shivered, slid into the car seat beside Elliott, slammed the door closed and locked it.

Chapter 15

"Drive." I said as soon as I could assemble my wits, my voice sharpened by fear.

Elliott fumbled to start the car. "Are you alright? What happened in there?" he said, as we turned the corner onto the main road, clipping the kerb. "Jesus, Sam, talk to me. What the hell happened? I saw him come back . . . Jesus." He wiped his palm on his trouser leg. "I didn't know whether to come in there and get you, or stay in the car . . ." He ran a hand through his hair. "I figured I'd give you another couple of minutes and then I was going to come in, regardless—"

"You were right," I said quickly, stopping him in full flow. "They've changed somehow. His mother admitted it to me. He used to be a quiet boy with a bad heart who lived at home with his parents. Since the last visit to the hospital, the time he nearly died, or actually died, he's changed. He's altered his physical appearance and is behaving differently – he brought a woman home and shagged her while his parents were both downstairs."

Elliott looked across at her and raised an eyebrow.

"Quite. Judging by the setup there, and believe me you couldn't find a more straight-laced family, that's not the sort of behaviour they're used to. I mean, his mother uses a teapot and cosy, for God's sake, and the time I saw him in the hospital he was wearing Star Wars pyjamas."

"Okay," Elliott said, focused back onto the task at hand. "Okay, so we now have two people we believe to have active virus with reports of behaviour change. We need to find more." He pulled up in front of his house.

"How do you propose we do that?"

"I don't know. I mean, if we're seeing it here, we can't be the only ones. There are reports of all the samples globally containing the virus. If the trigger is what we have suggested it is, then we need to connect with other places, because there must be others who are picking up on this."

"Why would they link it to the virus? I mean, it's only because we randomly connected and you know a microbiologist that we even thought to look. Behaviour change is not uncommon after trauma, especially head trauma . . . or at least not unheard of."

"You're right, they may not have made the connection to the virus . . . we just need to make the connection for them. First, we need to find families that are trying to cope with their loved one having had a personality shift."

"Have you got any buddies who deal with this?"

"A few from med school. I'll try and track some down."

"I'll take a look at a few chat rooms online. You never know, if people are struggling they may look for anonymous help there."

"Good idea." He switched off the engine and we both got out, but stopped when we saw two shadowed figures waiting for us on the doorstep. I breathed a sigh of relief when I realised both were too stocky to be Edward. A couple of steps towards them and I recognised the larger figure as the police officer I'd met, Frank Murray.

"Good afternoon," he called from the doorstep, his colleague moving to his side as we approached.

"Officers," Elliott greeted them. "What can we do for you? Have you picked him up yet?"

"We have had a chance to speak to Mr Patterson. That's why I'm here," Murray confirmed.

"Won't you come in?" Elliott fished out his key and opened the door, then ushered us all inside. I didn't miss the way Murray stared at me when he stood back to let me pass. He thought I hadn't noticed. It didn't feel like a friendly look, in fact, I got a bad vibe from the pair of them. His partner hadn't spoken a word. It made me wonder what Edward's version of events had reported, a twist of anxiety gripping my already fragile stomach.

By the time we were all seated and Elliott had made us the obligatory cup of tea, the tension in the room was thick.

Elliott looked at Officer Murray. "So, do you mind telling us what happened when you picked Edward up?" he said, our cups cooling on the table in front of us.

"We located Mr Patterson at just after eleven this morning. He was staying with a friend. We questioned him about your allegations." He paused, looking over at his colleague before pulling out his notebook, as if for reference, then returning his cool gaze towards me. "I need to inform you that Mr Patterson refutes the claim that he tried to strangle you. In fact, he claims you are paranoid and delusional, Ms Davis."

"He's lying!" I said, incensed. "You can see the bruises yourself." I pointed at my neck.

"Mr Patterson claims you did that to yourself. He alleges that when he tried to finish the relationship with you, you were so upset you claimed you would hurt yourself if he didn't stay. In fact, he claims that you did indeed hit him, but that you did it because you were jealous of his new relationship."

"That's a complete lie! He attacked me when I refused to have a baby with him. He tried to strangle me. I hit him to protect myself."

"So you say, Ms Davis. But I have to tell you, if you did hit him – in the manner you described – there was no evidence of it. He had virtually no bruises, only a minor abrasion on the side of his head, and certainly nothing that fits with your version of events."

Elliott sat in silence, watching the exchange as Officer Murray continued, "I have to warn you, Ms Davis, Mr Patterson accused you of being unstable, that your jealousy had pushed you over the edge. He was concerned you would do either yourself or one of them harm."

"Jealous!" I had to laugh. "I was the one who finished the relationship with him originally . . . Hold on, you said one of them? One of whom? Who are you talking about?"

"We located Mr Patterson with Ms Serena Sutton. She claims they were together when you allege the attack took place–"

"She's lying!" I cried. "It happened exactly as I said it did . . . she's lying . . ." I could already tell he didn't believe me.

"Mr Patterson asks that you remove the remainder of your possessions from his apartment as soon as possible and return the key. He's threatened to take out a restraining order if you persist in harassing either him or Ms Sutton. I would strongly suggest that you be accompanied on any visits to the apartment."

I looked at Elliott, who had still to say anything, then turned my attention back to the officer. "I don't need anything . . . I collected everything important this morning. He can keep the rest. Believe me, I have no desire to see him ever again. Here . . ." I said, rummaging in my bag for the key to the apartment, hands trembling as I detached it from the keyring and held it out towards him. "Take the key. You can give it to him yourself."

He took it from me. "Well then, I believe that brings everything to a close." He stood.

"What about my allegation that he tried to strangle me? He just gets away with it?"

"Ms Davis, there is little evidence to support your allegation. You are, of course, welcome to proceed with the charges if you wish, but based on what I have seen so far, I believe your chances of success are slim: Mr Patterson has an alibi for the time you say the incident happened, and there is no physical evidence that cannot be given an alternative explanation or that doesn't support Mr Patterson's version of events. In fact, being completely honest with you, I don't believe there is anything to suggest the events you described happened at all. Frankly, I think you're lucky Mr Patterson isn't pressing his own charges against you." I started to interrupt again, but he stopped me. "You seem like a nice enough person, miss. Maybe you should just put this bad relationship behind you and move on," he said, looking over at Elliott.

The three men stood. Murray nodded at me one last time before Elliott showed them out. The low mutterings of deliberately quiet conversation carried from the front door, and I knew, without a doubt, they were talking about me. Left alone, I reflected on the exchange, mortified to think the police believed

I'd made it all up. Worse, they thought I had inflicted the injuries on my neck to myself – was that even possible? – and that I had, unprovoked, attacked Edward. God only knew what Elliott thought. I could only imagine he seriously regretted letting a deranged woman into his life. For a moment, even I questioned my version of events.

I ran into the bedroom and started scooping up the few possessions I had left there – my shift dress and blouse from the day of the attack – it seemed incredible that had only been yesterday. Elliott walked in as I picked up the shoes. He stood watching me for a second before he asked; "What are you doing?"

"I'm so sorry, I'll be out your way in five minutes. Please believe me, I didn't do it to myself . . . I don't know why he's lying, but I didn't do what they said . . . I'll get my stuff from your car and get out of your hair. I'm so sorry you got caught up in all this shit." The words tumbled from me, uncontrolled, my cheeks heated with humiliation.

Elliott walked over to me and pulled me to my feet, holding both my hands as he looked at me. "I know you're not lying." His gaze seemed sure.

My fear and anger morphed into tears. A large tear ran down my cheek and dripped off my chin onto my chest. "How? How do you know?" I needed him to tell me.

"Well," he said slowly, "first of all, I know you. I've known you since before the attack, not well admittedly, even though you barely noticed me. Even back then I could see the sort of person you were. The person you still are. It's what attracted me to you in the first place," he admitted, blushing as he stroked the back of my hand with his thumb. "You're solid and strong, not the sort given to jealous rages." He smiled and took a deep breath before he continued; "Secondly, I knew about the state of your relationship well before the attack . . . and why. His story doesn't make sense. He's been all over you these last weeks, you said so yourself, and now suddenly he's all about this Serena woman? Seriously? It just doesn't add up. I'm sure your friends would say the exact same thing. And then there are the injuries on your neck. The bruises show a clear handprint. You have small hands, Sam, and the bruises suggest a much larger grip – we could prove it if we needed to – let alone the likelihood of anyone actually trying to throttle themselves. It just seems so unlikely. Finally, even if it were possible that you had, you forget we still have the wooden elephant. That proves your version of events. No one who'd been hit on the head with that lump of wood – twice – should be walking and talking a day later."

"The elephant!" I'd forgotten all about it. "We need to take it to Frank Murray. You're right, we need to show him he's wrong."

"We could do that," Elliott said slowly, "but just hold on a minute. We need to think about this first. The elephant proves your version of events, it's true, but this whole situation is bigger than just your attack. If what Officer Murray reports is true, then you hit Edward over the head with a large lump of wood and now, only a day later, there is virtually no evidence of it. Somehow he's healed sufficiently to mask his wound. In the same way he healed his lacerated liver. As I said, there's more to this than just what he did to you, awful though that was. We need to figure out what the fuck they are and, more to the point, what they want."

Chapter 16

I stared at Elliott as I considered what he'd just said. Edward had changed, that was irrefutable, but the meaning behind that change was less clear.

"Right now Edward and Richard don't know we suspect there is more to this than your failed relationship," Elliott said. "I'd like to keep it that way."

My eyes sprang to meet his. "You think they're all dangerous?"

"I don't know." He sighed heavily, running his hand through his hair. "I do know he tried to strangle you. I also know Richard freaked you out and, no offence, but you're hardly a complete pushover as girls go."

I grinned, despite the serious tone to his voice. It broke some of the tension. Until he spoke again.

"Look, I just don't want to risk taking them on until we know what we're dealing with."

"Then why the hell are we taking them on at all? We should be telling someone . . . the police, the army . . . I don't know . . . someone!"

"And what exactly would you tell them? That your boyfriend had a personality change after surviving a life-threatening accident? It's hardly something that's likely to set alarm bells off."

"But the active virus in their blood – that's something."

"Once we put that out there. We need to be damn sure we know our facts." He took a long, tired breath. "Look, I need to catch up with Malcolm and see how he's getting on. See if you can find any other people reporting personality changes and if they survived some sort of life-threatening episode. We need to prove the link, and we need more people than just us reporting it."

"We should find someone who's dying and see if they come back to life – that would prove it," I muttered, irritated that he couldn't see we were not equipped to handle this alone.

Elliott sat back in his chair. "That's not a bad idea."

"I was joking – that's just sick."

"But it would prove the point," he argued. "If someone with a terminal illness recovers, then people will have to pay attention. I'll give it some thought."

It was all too much. The experience at Richard's house, the police, and now Elliott suggesting we should watch people die to see if they came back to life. Fatigue hit me, and my body sagged. "I need a break from all this," I told him. "I'm going to lie down. I've got to get my head together – this has all been too much to take in for one day. When I wake up, I'll do some research, just give me some time to get my head together."

His gaze softened. "Sure," he agreed. "Go and lie down. You look bushed. It's not surprising. Your body's been through a lot. Everything else can wait." He pulled me into a hug and pressed a gentle kiss into the top of my head. Comfortable, for a moment I let myself rest there, safe within his arms. It soothed me like an emotional balm. His strength, the press of his hard chest against me, reassuring. I liked it too much.

I mentally shook myself and pulled away. Only a few days ago I'd been willingly having sex with Edward, even contemplating having a child with him, and now I was already physically responding to Elliott? And I'd thought Edward had a problem! Maybe I was the sick one.

I stumbled as I took a hasty step back, nodding at Elliott before scurrying off to my room, refusing to acknowledge my feelings of guilt at the confusion I'd seen on his face, his arms dropping back to his sides. I lay on top of my duvet trying to sleep, berating myself and my fickle heart for even considering succumbing to temptation, and trying to ignore the troublesome inner voice that told me I hadn't loved Edward for a long time . . . if ever. We had shared physical intimacy but not emotional. Did that make a difference? I didn't know. Was I lying to myself? Until he'd tried to strangle me, Edward and I had been becoming closer again. What I did know for certain was that starting something with Elliott when my life was this fucked up was definitely a bad idea, however tempting he might be. With thoughts of what a relationship with Elliott might be like, I finally fell into a restless sleep.

***

I woke to silence.

I cringed as I recalled Elliott's and my awkward separation hours earlier. It worried me that things might continue in the same vein. If that were the case, I needed to find another place to stay – soon. Jesus, if I kept having thoughts about Elliott like the ones that had just filled my dreams then I needed to find somewhere ASAP. What the hell was I doing here anyway? Living in the house of a virtual stranger, chasing down conspiracy theories? But he didn't feel like a stranger; in fact, he felt more real than many of the other people I called friends these days – except maybe for Heidi.

I was hopeful Heidi would be back any day. She and Paul had to have nearly finished their Italian shagathon and, with any luck, they'd be willing to let me stay with them until I sorted myself out. Paul would doubtless be less keen on having me under their roof for any length of time, so it would only be a very short-term solution. Then again, if they were shagging every chance they got, I had no desire to be under their roof for long either. I needed to find an apartment or room of my own to rent.

I wandered out into the lounge and found a note propped up between a decorative glass bowl and a coaster on the coffee table. It seemed Elliott had been called into work while I'd been asleep – some sort of surgical emergency. My emotions bounced between pleased to avoid any further awkwardness and disappointed not to see him.

I found the coffee machine and started to make myself a strong cup. It was a good idea in theory, but as soon as I lifted the cup to my lips the smell didn't appeal, and I found myself pouring what remained down the sink. Instead, I reached for the orange juice, enjoying the cool, sharp sweetness as it washed away the last vestiges of sleep from my mouth, including a persistent metallic taste, and soothed the ache in my throat. As I powered up my laptop, I grabbed an apple, and nibbled at it while I waited for the system to load.

The Google logo flashed onto my screen. I hesitated, wondering what to type into the search box, eventually settling on "personality change after illness or accident". I found a surprising amount of information. I read through the different types of personality changes, as they described the categories: Confusion or delirium, delusions, disorganised speech or behaviour, hallucinations or mood extremes like depression. I discounted the first four topics and focused on the last one. Again, there could be any number of causes, from the use of drugs, to mental disorders like schizophrenia to disorders that directly or indirectly affected the brain. I noted that concussions and liver disease were both listed. From what I read, it would be terribly easy to dismiss Edward's changes as being a direct result of his injuries from the accident, if one were so inclined. Elliott had been right not to rush to the authorities. We would have been laughed out of the place.

I moved on from the medical descriptions to sites where people raised concerns about changes in relatives. Some were clearly associated with other causes, like severe illnesses known to affect the brain, but one or two seemed less obvious. I filtered the ones I was interested in by date and concentrated on those seeming to be from after the date of the accident. There were about six in total that appeared unusual and couldn't be easily explained away. One in particular could have been written by me: a young woman named Clare described how her boyfriend had suffered a major fall during a rock climbing expedition. They'd been out together, it was a shared passion, when a small rock fall had caught them, some of the falling boulders hitting her partner on the head. He'd fallen from the line, dropping about thirty feet. No one had expected him to survive the accident. He hadn't been wearing a helmet, and several critical bones had been shattered in the fall, but amazingly he had lived. So far, so good, one would have imagined, but the woman went on to describe how her partner had completely changed. He no longer seemed interested in getting back out climbing. He insisted he wanted to stay at home and start a family. The woman said this would be understandable, to some extent, after such a life-changing experience, but he knew she couldn't have kids. He'd always known, from when they very first got together. It was something they'd discussed at length, a genetic condition which prevented her from ever conceiving. They'd always agreed that if they ever decided a child was something they wanted, they'd be happy to adopt. Now, since the accident, he'd asserted adoption was no longer an option. He wanted his own child and had therefore insisted they needed to finish their relationship. Understandably she was devastated and looking for answers to explain why her lover had undergone such a complete transformation, needing to understand if there was any hope he might revert back into the man she loved.

I scanned the comments below. There was the usual comforting "it's normal after an accident" fare, insisting he'd become more himself over time as his brain recovered from its trauma. Some suggested depression and unexplained bursts of anger were common after serious illness or accidents as the person came to terms with everything that had changed in their life, and to "hang on in there". Easier said than done, I imagined. From what I'd read during my research already, I knew his symptoms were common in this sort of situation, but something about this read differently to the ordinary cases. This guy had made a complete physical recovery. It was almost miraculous. The depression people normally suffered came about as a side effect of needing to adjust to the physical and lifestyle changes the accident had forced upon them. This guy didn't have that problem. Clare had also replied to a question about anger, saying he'd become almost violently angry when she'd reminded him about her inability to have children, telling her she was "useless" and a "waste of space". Her hurt bled into her words. I typed a quick comment, calling myself "kindredspirit"; *I'm facing a similar situation following an accident. Maybe we can support each other?* I left her an email address from a new Gmail account I set up quickly. That way if a load of other people wanted to spam me it would be easy to delete the emails. It also made it more difficult for anyone to trace me. I was becoming paranoid.

I scanned the other people that seemed to meet my criteria and sent similar notes to them all. Happy I'd done what I could, I sat back and contemplated what to do with the rest of my time. I clicked into Outlook and read a few work emails, which depressed me as I read through the list of outstanding demands that had piled up in my absence. A note from HR warned me I had reached the limit on my paid sick leave period and that any further absences due to illness would be unpaid until the end of the year.

Discouraged by what awaited me on my return to work on Monday, I picked up my camera and took out the memory card. I plugged it into the laptop and started to download pictures, deleting any that were not up to my exacting standards. The wedding pictures had already been taken off when we'd seen Victoria at the bar, but there were loads from when I'd taken shots in the park, and a few more recent ones from inside the apartment. I'd always preferred taking pictures of people, although I did have some landscapes in my collection too. I liked images where the people resembled the paintings of old, still-life portraits capturing a moment in time. I paused when I reached some of Edward – taken only a few days ago – when I'd been playing about with my camera. Given what had passed since then, it felt like a lifetime. I took in his familiar features in the many different frames I'd taken, stilling when I reached one where he'd been gazing straight into the camera – straight at me. He'd fucked me moments after I'd taken the picture, and his intention bled into the expression I'd captured. This was not the image of an unhappy man, already in a relationship with another woman, looking for a way out. I stared at the picture a moment longer, before pulling up a folder from the wedding. I filtered through the pictures until I found one of Edward that I'd taken at the table during the reception, and then arranged both images so that I could view them side by side. The difference was immediately stark. An "otherness" seemed apparent in the more recent picture that hadn't been present in the wedding photo. Like the difference between a huskie and a wolf. If I had wanted any more proof of the differences I had seen in him, the evidence sat here in front of me.

My head started to pound, as if in response to the strain of trying to understand the differences between the images. I staggered into the bathroom in search of some paracetamol.

Unsuccessful, I collapsed onto the floor, feeling sorry for myself as I cursed Elliott for not keeping any drugs in his home. My head continued to pound its steady beat.

I was resting my temple on the cool rim of the bath, some small part of my mind grateful for the obvious cleanliness around me given my inability to lift my head, when Elliott returned.

When he didn't come to find me, I pulled myself to my feet. I cupped some water in my hand and brought it to my mouth, swilling away some of the fur that carpeted my tongue. I looked like shit. The light in the bathroom shone uncompromisingly bright, there was no hiding the dark bags under my eyes and the haggard sallowness of my complexion. I'd also lost weight. I ran my fingers through my hair, trying to tame it, before gripping hold of the door, pulling it open and walking out into the lounge.

Elliott crouched over the laptop, staring at the images of Edward.

Chapter 17

"He looks like a completely different man," he said as I approached, his eyes flicking between the two pictures. "Sure, the physical features are all in the same place, but how he's using his muscles, the way he's responding, he looks so different."

"I agree."

Elliott stood, turning to look at me. "God, you look awful, Sam. Are you okay?"

"Not really," I admitted. "I feel like shit. Do you have any headache tablets?" He looked concerned walking over to me and pressing the back of his hand against my forehead. "I think maybe I've picked up a bug. My head is killing me."

"You're not hot. You've been through a lot over the last few days. It's bound to take it out of you." He walked into the kitchen, returning with a glass of water and some pills. "Maybe you need to take it a bit easier?"

"I've been asleep loads. I'm not sure how much easier I can take it without putting myself into a coma," I said with a weak laugh. "Anyway, I'm all out of paid sick leave at work, so I have to be better by Monday." I paused, wondering how to say what I needed to.

"Spit it out," Elliott said, frowning at me.

"What?"

"Whatever has you chewing your lip like that."

I unclenched my jaw, releasing my lip. "I'm going to look for somewhere else to live as soon as I can. I'm sorry to be imposing on you like this."

"There's really no rush."

"You've been amazingly kind to take me in at all. You barely even know me, and then there's all this . . ." I pointed towards the images of Edward on my laptop.

"Really, you have nothing to apologise for. I offered."

"And I appreciate it, but I think I need my own place. I'm hoping Heidi will be back by Tuesday and I'll be able to stay there until I find something of my own."

"As I said, I'm happy to have you here." His cheeks coloured a little as he added, "I like having the company." He paused, eyes fixed upon some intriguing spot on the carpet, then he looked up at me again. His frown deepened, seemingly concerned with what he saw. "Can I make you something to eat? Or a cup of tea?"

"Sure," I agreed, both of us happy to let him move the conversation on. He vanished into the kitchen again, emerging five minutes later with two steaming mugs.

"I didn't know how you took it, you usually have coffee, so I guessed milk but no sugar."

I smiled. "Perfect." He placed a cup down on the table in front of me.

"So," he said, sitting down beside me on the sofa. "I talked to a friend of mine. I was thinking about what you said, about seeing it happen – seeing someone come back to life – and I think I've found a way we could do it."

"Are you serious?" It was hard to know whether I was more shocked or horrified.

"No, listen, it's not as bad as it sounds."

"Watching people die is not as bad as it sounds?" I asked, incredulous.

"Really. I've got a friend who works as a doctor in a hospice. Some of the patients have no friends or family, no one to be with them in their last moments. The staff are pretty stretched, as you can imagine, so people can volunteer to be there – just because it's a scary thing to die alone, and no one should have to." He echoed the same thoughts I'd had when Edward had been so ill. "Having someone there to hold your hand can make all the difference in the peacefulness of the passing. I just thought we could volunteer. It would be a decent thing to do, but we could also test our theory at the same time."

"I don't know." The prospect of watching someone die, even if I didn't really know them, horrified me. "What with everything I saw Edward go through, it's all still a bit raw. I don't know if I can do that for someone else right now."

"I understand," he said quickly. He patted my arm. "I'll go on my own." I felt bad for letting him down.

"Wait," I said. "Let me think about it for a bit. When were you thinking about going?"

"Tonight."

"Tonight? Oh my God! Why so soon?"

"Well, my friend mentioned there's a man likely to die soon who fits the bill exactly – no family, no friends. He's not likely to survive much longer. He's got terminal lung cancer, with secondaries just about everywhere else now. Plus, I have this feeling the longer we leave all of this, and the more time that passes before people cotton on to what's happening around us, the worse the position we're going to be in. If this is happening everywhere, all over the world, then think how many people might be affected before we have the chance to stop it. The longer we let it go on, the harder it will be to go back to anything resembling normality." I knew he was right, but I was still terrified at the prospect of watching someone die – again.

"What if I can't handle it?"

"You don't have to be there at all. And if you do come, and it gets too much, you can leave. I'll stay. I'm more used to seeing death than you are."

"Jesus, I don't know how you do it."

He shrugged. "Death is part of life."

"Maybe not. Not anymore," I muttered, thinking about Edward.

"And that truly terrifies me," Elliott admitted.

"Eternal life?" I said facetiously.

"Or eternal death. We don't know what we're dealing with right now."

"God, this is surreal." My laptop pinged as a new email came in. Needing the distraction, I wandered over to it. It was in my new Gmail account, from the girl I'd contacted, Clare.

Dear kindredspirit, I got your message. Thank you. Can you give me an outline of your situation? I've had too many nutcases contact me to trust anyone now. Thanks, Clare

It was fair enough that she was suspicious of me; after all, I'd randomly contacted her through the internet. I could be any kind of freak. We'd all watched *Catfish*. "Who is it?" Elliott asked, peering over my shoulder.

"A girl I found on a website about personality change. She sounds like she could have been affected like me." I explained what had happened to her, and her partner, as I drafted a quick response describing the situation between Edward and me. I left out the attempted murder. I didn't want to frighten her off completely.

"Sounds promising," Elliott agreed as I pressed send. I turned and faced him. He had been standing so close to me that when I turned we finished up with our bodies only centimetres apart. The physical jolt from his proximity made me jerk. His face flushed, and he took a step back. It was oddly endearing.

"I'll come," I promised in a moment of rash spontaneity. Elliott looked confused. "Tonight, when you go to the hospice, I'll come," I clarified.

"Are you sure?"

"Yes. You're right, there's more going on here than it seems. Someone has to shine a light on it all."

"If you want to leave at any time it'll be fine. You only have to stay for as long as you're comfortable."

"Thanks." I smiled at him, and he smiled back. I tried hard not to notice the dimples in his cheeks, telling myself sternly that the last thing I needed to add into the current toxic mix of my life was any more hormones.

***

Four hours later we walked through the doorway of St Francis' Hospice, as I tried to quell the rising swell of nausea that threatened to overwhelm me as soon as the smell of disinfectant, with undertones of decay, assaulted my olfactory system. Elliott paused to speak to the nurse on reception, who smiled over at me as soon as he explained who we were and what we were there for. She called to a colleague, who led us along the corridor to a door. The nameplate declared its occupant to be Victor Holmes. The door was one of many – I tried not to think of the dying people lying in their beds inside every room. Instead, I attempted to calm my nerves, which were currently performing the conga around my intestines, by taking some deep breaths and rolling back my shoulders. I took a final deep breath, then I stepped into the room.

It looked like any other bedroom I'd ever seen; the sort of generic guest room your mum might have for occasional visitors – I knew my mum used to when she was alive. It wasn't at all the clinically sterile hospital room I'd expected. There were wooden blinds on the windows and a sofa in the corner, complete with a throw cover and cushions. The fixtures and fittings were more Laura Ashley than Staples. The only anomaly was the hospital bed.

My eyes were drawn to the small figure in the bed, his body shrivelled by both his advanced age and his disease. It was obvious the cancer had wiped-out the last of his strength. His breath rasped as he gasped air into his diseased lungs, and, for a moment, I was transported back to Edward's time in the hospital. But this felt completely different.

The man in the bed stirred and opened one watery blue eye, his gaze fixing on Elliott. He tried to speak, but Elliott put a hand out to stop him, saying; "Hello, Victor. I'm Doctor Elliott Harvey. We thought you might appreciate a little company this evening." He looked over his shoulder at me as he said it, giving me an encouraging smile and gesturing for me to move closer.

I took a couple of steps forward, stopping just behind him. Elliott moved to sit in one of the two chairs immediately beside the bed, indicating I should do the same. I hesitated.

Victor's tired, pain-laden eyes landed on me, and for a moment they widened. Then he reached up to take the mask from his face, clawing at it with his weakened fingers. Elliott tried to stop him, but it just made Victor more distressed, so instead, he helped him move it away from his mouth so he could speak.

"Martha," he wheezed, pausing to gasp for air, his eyes fixed on me as if he were afraid I might vanish. "You came. You promised you would." He stopped to cough, then gasped in a wheezing breath. Elliott attempted to replace the oxygen mask, but Victor was having none of it. "Come closer," he begged, "so I can see you properly." He believed me to be someone else. Someone important to him. I hesitated, unwilling to mislead him but equally unwilling to upset the man in his final hours. With a glance at Elliott I shuffled forward. Elliott stood from his chair and moved out the way, sitting down in the one alongside it. I ran a hand through my hair, before taking the seat directly beside the bed.

"You don't have to do this, Sam," Elliott whispered, with a gentle touch on my shoulder. The old man reached for my hand which still rested in my lap. I allowed him to take hold of it and tried not to shudder as the cool, bony appendage pressed against my palm.

"You always said you'd be here for me," Victor said, his eyes fixed upon mine as his breath continued to grind in and out of his chest, the rattle on every exhalation a constant reminder of his disease and impending death. This time, when Elliott reached to replace the mask, he didn't struggle, content just to have my hand within his own. I envied whoever had earned the devotion that Victor now lavished upon me with only a look. Tears brimmed in my eyes as he smiled from beneath the mask, looking at me until his eyes grew heavy and sleep took him. He didn't let go of me all the while he slept.

"He's going downhill," Elliott said, several hours later, after a nurse had been in to check his vital signs. They'd been coming and checking on him every fifteen minutes. One of them had explained that he was deteriorating fast and they didn't expect him to last the night. After the most recent visit the nurse had whispered into Elliott's ear. He'd nodded. "He's going downhill. It won't be long now."

I could see it, his breathing now so shallow that at times I had to look for the slight movement of his chest to know he still lived. "Is he in pain?"

"No, he's unconscious. They're managing his pain." He pointed at the cannula in Victor's arm where the nurse had been administering drugs periodically through a pump system. "He's not likely to wake up again. You can let go of his hand if you like."

But I couldn't. Not really. I owed him this much if I was going to share the moment of his death. And, if it gave Victor any comfort, then really it was the least I could do. The feel of the small hand within my own no longer unpleasant. It felt good, like I was doing something positive, something I could be proud of. I hoped someone might be willing to do the same for me one day.

When the nurse came back ten minutes later, she told us that he'd passed. Shocked, I felt guilty I hadn't registered the transition from life into death, the difference so slight yet profound. The silence after she switched off the oxygen machine seemed overwhelming. Elliott and I both stared at him, waiting for the moment when the virus would activate, but nothing happened. Victor continued to lie there, a peaceful expression on his face, released from the painful life that had held him captive these last months.

"I don't understand," Elliott whispered, as I wiped a stray tear from my cheek.

"What's not to understand," I said, angry that his obsession with the virus had become more important than marking this important moment in Victor's life, "he's dead."

"But why? Why hasn't the virus activated?"

"I don't know, Elliott," I said, the tears falling more rapidly now. "Can we go, please?"

"I'll just take a quick blood sample." He pulled a vial from his pocket, extracting a small sample of blood for analysis from the arm I wasn't holding.

I released Victor's hand gently, placing it carefully onto the bed beside him, and brushed my tears away with the back of my hand, before bending and kissing him gently on the forehead. I ignored the feel of cooling skin against my lips. Behind me, Elliott muttered all the while about why the virus had not activated. Frankly, at that moment, I didn't give a shit about the virus.

Happy I had done everything I could, I stood, brushed myself down, and then walked out of the room without a backward glance.

Chapter 18

"I'm sorry, Sam," Elliott said when he reached the car. He slipped a hand around my waist and pulled me into his chest for a hug. "I'm sorry, I didn't think." I sobbed as he held me close, the smell of him, his vitality, comforting after what we'd just seen. "I forget what it's like to experience death. It's such a part of my job that sometimes I forget what it really means." He pressed his nose into my hair and took a deep breath. "What you did in there for him was beautiful. You made his passing as good as it could be in the circumstances. You gave him peace."

I nodded. I knew my being there had helped in some small way, but it had taken a toll. My body now weighed down with melancholy. I couldn't imagine how the nurses who worked there did that every single day.

Elliott saw me into the car, closing my door before pulling out his phone from his pocket. I heard him explaining to someone what had happened. "I'll drop the sample round on our way home." Malcolm, I had to assume.

We stopped at a nondescript apartment block for Elliott to run the sample in, and then drove back to his house. I was so tired by the time we walked through the door, it was all I could do to brush my teeth before falling into bed. My perpetual bone-numbing weariness worried me until I realised it was nearly two in the morning. Elliott stuck his head around the door as I pulled the duvet over myself. "You okay?"

"Yeah." I sniffed, trying not to let the tears start up again, as I worried who would sit and hold my hand if I were dying. The fear of dying alone spilled out as more tears. A little sob broke free.

"Sure?" He sounded worried, moving closer. He dithered beside the bed, looking uncertain how to proceed with the overtly emotional female wreck in front of him. I continued to cry, seemingly unable to stop myself now I'd started. With a muttered, "fuck it," the bed dipped as he lay down beside me and pulled me into his arms. He lay on top of the covers, while I stayed underneath, but I appreciated the comfort he offered. He stroked my hair, promising me everything would be alright, until finally, I fell asleep.

I woke once in the night, convinced I still held onto Victor's cold, dead hand, until it moved and I realised the hand I held belonged to Elliott. It was cold because he still lay curled in a ball above the duvet. The night air felt cool; certainly too cold to go without any sort of covering. I pulled the duvet out from beneath him and then resettled it above the pair of us, before curling up again in my half of the bed. He stirred slightly when my body brushed against his, muttering my name in his sleep. The warmth generated by our bodies soon pulled me back into sleep and, for the first time in a long time, my dreams were only filled with happy images.

***

I was too hot when I woke. I lay still for a moment, trying to collect my thoughts as memories from the day before tumbled into place. A hand moving against my breast caused the last vestiges of sleep to evaporate as I became aware of the other physical presence in the bed with me. His body was pressed behind mine, arm slung across my chest, hand resting on the aforementioned breast, and a firm erection against my buttocks. A flush of desire washed through me. But it was too soon. Guilt at my fickleness doused my lusty thoughts and sent me wriggling from under his arm as I tried to get out of the bed without waking him. Once accomplished, I couldn't help but pause to look down at his sleeping form.

He was quite a sight to behold, a feast for the eyes, everything light to Edward's dark. His golden hair, tousled from sleep, gave him a boyish look further enhanced by the long dark eyelashes that rested upon his cheeks. When he was awake they framed his beautiful blue eyes, but now, asleep, they were a wonder by themselves. His lips appeared pink and entirely kissable, and a soft stubble dusted his cheeks and chin. I resisted the urge to bend down and brush my cheek against his before kissing him. His eyes started to flutter slightly, still closed, as he began to stir. I must have disturbed him when I'd slipped from beneath his arm – either that or he had sensed me staring at him. Quickly, I grabbed some of my clothes and headed into the bathroom. When I returned to the room twenty minutes later, he'd gone.

I finished getting ready and then steeled myself to face him. With my shoulders back, I walked into the lounge to find no Elliott, just a note waiting for me next to a still-steaming cup of coffee. He'd already left for work, the brief words telling me he'd overslept and had to rush off, but that he would be back later, after his shift was completed. I collapsed onto a chair, allowing the cortisol from the stress I hadn't even realised I was feeling to seep slowly out of my body. Strangely crushed, I contemplated why he'd been so desperate to avoid seeing me he hadn't even bothered to brush his teeth or call out a goodbye. Then I scolded myself for caring. He was only a friend helping me out in my time of need – yeah, right. That might have been his feelings on the subject, but my hormones seemed to have other ideas.

My stomach rumbled, distracting me from my inner turmoil. I'd barely eaten anything over the last four days, I needed to get something inside me, and soon. I stood, made my way into the kitchen and rummaged in the cupboards until I found some eggs and bread.

Ten minutes later, I sat down to eat some scrambled eggs on toast. The coffee remained untouched. I helped myself to some more orange juice, deciding I needed to do some food shopping later to replace everything I'd eaten. I'd get something I could make him for dinner as a way of saying thank you, I decided. I prayed it wouldn't be awkward between the two of us after last night, telling myself we'd done nothing wrong. We were just two friends, and he'd done a great job of consoling me after what had been a pretty crap few days, nothing more. The lusty thoughts I found myself having about him were just a result of the kindness he'd shown me since Edward's attack . . . nothing more . . . really, nothing more.

By mid-morning I'd cleaned the apartment, done all the washing I'd found in the washing basket in the bathroom, and had put on my jacket ready for the quick trip to the shops, when my mobile rang with an unfamiliar number. I answered with some wariness.

"Hello," a voice said. I didn't recognise it. The person on the other end seemed to be whispering.

"Yes?"

"Samantha? Is that you?" a now identifiably female voice asked.

"Yes, speaking," I replied. "I'm sorry, who is this?"

"It's Mrs Rawson. Richard's mother."

"Oh, Mrs Rawson. How are you? I'm so glad you called me. I wanted to apologise if I caused you any bother after my visit yesterday. I didn't mean to upset anyone–"

"Samantha, I'm frightened," she interrupted, with a small whispered sob.

My heart rate accelerated at her words. "Frightened? Why on earth are you frightened?"

"It's Richard. He was so angry after you left. He won't let either of us leave the house, not even to buy milk. He physically barred the way when I tried to ignore him, he pushed his father over when he came to my defence. Rupert isn't strong; he hurt himself when he fell. Richard doesn't know I have a mobile telephone handset in my bedroom, it's a cheap one I picked up from Tesco when the landline was blown down after a storm once. I had your card . . . I didn't know who else to call."

"Why won't he let you leave the house? What did he say? Where is he now?"

"He's out in the garden. I told him I was going to have a bath, I locked myself in here to call you."

"Why has he locked you in, though?"

"He was shouting that you were interfering. That you'd poisoned our minds, and now we couldn't be trusted. His father's not a well man. After the fall . . . well, I'm worried what this might do to him."

"You need to get out." I paced around the room, feeling helpless. "Now. You need to get away from Richard while he's out in the garden. Go to a hotel. There's something wrong with both Richard and Edward. I can't explain it yet, but I think you're in danger–" My words were cut off by a loud noise in the background, and then the line went dead. "Mrs Rawson!" I shouted into the phone. "Mrs Rawson?" Nothing, just the sound of static on the line.

Without thought, I snatched up my bag and ran out of the door. My car still sat where we'd left it. I was relieved Elliott hadn't used it to get to work; he must have taken the bus, as his own car was still in the staff car park at the hospital. Fumbling with the keys in my haste, I started the engine and headed back towards the house I'd visited only yesterday. The closer I got, the more I became aware of a buzz of excitement on the streets. Increasing numbers of people milled about. Something had happened, something big enough to provoke the inhabitants to step out from behind their privet hedges and talk to one another. It was a bad sign. Two turns later and smoke billowed across the road, drifting from a north-easterly direction. The same direction I was trying to head in. In the distance, as I waited impatiently at a junction for the traffic to clear out of my way, approaching sirens howled.

I reached the turning for the Rawsons', to find a policeman unravelling a roll of police tape, cordoning off the road. Another officer stood in the middle of the lane, turning traffic and curious pedestrians away from whatever had happened beyond. I wound down the window as I reached him, the officer bending to speak to me. "What's happened?"

"We think it was a gas leak, ma'am. We can't let anyone down there until the fire is under control. Sorry."

"Was anyone hurt? Did everyone get out?" I dreaded his response.

"It's too soon to tell, ma'am. We'll know more once the fire brigade have the incident under control. Now, if you don't mind moving off, please . . ." He stood upright, dismissing me.

I wanted to tell him I knew who had caused it – there was no doubt in my mind the explosion had happened at the Rawsons' – but I knew if I claimed to know something I'd come across as a crazy woman. I moved the car further down the road, then pulled over and got my phone out. As I scrolled through my contacts to find Elliott's number, two ambulances and three fire engines turned into the street behind me.

"Sam?" Elliott answered on the second ring. "What's wrong?"

"Oh God, Elliott, it's the Rawsons," I sobbed. I told him about the call from Mrs Rawson and what I'd learned since.

"Jesus," he whispered when I finished. "Where are you now?"

"I'm parked on a road just off their street. I wanted to check if they were okay. God, Elliott, I'm scared. I think he killed them. I think he killed them because of me."

"You don't know that, Sam."

"He was keeping them prisoner because I went there, she told me that. What else am I supposed to think?"

"I don't know." I visualised him running his hands through his hair. He took a deep breath. "Jesus, Sam. Look, you need to get to somewhere safe, somewhere he doesn't know. Go back to my apartment and don't leave. Don't let anyone in, and don't answer any calls from numbers you don't recognise. In fact, turn your mobile off and only use the landline for now. I'll call and check in with you in thirty minutes. Get home . . . please," he added at the end. It was his pleading tone that had me agreeing finally.

I disconnected the call, switched off my mobile and started the engine. I threw the car into a three-point turn and pulled away, back in the direction I'd come from. I slowed as I passed the bottom of their road, as did the rest of the traffic given the large presence of emergency services in the vicinity. A sizeable crowd had gathered in the short time it had taken for me to call Elliott. I peered through the small gaps, between the people gathered at the cordon, catching only glimpses of what was happening beyond. The flash of a smallish figure wrapped in a blanket confirmed what I already knew. Richard had survived.

Afterwards, the journey home was a blur as my mind ricocheted through the implications. Initially, the guilt almost paralysed me. Somehow, I parked the car and made it into the apartment. Once inside, I ran into the lounge and turned on the television, scrolling through the menu until I found the rolling news channel.

The breaking news banner announced the explosion, presumed to have been caused by a gas leak, and the fear people may have been killed, but I had to wait while they finished reporting on some of the atrocities happening in the Middle East for a report. I looked at my watch; it was nearly quarter past the hour, so I knew the headlines would be repeated shortly. Finally, the story finished and the cameras returned to the newsreader in the studio. His headline about the gas explosion was third in order of importance. When he said, "at least two people are feared dead," I threw up, only just making it to the toilet in time to empty the vomit filling my mouth before heaving spasms took over my body again.

The sound of the landline's insistent ringing roused me from what had become a comfortable spot on the bathroom floor. After I'd stopped being sick, I'd curled up and cried. I wondered, as I lay there, if I my tears were for them or me. Only guilt at the thought of how much Elliott would worry if I didn't answer the phone had me moving at all when the ringing stopped, and then started again immediately. "Samantha! Thank God!" he said, as soon as I answered.

"Sorry, I was in the bathroom."

"Are you okay?"

I thought about that for a moment. "Not really. They're dead, aren't they?" My voice sounded flat and unemotional.

"Yes," he confirmed. "They brought the bodies in, they were pronounced at the scene. There was someone else, though."

"Richard?" I said, my voice barely a whisper.

"No, I haven't seen him. A neighbour. He got caught in the explosion and suffered severe burns and crush injuries from falling masonry."

"Why are you telling me this?" I said, finding myself annoyed at the excitement in his voice.

"Sam, it happened again. I saw it this time. The guy flatlined as soon as they brought him in. We worked on him for nearly twenty minutes before he was pronounced, but then, just after they called him, his heart started again. I watched it happen. We're not imagining this, Sam."

"No," I agreed. My voice sounded strange. Cold. An icy rage had replaced my fear. "We're not imagining this. We're not imagining that these people seem to be coming back from the dead. We're not imagining that the man who looked like my douchebag of an ex-partner tried to kill me. We're not imagining that Richard has killed at least two people, and we're not imagining that he did that once he knew we suspected something was different about him. You'll forgive me if I'm a little less excited about all of this than you are." And with that I put the phone down and went to bed.

Chapter 19

When Elliott came home he was not alone. It was late, after midnight, and I'd spent the day absorbing the evolving news story about the gas leak. I hadn't been able to sleep, despite having lain on the bed tossing and turning for nearly an hour. Instead, I'd got up and settled myself on the sofa. Every new snippet of information, offered in intervals over the course of the day, held me transfixed in front of the TV like a junkie waiting for another hit. After each one I promised myself I'd watch only a few minutes more, until some new revelation left me gagging for another injection of headlines.

I watched the eyewitness accounts of a fireball seen coming from the back of the house. Then the names of the victims, Mr and Mrs Rawson, were released, accompanied by a grainy photo of them taken at the Jubilee celebrations. The survival of their son had been pronounced "a miracle", as had that of the neighbour, Andrew Darcy, despite the severity of his injuries. Generally, people seemed grateful it hadn't been much worse given the size of the leak. It was assumed that the pipes feeding their range cooker were somehow at fault, but nothing could be confirmed until a full investigation had been conducted. I knew they were wrong. I knew Richard had made it happen somehow.

I was sitting in the dark, the room lit only by the red glow coming from the BBC News channel branding, when they walked in. "Are you okay?" Elliott asked from the doorway, Malcolm at his shoulder, as he took in my unmoving form shrouded in the darkness. "Mind if I turn the light on?" he tried again when I didn't respond.

"Sure," I grunted, irritated by his question. "I'm going to bed anyhow."

"Are you okay?" he asked a second time, after he'd turned the light on and looked at me properly.

"Stop fucking asking me that!" My anger bubbled to the surface, as I shot to my feet and strode across the room towards them. Malcolm retreated a couple of steps. "No! For your information, I'm not okay. Two people were killed today, and I think it's my fault. I'm guilty and angry and scared. So no, unsurprisingly, I'm not fucking okay."

Elliott grabbed me by the shoulders when I tried to push past him. "I get it," he said, his voice quiet as he held me firm. "What you're feeling . . . I get it. I'm feeling it too. Sure, I haven't got the same personal connection to this you have, but it's freaking me the fuck out when I think about what all this means. So, I get it. And right now, I need other people around me who understand why we should all be freaked out, and so do you. We're safer together . . . We're close, Sam. We're close to having enough to tell people about it." His words were like a slap in the face.

"What have you found?" I asked, looking from Elliott to Malcolm, who stood a few steps away from us, looking at me as if I were a wild animal that might attack at any moment. "What have you found?" I said, directly to Malcolm this time.

"Oh, um ..." He pushed his glasses up his nose as he stepped fully back into the room. "Well, you see ..." He fidgeted, his hands twisting in the glare of my attention, looking unaccustomed to dealing with overtly emotional women.

"Sit down, Malcolm," Elliott suggested kindly, trying to put him back at ease. "Will you stay and listen to this, Sam?"

I nodded and moved back to one of the armchairs.

"Drink?" he asked us both once we were seated. We shook our heads in unison. "Okay, well let me start this by repeating the fact that I saw it happen again today. It was unequivocal. The guy came back from the dead, and this time I wasn't the only one to notice it. The other medical staff were freaked out – several mentioned other patients they'd seen it happen to recently. We're not the only ones noticing this now." He turned to Malcolm. "So, what have you found?"

"The link is indisputable. I searched the data, looking at hospital activity codes for any kind of resuscitation-linked activity, regardless of eventual outcome, and let me tell you there was a lot."

"It is a hospital," I said drily.

"Yes, well, anyway, there was a drop in the expected rate of death in the population from the norm." We both nodded at him to continue. "When I looked at the data, there was a clear group that stood out: males, under sixty."

"What about them?" I prompted.

"None of them died."

"None of them?" Elliott echoed.

"Nope, not one. It really is most unusual. In the last three or four months, since exactly the date of the fog, not a single male under sixty has died at the hospital."

"What does that mean? Could it just be some sort of a freaky coincidence?"

"I don't think so. I've looked at twenty percent or so of the blood samples of the males affected, and all of them show active virus. When I compared it with an equivalent sample of other age groups and genders, none were affected, and the mortality rates followed a normal distribution. I think we have our proof, ladies and gentlemen."

For a moment, Elliott and I sat there in stunned silence, while Malcolm puffed his chest out, looking pleased with himself. It took me a while, but I managed to coalesce a sentence from the questions that were bouncing around in my head. "So, the virus really is bringing men back from the dead. Why? Why only men?"

"We still don't know that yet."

"How many men are we talking about?"

"Well, roughly two hundred and thirty thousand-ish adults die in hospital every year in England. You have to assume roughly half of those will be women, and then some will fall outside the age parameters, but we're still talking . . ."

"Lots," I whispered. "And those are just the ones who are in hospital. In England. This was worldwide. Jesus." I turned to look at Elliott. "We have to tell someone. I think these people might be dangerous. I know Richard and Edward are. There could be so many of them . . . all men, all young and strong. Who are they? What do they want?"

"We still don't know any of that, but I think you're right," Elliott agreed. "We have to talk to the authorities. Malcolm, can you write up your paper with all the evidence as soon as possible? We'll take it to them as soon as you're done."

"Who, though?"

"I don't know; the police, the Centres for Disease Control or the Health Protection Agency. If they won't listen, we'll talk to other medics or the WHO. We'll talk to everyone until someone pays attention, but we need the data, Malcolm."

"You'll have it tomorrow," he assured us, standing and brushing himself down. "On that note, I need to get home if I'm going to get this written up."

We said our goodbyes, Elliott's words from before about us being safer together making me nervous as Malcolm left. I couldn't shift my feelings of paranoia.

By the time we closed the door, having made plans to meet again tomorrow to agree what we would do next, the clock showed it was already past one in the morning.

"Are you okay?" Elliott said as we returned to the lounge and sat back down. "I'm sorry I couldn't come home when you called earlier – I wanted to – we were all on standby after the explosion in case there were lots more casualties . . ."

"Really, it's fine," I assured him, wishing it didn't feel like a lie. "I need to stop being so dependent on you. I couldn't think who else to call when I realised what had happened." I hated how needy I sounded.

"I like it. I like you coming to me. I'm glad you called." He reached out and took hold of my hand. "You still look a bit pale. Can I get you anything?"

"I'm as okay as I can be, all things considered, Elliott. I've been having sex with a man who meets the basic entry criteria for being classed as a zombie. It's bound to make me feel a little out of sorts."

Despite everything, Elliott smiled. "I'm sure if he'd had a shuffling gait and smelt of decomposing flesh, you'd have been on to him sooner."

I slapped him on the arm as I choked, "I'll have you know it's no laughing matter."

"You're telling me," he said with a laugh. "You passed me over for the walking dead! How do you think I feel?"

"I didn't pass you over," I defended myself. "You never offered . . ."

"You knew I wanted you, though." His voice turned quickly serious, his eyes intent. "I wanted you from the very first time I watched you do a presentation. I can't remember a single thing you said about the drug, but I remember everything about you; what you were wearing – a black pencil skirt with a fitted white blouse and a pair of killer heels, in case you were wondering – how, when you smiled, I felt torn between awe at the way it lit up your face and rage at the guy you bestowed it on. I don't think I uttered a word the whole time you were in there; you stunned me into silence. You were so cute, awkward to even be there. You kept apologising for taking up our time. I don't think I've ever seen anything more adorable. And most of the other doctors felt the same way. Didn't you ever wonder why your lunch meeting presentations were so well attended?"

"Well, no," I said, bemused. "I always assumed people liked my Marks & Spencer sandwiches."

"Ah, well, it could have been that too, at least for some of the women. For the majority of the male population, I can guarantee it was for the simple fact that you are quite the most stunning woman I've ever set eyes upon. Add to that you're intelligent, funny and nice with it, and you're talking the full package. What's not to like? When I walked into the waiting room and found you there, waiting for Edward . . ." My cheeks heated as he stared at me, his eyes drifting down towards my mouth. "To say I was gutted is an understatement." Before I could respond, he leant in and kissed me.

His lips were soft and tentative, as if he expected me to pull away. I didn't. It felt too good. I couldn't deny I'd thought about this happening. I'd imagined it, even before Edward and I separated. All those moments at the hospital, the looks we'd exchanged, the attraction between us undeniable. Even Edward had picked up on it. Now that we were kissing, something ignited within me. When his hand threaded around my waist, I allowed him to pull me closer, his chest pressed against mine. Our bodies twisted towards one another as the kiss deepened. Only when my hands wanted greater access to what lay beneath, did he finally break the contact and pull away with a groan. "I'm sorry," he gasped, his breath coming fast.

"Why? I was as invested in that as you were."

"I just need to be sure that you actually want this, want me. With everything that's happened in your life."

"I want you," I said, "but it's true, my life is about as fucked up as it's possible to be right now. Wanting you is one of the only things I am certain of."

"I don't want to share you. I'm serious about this, about you. I'd rather you said now if all you're looking for is someone to take your mind off Edward."

"We'd been struggling for a long time, you know that. I stayed through guilt, nothing more. I won't lie and say I didn't start to like the new version of him, but I wish I'd never slept with him again. It's complicated." Elliott's face fell. "I like you, Elliott, I do. More than that, I trust you. That's a huge thing for me right now. But I'm a mess," I said. "I think you're a fool to want anything to do with me."

"I've always been a fool," he said, with an uncertain smile. "Look, I want to try this, but I think we should take it slow. It's the only way we stand a chance with all the craziness going on around us. I know we've jumped ahead a bit with you moving in, but I don't think that means we have to rush everything else."

"I can move out," I said quickly. "I should move out. Heidi–"

"I don't want you to move anywhere. I want you here, where I know you're okay. I won't rush anything else, but please, stay here with me until we know everything is sorted out, at least."

I thought about it. I'd still not heard from Heidi. I had no idea if she'd even returned home from Italy yet, so I didn't have anywhere else to go. That still wasn't a good enough reason to stay. I looked at Elliott again, allowing myself to really look at him; his intense blue eyes, intent on me, the colour I imagined the oceans I'd always dreamed of swimming in would look, windows to the soul of the man within. I could see kindness, gentleness, even more, within them. He felt safe, like home.

"If you're sure you really want me to, I'll stay," I promised. His smile eclipsed any last reservations I may have had.

Chapter 20

Sharing the bathroom the next morning, as we both got ready for work, was strange. In so many ways our relationship already had many of the intimacies of a longer-term relationship, and yet we were in the early stages of whatever this thing between us turned out to be. I giggled as he nudged against me at every opportunity, brushing past as he made excuses to fetch items on the opposite side of the room. I stole glimpses of his body as he showered, which only strengthened the desire to touch him. I knew I had the same effect on him.

"I want to take you out to dinner tonight," Elliott announced, pulling me against his chest and kissing my just-glossed lips, as I finished up the final touches to my makeup.

"What about Malcolm? Isn't he coming round? Don't we need to plan things?" I said, brushing the residue of my gloss from his lips with my thumb. His teeth caught the pad and bit down gently, making me gasp. His eyes darkened at the sound, his pupils expanding, as the sexual tension in the room thickened. If he kissed me now, I wasn't sure I'd be able to stop it from going further. Last night we'd managed to step away from one another, and sleep in our own rooms. I didn't know how long I would be able to last with that arrangement. I was horny. With the way he was looking at me now, I was done for if he even tried to kiss me.

Elliott groaned and, with steely resolve, stepped away and looked down at his watch. "We both need to get dressed and go to work before we lose our jobs." His husky voice told me plenty about what he'd rather do. My lips opened slightly, my nipples tightening in response to his unspoken words. "Jesus, Sam," he groaned, taking a step towards me, as he allowed the towel to drop, his hands reaching.

His mobile ringing from the other room broke the spell.

He stepped away again, sporting a large erection which I stared at unashamedly, before he grabbed his dropped towel and sprinted into the other room. My body pulsed for him, the heat he'd caused seeping away slowly.

He wanted to take it slow, and what had I done? Thrown myself at him. I grabbed my things and slipped into my bedroom to dress, irritated with myself, the low murmur of his side of the phone conversation carrying from the lounge. I plaited my hair quickly and then slipped into my favourite black pencil skirt and the white blouse he'd mentioned I'd been wearing the first time he saw me. I was slipping into a pair of heels when he finally stuck his head round the door, now sporting a shirt and chinos.

"Damn," he said, as soon as he saw what I was wearing. "You did that on purpose." He stalked towards me. "How the hell am I meant to concentrate on saving people when I know you're out and about looking like that?" He ran a finger down the skin exposed at the neck of the shirt.

"I'm wearing it for your benefit."

"I hope so. I told you, I won't share. Will you wear that tonight for me too? I said we'd meet Malcolm back here after our meal. It's taken him longer than he expected to pull all the data together into a report. We'll see him here about ten. Are you okay to meet me at this restaurant after my shift at work? About seven-ish?" He handed me a piece of paper with an address on it.

"Sure. I'll look forward to it," I said, my voice husky and turned on. My libido was out of control.

"Damn," he groaned again. He kissed me on the cheek, offering a last look of regret, before he ran out the door. I smiled to myself, certain that by tonight either our relationship would have moved on a step or I would be unpacking my Rabbit. As far as I was concerned, with the way I felt, "taking it slow" was overrated.

***

Work managed to be as hideous as ever. My shoes pinched relentlessly, reminding me why I never usually wore them for work. They rubbed their nasty hard edges against the soft, pink parts of my feet, until my feet were shredded. By lunch, I had to stop and pick up some plasters. I sat in a café, liberally applying them over the reddened patches, contemplating whether flip-flops would be likely to have the same effect on Elliott at dinner tonight. My phone rang, Heidi's name flashing on the screen.

"Oh my good God," she began, as soon as I connected the call, "I've got cystitis from too much sex."

"Is that good or bad?"

"Both. But it was fucking worth it. I swear to God if we didn't make a baby after all the sex we had over the last few days, then there really is no hope for us." She giggled, the sound light and joyous.

"I'm glad you had fun," I said, forcing myself to smile as I wondered how to begin telling her about what had happened to me over the last few days.

"Fun does not describe the frankly almost illegal amount of intercourse we had. But anyway, enough about me. How's things with you and Edward?"

"Yeah, well, about that . . ."

"What's the fuckwit done now?" I loved her a little bit more for assuming immediately any fault lay at his door.

"Well, he's moved Serena in, and now they're a thing."

"What! Who? You don't mean Serena from the wedding? You're all living together? When did this happen? What the fuck!"

"He found out I didn't want a baby with him, that I was on the pill, and lost the plot. He seriously tried to strangle me he was so mad. I hit him . . . It was a mess. Anyway, I thought I'd killed him, but it turns out he's fine . . . again. Then, the next thing I know he's shacked up with Serena, telling me I imagined the strangling part, and that I'm making it all up because I'm jealous of their relationship."

"What? That's crazy. I never liked him. He tried to fucking strangle you? Did you call the police? What did they say?"

"That there's no evidence he did anything, especially as Serena claims he was with her."

"That lying slut."

"Anyway, I figure I'm better off without him. I never intended to stay with him after the wedding. I only did because of the accident. So frankly, if she wants him, she's welcome to him."

"But what about all the 'marriage and babies' shit he was coming out with the other night? That's a bit of a turnaround, isn't it? This is fucking crazy. Where are you even living?"

"Well, umm, the thing is Elliott helped me out with a room."

"Elliott?" I could feel her mind reeling through all the people called Elliott we'd ever met. "Hold on, you don't mean Doctor I'd-look-good-on-a-surfboard Elliott, do you?"

"I do," I admitted.

"Well . . ." My friend was lost for words, which had to be something of a first. "Well," she eventually said again. "I've got to say I'm impressed."

"It's not like that. He's just helping me out."

"Sure . . ." She dragged the word out for an unnecessarily long time.

"Well, it wasn't," I admitted. "It might be heading that way now."

"You are a dog," she said with a hearty laugh. "Still, with the way Edward's behaved, who can blame you? I still can't believe he's moved on to Serena after all his declarations the other night. The guy will give himself emotional whiplash if he carries on like that."

"As I said, she's welcome to him. He's changed, Heidi, and not in a good way. I can't explain it right now, but I will. In the meantime, I seriously think he's dangerous, so just steer clear of him."

"You don't have to worry about that." She laughed again. "I always thought he was a tosser. I only put up with him because you seemed to like him, and even then it was begrudging – especially after he started shagging other women." I had to laugh at that. "So, when am I going to see you? Are you free tonight?"

"No, not tonight. I'm meeting Elliott."

"What do you mean you're meeting him? You live with the guy already."

"We're going out to dinner together. Nothing has happened between us yet. Not really," I hedged, thinking about the kisses we'd exchanged.

"Whatever. I think it's cute. Perfect rebound fodder. I can't imagine Edward will like it, though. He was always fine with you not being that into him when you were together and it was him flirting with other women. You might find he's different when the shoe's on the other foot. Does he know you've moved on?"

"No. But I don't plan to see him, so I won't need to worry. And neither should you – see him, that is."

"No worries there," she assured me.

We finished the call, making some tentative plans to meet at our favourite wine bar in a couple of evenings' time. I looked at my watch. It was already after two, and I had no appointments in my diary for the rest of the afternoon, which meant hours of fruitless wandering around hospital corridors, or ... A quick glance out of the café window showed me the weather was great. I glanced at the work emails that had come in on my phone, seeing nothing unduly alarming or urgent, and made a spur-of-the-moment decision to head outside. I knew my camera was in the boot of the car; I had the urge to take some pictures.

Half an hour later, I situated myself on a discreet park bench, nestled beneath the sweeping branches of an old oak tree, taking photos of anything and everything around me. Once again, the good weather brought people outside, so there were lots of subjects to choose from. My phone buzzed – my manager – but I ignored it, telling myself I'd pretend I'd been in the hospital and needed to have my phone on silent. Instead, I focused on the people around me – a mother and her toddler catching my eye first. Her rigid posture and jerky arm movements, as she gesticulated at her wayward child, suggested she was having a bad day. The child turned and laughed, delighting in ignoring her. He darted past a group of people, sitting under another of the perimeter oak trees. I lifted my camera and focused in on them.

Snapping frame after frame, I couldn't work out at first what had caught and held my normally wandering eye. Only when the child ran past the group a second time, back into the arms of his relieved mother, did I realise all the seated adults were male. Of itself that would be nothing unusual, except that this time of day, midweek, was usually the preserve of mothers and their preschool children, the elderly or unemployed. The gathering beneath the tree looked like none of the stereotypes. Too young to be retired, clean and well dressed and with no evidence that any of the nearby kids belonged to them, they were an unusual collection of assorted ages. My view of them was apparently shared by the local mothers who, now I looked more closely, were eyeing them warily and giving the group a wide berth. The first woman I'd noted picked up her child and moved him away, looking over her shoulder as if to check no one was following them.

I shuddered. Could they all possess activated virus? Could there be so many of them already? None of the men looked familiar. I focused in on the faces again, taking an image of each in turn. There had to be over twelve of them. My thoughts turned to Richard and Edward, and suddenly I didn't want to be anywhere near these men. I scanned the vicinity to be certain no one watched me, before standing and making my way back towards my car. I wanted to run, but feared drawing attention to myself so held my pace steady, checking the face of every man I passed, paranoid they might be someone I knew. I berated myself, wondering what it was I was afraid they might do. And then I remembered the Rawsons. Only when I got back in the car, and locked all the doors, did I finally feel secure. My accelerated heartbeat thumped in my chest, keeping me on edge as I took deep breaths, willing my hands to stop shaking long enough that I could drive.

The shrill ring of my phone cut through the silence and lifted me vertically off my seat in terror. It was my manager again. "Sam, where the hell are you?" he barked, as soon as I answered.

"At St Richard's, my phone was on silent. I'm only just back in the car," I lied, crossing my fingers as if that made it okay.

"I've been trying to get hold of you all day. We have a meeting this afternoon. You've got twenty minutes to get yourself here; it's compulsory attendance. Don't you read your fucking emails?" It was unusual to hear him swear.

"Where?" I asked blankly, as I scrolled through my unread emails on my phone, trying to find the one I'd obviously missed. Sure enough, it was there, the red exclamation mark beside the subject heading marking it as urgent.

"Hilton. Get here fast," he said, and cut the call.

I gunned the car out the car park, making the half-hour journey to the hotel in the agreed twenty minutes, and arriving into the dark, windowless meeting room only five minutes late. My manager scowled at me as I took a seat in the back row next to one of my colleagues. "What's going on?" I whispered, as one of the senior directors stood at the front with a PowerPoint slide bemoaning the lack of NHS funding for new medicines due to continued budget cuts.

"Restructure," she whispered back. I raised an eyebrow. "You haven't been around much recently, but there's been loads of stress about our performance. Sales are seriously down for some reason, but no one's sure why. We're miles behind plan. They just can't keep us all and make any money."

Sure enough, as she whispered the words a slide flashed up on the screen announcing that "changes" were needed to meet the current shortfall. Three slides later, it was revealed that the "changes" they intended to make included axing our entire division. No wonder my manager had been in such a foul mood.

As we drifted away from the meeting, on immediate garden leave with a months' notice, I wondered why I didn't feel inclined to huddle with my colleagues to bitch about how unfair it all was, and collectively worry about what we'd do next. Relieved at being released from a job I hated, I knew I should be worried about how I was going to feed myself. But there were more important things going on that needed to be dealt with first.

My mind scrolled through the implications of the sudden drop in sales. Could it be the result of the men with activated virus no longer needing the medicines people usually relied upon to keep them alive? What did that mean about the scale of activated virus now present within the population? Again, I thought about the large group at the park. I examined the faces of the people around me – were any of them here? How would I know? I wanted to go home.

***

By seven I sat in the restaurant at the table Elliott had reserved, waiting for him. Having placed my fear in a mental compartment entitled Can't Do Anything About This Right Now, I found myself oddly euphoric after the news from the meeting earlier. That good feeling lasted right up until the point Edward and Serena walked into the restaurant, arm in arm. She clung to him possessively, leaning into him, laughing at something he'd said. In contrast, he had the odd, glassy-eyed expression I recognised well from our years together – it meant he was only half listening to whatever she was saying. Given what I recalled of the conversation over the table at the wedding, I couldn't really blame him. She was a pretty girl, but that was about all she had going for her.

I slumped down into my seat in the hopes they would walk past without noticing me, yet knowing how unlikely that was. Edward's head swivelled almost as soon as they stepped into the main dining area, fixing upon me. His eyes flared with what looked like irritation, followed by lust when he saw what I was wearing. He headed straight for me.

The waiter followed, struggling to redirect them towards their own table in the other corner of the room. "Samantha," Edward said, as soon as he reached my table, "what are you doing here?"

"About to have dinner, like you. Hello, Serena," I said politely to the now-silent but fuming girl at his shoulder.

"Samantha," she said in a clipped voice, as she gripped Edward's arm. "Let's go and sit down, sweetie."

He ignored her. "Who are you here with? Heidi?" He looked around.

"No." I chose not to elaborate any further. "I'm glad to see you both looking so well," I said pointedly to Edward, raising one eyebrow. "Enjoy your meal." I picked up my menu and effectively dismissed the pair of them. Edward stood there for another moment, while Serena tugged on his arm, until he gave way and allowed her to lead them to their own table. Judging by the intent expression on her face, and her pursed lips, she was giving him a flea in the ear. It made me smile to watch them. Then reality landed and I grabbed my phone, texting *ABORT, ABORT, Edward and Serena here* to Elliott, but before I pressed *send,* he walked through the door.

My heart did a little jump in my chest as he saw me and smiled, exposing his dimples for all the world to see. He walked quickly to the table, bending down and kissing me full on the lips. "I've thought about nothing else but you in that sexy skirt and blouse since I left this morning." He kissed me again.

The press of his lips against mine obliterated all other thoughts from my mind. "Do we really need to eat?"

He grinned, clearly enjoying the effect he had on me. "We're taking this slow. I want to have a proper date with you first."

"First?" I asked, hoping he would add *before I take you home and make you scream my name.*

"First, before I take you home and make you come repeatedly."

That would do, I decided, grinning at him. "Oh, fuck, I forgot to say . . . I was texting you as you walked in. Edward's here."

"Edward?" The smile dropped from his face as he looked around the room, his body now rigid.

"With Serena. Over there in the corner. We can leave if you want?" I said. His face turned thunderous. The expression only eclipsed by the fury visible on Edward's.

"No, why should we?" he said, seemingly nonchalant. I sensed the tension within him, though. "Did he speak to you?"

"He came straight over with Serena as soon as he saw me sitting here. Asked me whether I was with Heidi. I told him no, but didn't say who I was with, and then wished them a nice meal. I was just texting you to warn you when you walked in." I held up my phone to show him.

"If he comes anywhere near you again—" His voice quivered with barely suppressed rage.

"He won't," I reassured him, placing a calming hand on his arm. "I'm with you. All night." I said it to distract him from Edward, and it worked. The testosterone that had been gearing him up to fight redirected itself towards me, and I found myself being kissed senseless until the waiter interrupted us with some discreet coughing to hand Elliott his menu. I had a feeling if that hadn't worked, he would have been tipping a bucket of water over us next.

"Damn right," Elliott growled at me, with a final scowl in Edward's direction before we both focused on enjoying our date.

I spent the entire meal feeling as if Edward's eyes were burning holes into the back of my head. Heidi's words from earlier kept running through my mind – but that's not Edward, I reminded myself. This guy had tried to kill me, whatever he pretended now.

"So, how was your day?" Elliott asked, and I liked how domesticated it sounded coming from him.

"Well, funny you should ask." I told him about the meeting I'd been called to earlier and what it meant for my job. He shrugged, reassuring me we'd manage fine without it.

"I'm not your responsibility."

"No, but you are my friend – hopefully more – and friends help each other out when they need it. I know you'll find something else. In the meantime, there's your photography," he suggested. "You could try and make something of that while you're thinking. From what I've seen, you're really good. Either way there's no rush – I was managing the mortgage before you arrived. It makes no difference to me. Plus, I like having you there."

"But what if I don't find any work and you end up hating me because I'm a sponger? What about the virus?" The time inched ever closer to the point we needed to leave and meet Malcolm. "We don't know what effect that's going to have on us or our jobs."

"We'll worry about that if or when we have to. They'll always need doctors ... well ..." He tailed off, realisation dawning that they might not need so many if half the population wasn't at risk of dying. "Regardless, you hated that job." There was no denying that. I told him my theory about the poor sales performance.

He listened intently. "If the effect is global that could be interesting to include in our data."

"Or I was thinking we should look at the performance of brands that primarily treat diseases that affect men in that age group. I know some people we could talk to."

When the time came to leave, he insisted on paying the bill. He claimed, as he pulled a few crisp notes out of his slim leather wallet, that, as this had been a date, he had a right to pay. I resisted briefly before accepting his chivalry, then made my excuses and headed for the bathroom. When I stepped out of the cubicle, Serena was waiting for me.

"Oh, hi," I muttered, as I tried to step around her towards the small washbasin.

"He doesn't want you anymore," she said, standing directly behind me.

"Well, that's good then, because I certainly don't want him." I squirted some soap into my palm and started to wash my hands, trying to be as quick as it was possible to be.

"That was pathetic, trying to make him jealous like that. You need to stop following him. It's creepy."

I stopped washing my hands and looked at her through the reflection in the mirror. "First of all, I'm not following him. I had no idea that he'd be here. For your information, not that it has anything to do with you, I'm on a date with my new boyfriend." Distracted, I squirted a second palmful of soap into my hands. "It is a complete coincidence we were here at the same time as you. The last thing I'm trying to do is make him jealous. I can assure you," I turned on the tap with my elbow to rinse. "You're welcome to him."

"He's told me how you won't leave him alone," she said, not letting the subject go. My irritation rose a notch as she pushed into my space; "We're incredibly happy together. He's said he wants to marry me. We're trying for a baby." She looked smug as she patted her lower abdomen.

I froze, standing upright as I stared at her, my hands forgotten as her words took a few moments to sink in. Fear sliced through my chest. Everything she'd said mirrored exactly what he'd said to me. I started making connections that terrified me. I walked backwards towards the door, my hands still slimy from the soap.

"You need to be careful, Serena. He's not what he seems. Before you do that with him, just . . . be careful," I said, reaching for the door, my hand slipping off the smooth metal handle.

"He said you'd try and scare me off," she crowed, as if I'd somehow confirmed something to her. "He said you were mental."

"I'm not mental," I argued somewhat pointlessly. "He's dangerous. You have to believe me. Don't have a baby with him—"

"You're evil!" Her eyes narrowed as she hissed. "You're trying to destroy what we've got any way you can."

"Oh, for fuck's sake, you've only been with the man a few days. You're fucking, that's all. Know what? If you're that keen, go for it. Frankly you deserve each other." I found I no longer cared if Serena hooked up with zombie Edward. I pulled the door open and fled out into the restaurant, grabbing a napkin off one of the tables as I passed to wipe my hands.

Elliott stood beside our table, the meal receipt gripped in his hand, nose to nose with Edward. "I'm sure there's some law about doctors running off with their patients' wives," Edward said as I approached. He looked furious, his fists clenching and unclenching.

"That's doctors not being allowed relationships with their patients. And she's not your wife. She's the woman who dumped you," Elliott replied, his voice deceptively calm. The waiter stood anxiously to the side of the two men, his eyes darting between them, sensing an imminent fight.

"Elliott, let's go," I said, as I grabbed his hand and tugged him out of the door of the restaurant. The waiter smiled at me gratefully.

Edward watched us leave, a scowl on his face. "See you soon, Samantha," he called. Elliott tensed, prepared to turn and argue.

"Come on, we have to leave," I said in an urgent whisper. "I just worked out what the link is."

Chapter 21

The fight seeped out of Elliott as soon as I said I knew what the link was. Instead, we hurried back towards the car park and our respective cars. Frustrated to have to wait to talk to him, now that I'd made the connection, I couldn't get home fast enough.

Edward stepped out the restaurant behind us, without Serena, but remained in the shadows watching. From the glow of the mobile phone pressed to his ear he was speaking to someone. I shivered.

"I'll see you back at the apartment," Elliott said, kissing me before he opened my car door. He waited for me to start the engine and pull slowly away before he moved off and got into his own vehicle.

I put my foot down. It seemed important I speak to someone about what I'd figured out soon – before anything happened to me. I parallel parked with unusual efficiency, slipped out of the car, locked it and fumbled inside my bag for the front door key Elliott had given me. A figure stepped out of the shadows. I screamed and took a step back, clasping the keys like a weapon between my fingers as I prepared to stab any would-be attacker.

"Sam, shut up, it's me, Malcolm," Malcolm hissed, stepping into the halo of the streetlight so I could see him properly. "Stop screaming."

"Fucking hell, Malcolm. You nearly made me wet myself."

"Where's Elliott?"

"Just coming. We had both our cars at the restaurant tonight. He came straight from work. Come on, I've got a key, I'll let you in." I walked towards the front door, feeling jumpy, wanting to get out of the open. Headlights appeared in the street behind us. I hoped it was Elliott, but didn't want to hang around just in case it wasn't.

Trembling a little, I opened the front door, flicking on the lights before we stepped into Elliott's apartment. I hesitated, waiting for the tell-tale sound of Elliott's key in the street door. When I heard it, I relaxed a little and led Malcolm into the lounge. "Tea?" I offered, knowing it was his tipple of choice.

"No, thank you, I'm fine."

"Sam?" Elliott called as soon as he walked into the hallway.

"In here, with Malcolm," I called back from the lounge, hugely relieved we were all home.

"Alright, Malcolm?" Elliott nodded at his friend, heading straight for me. "Jesus, Sam, that was a hell of a first date," he said with a laugh as he bent to kiss me. "So, tell me," he dropped down onto the chair beside me, "what have you worked out?" He looked over at Malcolm, on the sofa opposite. "Sam says she's worked out some sort of a connection," he explained.

Malcolm looked at me expectantly, as they both waited for me to explain.

"It was something Serena said when we were in the ladies together," I began, trying to hide the happy smile that wanted to curl the corners of my mouth as soon as Elliott draped his arm around the back of the chair, brushing against the tops of my shoulders. "She mentioned they'd been trying for a baby – she and Edward, I mean. At first I just thought "oh for God's sake, already?" I mean, seriously, a baby? They've only been together five minutes. But then I thought about it. It was all so reminiscent of everything he said to me after he'd recovered from the accident – a complete contrast to the man he used to be – it got me thinking. I think it's possible they need to reproduce themselves to survive. The virus only affects males, so they need us – women that is – to reproduce, so they can spread the virus, or DNA of whatever they are, to create new organisms. That's why they're all under sixty – or whatever age it was – it's prime reproducing age." I paused, breathless from rushing out my explanation. It sounded a bit mad now I said it out loud. "What do you think?"

Elliott and Malcolm were both still. I began to wonder if they'd actually heard me when Elliott finally said, "Fucking hell, I think you're right. It makes perfect sense. It explains so much: the age affected, their behaviour. If they reproduce, the adapted DNA will be passed to the offspring – at the moment they only have males, and that means they can't reproduce by themselves. They need women. Once they have mixed females, presumably they'll become self-sustaining. They're genetically wiping us out – at least they will eventually. We've been invaded."

Elliott and I pulled apart and looked at each other.

"I'm scared," I said. "This is so big. We can't leave it just between us any longer. It's past time to talk to some other people. People that can act to stop this."

"I agree," Elliott said quickly. "Malcolm, we need to get that report out. We need to send it tonight – we can't sit on this any longer." We turned and looked at him.

"Ah, well, that might be a problem." Malcolm shifted on his chair.

"Haven't you finished it?" Elliott said, not trying to hide his frustration.

"I don't have it."

"What do you mean, you don't have it?"

"It's gone."

"For God's sake, man, speak sense. Where has it gone? Have you sent it already? Where's all the data?" Elliott quizzed him, whilst I looked at Malcolm more closely. Then I saw it. He was different. I looked at him again and recognised the marks on his neck, bruising showing above the collar of his shirt. "Jesus, Malcolm, what's going on?" Elliott said, oblivious to the differences staring him in the face.

"It's not him," I said, releasing my breath.

"What do you mean it's not him? I'm looking at him for fuck's sake."

"I mean it's not our Malcolm anymore, it's one of them. Look at his neck." The more I looked, the more I saw the bruising – like mine – from someone wrapping their hands around his neck.

Malcolm, or the thing that looked like Malcolm, tilted his head and looked at me. "Edward said you were clever. Bravo on making the connections. Trouble is you're becoming a bit of a nuisance, both of you."

"What have you done with the data?" Elliott said. I could tell it was already futile.

"Destroyed it all."

"Why?"

"You were too close, too soon."

"We'll get it all again," I said. "It will be easy to replace."

"By that time it'll be too late. We'll be established. You were a bit too quick off the mark. You needed to be stopped."

"So one of your kind killed Malcolm?" Elliott said, staring at the man's neck. "Someone strangled him?"

"Yes."

"Why?"

"Strangling is relatively easy for us to recover from. The body is functional again almost immediately. He needed to be stopped, and an additional swift activation was a bonus."

"I've seen others like him! One of Edward's friends. It was like his personality changed overnight. He had marks on his neck too, I just didn't make the connection before. They must have killed him and then he activated too. They're killing people, Elliott." Fear sent ice racing through my body.

"Get out!" Elliott said to Malcolm, moving to stand in front of me. "I want you out of here now." His fists clenched at his sides.

"I'm going," Malcolm agreed too easily, appearing more sinister as a result. "I just wanted to let you know that there is no report. There is no data. There is nothing to prove what you think you know, and, even if you try to tell anyone, we're already everywhere." Malcolm stood, pausing at the door. "You know, you should be quite proud of yourselves. You caught on quickly, all things considered. At the rate you reproduce, you presented quite a risk to us for a while. Fortunately, the majority of your kind are physically weak and entirely too trusting. Elliott, we want you to become one of us. We think you'll be a popular addition to our numbers." Then he turned to look at me. "And as for you, Sam, we want you too, but not for quite the same reason." He laughed. There was none of Malcolm's geeky innocence in the look he gave me. He left me feeling dirty.

"Get the fuck out of here, now!" Elliott brandished a pair of scissors he must have found in one of the drawers on the coffee table, holding them aloft like a weapon. He dwarfed Malcolm's small frame, but I sensed his fear.

"I'm leaving, but we'll be seeing you soon, Elliott," Malcolm promised.

We stood in stunned silence until the front door closed. Then Elliott hurried out into the hallway. I heard him checking all the rooms, before he slid the deadbolt on the front door into place. Despite his efforts, fear still pumped through my body. The reality of what we faced hit me in a wave and my legs gave way. I collapsed heavily onto the chair, my breaths coming fast and ragged as my vision clouded, darkness threatening.

I became aware of Elliott beside me. "Breathe slowly, Sam. You're having a panic attack. Take slow deep breaths." He pushed my head between my knees, wiping the back of my neck with a cool flannel until I recovered enough to stand. He lifted me, hugging me against his chest, as he carried me into the bedroom.

"We're too late, aren't we?" I moaned. "They've won, and people don't even know it."

"Not yet they haven't." Elliott insisted. "We might not have the data, but we can still email what we know. Other people can look into it. They can't hide for much longer. It's already being noticed by medical professionals. The data is there if people know where to look for it."

"We need to do it soon . . . tonight." I couldn't say out loud what I really thought, I couldn't say that we needed to do it tonight because I knew there was a significant danger they'd get to him too. Then who would believe me? "Women," I said. "You need to tell *women*. They aren't affected by the virus. We can trust them. We don't know which men are affected. You might be talking to one of them even if they're pretending to be one of us." Thoughts tumbled out of me.

"Sam, I won't let them get me, and I'll look after you. Not one of them is going to touch you, I promise."

"You can't promise that." I smiled, but couldn't shake my sorrow. "One already has. And what about all the other women? What about all the babies they're making in them as we speak. How do we stop that?"

"There are ways," he insisted. "But not you. They can't have you. Not while I can stop them." He pulled me tighter against his chest, and I let him. I needed the comfort. I needed to forget for a while. My mouth sought his, needing to be closer to him. Legs entwined, we kissed, and the slow-burning attraction I always experienced in his presence ignited.

He sensed it too. His mouth grew more possessive as he unpeeled the skirt and shirt that I'd put on for him, what felt like a lifetime ago. So much had happened since then, little of it good. He was the one good thing in any of this, and I had no idea how long it would last, given what Malcolm had said earlier. My desperation to forget bled into my touch.

"No, Sam." Elliott broke away from me, stilling. "There's no hurry. I won't let them spoil this for us too."

He reached out and touched me gently, taking his time, stroking my hair, his fingers trailing down the side of my face, to my jaw, tracing my features with reverence. His eyes a deeper shade of blue, filled with love.

"That was beautiful," I told him afterwards, my body still humming with satisfaction.

"It was," he agreed. "Like you." He slipped off the condom, then pulled me close.

"The emails . . . we need to send them . . ." I said, as my need for sleep warred with my earlier anxiety.

"We will, in the morning. Tonight is ours. Nothing'll happen before then. Sleep." He kissed me on the forehead. I relaxed back against him, my head upon his chest, our breathing slowing until sleep came.

***

Pounding on the front door woke me. I sat bolt upright, terrified. "Elliott!" I cried out in alarm. He was already up and out of the bed, pulling on his trousers, hopping on one leg and then the other in his rush.

"Stay there," he said, before running out the room. I pulled the duvet around my neck, shivering as the cool morning air brushed over my exposed skin. Elliott called, "Who's there?" through the front door. The response was muffled, but the sound of him drawing back the deadbolt was unmistakeable. I looked around the room for some clothes to put on, but only found my skirt and blouse from yesterday. The rest of my stuff was still in the spare room.

"What the hell do you think you're doing?" Elliott shouted. "You can't just barge in there."

The door to the bedroom burst open, and three police officers stormed in. "Samantha Davis?" one of them said, looking down at me. Young and thickset, he had the appearance of someone who lived for these sorts of moments. His gaze raked over me, making me feel more vulnerable given my nakedness.

"Yes?"

"Samantha Davis, I'm arresting you on suspicion of the attempted murder of Edward Patterson. You do not have to say anything. But it may harm your defence if you do not mention, when questioned, something you later rely on in court. Anything you do say may be given in evidence." He paused to cuff one wrist as I stared up at him open-mouthed.

"Get your hands off her!" Elliott shouted. "She's naked, for God's sake. She's not resisting arrest. At least let her put some bloody clothes on."

"I haven't . . ." I paused as I thought about hitting Edward with the elephant. "I didn't . . ."

"Say nothing, Sam," Elliott said. "I'll find you a lawyer. Just say nothing until they arrive. Fuck!" He ran his hand through his hair. "Fuck, I'll get you some clothes," he said, looking to one of the other officers for permission. The officer in question nodded, and Elliott sprinted out the room, returning moments later with a pair of my yoga pants, clean knickers, a bra and an old sweatshirt. At least I'd be comfortable, I figured, as I hurried to dress. A female officer stayed in the room with me while I pulled my clothes on. Outside in the hallway, Elliott continued to argue about my innocence.

"Can I brush my teeth?" I asked the woman officer.

"No, I'm sorry, ma'am, we need to get you down to the station as soon as possible."

I shrugged the sweatshirt over my head and allowed her to fasten the other cuff, my hands now secured behind my back, slipping on a pair of flip-flops before she led me out the room. With one hand placed upon my shoulder, she steered me down the hallway, out through the door and down the front steps.

The scene in the street was mayhem. Police cars blocked the road as bleary-eyed neighbours wandered out of their houses in dressing gowns to find out what all the fuss was about. Several phones lifted in my direction as I emerged, capturing the moment of my humiliation for the YouTube generation. It seemed like overkill, considering this was me we were talking about.

The female officer led me towards a car, a second officer opening the rear door as we approached, gently pressing my shoulder down to encourage me into the back seat. I glanced back towards the house where Elliott stood, frozen on the doorstep. "The emails," I shouted out to him. "You need to send them. Now," I insisted. He nodded to indicate he'd heard, as I bent my body, allowing them to push me inside the car, before they slammed the door closed. There was, of course, no mechanism to open it from the inside.

***

Two hours later, I had been secured within a holding cell and was passing the time by counting ceiling tiles as I waited for their questioning to begin. At least that's what they'd told me would happen next. I'd been formally arrested on arrival, although I still didn't know what Edward's claims were against me. I'd seen no sight nor sound of the promised lawyer Elliott told me he'd call. The small room I was being held in was windowless, the smell of human misery permeating everything. I curled into a ball and lay there hoping for a miracle.

When the door did at last open, it made me jump; the locks retracted, grinding against the metal frame. I sat up as the door pushed open. Frank Murray stood there, his face expressionless. "We're ready for you now, if you're happy to be questioned, Ms Davis?"

"What about my lawyer?"

"He's just arrived. We'll send you to him in a moment. We don't want this to take any longer than it needs to, and I'm sure you're keen to get home too."

I nodded. I wanted this over and done with so I could get home and shower some of the holding cell stink off me. "Okay, well let's get this over with," I agreed, the thought of being able to wash and brush my teeth my primary concern.

Ten minutes later, I was taken to meet a small man dressed in an ill-fitting suit with a cravat. He carried a slim briefcase that he never opened, pulling out a small notepad from his pocket along with a cheap plastic pen. Surprised by his appearance I determined not to judge too quickly. Elliott would be looking out for me. "Ms Davis?" he said. I nodded. "I'm Arthur Stirling. I'll be supporting you during your questioning. Have you ever been arrested or questioned before?" I shook my head, and he looked pleased. "Good, well that speaks of a good character at least. Tell me, are you guilty?"

"What?" I said, slightly flabbergasted by the question when I realised he meant was I guilty of trying to kill Edward. "No! God, no."

"Well," he continued, "The best thing you can do is tell the truth. Hopefully we can get this all cleared up in no time."

"And you'll help keep me safe? Stop me saying something I shouldn't? I'm completely out of my depth here."

"The truth is your best defence." I wasn't sure that was correct; plenty of innocent people had been wrongly convicted. I knew he had to have been briefed on what I was being held for.

"So, what are they actually accusing me of?"

"It's concerning the accident you were involved in."

"The accident?" I sat back in my chair, taken by surprise. I'd been certain they were planning on pressing charges against me for hitting Edward with the elephant. I crossed my arms over my chest, trying to take a minute to focus on what he was saying.

"Yes, they seem to think you might have done it deliberately."

"Done what deliberately? Crashed?" I spluttered. "That's ridiculous. Why would I want to hurt myself? I was in the car too." He shrugged and said nothing more. "So how do we approach this, then? It's my word against his."

"Just tell the truth," he said again.

"So you keep saying. But you'll step in if they ask any questions I shouldn't answer, in your opinion, won't you?"

"Of course. I'm sure you have nothing to worry about."

I couldn't shake my anxiety at his overly relaxed attitude.

"Shall we get this over with?" he suggested.

"I suppose so," I muttered, feeling ill-prepared for what was to come.

Mr Stirling banged on the door to let the policemen outside know we were ready. They escorted us to another small room, this time with a table between us and the two chairs opposite, a recording device placed in the middle of the table. A CCTV camera watched with its beady eye from the corner of the room. We sat in silence until Frank Murray and a second man entered the room.

Any relief at seeing a familiar face quickly evaporated when he started to speak. "So, Ms Davis, before we begin I have to remind you of the following information: You have a right to silence, whatever you do or say can be used in evidence at court, and if you don't say something now that you later rely on in court you may be asked why you didn't mention it in the first instance. Is that all clear?"

"Yes."

"Good. Now, tell me, do you understand what you've been brought here and charged for?"

I looked to Mr Stirling. He nodded at me, gesturing for me to speak. "I know it's something to do with the accident I was in, but I don't know specifically why you've brought me here."

Frank Murray frowned at Arthur Stirling, before looking at me. "Mr Patterson contacted us late last night."

I said nothing, sensing less was more in this situation.

"He explained that his memory has been somewhat patchy since the accident, as I believe you were aware?"

I nodded to confirm I did know that.

"You nodded, Ms Davis, but I need you to confirm your response verbally for the sake of the recording."

"Oh, y-y-yes." I stumbled over my words.

"Yes what?"

"Yes, I knew he had some memory loss after the accident," I confirmed.

"Mr Patterson confirmed his memory has returned in full, finally, and he now recollects the moments prior to the accident." A sliver of fear threaded through me. "In your previous report after the accident you told us you were travelling back from a wedding you had attended in Brighton. Is that correct?"

"Yes," I agreed again, my eyes darting between the people in the room and the recording device.

"Don't be nervous, Ms Davis. We just need you to tell us the truth," he said, echoing the words Mr Stirling had said earlier.

I nodded. "So," he started again, "talk us through what happened after you left the wedding."

"You know what happened. You have my previous statement."

"Yes, but we'd like you to tell us again. Humour us."

"We left the wedding at about eight. I was driving. It was the day of the fog, so the visibility was poor."

"Had you been drinking?"

"No, because I was driving. You can check with the hospital – they took a blood sample from me."

"So, you were driving . . ." He gestured to encourage me to continue.

"I got onto the dual carriageway just outside Brighton, but when I went round a bend the traffic was stationary in front of us. I didn't have time to stop. I did what I could to miss everyone, but we clipped a car at the back and then we flipped."

"Okay. From the reports and photos I saw, you were lucky to survive."

"I was. We both were."

"Mr Patterson's side of the car looked as if it was much more damaged, was it?"

"Yes, because of how we rolled."

"Tell me, Ms Davis, how fast were you driving?" It had all been so civilised, we'd fallen into an easy question-and-answer rhythm, but when he asked me that, I hesitated.

"I don't know. I can't remember looking," I answered truthfully.

"Okay," Officer Murray moved quickly on, and I released the breath I didn't know I'd been holding. "Talk to me about what happened at the wedding. Mr Patterson said you had a bit of a disagreement."

I snorted at his description of what had happened. "A bit of a disagreement! He fucked someone else whilst we were there. I found them together and told him I was going home."

"So your relationship wasn't a good one?"

"Not really, not at that point. Not given his habit of sleeping with other women."

"That must have been upsetting for you," he said.

"I suppose some people would assume that, but not really, to be honest. It wasn't the first time. The relationship had met its natural end."

"So, he slept with someone else and you caught them at it, is that correct?"

"Yes."

"Were you angry?"

"A little, but mostly disappointed and hurt."

"Did you argue in the car?"

"Yes."

"How did you feel then?"

"How do you think? I felt cross."

"When people are in a heightened emotional state, they often drive too fast. Tell me, were you driving too fast?"

"It was foggy. It's hard to know. The fog made it disorientating."

"Did Mr Patterson ask you to slow down at any time, Ms Davis?"

I hesitated, looking over at Mr Stirling for advice on whether to answer. He nodded at me encouragingly. "I don't know. I'm not sure. A lot was said, and it all happened so fast." It felt like a fudge, but it wasn't a lie.

"Ms Davis, I want to remind you of the importance of telling the truth to us. Mr Patterson reports," he looked down at his notes, "that he distinctly recalls telling you to slow down. So, I want to ask you the question again. Did Mr Patterson ask you to slow down?" Again, Mr Stirling said nothing. I looked at him, waiting for him to step in and close the questioning down.

"He may have," I admitted finally, "but, as I said, it was disorientating in the fog. It felt faster than it actually was."

"Mr Patterson claims that he met Ms Serena Sutton at the wedding and recognised an immediate attraction. He admits they did indeed become intimate as you described. However, he claims he had been unhappy in the relationship with you for some time. He claims he had tried to finish the relationship on a number of occasions prior to the day of the crash."

"That's a lie!"

He ignored me, continuing; "He claims you threatened to make a scene at the wedding, so he agreed to leave with you, despite not wanting to, to avoid spoiling the day for the happy couple."

"That's a lie too."

"He claims you were seething with jealousy and driving erratically. He asked you to slow down, but you ignored him. He claims you told him . . ." Officer Murray looked down at his notes again for reference before continuing, ". . . that 'if you couldn't have him no one would' and then you deliberately steered off the road to crash, hoping to kill him."

"That's a complete lie! None of that is true."

"Ms Davis, did you attempt to frame Mr Patterson for an attack on you last Friday?"

"No, that was real. He tried to strangle me."

"The doctor who saw to your injuries has produced a report stating the injuries could have been self-inflicted. Were you so jealous of the relationship between Mr Patterson and Ms Sutton that you wanted to see him imprisoned rather than happy with another woman?"

"No. God, no. It's all a lie."

"Why, Ms Davis? Why is it a lie?" At that point, Mr Stirling, who'd been about as much use as a chocolate teapot, sat back in his chair and slowly unwound the cravat he'd been wearing. Underneath, highly visible bruising encircled his neck.

"You're one of them!" I pointed at him, my hand trembling.

"One of who?" Officer Murray asked gently as I continued to stare at Mr Stirling in horror. Realisation that they'd gotten to Elliott's nominated lawyer before he came to see me dawned. I was fucked. I needed to tell them what I knew.

"One of the people with activated virus. They're everywhere," I said.

"Who are?" He looked confused. I needed to start at the beginning.

"After the fog, people were infected by the new virus. Men, men under sixty. If they died or were killed, then the virus activated. It brought them back. It brought Edward back. He's one of them." I pointed at Mr Stirling. "Look at his neck."

"What am I looking at? What does it mean?"

"I don't know. They died – all of them – but the virus brings them back to life. That's what happened to Edward. He was different after the accident."

"How was he different?"

"He was nicer. He wanted to have a baby with me." In the back of my mind, I could hear how mad I sounded.

"So this virus made him nice and want a baby."

"Yes, no . . . I mean, it changed him. They want to reproduce the virus."

"Ms Davis, did you threaten Ms Sutton last night?"

"I didn't threaten her, no. I warned her what Edward had become. She told me he wanted a baby with her. I told her to get away."

"Okay, thank you, Ms Davis." He closed his notebook and stood. The second officer got to his feet as well, having never opened his mouth.

"What happens now? Can I go home? You have to believe me, I never tried to kill him. He tried to kill me if anything. Others of them are killing people."

"We'll see, Ms Davis. For your own safety, we'll take you back to a cell for now. I'm going to suggest we have a doctor come and see you."

"I don't need to see a doctor. I'm not ill," I insisted. But they ignored my protests, leaving me with a uniformed man who said nothing as he escorted me back to the holding cell.

Chapter 22

"Ms Davis, I'm Dr Nichols. I'm here to make sure you are entirely well and in a fit state to face the charges that have been brought against you."

"There is nothing wrong with me."

"Officer Murray reported you made some claims about a virus? Can you tell me a bit more about it?"

"You won't believe me either. No one believes me," I said, frustrated. "You need to speak to Dr Elliott Harvey."

"I will," he soothed, "but first I want to listen to what you have to say. I'm a doctor, so I understand things like viruses better than other people do. Explain it to me." He seemed kind . . . genuine. At least he wasn't looking at me like I was pond scum, which made a nice change.

We were sitting back in the interview room, the doctor had placed his chair beside mine, rather than opposite with the table acting as a barrier as Frank Murray and his silent friend had, making the doctor literally on my side. I hoped so, because there was no sign of Arthur Stirling, and I hadn't a clue when I was going to be allowed home.

"It came from the red fog," I explained. I was in deep now. My only hope was Elliott had sent the emails and that the information would hit the mainstream news soon. Then maybe someone would take what I was saying seriously. In the meantime, I took Dr Nichols through the information I had so far. To his credit, he barely blinked when I explained these were people coming back from the dead, that I thought we had been invaded, and that they were killing people to force them to change.

"Do you hear voices, Ms Davis?" he asked when I finished.

I slammed the table with my hand, making him jump. "You're no bloody different than the rest of them! No, I don't bloody hear voices. I told you, this virus is real. I'm not making this up."

"Did you want to kill Mr Patterson because he had the virus?"

"No, have you even been listening to anything I said? I didn't know anything about the virus then. I never tried to kill him. The crash was just an accident in bad weather conditions. I've never tried to kill Edward, well, apart from when he tried to strangle me, and even then I was defending myself. This is about the virus, not me."

"Ms Davis, I think you may not know it, but, in my opinion, I believe you could be very sick."

"I'm not sick."

"I believe that the sickness in your mind is making you believe things that are not real. It's what we call psychosis. I believe it's making you have delusions, and that you need to be treated for it, before you hurt yourself or someone else."

"I'm not having fucking delusions! This is real," I shouted.

"I know you believe that," he deflected.

"I want to go home."

"I'm afraid that won't be possible. I don't believe you are well enough to face trial at this time, but it will be my recommendation to the courts that you be committed for your own and others' safety."

"Committed? Oh my God, no. You think I'm mad? I'm not mad, oh God." I started to cry. He moved closer in an attempt to comfort me. Angry, I lifted my arms to push him away, catching him in the face with my elbow.

"Officers, now, please," Dr Nichols said, looking up into one of the CCTV cameras, holding a hand to his jaw. The door opened and two men in white medical coats entered with a trolley. "Please lie down, Ms Davis. Don't make this any harder than it needs to be."

"No, fuck no. I'm not going anywhere with you. I'm not mad, get your hands off me, I want to see another lawyer!" I screamed as one of the nurses reached to restrain me. He pulled my hands behind my back as the second man jabbed me in the neck with a needle. The effect was immediate, my legs sagging under my weight, held up only by the nurse restraining me.

Together they hauled me onto the trolley, the cool plastic sticking to my skin where my sweatshirt had ridden up behind me. My last memory was the feeling of hands gripping my body as they strapped me down.

***

I blinked my eyes open, and wondered if I'd died. Everywhere was white: the walls, the floor, the mattress and sheets on which I lay. There was nothing at all to orient myself by. No windows, no pictures, just an overwhelming whiteness. Even the robe I wore was white. I tried not to dwell on the fact that at some point I must have been stripped and re-dressed in the simple cotton outfit. My wrists bore evidence of having been secured, but otherwise I seemed to be untouched.

I lay there for a time, blinking myself awake as I gathered my wits and took closer stock of my surroundings. A fluorescent strip light ran down the length of the small square room, the plastic casing shadowed with the carcasses of the frazzled insects. I wondered how it might have been possible for them to even have reached the sterile cage in order to have become caught in the first place, given the absence of any windows in the room.

A camera blinked its small red eye from a vantage point high in the corner of the room, capturing my every movement – making sure I knew someone, somewhere was watching me. I strained my body, pulling myself to upright, ignoring my protesting muscles, to better look around at my surroundings. I found only two doors within my new white world: the one behind me looked like it led into a small bathroom, from what I could see from my vantage point on the mattress, the other had to be the way out.

My bladder pressed uncomfortably, reminding me of my immediate priority. That was the main reason I had awoken at all. I pulled myself to standing, leaning against the softly padded wall to stabilise myself, the motion making my head spin. Nausea rose, and I staggered into the small bathroom, only reaching the toilet in time for half the vomit to fall within the toilet bowl. The rest splattered across the floor and up the pedestal, creating a curiously attractive orange contrast to the otherwise monochrome colour scheme. Jackson Pollock would have been proud. I collapsed to my knees, being careful to avoid what was on the floor, and rested my pounding head on the seat. From this position it became clear what my eight-by-eight room actually was: a padded cell.

Once I'd relieved myself and cleared up the mess as best I was able, given the fact I had only toilet paper at my disposal, I walked back into the small room and stood below the camera. "Hey," I called into the lens, waving at the device. It was positioned too high on the wall for me to reach. "Hey, is anyone there? Can someone help me, please?" My head pounded with the effort, a physical echo marking every time I used my voice. "Hello?" I called again.

Five minutes later, or what I assumed was about five minutes, given that I had nothing to measure the passage of time, I'd still heard nothing. I strained my ears for any sounds of movement outside the room but the only sound was the thrum of my pulse in my ears. The continually blinking camera was the only sign that life continued at all outside of the room as it maintained its one-eyed stare. "Hey," I shouted again after a further five of my minutes had passed. "I'm serious, I need to talk to someone, or–" I hesitated. Or what? What was I going to do? What could I do? Where the hell even was I?

My internal rant was cut off by the sound of the door being unlocked. An electronic lock bleeped; six short beeps, followed by the longer tone that denoted a successful code entry, then the door clicked and opened inwards. I craned my neck to see who it was. Dr Nichols walked into the room.

"Ms Davis, Samantha, it's good to see you awake at last. You must have been tired. You slept for several hours."

"You stuck a fucking sedative in my neck. That's all. Where am I? What place is this? I want to speak to a new lawyer." I lunged forward and grabbed his arm. He shrugged me off quickly.

"Please lie back down on the mattress, Samantha. Let me assure you that if you display any of the aggressive behaviour you exhibited earlier, I will need to sedate and restrain you again. For your own safety, of course, as well as mine. It's a simple enough process to insert a catheter if we need to." He rubbed his jaw, clearly remembering the clout I'd landed on him earlier, then made a quick gesture to someone behind him, who must have been standing in the hallway out of my line of sight. A large man in a nurse's uniform entered the room, making it feel even smaller than it already was. In one hand, he held a mop and bucket, in the other a syringe. He looked at Dr Nichols, who nodded back at him, and quickly placed the syringe into his pocket before walking into my bathroom where he proceeded to clean the mess I'd missed in my earlier attempt at wiping up the vomit.

"Where am I?" I asked again, turning back to Dr Nichols.

"A safe place."

"Safe for whom? Where?"

"Does it matter?"

"How long do I have to stay here?" I thought of Elliott and how frantic he'd be about me.

"Oh, Samantha, I'm not sure you quite understand. You have been committed to my care for both your own and the general public's safety. That means you must stay here indefinitely. It's not so bad," he said, looking around.

"I'm not mad," I stated. "I know you think I am, but I'm not. You'll see."

"I know you're not mad, Samantha. Just inconvenient. And you annoyed the wrong person. So, you had to be stopped. Voila," he said with a flourish, sounding pleased with himself as he threw his hands up in the Gallic style.

"You can't keep me here. People will look for me."

"I think you'll find we can. You did a spectacular job of sounding completely delusional, with very little prompting on our part, I must say. It was simply marvellous. They couldn't get rid of you fast enough by the time you'd finished. As for whether anyone is looking for you; well, Elliott should be meeting with a little accident right about . . . now," he said with a look down at his watch. "You'd already been released from your job, so they're not bothered a jot, and the one friend you have in the world who cares about you is convinced you've run to ground with your new love interest. So, you see there really is no one worrying about you at all."

"What do you want from me?" I said, as I wrapped my arms tight around my middle.

"Apart from shutting you up for a little while, you mean?"

I nodded.

"Right now, nothing. For you to be forgotten. In the future? Well, all will become clear. In the meantime, relax." He laughed, and I wanted to hit him again, jerking forward in my annoyance. The male nurse was by his side in seconds, syringe in his hand. For a few moments we all stared at one another, then Dr Nichols walked to the door, unlocked it and paused to glance back at me. "I'll see you again when you've had a chance to reflect on your position here, Samantha. You're really very lucky compared to some of the others. Important people have laid claim to you. Anyway, for now all you need to do is . . ." He looked around the small room, "take it easy. Cool off a little," he said, waiting whilst the nurse collected his mop and bucket from the bathroom, before giving me a last grin and slamming the door closed behind them.

***

By what I reckoned was day three, I'd begun to sing to myself. The only break to the monotony of the endless empty hours came either when I slept or when the nurse brought in my food, which helped me to mark the time.

After what I believed was a week, I'd started to lose the plot. I begged the man, who continued to deliver my food every day, along with an occasional change of clothes, for something to fill my vast hours of nothingness. Even prisoners were allowed some respite from their incarceration – time in a yard, food in a canteen. I thought I remembered hearing some even had libraries. He ignored me, and as the days continued to trickle past I began to worry I really was losing my mind, or at least would lose it by the time anyone remembered me to realise I was missing. I questioned everything that had happened before I'd been locked up, and when I wasn't doing that, I worried what had happened to the people I cared about: Elliott, Heidi – it was a depressingly short list. The day I added Victoria, I knew I really had begun to lose my mind.

Time began to blur; a week turned into two and then more, and eventually I lost track. I slept and I ate. Most of the time after I ate I felt sick. Sometimes I vomited, like I had that first day, which made me wonder if they were putting something – maybe a sedative – into my food. I tried to exercise, doing press-ups and practising my kickboxing moves in the confined space, but most of the time I was so exhausted I gave up after only a few minutes. And all the while the blinking red eye of the camera watched me.

After one of my more spectacular vomiting episodes, as I lay exhausted, curled on the cool, tiled floor of the bathroom, the door bleeped. My mind registered the abnormality of the hour for a visitor. Too little time had passed since I'd been brought my breakfast. I knew I'd not slept since I'd last eaten and lost track of time as a result, as it had been the meal that had led to me being crouched over the toilet in the first place. I registered a presence above me and opened my eyes. "Are you ill?" Dr Nichols asked, as he peered down at me.

"Nice of you to finally notice. It certainly looks like it," I muttered, feeling too tired after my most recent vomiting bout to even lift my head. He harrumphed, as if I had been deliberately disobedient and made myself ill just to spite him. He reached down and took my pulse, before scooping me up and laying me back down on the mattress. He pulled out a syringe.

"What are you doing?" I cried, fearful he was about to inject me with some further poison. It was somewhat heartening I still possessed the will to live.

"Relax. I'm just taking some blood. We need to find out why you're ill." He tied a band around my arm, slapping my veins until they obliged, and then slid the needle into the purple shadow beneath my skin. I watched passively as my blood filled the small chamber. He replaced the first vial with a second chamber and filled that too, before removing the needle. He pressed some cotton wool against the still-bleeding puncture wound and folded my arm to apply enough pressure to keep it in place. "Good girl," he said with a smile, gazing down at me. "You really are quite lovely, you know," he said, taking hold of my jaw and turning it first one way and then the other. "Even sick as you are." I jerked away from him. "Anyway . . ." He leant over to pick up his vials, ". . . that's me done for now. We'll run a few tests and get back to you if there's a medication you need to take. Your kind is disappointingly fragile. Most irritating."

I said nothing as he exited the room and left me once more to my solitude. I dropped my head back down onto the pillow, enjoying the cool sensation as it pressed against my cheek, closed my eyes and slept.

***

Three days later, the door bleeped, announcing the arrival of a visitor – again between meals. I was feeling better today. I contemplated using my kickboxing skills to attack whoever it was, until the hulking nurse stepped in. The man was built like a brick wall. I knew my limitations.

"Stand up," he said. This was new; he'd never spoken to me before. "Stand up," he said again, when I did nothing, and only gaped at him. Clumsily, I forced myself to upright, pulling myself up from the low mattress, staggering at the unfamiliar sensation of being on my feet. He grasped my elbow and pulled me towards the door.

"Where are you taking me?" I gasped. He said nothing. It was funny, I reflected, that after all this time locked inside my cell, desperate to find a way out, the prospect of being taken outside now filled me with terror.

He led me down a white corridor, my legs feeling stiff and unused to walking as I forced them into action to keep pace with his long stride. Doors like the one to my own cell ran along the length. Presumably leading to rooms identical to the one I had been held within, each filled with someone like me, going quietly mad.

We turned a corner, and then a second, before we reached a door which led to a narrow staircase. He hurried me through and up the stairs, his tight grip on my elbow a clear reminder that I was still a prisoner here, ascending until the stairs finally stopped at another doorway. He entered another digital code, which unlocked the door with a shrill electronic beep, before pushing it open and leading me through.

Daylight hit me first, my eyes squinting closed in the unfamiliar brightness after the dimmer artificial light in my cell. As my eyes adjusted, the high ceilings and grand architecture came into focus. I appeared to be in some sort of country estate house, if the artwork on the walls and busts arranged on plinths up the grand, wide staircase that now swept upwards ahead of us were anything to go by. I figured I'd been held in the old servants' quarters which they'd adapted into cells.

The nurse led me along another hallway, past numerous rooms I only caught glimpses of, until we arrived into a lounge area. Seven women reclined on plush armchairs. Several more were seated at a large table having what looked like breakfast. It was breakfast time. I hadn't known for sure. I tensed, ready to call to them for help, but my captor's hand tightened painfully on my elbow, threatening unspoken repercussions, so I hesitated.

We walked across the room, the women's eyes barely lifting to follow us, curious but unafraid, then out a door on the opposite side of the room, along another corridor. The place seemed vast and built like a warren. I had little chance of finding my way out again on my own. I looked at the windows we passed, figuring they were my best hope.

Pushing through some heavy fire doors, we entered a newer part of the building. It appeared to be a later extension, the hallway again lined with rooms protected by entry codes, reminiscent of the area I had been housed in. I assumed more doors meant more cells, but when we passed a room that had been left open, instead of a cell like mine, I caught a glimpse of a well-furnished bedroom with a vast double bed. These occupants weren't prisoners.

We turned another corner and then stopped by a door that had Dr Nichols' name on the outside. The man knocked sharply. "Come in," Dr Nichols' voice called from within. The man turned the handle and pulled me into an examination room. It was exactly like any other clinical room I had seen during my career, complete with a medical examination table in the middle.

"Ah, Samantha," he said, looking up. "Good, good. Please climb on." He pointed at the table.

"No!" I stepped back, my back hitting the nurse's chest.

He frowned at me. "I'm not asking you, I'm telling you."

I shuddered. "And I'm telling you there's no way I'm letting you examine me on that."

"You want to find out what the matter is, don't you? Want to know what's been making you so ill?" It was true, I did want to know. I couldn't ignore the fact there was something wrong with me.

I climbed up reluctantly, convincing myself I could use the time to plan an escape. There had to be some way out of here, especially since the room was on the ground floor. I was hopeful, if at any point the nurse left, that I could overpower Dr Nichols.

That was until another knock sounded on the door. The person on the other side didn't wait for a response from Dr Nichols, opening the door immediately after knocking. Richard walked in, and hope fled.

"Get away," I cried, scooting off the bed and using it as a barrier between us.

"Now, now, Samantha. No need to be like that. How are you feeling?" Richard said.

I glared at him. "What do you care?"

"Oh, I care very much. You're very precious to me."

"Yeah, right. Fuck off."

"Vulgarity doesn't suit you, and as my mother would have said, shows a distinct lack of vocabulary. So please, Samantha, if you can't say something nice, please don't say anything at all."

"You killed your mother, so if you don't mind I won't take advice of any sort from you. What do you want? Isn't it enough that you've got me locked up here? Why do you need to torment me too?"

"We don't want to torment you. I've brought you a visitor. Come in," he called over his shoulder. Edward walked into the room.

"Hey." He smiled at me. "Come and lie down, Sam," Edward said, his voice gentle as he patted the bed. He looked pleased to see me.

"I'll stay where I am, thanks." I was trapped in a room with a murderer and an attempted murderer. I scanned the room for anything I could use as a weapon. There was nothing. "Look, I don't know why you don't just kill me, same as you did with the others," I said in desperation.

"Oh, I thought about it quite carefully," Richard admitted. "You really have been a frightful nuisance with one thing and another. But, despite his recent temper tantrum, Edward was adamant he wanted to keep you. He seems to be fond of you, and finds you very attractive. We need to procreate, that makes you valuable. Not all your women are as willing, or as appealing, to reproduce with as you were."

"You're dreaming, aren't you?" I laughed at Edward. "You tried to kill me. Anyway, what about Serena?"

"What about her?" Edward looked confused. "She's nothing to me."

"Our men aren't monogamous, Samantha," Richard explained.

Anger surged. "Well, that should suit you down to the ground," I seethed to Edward. "Unless you plan to rape me, there's not a chance of anything happening between us. I don't consent. I'll never consent to any of you." I stared at them in turn.

"We'd much rather you were willing," Richard said, unconcerned. "It's so much more pleasurable that way. But if that's not possible, then we will do what's required to breed from the women here. We'll do what we have to do."

"So, you rape those women out there?"

"No, Samantha." He sounded amused by the prospect. "Believe me, they're very willing." He emphasised the word "very". My stomach churned. "We're building a fine breeding herd. Picking out the women with . . ." Richard paused, running his eyes down my body, "all the best assets. Most of the ladies are more than happy to have been chosen by us."

"Do they know what you are? What you really are?"

"No, not yet. Just that we're a group with an open attitude to sex. A group that focuses on celebrating and worshiping women, and allowing them to reproduce as often as biology will permit. Many women are more than happy to live this way, as you've no doubt seen on your way up here. We take care of *all* their needs."

I bit my tongue.

"But you see that's why we can't allow you to mix freely with the others yet." Clearly, I had more work to do on masking my emotions. "The time will come for telling the full facts, but not today. Anyway, enough of all that; we have a couple of pieces of good news to share with you." I held my tongue, waiting instead for him to continue. "First of all," he said, looking over at Edward, "we're hoping your other little friend will soon be among our ranks. I believe a group were expecting to intercept him today. Hopefully once he's here you'll be more inclined to participate in the fun."

Edward and I both scowled at him this time.

"Now, now, Edward. You know the rules here, we all have to share nicely." Richard grinned. "I might even like a turn with her myself at some point."

Edward took an immediate step forward, his lip curled, fists clenched at his sides.

Richard stood his ground, looking unperturbed, but his voice held an edge when he spoke. "Back off, Edward, before you do something you regret."

Dr Nichols stepped up behind Edward, a syringe in his hand.

"We really need to manage the jealousy and possessiveness traits in our people," Richard said to Dr Nichols. "All these hormones and emotions are really most inconvenient."

Dr Nichols nodded. "I know, it's a problem. I'm looking into it."

"In the meantime, Dr Nichols, why don't you share our other piece of delightful news? I can't wait to see her reaction." Even Edward smiled at the prospect of whatever they were about to tell me.

"Well," Dr Nichols began, pausing to clear his throat. "Well," he started again, "we analysed your blood samples. I'm sorry it took so long, but we've had a few issues that have kept us otherwise occupied. Anyway, I took your blood the other day, as you know. We look for any hereditary issues that might affect our breeding programme, as well as each female's general health status. Given you'd been so poorly I was concerned you may have a serious underlying condition. The good news is that you are a quite magnificent specimen. Just perfect," he added with emphasis.

I crossed my arms in front of me. Edward turned to scowl at the doctor.

Dr Nichols ignored him. "The even better news is that you're already pregnant."

Chapter 23

"I can't be, that's not possible," I said, my mind reeling.

"I think you can," Edward supplied with a cocky grin, his smugness reaching insufferable levels. "We really were very proactive in the bedroom if you recall?"

"I was on the pill."

"It's not one hundred percent effective, and you weren't on the pill from the start."

"I took the morning-after pill the first time we had unprotected sex. I didn't want your baby!"

"The morning-after pill has also been known not to be completely effective," Dr Nichols supplied, looking delighted by the news. "You're clearly very fertile. A real asset to our group. One of our first successes, we believe, although we hope to have a number following on close behind you." He rubbed his hands, looking gleeful at the prospect.

"I can't be," I whispered, my eyes fixing on Edward's. He looked oddly proud as he gazed down at me with a soft expression. "Are you sure it's yours?" I said, despite knowing it couldn't be Elliott's – we'd only had sex that one time a few weeks ago, and we'd used a condom. I hadn't slept with anyone else.

Edward was around the table and beside me in a flash, his face twisted in rage and jealousy. "Who else did you fuck apart from that doctor?" His hand hung in the air, poised to grab my neck, his breathing ragged as he tried to control himself.

"Back off, Edward, before you end up killing her and the baby. We know it's yours," Richard said, sounding bored.

"How? How do you know?" Edward stepped closer to me so I knew the immediate danger hadn't passed. I stayed pressed against the bed, his eyes never leaving mine.

"There are viral traces in her blood," Dr Nichols informed us. "They've entered her system via the embryo. It means the embryo has to contain traces of our DNA, because it can't be transmitted via droplets like it was in the mist to the male population. There's no doubt it's yours, Edward, so look after her please. At least until she has it, and even then . . . We're not sure what the miscarriage rate will be with the combination DNA offspring and, until we know how to select out the suitable breeding partners, we need to look after the women who prove able to carry. We need to protect them and their babies until we have more data. So far very few seem to be progressing past the six-week stage before the pregnancy self-terminates; it's very frustrating. From the blood tests, we believe Samantha may be considerably further along than that, which makes her rather special."

"She is," Edward agreed, reaching out to cup my face gently. I flinched, staggering slightly as the adrenaline left my body in a rush, taking all my energy with it. He scooped me into his arms and placed me carefully on the bed.

"Bring over the machine," Dr Nichols instructed the nurse.

"What machine? What are you going to do to me?" I said, frightened again now.

"Calm yourself, Samantha, it's not good for the baby," Richard soothed, his voice sending chills through me. "We just need to ascertain how far along you are. It's only an ultrasound."

The nurse wheeled the machine closer from its position against the wall. Dr Nichols took a second to switch everything on, before picking up the probe and moving to my side.

"If the baby is too early we'll need to carry out a trans-vaginal scan," he explained. I started to protest, there was no way I would let him stick a probe inside me, but he ignored me. "Lift your robe, please, Samantha."

I looked around at the other men in the room, unwilling to expose myself to them.

"Do you need us to do it for you, Samantha?" Richard laughed. "I know I'd be willing to volunteer." Edward scowled again. "It's nothing Edward hasn't seen before, and Dr Nichols is a consummate professional. I'm reasonably sure I can restrain myself."

"Pull the fucking robe up, Samantha," Edward said. I complied, hating the way all three of them eyed my small white lace knickers with hungry expressions on their faces. "Get on with it," Edward added, after he looked up and saw the looks on his companions' faces, his irritation directed towards them rather than me now.

Dr Nichols picked up a plastic bottle attached to the side of the machine and squirted some cool blue gel straight onto my abdomen, placing the probe into the middle of the mess and smearing it all around my lower belly. He pressed firmly, almost painfully, into my lower abdomen, directly over my womb, as his eyes flickered between my stomach and the screen. His forehead creased in concentration.

I stared at the swirling grey images on the screen, wondering what would happen to me if they found nothing there. My tummy was still flat; it was easier to deny everything than accept the horrific reality a baby would present. Then I remembered the tiredness I'd been feeling, the repeated nausea and vomiting that I'd put down to all the stress I had been under, the tender breasts and ill-fitting clothes, and my heart sank. It sank further when the sound of a galloping heartbeat filled the room.

"There," the doctor breathed, turning the screen so the rest of us could see better. We all peered at the monitor, a spectrum of emotions on our faces.

"How many weeks is it?" Edward asked, eyes fixed on the screen, a soft smile curling the corners of his mouth.

Richard's gaze held an intensity that was unnerving. I was as transfixed as anyone at the sight of the small life-form, identifiably a baby, flipping about inside my tummy, amazed I couldn't feel its internal gymnastics.

Dr Nichols clicked on various points of the baby's limbs and head, capturing the measurements. "I estimate between ten and twelve weeks," he pronounced finally. The men all sat back happily.

"Nearly into the second trimester, Samantha," Richard breathed. "Well done. That's extremely pleasing." Edward said nothing as he continued to stare at the screen. "Do you know what sex it is yet?" Richard asked.

"It's difficult to tell for certain until around the twenty-week point. I'll check weekly, though. As soon as I know anything, I'll let you know."

"If you manage a daughter, Samantha, you'll almost have made up for all the trouble you've caused us," Richard said with a laugh. "You'll both be the most precious females to our kind, which is ironic given how many times I've wanted to kill you." He looked between Edward and the doctor. "Look after her. See she eats well and rests. Nothing physically strenuous, and no more temper tantrums from you," he added, directing his cool gaze at Edward this time. "I want to know when she's into her second trimester," he said to Dr Nichols.

"I want her with me," Edward said, breaking his silence.

"No. We can't trust her yet. Let her stay in a room up here, by all means, but she needs to be locked in, until she learns her place. Then, if she's good, we can grant her some additional freedoms. In the meantime, you're welcome to come and see her whenever you wish. It is your child, after all. Well done," he said, clapping Edward on the back, as if he'd done something more notable than knock me up. "I'll contact the others," he continued. "We have a global council meeting planned for tomorrow. As far as I know, this is the first pregnancy to reach this stage. We'll need to find out what's made her different," he said to Dr Nichols.

"I'll look into it."

Richard left, and then we were just three. Or four, I realised. My gaze slid back to the screen, where the doctor continued to examine the baby. I tried to see what he could, but the details were lost on me. It looked normal: one head, two arms, two legs, nothing to suggest any sort of *Alien*-esque mutant planning to burst out of my stomach. As it started to suck its thumb, I reminded myself I didn't want this baby, that it was half one of them and could threaten our future. At the same time my hormones surged, I found myself oddly affected by the sight. I'd sucked my thumb until I was thirteen and had the overbite to prove it.

"Well, that will do for now," Dr Nichols said, as he wiped the gel from my belly with a paper towel, discarding it in the wastepaper basket in the corner of the room. He peeled off his blue latex gloves, disposed of them and then pushed the machine back against the wall. "Either the nurse or I will need to pop back to take some more blood from you," he said, looking at both Edward and me, "but I probably have enough for what I need today. In the meantime, can I get you anything?"

"I'll get her anything she needs," Edward said, before I could answer.

"I'll prescribe you some vitamin supplements and folic acid." He ignored Edward. "I'll see you soon, Samantha," he said, adding a wink.

"Leave – now," Edward said. The doctor nodded at him and grinned, throwing me another parting wink before he left the room.

When the door closed behind him Edward sat down heavily on the desk chair, rolling it over until he was beside the bed.

"Are they seriously going to leave me locked in a room for the next six months?" I said, wondering just how mad I'd be after that amount of time.

"If they have to. Like Richard said, once they think they can trust you you'll be able to start mixing with the other women, but you've been a pain in the arse so far. You'll need to change your attitude and stop fighting with Richard every chance you get."

"He killed people."

"Because of your interference. They didn't trust him anymore, something had to be done."

"He didn't have to kill them."

"They were old. It was easier."

"Wow, seriously? What are you? Some kind of Himmler virus, or something?"

"Himmler virus." He laughed. "I've missed you Sam. I remember why I liked you so much. You're so much more interesting than the other women I've met so far."

"I assume you mean Serena!" I snorted. "That's not exactly difficult. It was hardly her weighty intellect you liked about her in the first place. More like her ready, willing and able vagina."

He laughed again, before turning serious. "It wears thin after a while." He looked down at himself. "I prefer a deeper connection, more of a meeting of minds. It matters more than I expected it to. I'm not the only one. It's been a problem for a lot of us."

I laughed, but it sounded hollow; "Well, that wasn't my experience with you before. At the wedding, you seemed totally unconcerned who you were sticking it in." I turned away to hide the hurt thinking about that day still caused. The hurt morphed into anger and frustration. "How the hell did I end up here with you?"

"Sam, believe me, I, I mean Edward, had more of a connection with you than anyone else. He would have been pleased about this baby. *I'm* pleased about this baby. More than pleased."

I stared at him, struggling to find words. "How on earth can you know that? About before, I mean."

"There are echoes of him here," he said, tapping his head. "Memories, I guess, that influence some of my thoughts and responses. I can feel what he would've thought from the echoes of what he felt before. The synaptic pathways he developed remember his responses. So I remember them. He would've liked you to have his child. I like that you'll have my child." He reached out and rested his hand on my lower stomach, the soft touch incredibly intimate. My breath caught as his thumb traced the slight curve of my abdomen. His gaze slid from my belly to my face, eyes dark with emotion.

He tried to kill you.

I pulled away, slid my legs to the side and stood, pulling down my gown.

"You'd better show me to my new cell."

"Samantha—"

I held up my hand again to stop him. "The thing is, you're not Edward, are you? Edward is dead. You've just occupied his body, like a parasite." I shuddered, remembering his touch. "So I don't really care what you think he would've felt. Or what you feel for that matter."

"He'd already died. He didn't need this body anymore."

"Maybe, maybe not. You didn't give him much of a choice in the matter. Or me," I said, pointing at my stomach. "You didn't tell me, or any of the rest of the harem out there that you're trying to impregnate, that you're not fully human. That you're trying to breed your DNA into the human race. Tell me, will humans cease to exist?"

"We'll become a new species. A species containing all our genetic information. You might call that evolution."

"I would call it an invasion."

"Life will continue. It'll be better."

"Human life won't continue. You've been killing people to speed up the process of taking control. Hell, you nearly killed me."

"I'm sorry about that, Sam, genuinely. You made me so angry when I found the pills. I thought we'd connected. When I found them on the floor I saw red. It shouldn't have happened. It's taking me time to control the emotions this body feels. The strength of feeling overwhelms me sometimes. You provoke my strongest reactions of all."

"How did you heal yourself so fast after I hit you?" It had been something I'd wondered about since it had happened.

"It's one of the qualities we possess. It makes us more robust – means we can repair the bodies we occupy at their initial death more quickly."

"If I hadn't hit you, would you have killed me?"

"Yes, probably," he said.

"You've killed others?"

"No!" He sounded shocked at the suggestion. My scepticism must have shown. "Others have taken that approach. They're impatient to get control of the population before we're discovered. You're technologically advanced. It means we don't have much time to establish ourselves before we're discovered. With that, and your slow rate of reproduction, it makes this a difficult transition."

"Maybe we don't want to transition."

"I don't imagine most species would ever even know."

"I'm guessing most species are somewhat less evolved. If they're simple-celled organisms I'm not sure they'd care one way or another. Tell me," I said, as another thought struck me, "does that mean you've occupied other species, apart from humans, here?" He nodded. "Plants too?"

"No. We're only compatible with sentient lifeforms."

"You're being very open," I said suspiciously. I hesitated, "I'm never getting out of here, am I?"

"Why would you want to?"

"Why would I want to?" I echoed, incredulous. "You're keeping me a prisoner. What about my friends? Heidi, Elliott?"

"Forget about him."

"No. I won't."

"He'll be one of us soon anyway."

"So then you'll let him fuck me – as soon as I've had this baby – so I can pop out a new baby mutant nine months later?"

"No!" His face turned red as his anger escalated. "You're not fucking anyone else. Only me." He sounded determined.

"Then I face a future of celibacy, because I'm sure as hell not letting you anywhere near me again." My chest heaved with emotion, tears threatening. At least now I could blame the mood swings on pregnancy hormones. "I don't want you."

Edward stalked toward me, stepping into my personal space. "Are you sure about that, Samantha?" He lifted my chin with a finger, forcing me to look at him.

I tried to suppress the acceleration in my breathing as we stared at one another.

He dropped my chin and smiled, then turned and left the room.

When the door closed I collapsed onto the bed.

***

Two weeks later, my new prison was nearly as bad as my old. Sure, it was much more comfortable: well furnished, big double bed, large bath. I even had books to read. But the loneliness crushed me.

My only regular visitor continued to be the nurse, who arrived and deposited my trays of food, but never said a word. Otherwise, I saw Dr Nichols – one time – to collect more blood.

I'd used some of the time to think about my situation. I'd rationalised my physical response to the thing that looked like Edward – that's what I'd decided to call it now, so I didn't confuse what it was – blaming the entire incident on pregnancy hormones. It was well documented that pregnant women could become extraordinarily horny in the early trimesters. I figured that was what I was experiencing.

My predicament hadn't been helped by the sounds that filled the night, every night. It seemed the women who lived here were embracing a "free-love" lifestyle. I feared the consequences of the baby-boom that would likely follow.

In addition, my renewed solitary confinement gave me far too much time to contemplate the pregnancy. It occupied the majority of my thoughts. In my darkest moments, I'd considered the ways in which I could harm myself sufficiently that I would miscarry. That there was nothing in the room sharper than a paperback book was not coincidence, I feared. Neither were the locked windows. Suicide, by jumping to my death, had also crossed my mind.

But, in truth, I wondered if, given the opportunity, I would even be able to go through with it. I thought of Heidi, how much she wanted a child, and how she would feel if she knew I had thrown the chance of having one away. Then I wondered if she might already be pregnant too. How nice it would be to share this experience together. And it was certainly an experience. One of the books I'd been left in my room was *What To Expect When You're Expecting*. I'd become obsessed with reading about everything happening inside my body as the baby changed from being the size of a bean into a plum and beyond. All the symptoms I'd been suffering were recognisably caused by being pregnant: the ligament pains, the enhanced sense of smell, a sudden dislike of caffeine. All thanks to my bean. And, on occasions, I'd found myself cupping my lower abdomen and talking to the bean as if it could hear me. No, I didn't know if I'd be able to harm my baby now, even if I could find a way.

I also knew, from what I'd read, that I'd passed the first trimester purely from my symptoms. The nausea and vomiting had eased, and I felt well. Good, even. My thicker hair was shinier than before. I'd mentally calculated the date of my last period – excluding the light bleed I'd had just after I'd taken the morning-after pill, which, from what I'd read, was probably caused by the embryo attaching itself to the wall of my womb – and calculated I must be about fourteen weeks. The thought amazed me. At my lowest, I blamed Edward for the fact his child had held on in there despite my best efforts to prevent it. At other times, I felt what could only be described as maternal affection for my bean.

"Time for another scan," Dr Nichols announced arriving unexpectedly in my room one morning.

"Where's Edward?"

"How sweet! Do you think Daddy should be at the appointment with you? He's probably off fucking one of the other women, trying to get another one of you up the duff."

You don't care, think of Elliott, I told myself, trying to ignore the surge of bitter jealousy.

"Come on," he said, leading me out of my bedroom and back along the corridor towards the examination room. A woman stepped out of her room and stopped in surprise when she saw me.

"Oh, hi," she said with a big smile. "Are you new? Welcome. I'm Tara. I hope you'll come and meet everyone when you've finished with Dr Nichols. When did you arrive?"

"Oh, about six weeks ago." Dr Nichols tried to pull me along, but I dug my heels in, sensing an opportunity.

"Goodness, how come we've not seen you before?"

"They've kept me locked up."

She raised her eyebrows, looking to Dr Nichols for an explanation.

"She's pregnant," he said.

Her face transformed into a massive grin. "Oh, how marvellous. That's just wonderful. You clever thing. No one else is having much luck in that department. No wonder, you must have been feeling dreadful. Have you been resting?"

"Not now, Tara. Samantha needs to have her check-up. She'll be out later if she's feeling up to it."

"Oh, great. I can't wait. I want to know all about it. They all will. They're going to be so jealous of you. Especially Ella," she said with another grin. "Oh, I can't wait. I'll see you later. I'll come and find you afterwards." There was no stopping the woman. I said a small prayer of thanks to whoever was looking out for me. This might be my chance to get word to someone outside of here.

"Great, I'll see you later," I agreed before Dr Nichols could stop me. Then I allowed him to pull me into the examination room.

Chapter 24

"That was really most inconvenient of you, Samantha. Richard will be very displeased," he said, as he closed the door behind us.

"I don't give a shit."

He sighed. "Climb onto the bed."

I obliged without argument, but only because I wanted to see my bean again. He didn't wait for me to lift my robe, pushing it up himself before reaching quickly for the gel and then the probe. "Good," he breathed when my bean's staccato heartbeat filled the room. He clicked on the image on the screen, taking measurements, before sitting back, looking pleased. "Definitely out of the first trimester. I'd say you're just over fourteen weeks." His view matched my own. I smiled. "You're a remarkable woman, Samantha," he breathed. "Take your robe off."

"Why?"

"I need to check you're changing as you need to."

"I don't think you do." I said, arms crossed tight over my chest. "I've read about doctors like you. The kind who need to cop a feel of a woman's breasts when they've gone to see you with a sore throat. This is bullshit. Keep your filthy paws to yourself."

Irritated, he grabbed the neck of my robe and pulled sharply, but I anticipated the move and kept a tight grip of my own. The cotton garment tore in half, exposing my body to him. I grabbed at the pieces, holding them together to protect my modesty. I was damned if I wanted the pervert to see my unprotected breasts.

"Fuck off!" I shouted, jumping off the bed. "Fuck you!" He came towards me, and I immediately fell into a fighting stance, winding him with a sharp kick to the abdomen before I finished it with a knee to his groin. He crumpled to the floor with a groan.

"What's going on in here?" Richard demanded from behind me. I turned, poised to attack again, until I saw the hulking nurse with him.

"Your perverted doctor fancied a grope of the goods. I wasn't in the mood." I pulled the torn parts of my robe together with as much dignity as I could muster.

"Andrew, we talked about this. She's not yours, at least not whilst she's pregnant. You need to control yourself better than that. Get out of here," Richard said, his tone disapproving. "Recover yourself, then we'll talk about this again."

Dr Nichols stood slowly, a wince suggesting he was still in some pain, and limped his way towards the door, scowling at me as he passed. He paused in the doorway. "One of the girls – Tara – saw her earlier, when I brought her in here. They expect her to join them this evening. I told them she was pregnant which was why she wasn't with them yet. Tara was excited. I'm sorry."

Richard scowled. "You should have waited for us, Andrew. We could have avoided all this fuss completely. Still, no matter. She'd have had to join them at some point. How many weeks is she?"

"Fourteen based on my measurements."

"Good, good. That's excellent. The news is breaking tonight anyway. I'd planned to talk to the women myself before the report went out. Aiden is being interviewed in America at six pm Eastern Time. Ask the guards to prepare the cells for any troublemakers," he said to the nurse. He looked at me. "She can join us after we've broken the news. I'll do it at dinner. Make sure she has some clothes to wear and we can bring her out afterwards. It'll be a good distraction from the information. Tell the local networks we need a cohort here tonight. Security too, in case we have trouble."

My heart thumped. This was it. The news was breaking; people would know what walked amongst them. People would know I wasn't mad, that they were different – that we had been infected, or invaded, for want of a better word. I would be released because they would know I wasn't what they'd painted me as. Hope sparked inside me, until it was doused with the realisation, equally swift, that these men would never just let me walk away now. Not with the baby inside me. I was too important to the next step of their plans. I needed to get away. Being allowed out of the room was the first step to being able to escape.

I permitted them to lead me back to my room, determined to plan. Clothes were delivered shortly after with instructions from Richard to make myself presentable. I duly showered and dressed in the skirt and blouse provided, the elastic waist making space for my expanding waistline even though I had yet to produce an actual bump.

At around half past six they led me from my room and told me to wait with the nurse in the kitchen. People chatted in the other room, male and female voices, their conversation interspersed with giggles. The sound of women flirting; I recognised it only too well. I wondered if they would feel as flirtatious once they knew they were flirting with dead men.

"Ladies," Richard began, his tone authoritative, so different from the man he'd once been. "Ladies," he said again, pausing until the crowd quieted and the giggles ceased. "Thank you for your attention. I wanted to speak to you tonight before our meal and evening activities." One of the girls giggled. "I have important news to share. Two pieces, in fact. Tonight, one of our brethren in America is being interviewed on television. Many of you are aware of the discussion in the media about the new virus—"

I realised with a jolt the news was already out there, which begged the question: why had no one come for me? Did anyone even know where I was? Did anyone care? Where was Elliott? Had they got him?

Richard was still speaking. "Tonight, Aiden will lay out the real facts. That our people are indeed the product of the virus." Someone gasped, but Richard ignored it. "Naturally, people will fear what they don't understand. You, who know us best of all, know we're a loving people, men who only wish to cherish the women in our lives, women like you who come to us willingly. We're not violent." *Liar*, I wanted to scream, but I held my tongue. "We're a natural continuation of the human species, and together – with you – we'll make it even more able to survive in this world. Survival of the fittest, evolution, these are concepts Darwin taught you. We're the living embodiment of that idea."

"But they said on the news you came from people that died. Are you dead people?" a woman asked. I thought it might be Tara; she sounded a little afraid.

Richard laughed, but it held an edge. "Do I look like a dead person?" He laughed again, the group joining in this time. Reassured. "And now onto my second piece of news. Samantha, please join us." The man behind me shoved me in the back and I stumbled into the dining room where more than thirty people were seated around an enormous table. The male-to-female ratio equal. "Tara, I believe you met our lovely Samantha earlier?"

Tara, seated near Richard, nodded and smiled at me.

"Well, today we're pleased to announce that Samantha is fourteen weeks pregnant." There were gasps, a far greater gasp than the one that had met his announcement about the virus. A woman of around my age stood and stared at me with a look of desolation – she must have lost her own child, because nothing else could have prompted such a reaction – before she wailed and then turned and ran from the room. "Phillip, follow her," Richard said to the man who'd been seated beside her. He stood and left the room.

The rest of the table occupants stared at me; the men with lust, the women with undisguised jealousy. "Samantha gives us hope for the start of our new future. She gives us hope for what we'll become together and reminds us how important our time together is. My people . . ." He sounded exactly like the cult leader he pretended to be. ". . . let's eat now, and then we'll celebrate, giving thanks for the new future that's been shown to us. Samantha, join me," he said, patting an empty chair beside him. I moved to the seat as requested, scanning the faces in the room as I sat. There was no sign of Edward.

"Who did you sleep with?" the woman on the other side of Richard asked. By the very fact she'd sat beside him, this woman thought herself important. I'd clearly put her nose out of joint by falling pregnant before her.

"You must be Ella?" I guessed. Tara smiled from behind the napkin she held to her mouth, but I deliberately didn't look at her.

"How did you know?"

"Just a guess. You're very beautiful, it was easy to work out." I pandered to her ego, hoping she'd back off.

"You didn't answer. Who did you sleep with?"

"Me," Edward said, walking into the room. He came straight up to my chair, bent down and kissed me on the forehead. Several women sighed at the gesture. "Move," he said to the man beside me, who scowled up at him, but still stood and relocated to one of the earlier vacated seats.

In unison, the men rose and collected trays of food from heated plates at the side of the room. They then started to serve the women still seated at the table.

"Will you spend the night with me tonight, Edward?" Ella asked, leaning forward suggestively, her breasts threatening to spill out of her top. He looked at her and frowned, but said nothing, as he stood and collected a tray laden with slices of roast beef. He placed two slices on my plate, then two on hers. He returned twice more with green vegetables and potatoes, until a plateful of food sat in front of me. On each occasion he served me first, and then Ella.

She smiled up at him every time he looked at her, making an obvious attempt to garner some attention. I wanted to tell her she was welcome to him.

Richard never moved from his seat, seemingly amused by the whole performance, a smug expression on his face.

"I'm spending the night with Samantha tonight, Ella. Another time, perhaps?" Edward said finally, taking his seat beside mine and picking up his knife and fork.

"And me," several other women around the table called. Clearly his ability to make me pregnant was enough to class him as highly desirable in the eyes of the other women. I sat with a rod-like posture as every woman at the table, except for Tara, propositioned him. I tried to convince myself I didn't care; after all, this was the Edward I was more accustomed to. You'd have thought I'd have been used to it by now, this Edward was easy to hate.

"Why her?" Ella said, cutting into my thoughts. "She's already pregnant. Why waste yourself on her? You should share yourself around and sleep with someone else. That's what you taught us." She looked at Richard for support. He nodded.

Edward frowned at them. A muscle flickered in his jaw, a sure sign of his irritation. "I'll sleep with whomever I please, thank you Ella. It's not your place to tell me what to do. This child is a blessing; I want to make sure it knows it's loved and precious to me – to all of us. The act of loving the child we've created is as important as the act of conceiving the child. You should know better." He glared at her. "All our children are precious, a blessing, but especially this one – my first. Our first." He looked at me with a soft expression.

Ella fumed at being so publicly put in her place. I knew there was no chance we'd ever be friends now, not that there had been much of a chance before.

"You should fuck her," I whispered to Edward, as we tucked into the meal.

"I should fuck you," he parried, his gaze heated.

"No, you really shouldn't. Not ever again."

"I have fucked her," Edward said, his eyes fixed on mine, looking for my reaction. "I've fucked all these women, many times. It's my duty."

I flinched despite myself. Despite Elliott. It still hurt, even after everything. He still knew how to hurt me. I looked away.

"But none of them . . ." He grabbed my chin so that I was forced to look at his face. ". . . none of them gave me what you did. None of them made me feel the way you made me feel. None of them made me come like you made me come. Most of the time I have to think of you to be able to finish with the others." He spoke quietly, our bodies close together, my chest heaving as we stared at one another. I needed to clear my head of the effect he had over me.

I pushed my chair away from the table and stood, grabbing my plate. "I'm tired, I think I'll eat in my bedroom. I'll be out later to watch the interview," I said to Richard, uncaring that it would be the middle of the night for us. I needed to see what the media were saying and how their leader would persuade people that the prospect of this genetic blending wasn't cause for concern. Richard grunted, shovelling another forkful of food into his mouth.

I marched off in the direction of my room, the sound of a second chair scraping across the floor warning me I was being followed. I slammed the bedroom door closed behind me, placing my plate down on the small table beside the chair at the window, as the door open again. I swung round to see Edward striding towards me, as I'd known I would. Without a word, he pulled me against him and kissed me.

For a second I let him, then I remembered who he was – and who he wasn't – how he'd tried to throttle me with the same hands now cupping my face. My hand swung round and cracked him hard against his cheek.

He pulled away and smiled. "I love your fierceness, Sam. I hope our child has that quality." He placed his hand against my lower abdomen, I pushed it away. "Richard said you had another scan today. You're fourteen weeks?"

"Yes, I had a scan. Yes, I'm fourteen weeks. And then your doctor tried to sexually assault me."

"He what?" Edward exploded. I took a step back in the face of his immediate, incendiary rage.

"He tore my robe and tried to grope me. It was only because Richard arrived he stopped."

"Excuse me," Edward said, stepping back before he turned and slammed back out of the room. Shouting followed.

I didn't care.

I sat and ate the meal I'd brought back to the room with me, for once grateful to be alone. The beef tasted good, tender and succulent. I wolfed it down. It was the first meal I'd enjoyed so much in weeks. Months, even.

Finished, I leant back and enjoyed the sensation of fullness, my hands drifting to rest on my belly. Satisfaction suffused my body. Despite the absence of a bump, now I knew what I was looking for I could sense the changes happening to me. My breasts were noticeably larger. I wondered who it would most resemble – Edward or me. I hoped it would have Edward's looks if it was a boy.

Irritated, I put a stop to that line of thought. It continually surprised me I even considered the baby in that way. I should hate it, hate everything it represented. Instead, I found myself protective, despite its origins. I thought about Heidi, wondering what she would say if she knew. I imagined the hurt my having a baby would cause her if she weren't pregnant herself. The thought depressed me. I shook it off, determined to focus on the bigger picture. The interview.

Chapter 25

I sat in the armchair and willed the hands on the clock to move quicker. They didn't. More than once my eyes drifted closed, jerking open again when my head rolled and jolted me back into consciousness. The soporific effects of my early pregnancy combined with a full stomach were taking their toll.

From what I recalled, we were five hours ahead of New York in London – assuming I was still somewhere near London – so at a quarter to eleven I stood and opened the door to my room, half expecting it to have been locked. It wasn't. Edward was sitting outside the door, his back propped against the wall.

"What are you doing here?"

"Guarding you."

"From whom?"

"From everyone."

I laughed. "Who would want to bother with me?"

"You have no idea," he said, his voice flat as he looked at me. He peered at me more closely; "You really don't, do you?" I shook my head. "The men want you for themselves, and the women just hate that you're pregnant before them. You're not safe here."

"I'm already pregnant. Why would the other men want me now?"

"All our men want to be among the first to succeed in producing the next generation. It's hugely important to us. Most women seem to be reproductively hostile so far. It makes you very special. A prize."

"Thanks, but I'm not really interested in being your brood mare." I sighed. "I'm not safe anywhere now, am I? You made sure of that."

"I'm sorry, Sam. Genuinely. I wish things could have been different."

"Yeah, me too." I rubbed my hand over my face. "Listen, I want to watch that interview before I go to bed. I want to see what they're saying. Are you going to try to stop me?"

"No, of course not, but . . ."

"What?"

"They're out there." He nodded towards the lounge. "Some of them prefer to do it as a group."

"Do what?" I walked towards the lounge area, Edward close on my shoulder. I stopped when I reached the doorway of the lounge. It was an orgy. I didn't think myself a prude – I mean, I liked sex, particularly when it was done well – but this was way beyond my personal comfort zone. Those who weren't actively participating on the large daybed were watching, touching themselves. Ella had pride of place in the middle, three men in bed with her.

"You might want to tell them you can't get pregnant putting it there," I muttered, squaring my shoulders as I put my head up and walked past the scene.

"Edward, come and join us," Ella called as Edward shadowed me.

I wanted to slap her, again. "Really? He's knocked you back publicly once already tonight, are you going to make him do it again? Do you have no pride?" One of the girls in the room sniggered; It appeared I wasn't the only person who wasn't all that keen on Ella.

"Come on, Sam, the interview is about to start," Edward said, pulling me past the bed. "Ignore her."

I scowled, as she sat there unashamedly naked, her eyes willing Edward to fuck her. My palm itched. It was the sound of the television from the corridor beyond that reminded me of my priorities, and gave me the strength to walk away.

In the hallway, I headed towards the origin of the television noise, which thankfully overwhelmed the sounds from the orgy. I had no doubt Ella was putting on the show of her life, determined to make Edward believe he might be missing out.

I looked at Edward. The old version would never have been able to say no to a girl like Ella, if offered. This Edward was looking at me.

"What?" he said when he caught me staring.

"Nothing."

He smiled and grabbed my hand as we entered an already crowded room.

"Edward, Sam, just in time," Richard said from the front. "I saved you both seats." A path opened up for us to shuffle through. "Samantha, sit here," Richard said, patting the seat beside him. Edward manoeuvred me aside so I ended up beside Tara instead, placing himself in the seat next to Richard's. "As I said before, share nicely Edward," Richard muttered.

"Hi," Tara said brightly, I smiled, but was prevented from saying more when the introductory music for the news programme started and our attention was drawn to the screen.

"*Good evening and welcome*," the anchor-man said. I recognised him, a seasoned news pro for more than a decade. They'd pulled out the big guns for this interview. "*Tonight we have the first interview with Aiden Parrish, the self-proclaimed leader of the Homo Evolutis species. They're the group known to represent the men who've been altered by the virus that arrived in the fog.*" The camera shifted to focus on an extraordinarily handsome man. He possessed a wicked combination of chiselled cheekbones and a strong jaw, all enhancing naturally fair hair that had been swept neatly over to one side, framing bright blue eyes. He looked like a poster boy for the US military, and the kind of man most mothers dreamt their daughter would bring home. The women in the room unanimously sighed with pleasure – I could almost hear the eggs popping out of their ovaries.

"I'd make babies with him any day," Tara whispered, echoing the thoughts of almost every woman in the room.

"Wait and see if you still feel like that after you hear what he has to say," I whispered back, returning my focus to the screen. A second individual was being introduced. A woman – the interviewer named her as Doctor Reynolds. She looked severe and professional, dressed in an ill-fitting suit, not her usual choice of attire judging by the way she pulled repeatedly at the hem of her skirt.

Richard leant over. "Who is that?" he said to Edward. "What happened to Henman?" Edward shrugged.

The camera panned away as the presenter introduced some of the background to the discussion; showing pictures of the fog, citing earlier reports of how the virus had been initially identified as having arrived in the fog, and how activated virus had most recently been found in ten percent of male samples taken. I gasped at the figure.

Richard leant across Edward. "I think it's safe to say that's an underestimation." He smiled. "Our own people calculate we're running closer to thirty percent, and that number's believed to be rising rapidly. We estimate we'll reach an excess of sixty percent saturation in about six weeks, maybe sooner depending how this goes."

I stared at him, unable to speak for several seconds. "That can't be achieved naturally. You must be killing people to achieve a conversion of that rate." Richard smiled at me. My earlier meal turned over in my stomach.

"*Mr Parrish,*" the presenter began again, pulling my attention back to the screen.

"*Aiden, please,*" Parrish interrupted with a smile. He appeared depressingly presentable. I knew that would be enough for most people in this "spin over substance" society. You only had to look at our elected politicians to know that pretty liars won out most of the time over the honest but ugly.

"*Aiden,*" the presenter began again, with a warm smile. "*Tell us about the Homo Evolutis species. What are you, and where did you come from?*"

"*Thank you for inviting me, Robert.*" Aiden Parrish's voice oozed with practised sincerity. "*It's simple really. Homo Sapiens literally means 'intelligent man'. Homo Evolutis means higher existence. It was originally thought this next evolution would come about as a result of the way humans incorporated new technologies, but the virus acted as a more immediate trigger. We're a peaceful group of men who've been fundamentally altered by the recent fog virus – given birth to by it, if you like. It wasn't by choice. It just happened to be a selection of us that were affected. In every respect we're just like any other minority group. We want people to know about us because otherwise they'll fear us, and with fear comes repression and persecution. The media's been doing a good job of stirring up the masses and vilifying us to create a tide of hatred against our people. We're just trying to show the other side – seeking to put a face to our kind. We want to show we're just like them, we're trying to ensure we're not oppressed by others who, in their ignorance, wish to penalise us for our differences. We want to live our lives as peacefully as we can, grateful for the fact that life is still life, and it's always precious."*

Doctor Reynolds snorted at that comment, in perfect harmony with one of my own. I cheered mentally.

"Thank you," the presenter said, directing a scowl towards Doctor Reynolds. *"We'll come to you for comment in a moment, Dr Reynolds."*

She sat back in her chair, looking sullen.

"Please continue, Mr Parrish."

"Well, as I was saying, we represent a group of men who currently have no other voice. But we're not a threat."

Doctor Reynolds snorted again, this time louder. *"Really, Dr Reynolds,"* Parrish said, his hands out in a placating manner, *"I know you find this hard to believe, but we do just want to live our lives peacefully. We value the people in our lives, and the women who choose to share their lives with us are even more special. We worship them."*

Doctor Reynolds couldn't contain herself any longer, leaning forward with her finger wagging. *"You, sir, are a liar."* Her hand trembled with suppressed rage. She gave up trying to hold back her fury. *"Can you explain to the people watching how it is that this virus becomes activated in the first place?"*

Parrish frowned and leant back in his seat, arms crossed over his chest.

"Would you care to explain, Doctor Reynolds?" the presenter filled the silence.

There was no doubt she intended to, as she took a deep breath. *"It's been widely established, by my fellow scientists, that the virus becomes activated after the human body hosting it dies. We know this because of the analysis we have done. All the early documented instances were recorded in hospitals where resuscitation activity was required in what were deemed to be fatal circumstances. In every instance the patient died and then seemingly came back to life. It was some time after this that doctors began to make the link to activated virus. We have now seen this repeated in hospitals across the world. We even have it on film."*

The presenter looked amused. *"Are you telling me he's a zombie?"* he said, chuckling. *"Best damn looking zombie I've ever seen."* He laughed again. Parrish and most of the audience joined him.

Doctor Reynolds seethed. *"That's as may be. The fact remains that the virus only becomes activated in the eligible population after the death of the host, and the eligible population is males between sixteen and sixty, we believe. The very fact that you have suggested ten percent of the male population now register active virus, a number far higher than the natural mortality rate for that age group, suggests your people are killing our men to achieve a faster transition. The real question is why."*

"I can assure you—" Parrish began.

"I can tell you why they are killing men between these ages. Because these are the prime reproducing ages. They hope to pass the virus on to women in the next generation through their offspring. If you follow that line

of logic, where all men of reproducible age possess the virus and pass it on to their children, then there will be no individuals in future generations who do not possess the virus. The human species will be forever changed. The fact is we have been invaded. And just because they didn't arrive in spaceships shooting fire from the sky at the White House, we're sitting back and letting them get on with it."

"Really, Doctor Reynolds, I think you're being overly dramatic," the presenter looked at Aiden, seeming worried.

"Overly dramatic? I don't think so. Tell me, what is the average mortality for the age group you suggest that now has ten percent active virus?" She looked expectantly at Parrish, who said nothing, his lips clenched together. "Don't know? Well fortunately for the people watching I do. I make it my business to know. In 2013 in the U.S. alone there were two thousand, eight hundred and eight deaths per 900,000 population of males you mentioned. That's 0.3% of the population. Even if your estimation is correct at ten percent, and my own data suggests this may be a woeful underestimation, then something else other than natural causes is happening to change our men into people like you."

"Really, Doctor Reynolds, you have nothing to fear from us. We are a peaceful people. We only want to help this planet flourish. We're a natural evolution of your species."

"There's certainly nothing 'natural or peaceful' about you. I'd call you a parasite except you've already killed your host."

"We didn't kill the hosts; they died of natural causes. You might even say we've enabled these men to carry on with life when they would otherwise not have survived."

"There's nothing about the changes we've seen in our men that makes me believe this is a continuation of the life they lived before. Women all over the world are reporting that their husbands, fathers and brothers have significantly changed in personality from one day to the next. There are reports of it happening in men who were perfectly well, with no previous ill health or reported accidents. The only consistent sign we've heard about is strangulation marks to the neck. I believe you're killing our men and replacing them with your own. I repeat," she said, looking straight at the camera, *"we've been invaded."*

The television was silent, as the three individuals stared at one another, Doctor Reynolds' chest heaving after her passionate words. Then the screen went black. At first I thought Richard had turned it off, but it soon became apparent the network had gone down. The room remained equally silent, until Richard said, "Code black," and all the men swung into motion.

"Ladies, please return to your rooms," Richard said.

"What was that?" Tara sounded frightened. She should.

"Please, just return to your room, Tara," Richard said again, his voice cold.

"But what was that? What that lady said, about you guys and the virus. Was that true? What are you? Are you dead? Are you killing people?"

"Do we look dead, sweetheart?" One of the men leered at her.

"But you died to make the virus active?"

"What does it matter? I still make you feel good when I sleep with you, don't I? Go back to your room, honey. We'll be with you later."

Tara allowed herself to be led out. The other women put up next to no resistance as the men coerced them. Ella protested loudly from the other room when someone put an end to her sexploits. After a few minutes, only Edward, Richard and I remained in the small television room.

"We'll need to act more quickly than we thought. That was a disaster." Richard paced the room, I'd never seen him so shaken before.

"I don't know what Aiden thought he'd achieve by doing an interview with her," Edward looked concerned.

"It was never meant to be with her. We had one of our own set up to be interviewed with him. They must have cottoned on to him and made a switch at the last minute. It's a disaster." He stopped pacing and looked at Edward. "Well, what's done is done. You'll need to make sure this place is locked down. There may be some trouble with the natives. We'll need to get the women ready to evacuate. We can't wait any longer. Make sure the word goes out to seize control of the prisons, army and police. Governments are already in hand. Have the men transitioned, then move them out the prisons and get the women in. There's going to be some hysteria while they adjust. I want it squashed quickly."

Edward nodded while I stood there waiting for someone to pinch me.

"I'll check the status with the other countries, but the agreement was if the interview went dark then we'd move to phase two. You," he said, finally looking in my direction. "You need to come with me. Aiden will want to meet you."

"What does he want with her?" Edward stepped closer to me.

"Samantha here's the only woman we have at her stage of pregnancy globally. This species is proving hostile in every respect. We need to understand what it is that's different about her. Aiden's taken a personal interest. He'd already planned a visit. We can expect him here in the morning."

"I want to be there too."

"Edward, this is no time for you to become possessive about her. She's important for all our futures, not just your own personal needs."

"I want to be there," he repeated, looking stubborn.

"Fine, whatever. Get her back to her room and keep her calm. Keep all the women in early pregnancy away from any of the news outlets. Take the general Wi-Fi offline, just leave the secured network, and remove any other devices including phones. I don't want mass hysteria causing any more women to miscarry. How many do we have at the moment?"

"Apart from Sam? Only one. She's very early and on bedrest anyway. Two others were but have shown signs of bleeding. They should be unaware of all this unless the other girls have been in to see them."

"Well, make sure they haven't. And get Sam back to her room," Richard said, scowling.

I allowed myself to be led back through the now silent lounge area and along the quiet corridor to my bedroom. Occasional sounds of weeping drifted from the rooms beyond, as men milled around, their presence intimidating. The façade of the building changed in a moment from the happy harem it had pretended to be, to the prison I knew it was.

Chapter 26

A scream in the corridor woke me just as I was drifting off to sleep. I sat up with a jolt, slipping out of bed and pulling on my robe. It wasn't the kind of scream I'd been hearing nightly up until now. This sounded terrifying. I debated whether to go looking for its source as my heart pounded, the need to protect my baby foremost in my thoughts. A second scream had me moving anyway.

I looked out of my door. A girl lay on the floor, restrained by two guards, both twice the size of any of the women on this level, a third pointed a gun at her head. "Let me go," she said, sobbing. "I want to go home."

They held her in place, arms pulled tight behind her back, as she fought them. A fourth man slid a needle into her neck. She slumped into unconsciousness.

They hoisted the woman up between them and carried her back to her room. "Get back in your rooms," one of the guards said, as they stationed themselves at either end of the corridor, their automatic weapons resting across their laps.

I knew full well that now was not the time to make a stand.

The same scene repeated periodically throughout the night, each altercation ending the same way – with the female in question crying and being unceremoniously bundled back into her room, sometimes conscious but often not, the door slammed and occasionally locked behind her. After a while there were no further attempts to leave, and no more noise, allowing me to fall into a deeper sleep.

I woke to a bright morning, the dappled sunshine casting patterns on the wall as it filtered through the thin fabric draped across my windows. My bleary eyes tried to make sense of the shapes being cast, until I registered what had woken me in the first place: more noise outside in the corridor. This time it was the sound of people on the move.

I grabbed my robe off its peg on the back of the door, pulling it swiftly over my shoulders and securing the belt, before running a hurried hand through my tangled mass of hair as I pulled on the door handle, half expecting it to be locked.

The scene outside was chaos. Women in various stages of undress were being escorted by pairs of soldiers, protesting loudly about everything they'd left behind as they were led away; most still wore their nightclothes. A few had the sense to be visibly afraid.

"I'm telling you, Richard is going to be mad you're treating me like this. You're scum." Ella spat at one of the men holding tightly on to her elbow as he pulled her along. He said nothing, continuing to tug her sleeve, much to her obvious annoyance. Unlike some of the other girls I'd seen, she'd had the time to grab a short, silky, oriental-style robe and managed to still look beautiful, despite the early hour. She paused as she passed my door. "What are you staring at?" Then she turned to shout at the guard again. "Why is she allowed to stay? What's so special about her?"

Her companions stonewalled her. Uncertainty and fear had her pulling against her captors, until she caught sight of Edward further along the passageway. She yanked her arm away from her keepers, and ran into his arms.

He hugged her into his chest, soothing her, whispering something as he moved her hair away from her eyes and tucked it behind her ear. She smiled up at him, relaxing into his touch.

A twinge of irritation at the obvious intimacy between them twisted my stomach. Edward's gaze lifted and caught me staring. He pulled away immediately. Ella looked up when he detached her, her face immediately furious when she saw him looking at me. He handed her back to her keepers with a few parting words of reassurance, before heading in my direction.

I ducked back into my room and closed the door, still irritated by Edward's flirtation with Ella – and even more irritated that I was irritated. I moved quickly across the room, positioning myself behind the upholstered wingback armchair just before the door opened and Edward walked in. He paused inside the doorway, taking in my defensive posture.

"Where are you taking them?" I said.

"Somewhere safer. Somewhere we can protect them."

"Protect them? From whom?"

"From the people who want to stop us."

"Oh, you mean the good guys . . . or maybe girls."

"It's all a matter of perspective."

"It's a matter of right and wrong."

"Is it? I think it's more like shades of grey, but that's probably a conversation for another time. How are you feeling?"

"What do you care? Shouldn't you be running after your girlfriend? She didn't look too happy when she saw you coming to my room. She might not put out for you next time you want it. Then again, knowing the sort of girl she is, you probably don't have too much to worry about there."

"Samantha, are you jealous?" Edward looked pleased as he stalked across the room towards me. I clutched the back of the chair tighter.

"Of course I'm not jealous. I got over that a long time ago, given your proclivity for other women's vaginas."

"I've changed."

I cocked my head as I looked at him. "That's true, but not completely. You still like putting your dick about."

"I told you, it's our duty. We don't get a choice."

"Well, I do. And I choose not to have anything to do with you and your philandering ways. I think you'll find it's a major turnoff for a lot of women."

"You're the only one I've chosen. I'd only be with you if it were my decision to make. You have everything I could want in a woman." He paused. "I brought you something." He pulled a strap from his shoulder I hadn't noticed lying flush against his dark jumper. "Here," he offered, holding it out towards me.

It was my camera. I hadn't seen it since I'd been at Elliott's, all those weeks ago, but it was recognisably mine. I could see the worn patch on the cover from where it rubbed against my belt buckle when I carried it.

"Where . . ." I began, as I took it from him. "How . . .?"

"I asked Elliott for it, and he gave it to me."

"Elliott? Where is he? How is he? Has he been . . . changed?"

"No, still not one of us, despite Richard trying his best to get to him. He's being protected."

"Does he know where I am? What is he doing?"

"He doesn't know where you're being held. He does know you're with us, though, because I told him. He's currently a very vocal part of the resistance, leading the people trying to track down supposedly 'missing' women. Inciting the masses to mobilise against us."

"How come you saw him, then?"

"We bumped into one another when I attended one of the rallies his group had arranged. He saw me in the crowd and made a beeline for me." Edward moved closer to me, as I gazed down at the camera in my hand. He touched my face. "You inspire men to go above and beyond, Samantha. You inspire us to want to fight for you."

"Rubbish." I took a step back, pulling away from his touch. "You only ever wanted what you couldn't have. All the years I was with you, you were never bothered about me. As soon as Elliott expressed an interest you suddenly decided you wanted me again. It's too late, Edward."

"I've already told you, I may look like the man who wasted those years with you, but I am quite different. I know what you're worth. All the others can see it too."

"So valuable you tried to kill me?"

"That's my greatest regret. You know I've struggled to manage the emotional intensity these bodies feel. I'm getting there slowly, finding it easier every day, but you make me feel so much, Sam. That day I was so angry . . . so hurt after everything I'd believed we had between us. It was a horrible mistake. I threw everything we had away with one fit of rage. I wanted to hurt you as much as you hurt me. I wasn't thinking. As a result, I lost you. I'll regret that every day of my life."

He sounded so sincere it was disconcerting. I shook myself. "Why am I still here? Where are you taking the other girls?"

"You're pregnant, Sam. The pregnant women are staying here. We're taking the other women to somewhere that is . . . easier."

"Easier for what? To contain them? Shit, you're taking them to the prisons, aren't you?" I realised, remembering what Richard said about clearing the men out of the prisons. "So, you're going to lock them up and just fuck them whenever one of the males fancies the idea, and if they get pregnant they get to come back here?" He shifted, I'd hit the nail on the head. "You have to see how wrong that is, Edward. You have to–"

He turned, his head bowed. "I do see," he said. "I know you don't believe it, Sam, but I care about you. If you were among those other women I don't know what I'd do. I thought I was okay with it, but these feelings . . . There are others among my kind that feel the same way. Men who have memories of partners they still care about. You have to understand, I'm powerless right now." He whispered, his tone had taken on an urgency that made me believe there was at least some truth in what he was telling me. "I need a truce between us, for now anyway, while I try and work this out for you . . . for us. They're watching you, and me. This baby means too much for us to disappear without anyone noticing. Even Aiden Parrish is taking an interest in you. Until they can work out how to breed with the other women, there will be eyes on us."

"So? What do we do?"

"For now, nothing. We need to keep a low profile, stop them thinking about us so much. Let them get on with managing everything else. Not cause them any bother. If we spend the day together, let them see we're close again, that'll take the edge off. I want to stay nearby anyway – I don't trust most of these men around you."

"Can we leave the grounds?"

"No, not a chance. But we could go for a walk. You can bring your camera. It's a nice day. I could ask for a picnic."

It sounded nice. Too nice. I wondered if he was fooling me again.

The door crashed open and Richard marched in, making us both jump. Edward's guilty reaction persuaded me he was, in all likelihood, telling the truth. It also meant I needed to distract Richard's attention away from Edward before he noticed his excessive jumpiness. "Richard! Finished corralling your brood mares?"

"Ah, Samantha, if only everyone could be as fertile as you." He paused, looking at us properly. Edward looked tense. "What are you two doing?"

"Samantha was unsettled by all the noise; I was just calming her down for the sake of the baby. I planned to take her out for a walk in a bit. Why?"

"Aiden will be here by mid-afternoon. I'll need her back by then. Make sure you stay in the grounds."

"Of course," Edward agreed quickly. "Has everything gone to plan so far?"

"Yes. We're delighted. Martial law has been declared. We've taken over the leadership of the police, army and government, as well as all the main media outlets. It's very fortunate for us women failed to achieve the same number of leadership positions as their male counterparts. It makes our lives an awful lot easier. There are obviously some significant cells of resistance where women and unturned males are bunkering down. We'll flush them out eventually. Nothing to worry about at this stage." He smiled. "Aiden's doing another interview later. We're confident we'll shift opinion relatively easily. In the meantime we've maintained the supply of power and water, and the herd . . ." He looked at me, and I knew he was being deliberately provocative. ". . . are safely ensconced in their new home."

"And the other countries? Any reports?"

"Saudi barely noticed any difference. Reports from Europe mirror our own experience. Areas of excessive rurality are proving trickier because it's taking longer to get to all the male population. But we're getting better all the time at enabling a rapid transition. Your old company have been very useful, in fact," he said to me.

I had no idea what he meant, so I ignored him.

"Anyway, the U.S. and China are going to plan. We have the president now." I wondered if I'd wandered into a parallel universe as I sat and listened to Richard describe how they'd taken control of all the major players in the key power centres. "Still, it'll all be a waste of time if we can't work out how to breed with them." He stared at me again. "You really are extraordinarily important to us, Samantha. You have no idea."

"Yeah, well, this special person could do with some breakfast. Then you promised to take me out for a walk," I said to Edward.

Edward smiled. "My pleasure. There's a lake on the other side of the copse. You should be able to get some great pictures down there." I grunted, as Richard stared at us.

"You two seem to be getting on better," he said. "Don't forget you'll be required to visit some of the women at the centre later, Edward. With your hit rate, we can't afford not to share you around a little."

Irritation churned inside me. Edward was being farmed out as a stud.

"Of course," Edward said, as if it was the most natural thing in the world.

Richard laughed. "Well, my work here is done. See you later, Samantha. Enjoy your walk." He laughed again, and strode out of the room, not bothering to close the door behind him.

I swung around to shout at Edward, but he'd already moved, pulling me into his arms. He kissed me before I had a chance to say a word, stopping my protest in its tracks. When he pulled away, both of us breathless, he looked at me and said, "You're the only one I want, Sam, don't ever doubt that."

Chapter 27

Edward carried the picnic basket in one hand and clasped my hand in his other, as we tried to ignore the armed guards shadowing us. He insisted the hand-holding was necessary to deflect attention. I was left feeling uncomfortable with how natural it all felt. As if the last months had never happened. I reminded myself it was all unnatural, Edward hadn't held my hand in months before he'd changed.

We emerged beside a lake. Covered in waterlilies, like a scene from a Monet, I hummed to myself in pleasure, watching as dragonflies hovered over the flowers. I snapped photos, while Edward lay out a blanket on a patch of grass dappled with sunshine, and proceeded to unpack the food he'd sourced for the occasion.

Having rediscovered my appetite, I gorged myself, much to Edward's obvious amusement, before lying down on my back, to gaze up at the wisps of cloud drifting past overhead. It was easy to forget what was going on away from here.

"You would have never done something like this with me before your accident," I mused, breaking the easy silence.

Edward rolled onto his side, propping himself up on an elbow so he could look at me. "What do you mean?"

"A picnic? So not your sort of thing. I can't remember you ever choosing to spend time with me that didn't involve your mates, alcohol, and preferably other women being around too. Never happened."

"Why did you stay with me?"

"In the beginning it was good – it was great. Until you started flirting with other women."

"I can remember some of how I spent my time. He cared for you in his own way, though. As much as he cared for anyone. He didn't want you to leave him."

"Why are you so different now? I mean, you're nicer than you were. Why is that?"

"We're like any group of people. Some of us are nice, some are less so. You just happened to get a good one." He grinned.

"So you're a different person, then?"

He nodded.

"Just with his memory bank?"

He nodded again.

"It was good for a while. After the accident, I mean," I admitted. "I was happy with you. As happy as I'd ever been. I even considered having the baby you wanted. I just didn't know you'd already gone ahead and impregnated me."

"Are you happy about it? The baby?"

"Surprisingly, yes. I mean, I know what this child represents to other people, but to me it's just my child. Our child. It's hard for me to think about it any other way. I feel protective about it. I don't want anyone to hurt it. I just want to be allowed to be a mum, but I'm afraid they're not going to let that happen, are they?"

His expression clouded. "I don't know. I don't know what they'll do with it. Or you."

"*It's* our child. The violence I've seen – is that just you, or are you all like that?"

"I think we're all like that to some extent. I've seen lots of the guys lose it over small things. Their reactions are disproportionate. Like when I found those pills. I should've talked to you about it instead of trying to kill you. The red mist descended, and I lost control. Believe me though, I always cared for you, even loved you. The last thing I wanted to do was hurt you. I thank god I didn't kill you that day. I don't think I would've ever recovered."

"Of course you would have. You had the lovely Serena on standby."

He groaned. "That was Richard's idea. When I woke up in that pool of blood, I panicked and called him. He came up with the plan. She was a willing alibi, that's all."

"She was certainly willing." A thought struck me, something I'd been wondering for a while. "Are you immortal? I mean, I know you recover quickly from injury. But, can you actually die?"

He shifted, looking uncomfortable for a moment. "If you chop our heads off, or cause serious trauma to our brain – I mean literally smash it in – there's only so much our powers of regeneration can achieve. That would do it. Most other things, given enough time, we can pretty much recover from. We can't regrow limbs, obviously."

"Huh, you have more in common with zombies than I thought."

He laughed, then looked at me seriously. "We are hard to kill, though, Sam. You need to remember that if you ever have to take one of us on. You need to disable them and escape while they're recovering. Don't stay to watch. Promise me?" He stared at me.

"I promise." I laughed to diffuse some of the tension. "So how do you even know all this? I mean, who tells you?"

"I just do. We all just know. When we wake up, our purpose is . . . there. I don't know how to explain it. Maybe like salmon, or birds flying south. It's inside us."

"So won't you overfill the planet if you can't die? I mean, there's only so much space, and we're already pretty overcrowded in some places."

He laughed again. "I don't think so. Our ability to regenerate declines with age. Our lifespan is longer than yours, but we're not immortal. It just means we prolong the stage of life that's of most value – in terms of being able to work, reproduce and generally live a good quality life for longer."

"That's a definite upside," I said, thinking about the poor man I'd watched die in the hospice.

"Sam, our primary purpose is to reproduce. Like all species. That's all we're concerned about. It's unusual for us to become emotionally involved, the way that some of us have. We're the exception, not the rule. Most don't care at all. They want to reproduce. They want a generation of virus-carrying females."

"Then what? They'll kill the rest of us? Exterminate us?"

"It could happen. To anyone who gets in the way."

"Why? Why can't we co-exist?" I thought about the baby in my belly.

"I don't honestly know."

I sat up, finding the beauty of the scenery insufficient to forget what was happening beyond the walls. "Hey." Edward pulled me into a hug, my back pressed into his chest. "I didn't mean to upset you. None of it may happen. Your people may blend with mine without any bother."

I couldn't imagine it. I didn't want to be 'blended', and I was pretty sure others wouldn't either. "Regardless, I'll make sure you're okay." He turned me so I faced him. "Believe me?" He looked at me intently until I nodded. I believed he meant it, I just wasn't so sure he'd be able to keep his promise. "You're special,

Sam. To me, anyway." He bent forward to kiss me. I considered letting him, knowing his touch would feel familiar, perhaps comforting in its own way. It might help me forget everything happening around us. But I didn't want to forget Elliott. His mobile rang and saved me from the dilemma.

He broke away with a curse, fumbling in his pocket to retrieve the device, while I tugged at my clothes, berating myself for even considering letting him kiss me.

"Richard." He sounded annoyed and a little breathless. "What? Really?" He pushed himself upright. "Yeah, we can be back in fifteen," he agreed, resigned as he glanced down at his watch. "Yeah, okay." He cast a look in my direction. "I said okay." He disconnected the call, staring at the screen until he was certain it had cut off, and then looked up at me. "Aiden's here earlier than expected. He wants to meet you."

"What if I don't want to meet him?"

"He's not a man you get to say no to. I've only met him the once, but he's important. He's been directing the operations."

"Am I supposed to act as if I'm honoured? They'll be waiting until hell freezes over if so." I sighed. "Well then, let's get this over with," I said, standing to brush myself off as Edward bundled the contents of our picnic back into the basket. We walked slowly back to the house, Edward seeming inclined take his time.

Inside the house, men milled around the ground floor. I didn't see a single woman. Eyes swung towards us as Edward escorted me across the wide entrance hall. His grip on my hand tightened at the level of interest I attracted. My summer dress that had earlier seemed picnic appropriate, now felt revealing given all the eyes upon me.

We stopped at a door to a room I hadn't visited before, it opened to reveal a library. Shelves of books filled every wall, ceiling to floor, the space between furnished with green leather armchairs. Despite the warm day, someone had lit a fire in the fireplace, the room now stifling.

Richard, and a man I recognised instantly from the TV as Aiden, turned to us as we walked in. "Ah, Samantha, you're looking extraordinarily lovely," Richard said with a smile. I forced my cheeks upwards, into what may have been more of a grimace, my hand still clutched tightly in Edward's, before turning my attention to Aiden.

He'd been watching us silently. His gaze dropped to my belly, passed up over my breasts to my face, and then fell again to the hand that was still clasped within Edward's. "Aiden, this is Samantha, the girl I was telling you about. And Edward, our man who sired the child."

"Jesus, *sired?* Seriously?" It burst from me before I thought through the repercussions. Edward squeezed my hand sharply.

"She's unbroken?" Aiden said, with some surprise, his head tilted to one side as he looked at me again with even greater interest than before.

"We haven't had time. She won't cause us any trouble," Richard said, with a confidence I wasn't convinced he actually felt. I wanted to laugh again, but a second sharp squeeze from Edward warned me against any further outbursts. Richard must have caught the movement. "Edward, you're expected over at the compound. Go and see to your duties, please. We'll look after Samantha."

Edward hesitated, reluctant to leave me. This time it was me who squeezed his hand in reassurance. It would serve no purpose, I figured, to draw attention to ourselves unnecessarily at this point.

"Of course," Edward said briskly. "I'll see you later. Will there be a dinner?" he asked Richard.

"Yes. Be here for seven thirty. You can always go back to finish off any other women you want to service afterwards if that doesn't give you long enough now. You'll need to keep your strength up given the number of women we need to see to." Richard laughed. I tried to keep how sick the conversation made me feel from my face, but it was hard, and I felt certain I'd failed.

"Later, then." Edward nodded to the two men, before turning and leaving the room. He didn't look at me once. Just as well, as it turned out, because when I turned back Aiden's gaze was fixed upon me once more. I shivered despite the heat in the room.

Aiden stepped closer. I resisted the urge to step away, my hand dropping protectively to my abdomen. His eyes followed the movement. "How sweet," he said, smiling at me. "I must say, this is an unexpected pleasure, Samantha." He turned to Richard. "You never told me she was stunning as well as fertile."

Richard laughed. "You wouldn't be the first to mention it. There's quite a clamour to mate with her once she's had this one." Sickened, I scowled at him.

"Do we know why she's been successful where the others have failed?"

"Not yet. Our scientists are running tests. They think there may be something in her genes that makes her more compatible. She may be the key to unlocking the other women if we can establish what it is. In the meantime, we're trying to work up a plan to harvest her eggs after she has this child, so we can implant other women with her pre-fertilised embryos to see if that might work. And, of course, we'll be breeding more children from her directly. We're very hopeful. It's just frustrating how long they take to gestate. Such a waste of time."

"No hurry. We'll get there in the end." Aiden moved closer, so his breath feathered over my cheek. I turned my face very slightly away from him. He inhaled deeply. "I think I'll have her," he said. "We'll still need to harvest her eggs and complete the tests, but she'll stay with me, under my protection, until I decide otherwise."

"Don't I get a say?" The comment burst from me, unbidden. "I want to stay here." I wanted to stay near Edward if I had to be near any of them. It was funny how quickly your perspective could change.

Aiden laughed, eyes flaring. "She's got some fire. I like that. She's quite a treat."

"She is that." Richard smiled, but it didn't reach his eyes. He seemed irritated I was being stolen out from under him, it was clear Aiden held all the power. "You might want to see some of our other girls too. We have one other pregnancy in the house on bedrest – we lost one this morning, sadly – with two more confirmed today at the prison after their initial medical. They're expected back here at any time. It may be that one of them strikes your fancy more."

"It may be," Aiden concurred, before turning a dead stare straight at Richard and adding; "but I doubt it." He stepped towards the door, effectively finishing the meeting. "See she's moved to my room this evening. I want her dressed for dinner and seated beside me for the interview later. It'll be good for people to see a woman sitting beside me – being supportive." He left the room, and I dropped like a stone into an armchair.

"Well, Samantha, aren't you the lucky one? Our high commander wants you. As far as I'm aware you're the first woman he's chosen. You should be honoured. It pisses me off, of course. I was looking forward to thoroughly defiling you after you'd had that baby. Still, he'll tire of you before long, and then we'll all get a turn. I wonder what Edward will say." He chuckled. "I'll arrange for your things to be moved later. In the meantime, can I suggest you start to get yourself cleaned up? The interview is in an hour, at least that's when they want everyone downstairs. You'll need to be ready by then at the latest. I'll have a dress sent up for you. Peter!" he called, loudly.

A man stuck his head around the door. "Yes?"

"Can you take Samantha back to her room?" The man nodded.

I stood obediently and followed him out, my head filled with what had just happened. I couldn't quite decide what was more horrifying: appearing in an interview with the man responsible for the enforced evolution of the human race, or the fact he'd apparently taken me as his concubine. My hand moved protectively to the baby. The man called Peter glanced down and smiled. "I heard there was a pregnant girl at last. How far along are you?"

"Fourteen weeks."

He smiled again. "That's wonderful. Are you over the sickness yet? My wife was sick as a dog when she had our two."

"You have children?" I said, surprised.

"From before, but they still feel like mine. I still love them."

"How's your wife?"

"Not so good," he admitted, a worried frown replacing his earlier smile. "She's not too happy I have to be here all the time. She doesn't like what I have to do with the other women. I tried to explain it's not the same as with her, but she doesn't understand it."

"Most of us prefer to be monogamous. At least we set out to be. If you married her, then in all likelihood you promised to be faithful to her – or the man you used to be did. I can see why she might be struggling."

"But you're not? Struggling, I mean."

"Oh, I am," I admitted, "but for a different reason. Edward slept around before he had his accident. It's not so hard to imagine him doing it here too, I suppose. Doesn't mean I like it, although we'd already broken up." We reached my door, and he stood beside it while I turned the handle. "Be kind to her, Peter. She sounds like a good woman. You must have loved her once."

"I did. I do," he admitted.

I nodded, noting the sincerity behind his words. He was one of the 'others' Edward had described – one of the ones unhappy at having to walk away from the women they remembered that they had loved – just to further their cause. I squeezed his hand with affection before walking into the room. When someone grabbed me from behind, I gasped a quick breath as I prepared to scream.

Chapter 28

A hand clasped my mouth and stifled the sound before I had the chance to release it. Edward, I realised a second later, recognising the smell of his aftershave.

"Are you okay, Samantha? I thought I heard something," Peter's concerned voice called, as he started to open the door. Edward ducked to the other side, hidden by the panelling, keeping out of his colleague's sight. From the corner of my eye I saw him shake his head.

"I'm fine," I reassured Peter, my voice shaky from the fright. "I just stubbed my toe on the edge of the bed. It made me gasp."

"Okay," he said, looking down at my shoe-clad foot with some confusion. "Well, just ask someone to find me if you need anything. Anything at all." He smiled and I nodded, working hard to maintain my focus and not to look towards Edward's hiding place. Peter closed the door again, and I collapsed onto the bed as my legs buckled beneath me.

"Jesus!" I hissed at Edward. "What the fuck were you trying to do? Frighten the life out of me?"

Edward immediately looked concerned, rushing over to where I sat to place a hand on my belly. "I'm so sorry. I didn't think. Is the baby okay? Are you okay?"

"We're fine," I grumbled, praying it was true, surprised by the strength of my concern for the unborn child. "What the hell are you doing hiding in here? I thought you were supposed to be out servicing the herd like a good little stud."

"I already told you, you're the only woman I want to sleep with. I don't want any of those others, casually or otherwise."

"Won't Richard be mad with you when he finds out?"

"Probably. Hopefully he won't. That's why I was hiding in here." He rolled his eyes at me as if he thought I was being stupid. "Anyway, I needed to know what happened with Aiden."

"Not good," I told him, flopping back onto the bed with a sigh, knowing he wasn't going to like what I was about to say. "He has, and I'm quoting here, so don't shoot the messenger, 'taken me as his', whatever the hell that means."

Edward became very still. His stillness was almost more frightening than his anger had been when he'd tried to throttle me. I pushed myself up onto my elbows and looked at him. He remained like a statue. His voice was worryingly quiet when he did speak finally. "Tell me exactly what was said."

"He told Richard to move my things to his room. I'm expected to attend the interview he's giving, as some sort of companion, in . . ." I glanced down at my watch, ". . . forty-five minutes. Someone is going to deliver a dress for me any minute now, so I'm supposed to be getting myself ready." Edward looked ready to explode. "Jesus, Edward, I mean what the hell am I meant to do here? This is a freaking nightmare. It has to be. I'm being held in a virtual prison, for all the pleasant soft furnishings, surrounded by men who want to either fuck me or kill me. I'm pregnant with the first mutant DNA infected offspring, so I can't move anywhere without being escorted, and now they want to put me on TV as the supposed girlfriend of the King of the Mutant Zombies. I mean, seriously. What the fuck?"

"You can't go to him. You're mine."

"'You're mine'?" I laughed, the shocked sound exploding from me. "I tell you all that, I spill my guts about how fucked up my life is at the moment, and that's what you think the appropriate response is? 'You're mine.' Jesus, way to sound like a complete arse. Why am I even bothering with you?" I didn't know who I was asking – him or myself rhetorically. "Anyway, what's Aiden going to do realistically? I'm up the duff, for God's sake." I laughed again, sounding a little mad now.

"Do you think that would stop him? People have sex when they're pregnant all the time. He wants you. He'll use you and then pass you on once he's bored. It's what our kind do. There's a male pecking order. When we tire of a woman, we give her to another man lower down the food chain. It's what I did with Serena," he said, looking ashamed.

"Jesus, every time I think you lot can't make me feel any sicker, you manage to reach a new low. What about my baby? Would they hurt it?"

"It's our baby ... but no, I don't think so. It's too important to their plans."

I sighed, feeling too weary to think about the potential implications any longer. "Look, I need to shower. If I'm going to be forced to appear on TV I'm damned if I want to do it with greasy hair. I'll think about everything whilst I'm in there. If someone knocks at the door, hide."

An hour wouldn't have been long enough to remove the build-up of stress-related cortisol in my system – I only had ten minutes at my disposal. Edward slipped into the bathroom five minutes into my ablutions, further diminishing the shower's relaxing qualities. I assumed from his silence he was avoiding being seen by whoever had brought me a dress to wear. But, long after the delivery person would have left, his dark, possessive eyes watched me, making me squirm.

By the time we emerged from the foggy bathroom, me cautiously leading the way, a beautiful red dress had been laid out on the bed, accompanied by some matching underwear. It had a '50s feel to it. I worried that my waistline would not be able to cope with the restrictive structure but found myself pleasantly surprised by how well it fitted. There was no evidence of any emerging baby bump. Ten more minutes spent plaiting my hair and applying some mascara and lip-gloss meant my time was practically up. I still had no idea how I planned to manage the situation with Aiden.

Edward watched me in silence. "Take off your knickers," he said suddenly, as I stood and contemplated the heels that had been provided. They'd clearly been designed and chosen by a man who would never have to cram his feet into the torturous four-inch-heel contraptions.

"Really, Edward. Not funny, not now," I snapped, sitting to force the first shoe on.

"I'm not joking," he said. He pulled out his keyring and snapped open one of the sharp blades on the Swiss army knife he always carried attached to it. "Take off your knickers. Hurry," he said, when I gawped at him. "Someone will be here for you any minute."

"What are you going to do?" I said, even as I acquiesced, slipping the lace boy shorts down over my hips. With one swift motion Edward sliced his palm open with the edge of the blade, blood spilling immediately from the wound. "Fucking hell, Edward!"

He ignored me, grabbing the lace briefs and smearing his blood over the crotch area. "If he touches you, you tell him you're bleeding. Okay?" he said, looking at me. "Okay?" he said more urgently, when I didn't respond. I was still transfixed by the blood pooling on his hand. As I watched, the wound started to heal itself. "Samantha, focus. You need to put these back on." He thrust the knickers back into my hands.

A knock at the door had me scurrying into the newly soiled item and forcing the second shoe onto my foot. "Just a second," I called, as I tugged everything into place, turning when I was done for a final check in the mirror. I waved at Edward to hide in the bathroom before opening the door. Richard waited on the other side.

"Samantha, you look a picture. Come along, we have an interview to prepare for."

"I don't want to do it."

"Unfortunately you don't get a say. You just sit there prettily and let Aiden do the talking."

"I don't want to do it," I said again. "Actually, let me be clearer . . . I refuse to do it."

"I had a feeling you might say that. I've brought a little incentive along for you." He smiled, looking unconcerned.

My stomach lurched, sickeningly. "What do you mean 'an incentive'?"

"Well, come along with me and you'll see. We're all set up in the library." He pulled me with him, and I stumbled along in my too-high heels as he walked at a surprisingly fast pace given his short stature. "Do you have any idea where Edward is?" he asked, his voice deceptively casual. Anger simmered beneath the pleasant veneer.

"No, why?"

"Oh, just that he never arrived at the prison. We have to be so careful with all the extremists around. They keep attacking our men. Very annoying. Thank God for the curfew."

"Well, I have no idea where he is. Screwing one of your harem, I assume." I prayed my voice resembled something close to normal and he couldn't feel the jump in my pulse.

"You really do look delicious in that dress," he said with another sideways look at me. "I thought it would suit you." I determined to throw the dress away at my earliest opportunity now I knew he'd selected it for me. "Here we are," he announced when we reached the library, pushing the door open, then standing back so I could walk in first.

Three chairs had been positioned under some lights, a couple of cameras focused upon them. A number of people were milling about, setting up and checking equipment. The earlier fire had burned down but continued to give off copious amounts of heat from the still-glowing embers. That, the lights and the number of bodies in the room made the temperature unbearable. I retrieved a small book from one of the shelves and fanned myself with it as I was ushered towards one of the chairs.

Aiden was already sat in one, talking to a man in a smart navy suit standing just to the side of him. I guessed him to be the interviewer. It didn't surprise me that it was a man again – one of them, I presumed.

"Samantha, you look delightful," Aiden said as soon as he noticed me standing awkwardly to the side of him. "Come and join me." He patted the seat beside him.

I turned to look at Richard, preparing to object again.

Richard nodded over towards the corner of the room. I turned my gaze in the direction he'd pointed to see Heidi standing in the shadows. She was surrounded by two armed men, a gag bound tightly across her mouth. "Heidi?" I gasped.

Richard nodded to the guards, who removed the fabric ties from around her mouth. "Sam?" she said shakily.

"What are you doing here?" I turned back to Richard. "What is she doing here?"

"I thought you might need a little incentive to co-operate. She's it. We picked her up when we realised your importance to us. It was delightfully easy. Thought she'd be a handy addition to the herd anyway. Trouble is, she's infertile – we found it out at her first health assessment – so she's practically useless. Her only value is if she helps focus your mind. So really, Samantha, the ball's entirely in your court. If you do what we ask, then she'll be allowed to stay. If you don't . . . well, she's what we'd refer to as dispensable. The man she was with – Paul? – I think we've done him a favour. He seems delighted to be servicing the herd. Taken to it like a duck to water." Heidi was crying now. Her swollen red eyes suggested she'd been doing a lot of that.

"Shut up, you arsehole!" I shouted at Richard. I tried to move across the room towards Heidi, but two men stepped into my path.

"If you sit and do what we ask, Sam, then you can have your little reunion afterwards. She can even attend the dinner if you like. As I said, the choice is yours. I'm a reasonable man, after all."

"You're sick, the lot of you."

"Ah, but we're not. We're really quite disgustingly well. Far healthier than most of you overweight, germ-laden, cancer-ridden Sapians. You really are the most terrible abusers of your bodies. In my opinion you didn't deserve to keep control if you couldn't take better care of them—"

"Enough, Richard. Please, you've made your point," Aiden cut in. "Don't antagonise her further. Samantha," he said, looking at me again and patting the chair beside him.

I watched, tears rolling down my cheeks, as they replaced the gag over Heidi's mouth. Her eyes widened with fear. My brave, feisty friend looked broken.

"Samantha," Aiden said, and this time there was no question that it was an order and not a request.

I walked to the chair and sat down, casting a final glance over my shoulder towards Heidi, trying to tell her with my eyes that she'd be okay. That we'd be okay. But I wasn't sure I believed it myself.

Aiden gave a final brief to the interviewer, a thin, mature man I realised I had seen on BBC documentaries, and then an anticipatory silence filled the room as someone called; "Quiet, please, and . . . roll cameras."

I focused on a spot on the carpet. I refused to look at either the interviewer or Aiden, however pleasing to the eye he might be. I listened, trying not to give any sort of reaction, as the interviewer again introduced the known facts about the virus. He emphasised the fact that a person had to be mortally wounded or ill for the virus to activate. What I hadn't heard before, and what had me lifting my head to stare finally, was his summary of what had happened since last night's interview. He described a situation of civil unrest across most of the world, which had forced many countries to enforce martial law. The U.K. specifically had a 9.30pm curfew, and any large gatherings of women were being broken apart, by force if necessary, with the ringleaders taken into custody. "Aiden, what would you say to the people that want to incite violence out there?" the interviewer asked.

"Well, Terry, I'd ask them to think again. We're a peaceful people. We don't want anyone to get hurt. I understand why people are anxious, even frightened, about what they have seen happening, and what they've heard about us, but I can assure you they have no need to be. We want a peaceful resolution to this situation. At the end of the day we're all human beings. There may be some small genetic differences, but that doesn't mean we can't get along together. Think of it like species of dogs – there are differences, but when you really get down to it they're all dogs. We just want to be allowed to live our lives peacefully alongside everyone else."

"So why do you think people are so angry?"

"At the moment they're afraid. Once they see there really is nothing to worry about, things will calm down again and life will go on as before. That's why we need to get control of the situation, for everyone's safety, before too many more people are hurt unnecessarily. We can't have women attacking men unprovoked on the street. It's not civilised. So we're acting to ensure it doesn't happen."

"And the camps that have been set up?"

"Those are to separate out some of the women who have been particularly troublesome. We find if we remove the ringleaders, then the situation usually calms very quickly. Because the bottom line is most people are reasonable. Even women." Aiden smiled at his own supposed joke, and the interviewer laughed along with excessive glee. I wanted to smack the pair of them. "But I'm taking the best advice on how to calm our womenfolk," Aiden continued. At this point he reached down and took hold of my hand. I stared up at him in shock. "If only everyone could get along like Samantha and me, I think the world would be a much happier place." He patted my hand, gazing at me with a tender smile on his face, as I gawped at him in shock. "Samantha's been explaining to me how women think, what is really important to them. Believe it or not, we live to make you happy," he said, grinning at me this time. "We practically worship you." He lifted his gaze slowly from my own startled face to look back at the interviewer. "I fervently hope we can find a way through these sticky times soon so we can get back to what is actually important here – living our lives, looking after one another, and loving and nurturing our families." He lifted my hand on his final words and pressed a kiss to the back of it. My eyes widened with renewed shock as he looked across at me as if he loved me. The interviewer closed the interview, thanking Aiden for his time, before trailing what would be featured on the next programme. And then it was done.

Aiden dropped my hand and stood. He thanked the people in the room quickly before striding towards the door, turning at the last moment to tell Richard, "I need to make a call. Have her seated beside me at the dinner. I want her ready and beside me at all the public events we have scheduled over the next few weeks." Richard's eyebrows went up in response. "Will that be a problem?" Aiden asked, his tone making it clear he expected only one answer. I wanted to scream at him, 'What about me? What about what I want? What about what I think?' but I knew my opinion meant nothing, no less a prisoner now than I had been in the cell.

"Of course," Richard confirmed, smiling. He didn't mean it; the smile never reached his eyes. As soon as the door closed behind Aiden, Richard turned to me. "Come along. Bring her too," he said to the guards beside Heidi.

Richard led me, with Heidi and her guards close behind, back to the television room we'd sat in the night before. "You have half an hour until you're all expected for dinner, I'll come and get you," he said, turning a key in the lock before opening the door. "Until then I thought you might like the chance to reacquaint yourself with your friend." He nodded at Heidi. "After all, I'm a man of my word, and you did as I asked beautifully. The way you do everything, Samantha. Oh," he said, as he turned to leave, "there's a couple of your newer friends in there too. Lock them in and see that no one leaves," he instructed the two guards as they manhandled us inside.

Ella and Tara were slouched in chairs in front of the TV They both looked up as we stepped into the room. "Sam," Tara said, looking relieved to see me. Ella looked less pleased, her resting bitch-face becoming even bitchier. I ignored them and moved straight to Heidi, who was making gasping sounds through her gag. She looked like she was having a panic attack, her chest heaving as her eyes began to roll wildly.

"It's okay, we'll be okay," I soothed her, making promises I had no idea how I was going to keep as I attempted to untie the knot at the back of her head, releasing it enough I could untangle it finally. She gasped for air when I removed the ball of fabric they'd stuffed inside her mouth. "God, Heidi, I'm so sorry. I'm so sorry you were caught up in all this." I clasped her to me as we both sobbed, feeling her arms latch on just as tightly. All the fear and anger I'd been holding in for so long released.

After what had to have been over five minutes, we calmed enough to pull apart and look properly at one another.

"Have you two finished? Thank fuck for that. I can't hear the bloody television," Ella said.

"Are you okay?" I asked Heidi, looking at her red, puffy eyes and tear-streaked face.

"I think so. God, I didn't think I'd ever see you again. I didn't think I'd see anyone. I thought they were going to kill me." She let out another little sob, and my own eyes filled with tears again. "They took me from outside Elliott's flat. It wasn't long after they'd arrested you. Elliott called me in a panic. He'd found your phone and was calling everyone he could think of to see if anyone could help. No one knew what had happened to you. All the authorities would say was that you'd been committed, considered a danger to yourself and the public, but we didn't know where. No one would tell us anything – where you were or what you'd been diagnosed with.

"Elliott told me about what you'd found out – the virus and everything. He'd been emailing everyone with what he knew.

People started to listen. Then it hit the media. That's when things changed. Sam, they took control. They're everywhere. On the TV they made it sound like they wanted to live alongside us, but they don't. They want it all."

"So when were you taken?" I asked, desperate for a glimpse into what had been happening in the outside world since I'd been held captive.

"About a week or two after you were. I was at Elliott's place, as I said. We'd been discussing what we could do. Women were starting to mobilise and form collectives to protect themselves, along with any men who were shown to be virus inactive. There was a media campaign, to make more people aware, using the internet mainly – men control all the primary media outlets. Elliott was at the centre of a lot of it."

"He was still okay, then? They didn't get him?"

"When I last saw him, he was. They tried a couple of times, but he's got protection around him now. They didn't succeed last I knew. But that was a while ago . . ." her voice trailed off.

"And you? What happened after they took you?"

"I was taken to a cell. It was a padded room." She wiped tears away. "They took my blood. Tested me for God knows what. Then, less than a week later, men started to visit me. I begged them not to, but they didn't give me a choice." Her head dropped to her chest, and she started to cry again as she described days of being systematically raped.

I listened, horrified. My own experience benign by comparison. "What happened after that?"

"They knew I was your friend. That guy, Richard?" I nodded. "He's an evil son of a bitch." I nodded again, clenching my jaw. "He came and told me the blood tests had shown I'd had an early menopause," she sobbed a bit again on the words. "I had no idea. Richard told me I was a complete waste of space and that they'd get rid of me if it wasn't for you. I don't understand any of this."

"Oh, Heidi! Oh God, I'm so sorry."

"Why, though? Why you? What have you done?" Nausea threatened. I couldn't tell my best friend, my friend who'd been desperately trying for a baby for months only to find out she would never have one of her own, that I was pregnant . . . with Edward's child.

"Oh, for fuck's sake, it's like an episode of *EastEnders*," Ella said. "Your dear friend is pregnant. Did she not tell you?"

Chapter 29

"We all are," Ella added, looking smug.

I looked at Tara in shock, and she nodded, before I turned my attention back to Heidi.

Heidi stared at me open-mouthed. "You're pregnant?" She looked like I'd just kicked her in the teeth.

"I didn't plan to be," I felt obliged to say, but that just sounded worse when she had so badly wanted a child.

"How? Did they rape you too?" She looked stricken for a moment, as her hand reached towards mine.

"No . . . I, I wasn't raped," I said quickly, and Heidi's hand dropped like a stone to her lap.

"Then how? Is it Elliott's?"

"No." I struggled to say the next bit. "Edward's."

"Edward's? You slept with Edward again? I thought you were with Elliott." A note of disapproval coloured her voice.

"It was from before. When Edward and I were sleeping together. I didn't know. You remember what he was like then. I took the morning-after pill after we had unprotected sex that first time, but it didn't work. Then I was on the pill. I wasn't trying to get pregnant. I didn't even know I was until they told me. They did a blood test – like they did with you."

"You weren't trying . . ." She sounded broken-hearted. "It's one of their babies?"

"Yes." I placed a protective hand over my belly. She flinched as I did so.

"How many weeks are you, then?"

"Just over fourteen."

"God, already? And it's really one of them?"

"I don't know about that. All I know is it's mine."

"But you never wanted a baby. You never even wanted to get married. What happened? Why the big turnaround?" She sounded angry now. Hurt.

"You're right. I didn't want a child, or a relationship with Edward, or at least Edward as he was before the accident. But it happened, and now I have to live with it. I thought about getting rid of it, but . . . I can't. It's my baby too," I tried to find the words to explain.

"Elliott said they're trying to get women pregnant because they need the combined DNA so they can completely wipe us out. You're helping them."

"Not helping them. Just pregnant."

"These babies will help them," she insisted, looking round at the others in the room. "That's why they need me here – to make sure you toe the line," she realised. "That's why he wanted you on the film with him. But, why you specifically?"

"They're having trouble getting women to conceive, and even if they do they rarely seem to get out the first trimester."

"Except you."

"Except me."

Heidi stood, and turned to Ella and Tara. "How far are you two along?"

"Six weeks," Tara said. "She's the same. We only found out today when they tested us all at the prison."

"And were you raped too?" Heidi asked, looking sympathetic.

Tara blushed, while Ella just laughed out loud. "No, honey," Ella said before Tara could get a word in. "There was no raping here. I was quite willing. These guys aim to please, if you know what I mean, and they pleased me a lot. They're going to be the powerful ones around here pretty soon, if they're not already, and I aim to make sure I'm right there with them doing anything – and I mean anything – they want."

"Seriously? You don't care what they're doing? They're destroying the human race, killing our men – you're okay with that?"

"From where I'm sitting there's no difference. Men in positions of power or men in positions of power. Only difference is these ones value the commodities I've got – sex appeal and working ovaries." Heidi flinched as Ella continued; "If they want to make little mutant babies, then I'll be happy to help, in exchange for being kept nicely. I don't see it really makes any odds which type of man is screwing me." Heidi and I both stared at her in horror.

"I wasn't raped," Tara confessed, her voice softer than Ella's. "I met a guy I liked – first one in a long time that wasn't a shit. He treated me real nice, then invited me to come here. The other men were nice too. They explained they like to be with women, that they were relaxed about monogamy. My friend persuaded me to try. I ... I ..." she stuttered. "I hadn't been treated so nicely by men before. Most of my exes were arseholes who took what they wanted and then vanished. These guys weren't like that. They really seemed to want to look after the girls. I thought it was okay." She looked at us, seeking some sort of understanding. I'd seen it; I knew some of the girls had been happy with the set-up. "But at that prison I saw another side to them," Tara said. "The side you saw." She looked at Heidi. "Women were being held there unwillingly. They were taking women, with no respect, whether the woman wanted the man or not. It was shocking. I was only saved because I tested positive in the pregnancy test. They brought us straight back here," she said. I shuddered thinking of all the women being held at the prison. And that was only one prison; this situation was repeating itself all over the country, possibly the world.

"This place is where they're bringing any local pregnant women," I explained to Heidi. "They have cells here too, that's where I was first held when they arrested and committed me – like you – until they discovered my pregnancy. The rooms upstairs may be nicer, but don't be under any illusions. It's still a prison."

"Have you seen Edward?"

"Yeah, he's been around here too."

"Elliott was looking for you. As far as I know he's still looking for you."

Thinking about him sent a pang of longing through me.

"After they arrested me I never stood a chance. They'd stitched me up. Even the lawyer Elliott arranged for me was one of them. As you say, all the men are in the positions of power. They've taken control, barely even needing to lift a finger. All they needed to do was transition the man in the position of authority – they've been doing it by strangling them."

Heidi nodded. "Yeah, we worked that out too."

"We're screwed," I said, and Tara nodded.

"Maybe not," Heidi suggested, bringing our attention back to her. "Before I was taken, women had started to gather in strongholds. Female-only strongholds that were defendable. They'd formed a number of collectives. Those are just the ones I know about. Women were being encouraged to fight back, to not allow themselves to be used by these creatures. If we can get out of here, we could go to one of those camps."

"If we can get out of here. That's a big if. Have you seen all the guards they have on us?"

"Some of us don't want to get out of here," Ella said. "I won't help you."

"Fine, you can have them all to yourself," I spat at her. "That should make you Queen of the Zombies. A role that's perfect for you from what I've seen."

Tara sniggered. Even Heidi smiled.

"Yeah, well, you're forgetting that right now you're a hot commodity," Ella said. "Even Aiden wants you, although God knows why. They're never going to let you out their sight until some of the rest of us go beyond the first trimester. So you'd better make yourself comfortable. I can't see you getting out of here anytime soon."

"We'll see," was all Heidi said. She was stopped from saying any more by the sound of the door unlocking. Richard appeared, with Edward.

"Ladies, sorry to break up the happy reunion. We're needed at dinner," he announced. Edward waited behind him, silent, his eyes fixed on me.

"Edward," Heidi said, "how lovely to see you again. And looking so well."

He gave her a pained smile, unable to miss the sarcastic tone to her voice. "Heidi. I heard you'd arrived. It will be nice for Sam to have you here."

"I hear congratulations are in order," she said with a bitter laugh.

"Twice over, actually." Ella grinned. "I have reason to believe this baby is Edward's too," she said in a voice so smug my skin shivered. Anger flamed inside me. Her smile broadened when my own expression dropped, knowing she'd scored a direct hit.

"You don't know that, Ella." Edward looked furious.

"I'm six weeks', darling. You know that fits with our weekend together. You just couldn't leave me alone could you, baby? We had sex more over those few days than I had the rest of the month. I couldn't get enough of your big cock . . ."

"Enough!" Edward roared.

"Fucking hell, you haven't changed," Heidi said. "You always were a complete dog. You'd stick your dick in any old skank. You've really scraped the barrel this time." She sneered as she looked Ella up and down with disdain. "Come on, Sam, we're expected at dinner," she said, taking hold of my arm.

My eyes filled, both because I was grateful for Heidi's staunch defence of me, despite everything she'd just heard, and because he'd hurt me – yet again. Of all the women he could have got pregnant, it had to be her.

I let Heidi lead me out into the corridor, Richard stepping back to let us pass. "Sam," Edward said as I walked past him. He reached a hand out, but I jerked my arm away from his grasp. "Sam!" He sounded angry now.

"Edward, walk with me," Ella cooed.

He ignored her, closing ranks behind Heidi and me, walking beside Richard and leaving the guards to see to Ella and Tara.

Only when we reached the entrance hall did I realise I had no idea where we needed to go. "This way, ladies," Richard said, taking hold of my arm and leading me up the stairs to a set of ornately carved wooden doors. He pushed them open with a flourish. Inside revealed a large dining room, the table centre stage, made of what looked like polished walnut. The walls were a rich burgundy colour, papered with a flock design. To my eyes it looked like blood. Everywhere else was gold leaf. Opulent and overbearing, it felt as if I'd walked into an autopsy.

Richard led me to the seat to the right of the head, and Edward immediately assumed the position to my own right. Without being asked, Ella moved to the position to the left of the chair Aiden would fill. It seemed given a choice between Aiden and Edward, Ella would pick the head man every time. Heidi sat beside Edward, and Richard beside Ella with Tara to his left, collectively filling six of the twenty seats at the table. As we waited, men drifted in and occupied the remaining chairs. Aiden arrived ten minutes after everyone else and took the final place.

His gaze swept around the table, pausing briefly on Ella before stopping on me. He smiled. "Good evening, everybody. Apologies for the delay to the start of our meal. I'm delighted to inform you we have now taken control of all the G12 countries. We're well on track with our plans. Please, let's take a moment to celebrate. Champagne," he said to one of the waiters hovering at the side of the room as he pulled out his seat and sat down. He waited until all the glasses were filled and then raised his own, announcing to the table; "To the future." "The future," echoed back from around the table, the men all smiling at one another. Only Heidi and I failed to raise our glasses. Once he'd place his glass back down Aiden turned to me, as conversation broke out along the table.

"You don't wish to toast our future?" he asked me quietly.

"Not the future I've seen painted by your people so far," I said, holding his gaze with my own. There was a hardness to his otherwise attractive veneer.

"Can I ask why not?" He seemed genuinely interested, but a warning squeeze on my leg from Edward suggested otherwise. Past caring, I rammed my leg up towards the table, crushing his hand in the process, before turning my back on him to face Aiden. Aiden must have caught the wince on Edward's face, because he raised an eyebrow at me in amusement. "So?" he said again.

"Do you really think that oppressing women, forcing them against their will, raping them, making them nothing better than slaves is a future that I, or many other women, would willingly sign up to?"

"Some of us are happy to submit to you," Ella said in her whiniest, most sycophantic voice.

Aiden ignored her. "So tell me. Putting what has happened to one side, what is it about what you have seen our people do that makes this future so unpalatable?"

"But that's the point. You can't just 'put all that to one side'. You've kept me prisoner. You've raped my friend and threatened to kill her if she didn't make me behave as you wished. You're holding women at a prison and forcing them to get pregnant. Those are the things I already know of, and that's just while I've been held here for the last six weeks or so. Even the men who came from settled, monogamous, happy relationships – you've torn those apart, forcing them to break their marriage vows."

"Do you think if we allowed women to have relationships in the way they were more used to, they would be more accepting of us?" He moved slightly to the right, allowing a server to place a starter of a selection of cold meats onto the plate in front of him. "Thank you," he said, taking a moment to look up at the man who had served him. "So, do you?" he asked again, looking at me intently.

"What? Well, yes."

"And if I told the married men to service only the women they are married to?"

"It would be a start," I agreed, thinking of the man – Peter – I had met earlier.

"I've heard this has been difficult for some of the men. We're not usually monogamous, but it seems the nature of your people is sufficient to overcome our own natural inclinations."

"Not all our men are monogamous either," I said, my message intended for Edward.

"Yes, well, I think for those who wish to be, monogamy should be allowed. Certainly, those who are married or in a committed relationship. For all others we will make it as easy as possible to have intercourse with as many people as they wish. That is our nature. Contraception will be outlawed and intercourse encouraged from the age of sexual maturity. Provision will be made to care for any offspring we create, with the choice given that either the mother can care for the child herself, with financial support provided, or else the child will be cared for by others who wish for a child in their lives but are unable to produce one themselves. I believe there are many among your kind afflicted by such problems, are there not?" I looked at Heidi, who was now staring at Aiden with awe.

"Yes," I agreed slowly. "I think that would help."

"Then that's what will happen. Richard," he said, "ready the necessary papers. We'll need press releases to accompany the statute amendments. It should help silence some of our religious opponents, so make sure they know first. Ensure the right individuals are in place to push this through with the minimum amount of fuss, and make sure all our people know of the changes. There should be no women forced to do anything they are not happy to do. The only women who remain locked up should be the women who openly organise against us. Oh, and make it clear that these changes occurred thanks to the wisdom of Samantha here," he said, patting my hand. He left his hand placed over mine as he said; "It's her guidance that will ensure the amicable blending of our species. Our people owe her a debt of thanks."

I stared at him, I had a feeling my mouth was probably open, as Richard stood and hurried from the room to make the necessary arrangements.

Silent for the remainder of the main course, Ella used the time to attempt to charm Aiden. She came across as vulgar and easy, and he tired of her quickly, clearly suffering the remainder of the meal out of courtesy.

"Sam," Edward whispered when Ella had launched into yet another dull story about some C-list celebrity she had once met and slept with. I ignored him. "Sam," he said again.

"What?" I swivelled on my seat to look at him. "What is it now? What could you possibly want to talk to me about? There is nothing left for us to talk about."

"I will not let her sabotage us," he insisted. "You knew I slept with those women. All of them. You heard Aiden – it's what we were instructed to do. If the child is mine . . . well, I doubt it is, frankly. She's had more dicks in her than I've had hot dinners. It is only the fact we don't sicken from sexually transmitted diseases that meant I didn't use a condom before I went anywhere near her."

"I don't want to know about it," I said. "I certainly don't want to talk about it. I knew what you were like, especially at the end of our relationship. You were wrong to assume I'd forgive and forget. I have no doubt enforced promiscuity wouldn't have been a hardship for you, that's for sure. But . . . what I find especially hard to forgive is that you made *her* pregnant," I said, making it crystal clear exactly what I thought of Ella. "As irrational as that may seem, I find the fact you made anyone else, especially *her*, pregnant unforgiveable." It was completely irrational, given the current situation, but I knew as soon as the words came out my mouth that it was the truth. Edward stared at me, looking stricken.

"Samantha," Aiden said quietly behind me, "if you've finished your meal, allow me to see you settled for the night. It is not good for you to make yourself so upset in your condition." I looked down at the untouched plate in front of me and back at Edward, whose expression beseeched me to stay. Heidi caught my eye and nodded.

"Yes, please," I said to Aiden, standing. "Heidi, I'll see you tomorrow." I looked towards Aiden for confirmation.

"Of course you'll see her tomorrow," he said. "Come, my dear." He put his arm out for me to hold. I'd barely touched him before Edward shot to his feet, moving to stand between Aiden and myself. "Edward, what are you doing? Think very carefully before you do anything stupid," Aiden warned him.

"Your proclamation tonight, did you mean it?"

"Which one? Regardless, yes, I meant all of them. To which one were you referring?"

"The one about monogamy. Samantha, she's mine." Edward's chest rose and fell rapidly with the strength of his feeling on the subject.

"Is that so? It didn't sound that way to me. If I ask Samantha what she thinks, would her answer be the same, I wonder?" Both men looked to me for a reply.

"Edward has never managed monogamy in his life. I'm tired, Aiden. I'd like to go and lie down, please."

"Of course, Samantha," he said, moving past Edward to take a hold of my arm again. This time Edward did not stand in his way.

As we left the room Ella said, "Come here, Edward, I know how to make you feel better."

Chapter 30

It was only as Aiden led me down an unfamiliar corridor, stopping at a door to a room I'd never visited before, that the phrase *out of the frying pan, into the fire* came to mind. We'd been accompanied by two guards, who insisted on checking everything inside was safe before indicating we could enter. "Come along, dear," Aiden said.

"I ... I ... I'd prefer to go back to my own room," I said, as concern at the situation I now found myself in had me hesitating in the doorway.

"Samantha, I thought we'd discussed this already. You're to stay with me. I am best placed to keep you safe. Now stop your silliness and let's go to bed. We need to get to know each other a little better." He moved behind me, placing one hand against my lower abdomen and the second against my hip, pressing me back against him as he leant in towards me, his face burrowing into my neck. "This could be good, Samantha, you and me. I can feel it. Together we'll make better decisions for everyone. We already have." His lips caressed my neck, as my body froze.

"You promised you wouldn't force anyone." I thought of Heidi and what she'd had to endure and tears threatened as my fear escalated, my raised pulse nothing to do with arousal.

"Rules don't apply to me."

"Please, don't do this," I whispered. Then again, louder, I said, "No. Stop," as I tried to slip from his hold.

Aiden ignored my protests, maintaining his grip as he slid a hand lower until his arm slipped behind my knees and he swept me into his arms, cradling me as he carried me into the room. Fear froze me, leaving me unable to respond in any way, even as he placed me on the bed. He pulled me into a seated position as he unzipped and then removed my dress, before moving to undo the clasp on my bra. He smiled as he removed it, pausing to trace a finger over one of my exposed nipples.

My breathing escalated, panic threatening, as his fingers slid into the sides of my knickers and pulled them slowly down my legs.

Adrenaline kicked in. I prepared myself to fight, wondering what a naked woman could do against a six-foot-something man. I scanned the room for anything I could use as a weapon. Barring challenging him to a pillow fight, I didn't find anything.

He froze. "Samantha, you've been bleeding." He sounded horrified as he stared at the gusset of my knickers. My adrenaline ramped up a level, as fear for the safety of my child overrode concerns for my own wellbeing. I sat up quickly, unconcerned now about my nakedness. Then I saw what he was looking at – the blood Edward had placed there earlier, now darker where it had dried. My relief was immediate. Aiden, oblivious to my own emotions, jumped off the bed. "Get the doctor," he shouted to one of the guards in the hallway as he ripped the door open. "Tell him it's an emergency."

"Are you okay, sir?" the guard responded.

"Just get the fucking doctor. It's not for me, it's for the woman. Tell him she's losing the baby." Then he slammed the door closed again. "Lie down, Samantha," he said, with a look of concern. "You need to keep calm." His own voice anything but. "It'll be okay. You'll be fine, and so will the baby." He continued to try to reassure me. If I hadn't known there was nothing wrong with the child I'd have been truly terrified. It gave me a glimpse into just how important this unborn baby was to them. That, more than anything else, terrified me.

The sound of running in the corridor followed, moments before the door burst open. A panting Dr Nichols arrived first, Richard close behind. Edward appeared seconds after. His gaze appeared less panicked, although fury took over as he looked at my state of undress. I grabbed hold of the sheet and tried to cover myself from their scrutiny. "For fuck's sake, give her something to cover herself with," Edward said, with barely controlled rage. Aiden unhooked a robe from the back of the door and passed it to me while Dr Nichols inspected my underwear, Richard at his shoulder.

I slipped the robe on quickly, while the doctor called to the guards to fetch the portable ultrasound machine, his brow furrowed with concern. "How long have you been bleeding, Samantha?"

"I don't know. This is the first I knew of it."

"So you haven't seen any other blood on your trips to the bathroom?"

"No, nothing."

"Any other discharge at all?"

"No. Just this blood, and I didn't know that was there until Aiden saw it."

"Had you had intercourse?" the doctor asked Aiden. Edward bristled, his fists clenching by his sides.

"No. I saw the blood and called for you."

"What about you?" Dr Nicholls asked Edward, who replied with a terse shake of his head, as he continued to stare at Aiden.

The door opened again, bringing a halt to the accusatory exchange, as the machine was wheeled in. Dr Nichols grabbed it and quickly switched everything on, wheeling it over to the bedside. He pushed my robe aside, uncaring of my nakedness, as he doused my lower belly in the cool blue gel. Seconds after he had the probe pressed against me. The strong sound of my child's racing heartbeat filled the room, and the men collectively sighed in relief. "Thank the powers," Aiden murmured, surprising me when he pressed a kiss against my forehead.

Edward growled, "Haven't you already done enough?" before moving protectively beside me. "You need to leave her alone if she's bleeding," he said, looking to the doctor for confirmation.

"Edward has a point. If the pregnancy is at all unstable, I would recommend avoiding intercourse, at least for a couple of weeks, until we can be confident the baby is secure. It is too important for us to risk. I prescribe at least a week of bedrest. We can review the situation in a week if there has been no further bleeding."

"Can I move back to my own room if I have to go on bedrest?" I asked Aiden, pulling the robe tight around me again once Dr Nichols had wiped the excess gel from my stomach. "I'd be more comfortable there." Aiden stared at me intently, making me worried he'd smelt a rat – that I'd suggested the return to my own room too quickly – terrified he'd caught wind of our ploy.

"For now," he allowed finally. "Watch her," he said, looking at both Richard and the doctor. "I want to be certain she is well looked after. I will still need her presence at any interviews I need to do."

"We'll make sure she has someone with her at all times," Richard agreed quickly. He looked at me, his gaze unblinking as he said, "She'll never be alone." It sounded like a threat.

"I'll take her back," Edward said, moving closer to me and making as if to scoop me off the bed.

"No," Richard said, "I'll do it. You're needed by Ella." I stiffened at the girl's name, as did Edward. "She was keen you should spend the night with her tonight. We need to ensure we keep our pregnant women happy if we're going to breed successfully."

"The chances of that being my child are slim to nothing. Or at least, how many men are there at this house? A couple hundred to one. You know as well as I do she has slept with every willing man here, which has been every man – yourself included. It is not my child. She's jealous of Sam and trying to cause trouble."

"Regardless, I think we need to keep her happy until the pregnancy is secure, so go and see her," Richard said, moving to pick me up. I shuddered as his arms wrapped around me. Edward ground his teeth as Richard carried me out of the room.

"I don't know how you did it," Richard whispered, as he walked back towards my own room, a guard walking behind us, "but I know you made this happen. Don't get any ideas, Sam. I'm watching you. Watching both of you."

"Richard, you're becoming paranoid," I said with a laugh, praying my voice didn't sound too high the way it normally did when I told lies. "Just because you're always trying to get one over on people doesn't mean we all are."

The guard opened the door to my room and Richard swept us inside, depositing me on my bed. "You'll stay here, Sam. Alone. Perhaps it will give you a chance to reflect on what side your bread is buttered. You have a chance to be something special in this new world, and you're squandering that chance. You could learn a thing or two from Ella, you know."

"The only thing I could learn from Ella would be how to treat sexually transmitted diseases. She has to be something of an expert."

"Regardless, you'll remain here. Alone."

"Can I see Heidi?"

"Well, that all depends on how you behave, doesn't it," he said, storming out the room, leaving instructions with the guards as he passed that I was never to be left unguarded and to ensure I had no unapproved visitors.

***

The first day dragged with nothing and no one to distract me. My only visitor was Dr Nichols, who came by twice to listen to the baby's heartbeat. Edward tried to visit, but the guards turned him away, his voice raised in aggravation. By the second day, despite being bored out of my mind, I became more concerned about what was happening to Heidi. When the doctor visited I tried to enquire, but either he knew nothing or he too had been sworn to a vow of silence. When my evening meal was delivered, I was grateful to see Peter's familiar face.

"I wanted to thank you," he whispered as he placed my tray down on the small table by the window. "Thanks to you I've been taken off servicing the herd. My wife is so much happier. Really, I can't thank you enough for making the case to Aiden."

"It was the right thing to do," I assured him. "For your people and mine. If there is ever going to be a way we can live together, we need to understand one another better."

"Yeah, well, there's not much sign of it yet."

"What do you mean?"

"There's been violence. Lots of it. Raids on the herd holding locations. Attacks on some of the government stations. The opposition are better prepared than the leadership imagined they would be."

"Didn't expect women to have it in them to resist, did you?"

"As I understand it, it's not a common experience in these situations."

"So women are really fighting back?"

"They are, with some of the men who have not been turned."

I looked out the window at the tranquil grounds, finding it hard to believe. A kernel of hope lit within me, though, as I pondered what I could do to help them. "What about here? Has there been any trouble at the house?"

"Not yet, but we're on high alert. Don't worry yourself though, we'll keep you safe." I stared at him, wondering how he could imagine I would ever want to be kept a 'safe' prisoner here, rather than be free amongst my own kind. "Anyway, eat up," he said, looking down at the cooling plate of food. "Richard said your friends could come and see you later."

"Friends?"

"Heidi, is it?"

I nodded, relieved to hear she had been kept here and was seemingly well.

"And Ella and Tara."

I refrained from correcting him for describing Ella as a friend. "When?"

"Tonight. They're bringing a TV and DVD player. Apparently they have plans for a chick flick night or something. Sounds horrific if you ask me."

"I agree," I muttered. It sounded like something Heidi would enjoy, but was my idea of hell. I'd rather have gone to a kickboxing class.

***

By the time the girls rocked up with the TV I was so bored that even the idea of a girls' movies night sounded good. Heidi hugged me tightly when she walked into the room. "Have you been okay?" I asked her. "Have they left you alone?"

"Yeah. Now they know they can't get me pregnant, they don't really bother with me. I can't leave, but they don't touch me."

"How are you?" I asked Tara. She looked pale and a little withdrawn.

"Not so good," she admitted. "I've had some cramping today. I think I'm going to lose the baby."

"How do you feel about that?" I asked, remembering my own surprise at how bonded I had immediately felt to my own baby. Tara was a similar age to me.

"Oh, not so surprised. This is my second pregnancy since I've lived here. Last time I got to about this stage, and then I lost it. I'm learning not to get my hopes up."

"Second?" I said, surprised.

"Yeah. It might even be Ella's third," she whispered, looking over at where Ella had made herself comfortable on the bed, while Peter pottered about setting up the DVD player. Ella had ignored me since she walked in. "None of us go much beyond six weeks usually. Often earlier. You're the only exception. How are you anyway? Any more bleeding?"

"No," I said, feeling guilty for worrying them. "No, I've been fine and the baby is still fine."

"Would you be sad if you lost it?" Heidi asked.

"Yeah, I would," I admitted.

"It would solve a problem, though. Without your baby, they seem unable to reproduce. It throws a spanner in the works as far as their invasion is concerned."

It was true. I represented a future I found as unpalatable as anyone. But it was still an innocent child. My child – to love and protect. It was still a life. I explained how I felt to Heidi. "I get it, I do," she admitted. "If it were me, I know I would want to keep it too. I understand. I just don't know if everyone else will feel the same way."

We were prevented from talking further because Peter had finally got the film working. Ella huffed as Heidi and I piled onto the bed beside her, while Tara sat on the chair. "Enjoy, ladies," Peter said with a smile, as he left us to it. We'd watched about half an hour when Tara excused herself to go to the toilet. When she emerged, I took one look at her face and could tell the news was bad.

"I'm bleeding heavily," she said.

"Are you okay? Can we do anything?"

"No. I'll go and find the doctor to confirm it."

"I'll come with you," Heidi offered. "You shouldn't be alone."

"Thanks," Tara said, her eyes bright with unshed tears. "I appreciate it." The pair left. I heard them explaining to Peter what was happening. Ever the gentleman, he offered to escort them. It left Ella and me alone for the first time.

I tried to focus on the film, but Ella's eyes never left me. Eventually I couldn't ignore it any longer. "Have you got a problem? What are you staring at?" I asked.

"I don't know. It hasn't got a label on it."

"Oh, grow up, Ella, for God's sake."

"You don't get it, do you?" She stood, and looked down at me, her face twisted with hatred. "You've got them eating out the palm of your hand, and you don't even appreciate it! You don't deserve to be the only one able to carry their child. It's not fair," she said, her voice rising. I found myself wishing Peter were still outside.

I stood, placing the bed between us, my anxiety ramping up a notch with the direction this conversation had started to take. "If none of us can carry a child, you shouldn't either," she said, walking slowly around the bed towards me. The film continued to play in the background, masking the sound of our conversation.

"What are you talking about, Ella? You're pregnant too."

"See, that's the problem. I'm spotting. I've been here before. Next comes heavier bleeding, and then . . . no baby."

"Ella, I'm sorry, I didn't know. Why didn't you tell me? Tell anyone? Do you want me to call for the doctor?" As much as I hated her, hated what she'd done with Edward, the larger part of me was still sorry to see her going through yet another miscarriage, if what Tara had told me earlier was true.

"See, you're glad. Because of Edward. Just so you know . . . he liked fucking me. Whatever he said to you, this was his child. He couldn't get enough of me."

"Okay, whatever. Look, I'm sorry you're losing the baby, but there's no need to be a bitch to me about it."

"See, I think there is. Because it's not fair. If I can't have this child," she said, moving in front of me, "then I don't think you should have that one either." Her fist shot out without any warning, punching me straight in the lower abdomen. Pain radiated through me.

"Fuck! No, stop!" I said, bending forward, trying to protect my baby. Further blows rained down on my head, legs and arms as she continued to punch, kick and slap me.

"It's not fucking fair!" she screamed.

Something in me snapped. Fortunately, apart from the first hit, when I'd been unprepared and she'd landed the blow squarely on my lower belly, most of her hits were weak. She hit like a girl. But I knew that, before long, she would find something to hit me with. And if she got a hit to my head I could be in trouble, left unconscious and unable to defend myself or my bean. I needed to act. Calling on my kickboxing skills I got myself into a defensive stance, parrying her blows before landing my own uppercut followed by an elbow into her chin. She reeled, wobbling on her feet, as I finished her with a roundhouse kick straight into the side of her abdomen. For a second or two she stayed upright, before crashing to the floor, taking the small table with her. My immediate sense of relief halted at the sight of the growing pool of blood that seeped from between her legs. Worse was the sound of her scream accompanied by the wailing shriek of an alarm.

Chapter 31

Initially my only thought was 'Oh God, what have I done?'. Then I rationalised my fear. It had been her or me. Self-defence. I wasn't going to apologise for defending myself. Ella's initial scream had reduced to a moan, as she clutched her stomach. "You killed it," she wailed. "You killed it."

"You were already miscarrying. You said so."

"I'll have you tried for manslaughter."

"You attacked *me*."

"Prove it," she said, before taking a big breath and letting out the most ear-piercing scream I had ever had the misfortune to hear. The wailing alarm continued in discordant harmony in the background, while I held my hands over my ears and wished it would all shut the hell up for a moment so I could think.

To my surprise no one arrived in response to Ella's piercing scream. Then, shots were fired outside. I ran to the window. Sure enough, shadowed figures dressed in black swarmed at the gates. They were carrying weapons. An explosion blew the vast metal gates inwards. Armoured vehicles poured through, tearing up the gravel drive, stopping at the entrance to the house. People fired at them from the building.

"What the fuck's happening?" Ella said, when she stopped screaming to draw breath, the sound of gunfire unmissable now it was so close.

"The cavalry's arrived," I said. On cue the door to my room burst open and Edward appeared, looking wild.

"Sam, we need to leave, now," he said, ignoring Ella on the ground.

"Edward, she killed our baby!" Ella sobbed.

Edward glanced down at her for a second and then back at me. "Now, Sam."

"Where are we going?"

"To the safe rooms. We need to regroup and allow the men to clear the threat from the house and grounds."

"Who is it?" I asked, looking back towards the window and the sound of increasing gunfire beyond.

"The resistance. They've been trying to take out all the big centres over the last day or so. Trying to take the leadership out where they can. They've struck gold this time with Aiden here. We need to get out of this room and down to the safe rooms. Richard and Aiden are overseeing the evacuation, and they sent me to get you and the other girls. Come on!"

"I don't want to go with you." He recoiled, looking hurt. "To the cellars," I qualified, "with Richard and Aiden."

"What do you mean? What do you want to do?"

"Stay with the resistance."

"Don't be stupid. They won't want you."

"What? What do you mean?"

"The baby, Sam. They won't want to allow you to have this child. Our child. They'll force you to terminate."

"No . . . I mean . . . they can't – I'm too far along, aren't I? I mean, why?"

"God, for an intelligent woman, you are being really stupid. We don't have time to talk about this right now. Anyway, Richard and Aiden are not about to leave you behind up here, and I'm not in a position to take them all on," he said, grabbing my hand and pulling me towards the door.

"What about me?" Ella croaked from her foetal position on the floor.

"You can burn in hell for all I care," Edward said.

I hated the girl, but it seemed a bit harsh. "Edward, she needs help. She's miscarrying. You'll have to carry her."

"If she stays here someone else will find her. Either them or us. I need to get you into a safe place until the house is secured." There was more gunfire, closer this time.

"We can't leave her," I said again, crouching down to put my arm under her arms and attempting to lift her off the ground.

"Oh!" she moaned, "you're hurting me again."

"Fuck, Samantha, you shouldn't be lifting her in your condition. Fuck!" He pulled Ella from me and hoisted her easily into his arms. "Come on," he said. This time I followed.

We exited the bedroom and bumped straight into Tara and Heidi, accompanied by Peter, hurrying back towards the room. They both exclaimed when they saw the state of Ella in Edward's arms. "All of you, this way," Edward said, nodding down the hallway. "We have to pass across the entrance hall to get to the stairway down to the cellars. Our men have it covered, but we can't hang about. Security are waiting for us. Come on."

When we reached the entrance hall, men with automatic weapons filled every doorway, panicked instructions flying between them. Shots fired immediately outside. As we assessed the distance to the cellar stairway, the carved oak doors blew to pieces in front of us, and the resistance broke through.

"Get down!" Edward shouted, and we all hit the deck.

I landed hard, air whooshing from my lungs, lifting my head in time to see people dressed in black start pouring through the gaping hole left where the doors had once been.

The security from the house started shooting. Three men and a woman were hit in the first volley of shots. They went down straightaway, unmoving. "Keep down," Edward said, as the resistance returned fire.

We'd been stuck there for ten minutes or more when one of the men hit with the early shots started to move again. Then a second. Only the girl stayed down.

"What the hell?"

"They're using neuromuscular blocker darts," Edward said. I stared at him, trying to make sense of what he'd just said, and the implications if I was right.

"Neuromuscular blocker darts? You mean darts with anaesthetic in them?" He nodded, and I looked back at the woman I now knew was dying in front of us. Neuromuscular blockers were short-acting paralysing agents. They were used by anaesthetists during operations to keep the patient still during a delicate procedure. Without providing ventilation the paralysis would cause the person's lungs to fail to inflate, meaning the person would suffocate. The entire time they would be awake but powerless to help themselves. It didn't take a huge leap in thinking to realise that if the person who suffocated was a man it would mean only a short wait for the virus to activate, with no traumatic injury to recover from. As I thought this through, the men, who were now back on their feet, turned and started shooting in the direction they'd come from. At their own people.

The rate at which it had all happened was terrifying. A new expediting of the transition process. "You knew they intended to do this?" I asked Edward. He frowned at me. A remembered conversation with Richard played at the edges of my mind. "You gave them the idea? Because of my job?"

"Not now, Sam."

"Oh my God, that's barbaric. They'll know the whole time that they're dying. Their brains will be awake, but they'll be powerless to do anything or tell anyone about it. That's horrific."

"They'll re-awaken."

"Only the men will," I said, looking at the body of the woman. "And as one of you, not as themselves."

"It's still life."

"It's still murder." We stared at each other, at a stand-off, until a cry of 'grenade, get down' effectively finished the conversation. The blast wave from the explosion seconds later blew me backwards, my head hitting the wall behind us, sending me straight into unconsciousness.

***

"Pick her up and carry her!" a frantic voice yelled. It sounded female. Hands grabbed my arms and legs.

"I'm okay, I can walk on my own. Help her!" Someone said – it sounded like Heidi. I hoped she might walk away from this.

"What about this one? She's still alive." a voice said.

"She's bleeding too heavily. She won't make it. We'll have to leave her here. The other one is already dead." Did they mean Ella, Tara, Peter or Edward? A wave of sorrow washed over me at the prospect of my child never meeting its father. "They're re-grouping. We need to get out of here now," the woman's voice again. "This is the one we wanted." I felt myself being carried over someone's shoulder, jerking me around as they ran, the pain in my head blinding with every jolt, until oblivion took me.

***

I blinked awake again, in a vehicle of some kind. Two people were crouched over me. "She's waking up," the woman closest to me said. She was dressed in black, like they'd all been, but she had the symbol of a red cross on her sleeve. A medic.

"Sam?" a voice I remembered said. I tried to keep my eyes open, meeting the blue gaze of the second person.

"Elliott?"

"Thank God, Sam. You're okay. We've got you now. We're taking you somewhere safe." Guns fired, the motion of the vehicle erratic as it evaded the attack.

"I've lost my shooter. I need help up here until we get past the barrier," a voice called from above. "They're trying to get around us. I've never known them to fight back so hard. We must have something they really want this time."

The woman looked at me. "You go up, Elliott," she said. She might have been a medic, but her tone of voice made it clear she was also in charge here.

Elliott looked at me for a moment. "I'll be back, Sam. You're safe now. We'll make sure of it." He pressed a gentle kiss to my forehead before disappearing through a hole in the roof. Renewed shooting started above.

"How far to the barrier?" the woman called up.

"Five minutes. They're not letting us go. I've never seen them like this before."

The woman looked down at me. "Since you're the only stranger here, and I know they don't have special feelings about any of the rest of us, I'm assuming this devoted attention we're getting has something to do with you?"

I stared in response, remembering what Edward had said to me earlier.

"Not talking, eh? You certainly inspire passion in people. Elliott has been obsessed with getting to you since I first met him. Put himself at risk more than once to find you. He's a good guy – you're a lucky lady. I hope you're worth the effort." We stared at one another for the longest time until:

"Shit, he's hit! Fuck!" the driver cried. I knew she meant Elliott. "We're through the barrier!" she yelled, screeching the car to a halt.

I heaved myself up, trying to ignore the wave of nausea that hit me from the movement. "What did they hit him with?" I said, as the second woman appeared, dragging the now-immobile Elliott through the hole with her. Behind the vehicle, gunfire continued.

"There's a dart here," the driver said, and my heart sank.

"It's a neuromuscular blocker. You need to intubate him now or he'll suffocate and then change." The first woman stared at me in shock and then sprang into motion. She had a pack out instantly, tearing it open before positioning herself behind him, tilting his head back with practised hands so his neck extended then slipping the metal device down his throat to expose his vocal cords. Seconds after, she slipped the tube down, attached the bag, and started pumping the life-saving oxygen into his lungs. I released the breath I'd been holding.

"Okay, Elliott, we've got you," she said, as he lay there unblinking at us. "This little lady just saved your life." She gave me her first smile. I nodded, the movement sending a blinding pain through my head, before blackness clouded my vision once more.

***

"She saved my life. What more proof could you need? I'd be dead and changed if it wasn't for her."

"She's been with them a long time, Elliott. Longer than any of the other women we've rescued. I know you cared about her, but we need to be realistic here. She wouldn't be the first woman to want to be on their side in all this."

"She won't. She was with me in the beginning. The information I found out – she helped me. Hell, they nearly killed her for it. They falsified reports against her, then had her committed. She deserves our thanks, not our condemnation."

"No one is suggesting we punish her. Hell, she saved you – she probably saved loads of men who would've been hit by those darts if we hadn't found out from her what they had in them." She hesitated. "But that doesn't mean she's on our side. She's been out of the loop for a long time ... more than a month. Things have moved on a lot. I just ask that you have a degree of caution where she's concerned."

I'd heard enough. Blinking, I opened my eyes. Elliott and the woman were seated beside me, this time in casual wear. The woman looked no less imposing for it. Elliott looked like a surfer. I smiled up at him. "Hi," I whispered, "I'm glad you're okay."

"I am, thanks to you. Hell, I knew that job of yours was good for something," he said with a soft smile. "How are you feeling? How's the head? You took a nasty injury to the side of your head in the explosion."

"I've still got a headache, but it feels better. Thanks for getting me out of there."

"It was the least I could do," he said, picking up my hand and holding it. "God, Sam, I'm so sorry. What you must have been through. If I could . . . I hate what they-"

"I'm okay. It was okay."

"It's not okay. Rape is never okay," he said, his eyes full of tears.

"They didn't rape me," I said, without thinking, needing to put his mind at rest.

"They didn't?" the woman said, surprised. I realised my mistake.

"Sorry, who are you?" I asked, trying to sit myself up.

"I'm Commander Amanda Stewart. I head up this resistance base. And I know you're Samantha Davis. So can we cut the pleasant introductions for a moment? Can you explain why it was that you were in the invaders' captivity for almost two months and yet you weren't raped?"

"Lucky, I guess," I muttered. "How is Heidi?" I asked, trying to change the subject.

"She's fine. All things considered," the woman jumped in before Elliott could answer. "She was raped. Repeatedly."

"I know," I said, meeting her hard gaze with one of my own. "Can I see her?"

"Soon. We need to speak to you first. The sooner you co-operate, the sooner we can decide what happens next with you."

"Am I a prisoner here?" I looked straight at the commander.

"I think you're what we would describe as 'helping us with our enquiries'."

"Not so different from them after all, then," I muttered. "Nice people you've got yourself mixed up with here," I said to Elliott this time.

"Sam, give them a chance. We want to help you re-settle, but you need to understand that people are afraid. They're suspicious of everything and everyone. Once they get to know you, it'll all be fine. Just tell them what they want to know and then we can go."

"Where were you planning to go, Elliott?" the commander asked him. "Where do you think you can go and be safe as a man these days? Most of the camps aren't even accepting men anymore. Too many are compromised and then attack from the inside. You're lucky we're still allowing you to stay here because of everything you've done. And the daily testing."

"Where are we?" I asked.

"Kent. One of the female camps." He looked at the commander. "Look, I know you've done me a favour, but it's worked both ways. You know me. I'm still who I was. I'm hugely grateful to you for helping me get Sam out, but if she's not welcome here, or if I'm not welcome here, then I'm happy to walk out the gate."

"I wouldn't recommend it. Since she turned up with her friend," she said, nodding at me, "there's been a group camped outside. There's definitely something she's not telling us. I just want to know what it is. I'd suggest you tell us before we have to resort to more drastic measures."

"Steady on," Elliott said, putting a hand up. "What the hell is this?"

"This is a threat to our security. I am responsible for all the people in this camp, so you'll forgive me if I don't worry too much about hurting your girlfriend's feelings here." She looked at me again. "So are you going to help us, or what?"

Chapter 32

"You sound just like them," I said.

"I don't really give a shit, to be honest. I just want to know how it is that you're the first girl to have come out of there without having been systematically raped."

"A couple tried. Edward stopped them," I said, thinking on my feet.

"Edward?" she asked Elliott.

"Her ex. He's the one who was turned originally – on the first day. It's how we connected – in the hospital after the accident. He was there with you?" he asked me.

"Did you resume your relationship with him?" she asked. "Did you compromise yourself?"

"Fuck off!" I glared at her. "I didn't sleep with him. I didn't sleep with anyone. He just didn't let any of the others get to me either. He was protective of me. They're finding the emotions of our kind hard to manage; possessiveness, jealousy, anger, they're hard for them to deal with. It seems I bring all that out in Edward."

"That's interesting," she said, looking up at a mirror on the wall that I only now realised was two-way. I wondered who we had as an audience on the other side. "What about Aiden Parrish? You and he were close, it seemed."

"I barely met the guy. He wanted me as a stooge in his interviews to make him look better. They didn't give me a choice. Told me they'd kill Heidi if I didn't play nicely. What did you expect I'd do?"

"See," Elliott said, looking at Commander Stewart. "That's what Heidi said too. They're telling the truth."

"Maybe so," she agreed. "But it doesn't really explain why her. I mean there were lots of women who were jumping for a chance with Parrish. He's got fan forums dedicated to him, despite everything we've told them. Why force her when he could have one of them?"

"She's gorgeous?" Elliott said, with a smile. I smiled back at him, knowing he deserved the truth. Knowing I was about to let him down badly.

"Yeah, whatever." The commander frowned. "The group announced a change in the laws — allowing married couples to be monogamous, banning contraception, that sort of thing. He claimed it came from you as an idea. Is that true? Was it your idea?"

"Kind of. I told them they didn't understand our women. That most preferred monogamy, especially if they'd bothered to get married. I was telling him off for the promiscuous ways of his people, but he saw it as a way to get people on-side."

"It worked. More people are siding with them as a result. It was the single most damaging move they've made in this campaign. We're weaker as a result, thanks to you."

"It was a conversation."

"You helped them. We have only your word for it you didn't intend to."

"And Heidi's. She was there."

"Your best friend. Tell me, what are you both hiding?"

"What makes you think I'm hiding something?"

"Years of practice in interrogation. Oh, you're being clever. You're almost telling us the truth. There's just . . . something slightly off I can't put my finger on." She was close. I could feel it.

"I'm tired," I said, needing some time and space to think. "Can I sleep now?"

"Sure. Elliott will show you to your room. We're not locking you in, but I'd ask that you remain inside until someone comes and collects you for lunch. I'd like to ask you some more questions this evening when we have some of your results back."

"Results?" My heart started to race.

"Yes, we run tests on all our people. We're in an enclosed space here, and there are not so many of us we can afford to have a serious infection go round. Biological warfare, given where they came from in the first place, doesn't seem beyond the question." I nodded, trying not to show my relief that they weren't specifically looking for a pregnancy.

"I'll walk you back if you're up to it?" Elliott asked. "Otherwise I can find a wheelchair for you."

"I'll be fine to walk," I said quickly. "It will do me good," I smiled at him. I knew it might be my only chance to talk to Elliott without people watching. I had no doubt that whatever room I had been given was probably bugged. I stood and let him take my arm, then shuffled towards the door. "Goodbye, Commander."

"I'll see you later, Samantha," she replied, making the innocuous words sound like a threat.

Out in the corridor, much like the ones that had led to the cells at the house, Elliott paused to hug me. "God, I missed you so much," he said, pressing his head into my neck. "I thought I'd never see you again."

"I missed you too," I admitted. "So much. But I can't stay here." I kept my voice in a low whisper.

He pulled away from me, looking shocked. "What do you mean?"

"Walk with me. I'll explain." I said quickly, aware of the cameras at the ends of the corridors focused on our every move.

"Are you going back to them? To him?"

"No, no, I'm not. I'll stay on my own."

"You don't know what it's like. They won't let you. Any woman not in a relationship with one of them gets rounded up and herded to one of the breeding centres. There's talk of that changing with the recent legislation amendments, but women are still watched closely for any signs of participation in the resistance. And they're still expected to make themselves sexually available. Where did you imagine you were going to live? I don't want to patronise you, but things have changed a lot since you were last out there."

"I don't know. I just know I can't stay here," I whispered.

"Why, Sam?" he asked, pausing outside the door to what I presumed must be my room, his face beseeching me.

I took a deep breath. I needed to trust someone, and Elliott had never let me down before. It was only a matter of time before any blood they had taken from me came back spilling all my secrets anyway. I leaned in to him, wrapping my arms around his neck in a hug, pressing my body against his and my face into his neck so that my lips weren't visible to any cameras. Elliott responded immediately, pushing his body back towards mine. "I'm pregnant," I whispered. "Fifteen weeks – from when Edward and I slept together after the accident. The morning-after pill failed. Heidi knows – I didn't, until they told me."

Elliott pulled away from me, his face stricken.

"Don't say anything," I begged him in a whisper, my eyes flickering towards the camera. It was a lot to ask.

I turned and opened the door to a room that closely resembled the cell I had been incarcerated in for the first month of my time with the others. White seemed the colour of choice for prisons these days. Walking in, I spotted the bed in the corner and headed for it, leaving a still-open-mouthed Elliott standing in the doorway. As the door slowly swung closed I still had no idea what he would do with the information I'd just told him.

***

Sleep eluded me. I knew I needed help from someone inside if I was going to get out of here. Even with that help our chances were slim. If I did get out the hope of then evading detection by Aiden and Richard, with all the detection agencies and networks of CCTV cameras at their disposal, seemed equally slim. I didn't know for sure what the women here would say to my pregnancy, but I could guess. I did know it would signify a shift in the battle, a gaining of ground for one side or the other. If my baby ceased to exist, then there would be no immediate threat to future generations of humanity . . . unless they could use my eggs and continue to try and breed from me. Alternatively, they could use me to understand what made me different in order to resolve the problem in the other women. It suggested Edward was right – these people would want me and my baby dead. I was in more danger now than I had ever been with Edward and the others. On the other hand, letting the others use me, my eggs and my children for their own ends held no greater appeal.

Whichever way I looked at it I was screwed. For now, my fate lay in Elliott's hands. He was a sweet, beautiful man who had looked after me, and I had rewarded him by being pregnant with another man's child. Life had dealt us a cruel hand. When the knock on the door came at midday exactly, I called 'come in' and then held my breath.

Chapter 33

Elliott stood at the door alone. His face looked harrowed. "Lunch?" he asked in a falsely bright voice, as his eyes flashed towards the camera above my head.

"Yes. Please," I agreed. "Let me just go to the bathroom and wash my hands." He nodded, and I slipped into the small en-suite, remembering a similar room I'd pebble-dashed in orange bilious vomit. I grabbed the soap from the side and lathered my hands, taking a second to look at Elliott through the mirror. He'd turned up alone. That might be a promising sign. He looked haunted, though. Anyone who saw him would know he knew something, and whatever the something was, it wasn't good. I grabbed a towel from the hook and dried my hands, promising myself a shower later, then turned and smiled at Elliott. "Okay?" I asked.

"Not really," he admitted softly. "Heidi's meeting us in the canteen."

"That will be nice." I smiled again. "I hear you got to know her a bit before . . . before they took her too."

"Yeah. I like her. She's a good friend to you." I knew he meant she was a good friend because she'd said nothing about my situation to anyone. My clever friend had clearly worked through what they might do to me if they knew. He offered his elbow and I took it, allowing him to lead me out of the room, along the corridor to a fire exit at the end. The prefabricated building I'd been kept in was situated in the grounds of the camp, within the protection of metal walls. Space must have been at a premium.

The camp had been set up around a stately home – again, the groups had more in common than they knew. Elliott led me into the main building and towards a large room that had been turned into a canteen. The room must have been a ballroom or banqueting hall in a previous life. "Heidi's there," he said, pointing to the corner, where sure enough Heidi sat alone, a tray of food on the table in front of her. "You go and sit down. I'll bring some food over for the both of us." Given the silence that had descended at my appearance, I couldn't sit down soon enough.

I made my way across the room, ignoring the whispers about me and where I'd been. I heard Aiden's name mentioned a few times and the word "concubine". "Sit down," Heidi said, as soon as I got close enough. "You're not safe here, Sam. They hate you. They think you're working with them. You need to leave. They don't even know–" I gave a quick shake of my head to shut down the conversation.

"I know," I said. "I told Elliott. I didn't know what else to do. I'm not sure he knows what to do now. I agree I need to leave, though." We turned to watch him as he weaved his way across the room towards us. Several women jumped up and invited him to share their table with them. I had a momentary flashback to Edward and Ella. Irritation twisted several faces after he declined politely, choosing to continue his slow path towards us instead. Given the paucity of men in the room (I counted no more than six in over one hundred people), I figured a gem like Elliott would be a hot commodity. He would have been at any time – handsome doctors rarely struggled to attract the opposite sex in my experience – but here and now he was in even greater demand. As a result, we were subjected to numerous scowling looks cast our way, all of which he remained oblivious to.

"Fish and chips for two," he said, putting the tray down in front of his seat, removing a plate which he placed in front of me. "You've lost weight. You need to eat more . . . to keep your strength up," he said meaningfully.

My eyes filled until my vision blurred, as he busied himself, collecting salt and vinegar. A single tear rolled down my cheek. I reached out and squeezed his hand before picking up my knife and fork and cutting off a corner of the fish, aware of people watching our every move.

"So what happened after the grenade went off?" I asked Heidi, needing a distraction. "What happened to the others?"

"Peter blocked me from the blast. He was unconscious but still alive, last I saw." She looked down before she added;

"Tara didn't make it. A piece of shrapnel hit her in the head. There was nothing anyone could have done."

"Oh my God!"

Heidi nodded. "She was a decent person. One of only a few in that place."

"Yeah," I agreed. "What about Edward?"

"He crawled away. I think he broke his leg. He tried to wake you up first and got very distressed when he couldn't. In the end, when it became clear you had a concussion and were out for the count, and he couldn't even stand, I told him to go. I promised him I'd make sure you were okay. The resistance were pouring through the door at the time, shooting anything that moved. They'd have killed him if he'd stayed."

I nodded. I could imagine, from what I'd seen before I'd been hit, how bad it had been.

"What about Ella?"

"She was bleeding heavily but still alive."

"How the hell any God saw fit to save Ella and take Tara I'll never know. There's no justice."

"Who's Ella?" Elliott asked.

"She's one of the girls doing exactly what your commander accused me of. She was a jealous bitch. A bit like some of the women in here." I cast a look around at the still-scowling faces that surrounded us. An escalating angry murmur started circulating in the room.

"I think we need to leave, Sam. I don't feel safe in here," Heidi said.

I nodded.

Elliott grabbed a plate of food, and as a group we stood.

"Leaving already?" a tall Amazonian-looking woman asked, standing to block my route from the room.

"We don't want any trouble," Elliott said, attempting to intercede on my behalf, as he stepped in front of me.

"Step away, handsome. Our beef isn't with you or the other girl. Just her," she said, squaring up to me. It was too soon after my concussion. My body barely had the strength to stand up for long, let alone fight this giantess.

"Ladies, stand down," a new voice boomed across the room. For the first time since I'd met her I found myself pleased to see Commander Stewart bearing down on us. "Elliott, escort Samantha back to her room. I'll see some food is brought to the three of you there." Gratefully we made our way across the room. Elliott ignored the outraged comments that followed when he placed a protective arm around my shoulders, leaving it there despite the significant animosity it directed towards him. I welcomed the comforting weight, having never felt quite so vulnerable before.

True to her word, the commander supplied us with food, but given the surveillance in the room any conversation we might have wanted to have was stymied. Heidi left first, leaving Elliott with me. He seemed unwilling to leave me alone, despite my assurances I'd be fine. Given the level of surveillance they had me under it was hard to believe much could happen. In the end, because the bed only had a single mattress and there was nothing else suitable to sleep on, he left me to rest, the excitement of the day finally catching up with me. "I'll be back later this evening," he promised, kissing me gently on the forehead. "Get some rest."

"Thank you, Elliott. For everything."

"It'll be okay," he murmured. "We'll be okay." He saw me into the bed, making sure I had everything I needed, before leaving me to get some sleep.

I must have drifted off fairly quickly. The next time my eyes opened it was to find myself being physically restrained, a hand clamped over my mouth. I struggled, but there were too many hands on me, tearing my clothes away until I was left with nothing. All my initial fear was for my baby, my exposed belly vulnerable if they chose to attack. Thankfully my still-flat tummy drew little notice. Once they had me naked, a wad of material stuffed into my mouth to prevent me calling for help and making me fear suffocation, they took pleasure in covering my nose and watching me panic as my lungs heaved for oxygen. There were so many women in the room, all jeering at me, leaving me helpless to defend myself. A lit cigarette pressed repeatedly into my arms and body. Terrified, my bladder released. "Stupid, dirty whore," the ringleader announced. "Standing in your own filth, like the rancid bitch you are. You were happy to fuck the zombies. Did you like having their rotten dicks inside you? Then you think you can come here and take one of our men? We won't let you taint him with your infected pussy. Women like you should be ashamed of giving in so easily. Sitting next to that leader like you were proud to be there. Helping them to seduce more women. You should be ashamed. People should know what you are. It's our job to make sure they know exactly what you are, and what happens to women like you," she said, her passion infecting the crowd, who roared in approval.

When she moved towards me again my fear escalated. In her hand she held an object – a razor. I feared she intended to cut my wrists or my throat; instead, when she was within arm's reach, she grabbed a fist full of my hair and started hacking at it. My hair proved to be too long and thick, so someone produced scissors, and as I was held there they hacked it all away, long strands fluttering to the floor, feathering out around me.

I closed my eyes, trying to tune them all out, the jeers and laughs fading into nothing as I focused myself inward. Survival; that was all that mattered. Life. Mine and my child's. The rest of it, the rest of them, could rot in hell. I'd fought to defend these women, and this was what they chose to do to one of their own. Hatred burned within me, white hot, smelting my core and reforming me into something solid and unbreakable. I would survive this. Whatever they tried to do to me, I would survive it.

In the end, my peaceful acceptance of everything they had to throw at me, every debased action, took away their enjoyment, showing them up as the animals they were.

They left me in a heap on the floor, covered in my hair and urine, my body bruised and burned. I curled into a foetal position, one hand resting on my belly, and blinked away my tears. Under the watchful gaze of the camera I closed my eyes and, in the silence that followed, felt the first flutterings of my baby inside me, telling me it was okay . . . that we had survived.

Chapter 34

"Sam, fucking hell, fucking hell!" Elliott said, when he walked into the room and found me. "What happened?" He dropped to the floor beside me and cradled my body in his arms. "Who did this to you?"

"Who didn't?"

"It's a fucking disgrace." He looked up at the camera, "a fucking disgrace." He lifted me gently. "Animals!" he said when he saw the extent of the burns on my arms and torso, as he carried me into the shower.

He washed me, tenderly, both of us sitting on the floor of the shower as he rinsed the marks of my mistreatment away before finding a razor and shaving my head until it felt smooth and even to the touch. "Still the most fucking beautiful thing I've ever seen," he said, his voice thick with emotion as he stared at me, the water cascading around us as he sat there fully clothed. "Are you . . . Is the baby . . ." he whispered, the sound of the shower masking our conversation.

"The baby is fine. They didn't know. We survived." He nodded.

"Are you ready to stand?" I let him help me to my feet as he turned off the shower and fetched a large towel to wrap me in. He dried me off gently, finding yoga pants for me to wear and a sweatshirt. He located a pair of trainers in the wardrobe, and some socks, and helped me put them on, before grabbing himself a dry pair of scrubs to replace his sodden ones. "Come on, we're leaving," he said, taking hold of my hand and leading me out the room.

"Where are we going?" I let him set our course. I had no fear anymore. I knew I'd survive.

"I have no idea," he said. "It can't be worse than here, though, can it?"

"No."

The wail of an alarm filled the hallway. "It's an attack," he said. "They've been building their forces outside the camp all day. I knew it would be soon. Their timing couldn't be better. There's a rear gate. I've got a key, and I left a car on the other side for us."

"How did you get a key?"

"It pays to be one of the only men in a six-mile radius who's still human."

I smirked. "Still rocking the surfer doctor charm."

He smiled. "Don't knock it. You love it."

"Yeah, I kind of do," I agreed.

We walked through the camp, calm amidst the chaos all around us, as automatic gunfire rattled near the front gate. My new hair style worked in my favour, making me less recognisable. Elliott pulled his hood up, so no one bothered us as we strode towards the edge of the camp. "You sure about this?" Elliott said, once we were outside and in the car, the key in the ignition.

"Completely sure," I said, with no hesitation. "What about you? You don't need to do any of this. They'll all be after us. I won't be able to hide the baby forever and the others won't give up trying to get hold of it. I'm their only successful pregnancy that's gone beyond the first trimester."

Elliott's eyes widened at the news. "The only one?"

I nodded.

"Why you?"

"No idea. Just lucky that way, I guess. Still want to come with me?"

He locked eyes with me, his gaze solid. "I'm all in," he said. "Always have been."

"Even with this?" I pointed at my belly.

"It's a piece of you. That's good enough for me."

"Okay then." I smiled.

"Okay then," he agreed, and started the engine.

Epilogue

I took a deep breath, pulling the bracing sea air deep into my lungs, wishing for the millionth time I had my camera with me, the landscape in front of me so spectacular I wanted to cry. Maybe it was just my hormones. We were somewhere in the northwest of Scotland. A place with few people and fewer CCTV cameras.

"Have you seen this?" Elliott held up a newspaper. I missed his blonde locks. In sympathy, he'd shaved his head. We looked like escapees from the cancer ward, but it meant we'd kept off the radar for the last six weeks. He'd bought us both a pair of Doc Martens and some skinny jeans, and told me we should rock the skinhead look. That had made me laugh, a lot.

The paper showed a picture of me. From before. And Ella. She was accusing me of killing her baby. Apparently, I was wanted for manslaughter. It didn't surprise me. Nothing surprised me anymore. It was a blatant ruse to get hold of me. Both sides were at it. Only the fact we looked so different had allowed us to evade capture for this long.

"So are we going to do it?" Elliott asked.

"It's not a reason. It shouldn't be a reason."

"It is a reason. It will keep you safer for longer."

"Can't we just keep wearing the rings and pretending?"

"We need paperwork. You know they've started checking."

"We'd have to give our names. Then they'd have us, and we'd have to run again. They'd look at CCTV images and know what we look like now. We'd be found."

"Maybe," he agreed after a pause. "I just kind of liked the idea anyway." He patted my now slightly protruding belly. "And so did Bean."

"If we marry it will be because we want to be married, not because we're hiding from anyone." The change in the legislation, allowing married couples to continue in monogamous relationships, was what had saved us. We were hiding in plain sight, wearing wedding rings and pretending to be a couple. For now.

"When we marry, you mean." He smiled at me, then something over my shoulder caught his attention.

"Time to go?" I knew the expression. We'd drawn someone's notice.

"Time to go."

We walked back to the car holding hands.

A light mist was blowing in from the sea – a sea fret. The rapidly cooling moist air a reminder of that day so long ago. The tendrils curled behind us, as Elliott accelerated away. I knew we'd be found . . . sometime . . . maybe soon. The odds were certainly not in our favour. But not today. I patted my tummy, feeling the baby kick back, and smiled. For now, life was good, and for that I was thankful.

The End

Coming Soon

Still Born

Author's Note

It takes a village to write a book.

It's not an original saying, but it is a truism. I couldn't have written this without all the help I received. Physically and emotionally.

First of all, Katie, you always give me confidence in my writing and help me to make it better. Nicky and Patrick, for helping me make it look professional, and designing me a wonderful cover.

Mum, I was ready to shelve this book. You made me believe it was good enough to put out there, and supported me to do so. Hurry up and retire so we can do this all the time.

My wonderful, wonderful critic partners. You came into my life just when I needed you. Now, I wouldn't be without you for the world. I'm looking forward to our trip – a lot!

Lastly, my husband. For putting up with me, when writing drags me away. For letting me believe I'm good enough and always supporting me. One day I hope I'll write a book as good as yours, if not as important.

They tell authors to stay in their lane, and not jump between genres. I'm really bad at taking that advice. Thank you to all my loyal readers who gave this a go, even though it may not be their thing. To everyone else . . . thank you for taking a chance on a new author.

There are so many others I could mention, but this already sounds like an Oscars speech. I'll stop now, and go and write the sequel.

In the meantime, please stay in touch and let me know what you think. Reviews matter a lot to all authors – Amazon and Goodreads are a good place to start.

You can also get in touch directly:

Twitter: @bellahartloves

Facebook: https://www.facebook.com/isobelhartbooks/

Website: www.isobelhartsbooks.com

Other books by Isobel Hart:

<u>Adult Contemporary Romance</u>
What Goes Around Comes Around (Lily's Story Book 1)
Full Circle (Lily's Story Book 2)
Compromise Agreement

<u>New Adult Contemporary Romance</u>
Cold Comfort (Cold Comfort Book 1)

<u>YA Urban Fantasy - Isobel Hart writing as O.C. Shaw</u>
Centurion (Part 1 – Gabriel)